Slavery and Identity

MIEKO NISHIDA

Slavery and Identity

Ethnicity, Gender, and Race in Salvador, Brazil, 1808–1888

INDIANA
University Press
Bloomington & Indianapolis

This book is a publication of

INDIANA UNIVERSITY PRESS

601 North Morton Street

Bloomington, IN 47404-3797 USA

http://iupress.indiana.edu

Telephone orders   800-842-6796

Fax orders   812-855-7931

Orders by e-mail   iuporder@indiana.edu

© 2003 by Mieko Nishida

The paper used in this publication meets the minimum requirements of American National Standard for Information Sciences—Permanence of Paper for Printed Library Materials, ANSI Z39.48-1984.

Manufactured in the United States of America

Library of Congress Cataloging-in-Publication Data

Nishida, Mieko, date
    Slavery and identity : ethnicity, gender, and race in Salvador, Brazil, 1808–1888 / Mieko Nishida.
        p.   cm. — (Blacks in the diaspora)
Includes bibliographical references (p.) and index.
    ISBN 0-253-34209-0 — ISBN 0-253-21581-1
    1. Slavery—Brazil—Salvador—History—19th century. 2. Slavery—Brazil—Salvador—Psychological aspects. 3. Slaves—Brazil—Salvador—History—19th century. 4. Slaves—Brazil—Salvador—Social conditions—19th century. 5. Slaves—Brazil—Salvador—Psychology. 6. Slaves—Brazil—Salvador—Emancipation. 7. Africans—Brazil—Salvador—Ethnic identity. I. Title. II. Series.
    HT1129.S2 N57 2003
    306.3′62′0981—dc21

                                                                                    2002010944

1 2 3 4 5   08 07 06 05 04 03

To the memory of my grandmother
Kikuno Nishida (1909–1989)

All my life I had been looking for something, and everywhere I turned someone tried to tell me what it was. I accepted their answers too, though they were often in contradiction and even self-contradictory. I was naïve. I was looking for myself and asking everyone except myself questions which I, only I, could answer. It took me a long time and much painful boomeranging of my expectations to achieve a realization everyone else appears to have been born with: That I am nobody but myself.

—Ralph Ellison, *Invisible Man*

Contents

Acknowledgments

This book narrates a peculiar sort of history of the New World's "peculiar institution." It is not about slavery per se; instead it presents a new interpretation of urban slavery in an Atlantic port city from the vantage point of enslaved Africans and their descendants during the slavery regime and examines these people's self-perceptions and self-identities in a variety of situations. Drawing on appropriate available primary sources, both archival and printed, this book discusses the perspectives of slaves, ex-slaves, and freeborn people of color and explores a number of factors that affected their lives and self-perceptions most critically.

Enslavement in Africa had detached these people from their communities and, together with the following hardships of the Middle Passage, had deprived them of considerable honor and dignity as human beings. They had been forced to give up their original identities upon enslavement. Having arrived in the New World, every one of them was placed in a situation of slavery. Inevitably all the enslaved human beings of African birth suffered enormously and sometimes despaired. But despite the hopelessness of their situation, they exercised their slight remaining power over themselves to create and re-create their own distinctive identities through their struggles for the recovery of their lost freedom and humanity. While avoiding romanticizing the past, this book reconstructs these people's stories of (re)creating identities within the context of New World history.

This book involves my own search for my identity. I was born and grew up in Japan, and eventually left for the United States to be enrolled in a Ph.D. program, without imagining what fate would await me. My geographical move from the Old World to the New World coincided with my disciplinary departure from anthropology for history. I have since sailed a long voyage to re-create myself as a historian of Brazil beyond and above my multiple "otherness." Although my name appears in print as the author of this book, I know that the book would never have been completed without many wonderful teachers, colleagues, friends, and family in three countries where I have lived: the United States, Brazil, and Japan. I remain immensely grateful to all of them.

First of all, I would like to thank two anonymous readers for their meticulous readings of the manuscript, followed by sharp critiques, insightful comments, and thoughtful suggestions for the successful publication of this book. I am very grateful to Professor Franklin W. Knight for his strong support, generous help, and warm friendship over the years. I thank Professor Anani Dzidzieyno for his help, friendship, and support, and all of our intercultural conversations on race, ethnicity, and gender in Brazil and beyond. I owe most special thanks to Professor William B. Taylor for teaching me history as a "series of miracles" and for reading several different versions of my manuscript with much care. Professor Joseph L. Love generously found the time to critique my entire manuscript. I thank Professor William E. Jackson for his unfailing faith in my work and me. James Sidbury has been an excellent critic and a good friend.

My thanks are due to Dona Edy Aleluia, Judith Lee Allen, Professor Iraci Del Nero da Costa, the late Professor Peter L. Eisenberg, Professor Jack P. Greene, Professor Mary C. Karasch, Professor Richard Graham, Dona Helena R. Guimarãos, Professors Takashi and Jandyra Maeyama, Jacira Almeida Mendes, Professor Joseph C. Miller, the late Sr. Teizan Nishioka, Tejumola Olanyian, Professor Anne Pérotin-Dumon, the late Professor Armstead L. Robinson, Sr. Aloisío Conceição Rocha, Mary F. Rose, Professor A. J. R. Russell-Wood, Professor Consuelo Novais Sampaio, Sr. Daniel Azevedo dos Santos, Dona Arlinda Séras, the late Sr. Tetsuya Tajiri, Professor Luís Henrique Dias Tavares, and Betty L. Whildin. I also thank David J. Bachner, Thomas C. and Muriel E. Beattie, Regan Brumagen, Mark Erickson, Lee and Joanne Fisher, and Amy Rosner for their friendship and support.

I am indebted to the wonderful staff of the public and private archives in Salvador and Rio de Janeiro, Brazil; the Carter G. Woodson Institute of the University of Virginia; and the Benson Latin American Collection and the Institute of Latin American Studies, both of the University of Texas at Austin.

My research and writing were funded by The Johns Hopkins University graduate fellowships; a predoctoral research fellowship at the Carter G. Woodson Institute of the University of Virginia; and a Rockefeller Foundation postdoctoral fellowship at the Institute of Latin American Studies of the University of Texas at Austin.

My thanks are due to the editorial staff of the Indiana University Press: Robert J. Sloan, Marvin Keenan, Kendra Boileau Stokes, Jane Lyle, and copy editor Carol Kennedy. I would like to acknowledge permission to reprint portions of several chapters that have been previously published in different forms: "Manumission and Ethnicity in Urban Slavery: Salvador, Brazil, 1808–1888," *Hispanic American Historical Review* 73, no. 3 (1993): 361–391; and "From Ethnicity to Race and Gender: Transformations of Black Lay Sodalities in Salvador, Brazil," *Journal of Social History* 32, no. 2 (1998): 329–348. Several quotes in the text have been taken from four great works of American fiction with permission, and I thank Random House Inc. for Ralph Ellison, *Invisible Man,* and Caryl Phillips, *Crossing River;* Atlantic Monthly Press for David Mura, *Turning Japanese;* and International Creative Management, Inc. for Toni Morrison, *The Bluest Eye.*

I would like to express my heartfelt thanks to Kevin P. Rauch, an astrophysicist who patiently guided me through to find my own "star" in the very dark sky. I'll always remember him saying to me, "Yes, you can do it!"

Lastly but not least importantly, my profound gratitude goes to my family in Japan for their unfailing support: Takako, Taketoshi, and Hiroaki Nishida, my parents and brother; and Kikuno and Kiyokazu Nishida, my late grandparents. This book is dedicated to my grandmother, who always believed in me.

Mieko Nishida

Abbreviations

Archives

ACMS	Arquivo da Cúria Metropolitana de São Salvador da Bahia, Salvador, Brazil
AINS	Arquivo da Igreja da Nossa Senhora do Rosário dos Homens Prêtos, Salvador, Brazil
AMCS	Arquivo Municipal da Cidade do Salvador, Salvador, Brazil
ANRJ	Arquivo Nacional do Rio de Janeiro, Rio de Janeiro, Brazil
APB	Arquivo Público do Estado da Bahia, Salvador, Brazil
ASPD	Arquivo da Sociedade Protetora dos Desvalidos, Salvador, Brazil
BNRJ	Biblioteca Nacional do Rio de Janeiro, Rio de Janeiro, Brazil

Journals

AAEB	*Anais de Arquivo Público do Estado da Bahia*
ABNRJ	*Anais de Biblioteca Nacional do Rio de Janeiro*
AHR	*American Historical Review*
HAHR	*Hispanic American Historical Review*

Slavery and Identity

Introduction

Identity is not given. It is one's situational synthesis of self in relation to others. Hence, one defines and redefines his or her identity in each specific situation/context, particularly in relation to other people's perception(s) of him or her. Yet, even if one does not seem to possess any political power to influence others, one does not necessarily always have to accept a label or category that the larger society imposes, most likely based on ostensible appearance or phenotype. The creation of identity is a constant negotiation of varying impressions. In other words, the creation of identity is by no means one's passive reaction to a specific environment. It is as well an active process of self-creation. Collective identity emerges only when some individuals successfully recognize their common traits as a group, beyond differences, and connect with one another in opposition to others. Therefore, identity, either individual or collective, evolves, transforms, disappears, and/or reemerges over time in relation to a changing context.[1]

These are the issues of identity that this book scrutinizes and emphasizes. In order to do so, I choose as my subject the powerless, who were simultaneously the ethnic/racial "other" in New World history, namely enslaved peoples of African birth and descent. This study discusses how such powerless individuals and their descendants, women and men, enslaved and legally free (freed and free-born), created and re-created distinctive identities in diverse situations during the slavery regime. My understanding is that a specific sense of self, namely identity, stimulates, encourages, and even forces the individual to make concrete decisions and to take certain actions. This study examines very carefully one's actions and behavior as the outcome or representation of his or her specific identity or identities, not the other way around.[2]

The city of Salvador, Bahia, Brazil provides us with a most provocative setting for our discussions on the creation of identity during the slavery regime. By the mid-1770s Salvador had grown larger than any city of British America and possessed a larger population than major British cities such as Bristol, Liverpool, Birmingham, and Manchester.[3] As an important Atlantic port city, Salvador maintained its lead over Rio de Janeiro as the most populated city of colonial Brazil until the late 1800s.[4] Urban slavery had developed in Salvador and had existed throughout the city since the early colonial period, and people of African descent have constituted the majority of the population in Salvador from the early colonial period until the present day. The unique urban setting of Salvador enabled enslaved Africans and their descendants to come into contact with each other on various occasions in the course of everyday life.

For this study I have chosen to focus on a specific time period, from 1808 to 1888, which may well be regarded as a most critical transitional period of Brazilian history, following the transfer of the Portuguese court from Lisbon to Rio de Janeiro. Upon arrival, at the demands of Great Britain, whose Navy escorted their move to Brazil immediately after the Napoleonic invasion in Portugal, the Portuguese court was forced to immediately open all Brazilian ports directly to the world market. This brought an economic boom to Salvador as well as other port cities of Portuguese America. Transition from mercantilism to free trade (1808) brought Salvador new economic growth; Bahian exports increased from a total value of 1,418 *contos* in 1808 to 8,178 *contos* in 1824, whereas sugar production increased from 20,000 *caixas* (boxes or crates) in 1808, to 29,628 *caixas* in 1818, and 33,000 *caixas* in 1833. Imports to Bahia also increased by 50 percent within the first year after the opening of the ports to free trade.[5] During the given period 1808 to 1888, the transformation of Brazilian society took place at two different levels. One was socioeconomic: transition from slave society to legally free society (1888). The other was political: transition from colony to monarchy (1822) and then to the Republic (1889). As a result of such drastic and rapid political and socioeconomic changes in the larger society, the characteristics of those of African descent in Salvador continued to change in accordance with the illegalization of the slave trade in Brazil (1831); the termination of the transatlantic slave trade (1851); and the destruction of Brazilian slavery, beginning with the enactment of the Free Womb Law (1871) and moving toward total abolition (1888) with the enactment of the Golden Law (Lei Aúrea) of May 13, 1888.

By focusing on a specific local setting for a specific time period, this book raises theoretically broad and historically important questions on slavery and identity in New World history. In the course of our discussions on the creation of identity, three important factors emerge and form the book's three major intersecting axes of analysis. They are ethnicity, gender, and race.

Studies on Identity

This historical case study focuses on the creation of individual identities; inter-relatedness among those who came to share the same identity; and the emergence, transformation, and disappearance of collective identities. This study follows such important questions on identity as those raised by British social anthropologist A. L. Epstein, concerning by what processes a "sense of collective identity" was "generated, transmitted, and perpetuated"; how new identities came to be formed and how they interacted with preexisting ones; and what were the "circumstances in which established identities" were "abandoned or simply disappeared."[6]

Anthropological Studies on Ethnic Identity

My approach to ethnic identity among the African-born population in nineteenth-century Salvador reflects urban studies of South-Central Africa by British social anthropologists at the University of Manchester. J. Clyde Mitchell discusses urban ethnicity in the name of "tribalism" from a "phenomenological approach, which takes into account the meaning of actions from the actor's point of view coupled with a situational approach in which the meanings are related to the actor's definition of the social situations."[7] An urban environment creates anonymity, which is the keystone of categorical interaction since it operates in public places or wherever the actors know little of one another.[8] Among the urban migrant population on the Copperbelt of Northern Rhodesia in the 1950s, more than one hundred "tribal" groups were reduced to a handful of "tribal" categories in accordance with two principles: geographical propinquity and cultural affinity.[9] Unlike "tribes" in rural areas, "tribalism" in urban areas was a situational phenomenon in response to urban African life, a category of interaction based on broad cultural differences but within an urban labor system. Thus Mitchell distinguishes "tribe" in rural areas as a structure from "tribe" in cities as a category. According to Mitchell, categorization is "a common reaction in a situation where social relationships are of necessity transitory and superficial while at the same time multitudinous and extensive."[10] In such circumstances individuals seek means of reducing the complexity of social relations with which they are confronted. Urban migrants achieve this goal by classifying the people around them in a limited number of categories. They draw a "cognitive map," using a variety of indicators, such as ethnic badges, to which individuals respond with the appropriate behavior.[11]

My discussions on the historical creation of collective identity have greatly benefited from the renowned historian E. P. Thompson's classical work, *The Making of the English Working Class* (1963).[12] Thompson defines class as "an historical phenomenon, unifying a number of disparate and seemingly unconnected events, both in the raw material of experience and in consciousness" and "something which in fact happens (and can be shown to have happened) in human relationships."[13] Thompson continues: "[C]lass happens when some men, as a result of *common experiences* (inherited and shared), feel and articulate the identity of their interests as between themselves, and as against other men whose interests are different from (and usually opposed to) theirs."[14] Accordingly, between the years 1780 and 1832, most English working people came to share a collective identity in common as a distinctive class against their rulers and employers.

The U.S. historian Herbert G. Gutman, highly influenced by Thompsonian theories of class formation, in his *The Black Family in Slavery and Freedom, 1750–1925* (1976), discusses historical processes by which slaves in the American South, "especially in the eighteenth century, had to forge new institutions and beliefs to sustain them in their oppression," and "some—not all, by any means—of these institutions and beliefs were formed and transmuted."[15] He presents his monumental book as "a special aspect of American labor history: those men and women who labored first in bondage and then mostly as half-free rural workers,"[16] and maintains that "the same kind of historical questions can be asked of slaves that historians could ask about any other exploited population."[17] This raises the question of whether slaves in the American South formed a social class as a working people, as was the case in England.

Anthropologists Sidney W. Mintz and Richard Price, in their book entitled *An Anthropological Approach to the Afro-American Past,* which was published coincidentally in the same year as Gutman's book, discuss the historical creation of African American culture, namely the creolization process.[18] By taking such a similar combination of phenomenological and situational approaches, as suggested by J. C. Mitchell,[19] Mintz and Price perceive the "creolization" of diverse African cultures under slavery not as the simple transplantation of Old World cultures in the New World but as a creative process.[20] Yet their model, largely based on the case of colonial Surinam, seems to suggest that creolization could be synonymous with the convergence of diverse African cultures under a slave system into a unified, singular "African American culture." Mintz and Price maintain that "the Africans in any New World colony . . . began to share a *culture* only insofar as, and as fast as, they themselves created them."[21]

Thompson, Gutman, and Mintz and Price all emphasize that human actions mattered in making history. By sharing the same experiences of being socioeconomically exploited (and sometimes even culturally deprived), people connected with one another, reduced differences among themselves, and eventually created a common collective identity. This process resulted in the formation of a distinctive social class, or the creolization of diverse cultures, in accordance with each context. This book will test whether these models of collective identity formation are applicable to the case of African-born slaves and their descendants who lived in a specific New World city during the slavery regime. Did all such exploited individuals actually develop a collective identity over time by being oppressed commonly as slaves and/or by being part of the population of African descent? Was it rather an outsider's relatively shallow observation and stereotyping of others based on their seemingly shared superficial appearance(s), or even on a romanticized imagination of the powerless as a collective entity?

In order to answer these questions we have to investigate and study the individual's self-perception(s) on individual terms, not as a member of a group to which she or he is (or was) supposed to belong. After all, identity often differs from a category imposed on the individual by the larger society, thereby inevitably creating a critical distance between self-perceptions and ostensible appearances. This is well exemplified by the anthropologist Stephan Palmié in his monograph on the development of new collective identity as "black" Hispanics in Miami in that group's relations with African Americans, as well as with lighter-skinned Hispanics who may pass as whites in the U.S. society. Palmié skillfully demonstrates that sharing the same phenotypes as "blacks" (by U.S. standards) does not, in and of itself, provide sufficient foundation for "black" Hispanics to share the same racial identity with African Americans.[22] For, as Anthony P. Cohen demonstrates in his theoretical monograph on the notion of community, "appearances are deceptive."[23] Suzanne Oboler discusses similar, intriguing conflicts between ethnic labels and individual and collective identities among the diverse populations of Latin American origins in her meticulously researched monograph *Ethnic Labels, Latino Lives* (1995).[24]

While greatly benefiting from the aforementioned major monographs by Thompson, Gutman, and Mintz and Price, this study challenges their linear models of collective identity formation by demonstrating that the historical creation of collective identity by no means took just one single process for the population of African descent who lived in Salvador during the nineteenth century. Despite the rapid creolization process after the mid-nineteenth century, all the free-born population of African descent in Salvador did not come to perceive/identify themselves as a homogeneous racial/ethnic group. This book will attempt to illustrate carefully the most intricate historical process of identity formation by African-born slaves and their descendants in New World history.

Race and Color in Brazil

Perceptions of race and color in Brazil differ considerably from the situation in the United States, despite the fact that they share the long history of African/black slavery in the New World.[25] Definition of who is black or not varies and is only culturally defined; there is no cross-cultural criterion. Sidney W. Mintz elucidates: "[A]nyone here [in the U.S.] who has *any* black ancestry is *defined* as black."[26] As for Brazil, as the Brazilian historian Emília Viotti da Costa cogently explains, when Brazilians and Americans speak of blacks, they mean different things. The former emphasize the individual phenotype, whereas the latter define race in hereditary terms: parentage, not appearance, decides who is white or black in the United States. Accordingly for Viotti da Costa, in Brazil the mulatto has been seen as evidence that the population was becoming white, whereas in the United States as becoming black.[27] In short, as Mintz accurately summarizes, black is "a *social* line, not a racial line" in both the U.S. and Brazil.[28]

In Brazil, unlike the case of the United States, recognition of variations in the physical appearance of the population of African descent has been varied and complex since the early colonial period. In New World slave societies, as David W. Cohen and Jack P. Greene suggest, during the early phase of the emergence of the free population of color (the first several generations), the complex, multitiered, color-coding system may have been operative in terms of marriage reference and social status. However, unlike many other New World societies, where these categories became vague and confused even during the first century of the institution of slavery, in Brazil this color-coding system continued to function throughout the colonial and imperial periods and has survived to a considerable extent until today.[29] For instance, according to Charles R. Boxer, in Brazil, as well as in Portuguese Asia and Portuguese Africa, *negro* (black), *prêto* (black), and *cafre* (Kaffir) were all pejorative terms, often synonymous with *escravo* (slave).[30] During the colonial period, Brazilian-born people of color were occasionally described with such ill-defined phrases as *trigueiro, corado bastante* (brown, fairly brown), *de côr fechada* (of a closed color), *de uma côr equívoca* (of a dubious color), *ao parecer branco* (white to all appearances), or *de côr fula* (of the color of the Fulah).[31] In present-day Brazil hundreds of terms of color exist, which are impossible to translate into English. The census of 1980 found 136 color labels for self-description, while in the National Household Survey of 1976, Brazilians responded with 200 color terms.[32]

In Salvador, throughout the slavery regime, the Brazilian-born individual of African descent not only was always referred to in terms of legal status but also was identified with a color, and such usage of color continued to divide the Brazilian-born population of African descent. In chapter 1, I will introduce to the reader the color terminology that was prevalent in nineteenth-century Salvador. Chapter 7, focusing on the free Brazilian-born population of African descent in the late nineteenth century, should enable us to understand race, color, and identity in present-day Brazil. In this book, whenever possible, I choose to avoid categorizing and referring to African-born peoples and their Brazilian-born descendants together as "blacks," which inevitably carries the perception of race and color prevalent in the United States. Furthermore, whenever necessary, I specify a place of birth, ethnic origin, legal status, or color in accordance with the original local (Brazilian and/or Bahian) usage. Only in the case of lay sodalities for the population of color and the colored militia regiments do I follow the preceding studies to employ the usage of "black" and "mulatto" sodalities and militia regiments to describe and distinguish them from each other and also from their white counterparts.

Structure of the Book

This book is divided into three parts, in accordance with the changing composition of the population of African descent: from being predominantly enslaved to free, and from being predominantly African-born to Brazilian-born. I present empirical evidence that clearly demonstrates that enslaved people of African birth and their Brazilian-born descendants created and re-created distinctive identities during the slavery regime, and I show when, how, and why the creation of identity took place.

Chapter 1 serves as the foundation for the entire study. It reveals the characteristics of Salvador, Bahia, and the transatlantic slave trade; discusses

urban slavery and slaveholding in nineteenth-century Salvador; and catego-
rizes people of color in Salvador.

Part I (chapters 2 and 3) focuses on the creation of identity by the enslaved African-born women and men of diverse ethnic origins as they interacted with the continuing influx of new arrivals from Africa. Chapter 2
examines processes by which African-born slaves created ethnic and gender
identities in New World urban slavery and emphasizes that the creation of
gender identity undermined ethnic solidarity among the enslaved population to a considerable degree. Chapter 3 discusses how new gender and ethnic identities came to be represented in various collective forms: gatherings
and groupings, mating and consensual unions, voluntary associations, and
slave flights and uprisings.

The subject of part II (chapters 4 and 5) is African-born peoples who
managed to regain their freedom in the New World. Chapter 4 examines the
re-creation of identity as ex-slaves. African-born ex-slaves, who could not
benefit from the practice of unpaid manumission, most commonly obtained
their freedom through self-purchase, occasionally by manipulating their
ethnic identities. Upon obtaining freedom they attempted to follow the
elite's behavioral patterns, such as slaveholding and multi-memberships in
lay sodalities, but their newly acquired freedom in the New World was never
to be the same as the freedom that many of them had experienced as free-
born people and had taken for granted in their native lands of the Old
World. Once they obtained freedom, the former slaves of African birth
sharply distinguished themselves from their enslaved counterparts.

Chapter 5 examines the rapid convergence of diverse ethnic identities
into a broader ethnic identity as African-born. The 1831 decree officially
banned the slave trade in Brazil, putting an end to Salvador's direct importation of African-born slaves, although a great number of enslaved Africans
continued to be imported to Bahia, albeit illegally, until the mid-nineteenth
century. The resident population of African-born ex-slaves faced new dis-
illusionment and frustrations. Their newly acquired freedom as ex-slaves
did not approximate the freedom that most of them had known as free-
born in their homelands of Africa; the larger society continued to perceive
African-born ex-slaves as a critical threat to social order because of their
cultural otherness derived from their foreign birth. Ultimately in 1835, under
the common banner of Islam, African-born ex-slaves united with African-
born slaves in 1835 to stage a well-organized, large-scale uprising. Known as
the Malê revolt, this uprising was predominantly a male phenomenon, as so
many previous rebellions had been. But because it involved both slaves and

ex-slaves almost equally, it was a unique kind of social movement. And it paved a way to other unique events. Some African-born ex-slaves voluntarily returned to their homelands of Africa, while others remaining in Salvador began to connect with one another through kinship and fictive kinship networks.

Part III (chapters 6 and 7) discusses the creation of a disparate identity by the Brazilian-born population of African descent. Chapter 6 shows how the Brazilian-born population created their identities in relation to the larger society's favorable treatment of Brazilian-born over African-born, of lighter-skinned over darker-skinned, and of women over men among the Brazilian-born population. The proportion of the Brazilian-born free population began to expand rapidly once urban slavery started to decline in Salvador during the 1840s. I examine how the Brazilian-born population of African descent re-created their identity in freedom, in relation to a changing socioeconomic and cultural context in the 1830s and 1840s.

Chapter 7 treats the creation of a racial identity by a group of free-born black men of Brazilian birth. In the last few decades of the slavery regime, free-born people of African descent distinguished themselves from the slave population, most of whom had been labeled as "blacks" by the larger society, and tended to identify themselves as "mulattoes," regardless of their visible skin colors and other ostensible phenotypes. Nevertheless, a group of free-born men of African descent with artisanal skills and substantial economic means chose a collective racial identity as blacks and transformed one of the two newly established free black lay sodalities into a new type of mutual-aid association exclusively for black Brazilian male citizens. But they did not allow women, as their wives and mothers, to become full members of their association. Their better socioeconomic standing enabled them collectively to choose to identify themselves as blacks, albeit by excluding others in terms of class and gender.

The concluding chapter summarizes and reexamines the major argument about the creation of ethnic, gender, and racial identities in slavery and freedom in the case of nineteenth-century Salvador, Brazil. The way Africans and their descendants behaved in Salvador clearly indicates that they were a highly resilient population who never lost their creativity either in the experience of the Middle Passage or in the centrifugal experience of slavery in the New World: those who speak of "way of death" and "social death" greatly exaggerate.[33] I end the study by examining its implication for our own "global age," a time when the creation—and loss—of racial, ethnic, and national identities is arguably our most important problem.

Santo Amaro

Cachoeira

San Francisco
do Conde

Maragogipe

Bay of All Saints

Itaparica

Salvador

Atlantic Ocean

Jaguaripe

Subaé River

Tararipe River

Paraguaçu River

Jaguaripe River

Jacuípe River

Joanes River

0   10   20 km

jmh

1   A "Capital of Africa" in Brazil

The city of Salvador, commonly called Bahia after the name of its state, is located on the southeastern shore of the Bay of All Saints (Bahia de Todos os Santos), and is situated approximately thirteen degrees south of the equator. Geographically speaking, the city is divided into distinct parts: the *cidade alta* (upper city) and the *cidade baixa* (lower city). Throughout the colonial period and the nineteenth century, the upper city, built on an escarpment about six hundred feet high, was a largely residential district for wealthy merchants as well as for Bahian sugar planters who resided in the capital city for part of the year. Many wealthy British merchants resided in Vitória parish with its church of Our Lady of Grace. The upper city also contained the cathedral (formerly the Jesuit College), the governor's palace, the Casa de Câmara (municipal offices), the Treasury, the Santa Casa da Misericórdia (Holy House of Mercy), and the monasteries of the Franciscans, Carmelites, and Benedictines.[1] The lower city, composed of the two parishes of Conceição da Praia and Pilar, is built on alluvial soil, with a rocky substratum, and occupies a very narrow strip along the bay. Traditionally, the lower city was the commercial district, containing the dockyard, the marine arsenal, the Alfandega or custom house, and markets, as well as the stores of merchants and spacious warehouses for the port.[2] In the nineteenth century, these two parts of Salvador were connected only by narrow alleys, which were "passable with great difficulty by carriages or teams."[3]

Visiting Salvador in 1856, the German traveler Robert Abé-Lallemant described the overwhelming presence of "blacks" in the city:

> No sooner has the traveler set foot in Bahia [Salvador], than he/she
> is struck by the inescapable fact that the public roaming the streets is
> exactly in keeping with the maze of houses and alleys. Indeed, there can
> be few cities so uniquely peopled as Bahia. If one did not know that this
> city is in Brazil, one would think it to be a capital of Africa and the seat
> of a mighty black prince. This is a city where it is easy for the newcomer
> to overlook the all-white population. Blacks appear to be everywhere.
> There are blacks at the beach, blacks in the city, blacks in the area of the

lower city, and blacks in the districts of the upper city. Everyone that runs, yells, works, carries, and fetches, is black. Yes, even the carriage horses in Bahia are black. At least, this was my impression. There are the unavoidable Bahian sedan chairs, the caderinhas used here as cabriolets are elsewhere, and for which blacks play at being horses.[4]

Abé-Lallemant, who characterized the city of Salvador as "a capital of Africa" in Brazil, was, in fact, one of many visitors from Europe and the British North American mainland who noted in their travel journals the prominent blackness of the population of Salvador during the nineteenth century. In their accounts of Brazil, many such foreign travelers expressed amazement at the numerically notable "black" population in Salvador and presented a stereotypical description of these "blacks" as possessors of a collective mentality, with common physical characteristics, who were eminently suitable as a labor force in such street activities as chair carriers working in gangs.[5]

Small wonder all these foreign travelers did not overly exaggerate the historical reality. In 1807, Salvador's population amounted to 51,112, which rapidly doubled by 1872, to 108,138.[6] Throughout the ensuing eighty years until the abolition of slavery in Brazil (1888), some 70 percent of the whole population of Salvador was officially classified as "persons of color (*pessoas de côr*)."

Salvador, Bahia, and the Transatlantic Slave Trade, 1549–1851

The City of the Savior (*cidade do Salvador*), founded by Governor Tomé de Sousa in 1549, was the seat of the captaincy of Bahia and the capital of Portuguese America until 1763, when Rio de Janeiro became the capital. Salvador was the seat of the governor-general or viceroy, as well as of the royal treasury and high court. The High Court of Appeals (*Relação*) started to operate in Salvador in 1609.[7] Salvador became a bishopric in 1551, and an archiepiscopal see in 1676, and came to be known for its reputed religiosity; it is said there are 365 churches in the city, one for each day of the year. Although Salvador was the name of the city and the captaincy was named Bahia, nomenclature has come to confuse city with captaincy, and the designation "Bahia" has come to be loosely applied to city, captaincy, and Bay of All Saints. Departing from this common practice of referring to both the city and the captaincy with the same term, I distinguish Salvador (city) from Bahia (captaincy, or province after independence in 1822) to avoid confusion.

Salvador developed as a major port city for the export of sugar and later (in the eighteenth century) of tobacco as well as for the import of human cargoes from Africa, with the Bahian Recôncavo as its agricultural hinterland. From the colonial period, the Bahian Recôncavo has commonly been called "the interior," despite the fact that many Recôncavo towns are located along or near the coast and are within a day's travel from Salvador. Stuart B. Schwartz interprets Salvador's relationship with its hinterland as a conceptual dichotomy; the city of Salvador has represented urban, cosmopolitan life, whereas the Bahian Recôncavo has been perceived as rustic, removed, and aristocratic.[8] Although wealthy Bahian sugar planters spent a large part of the year in residence on their plantations in the Recôncavo and developed tightly knit networks among themselves to form a dominant class characterized as the sugar oligarchy, they maintained their two-storied city mansions (*sobrados*) in Salvador for their own and their respective families' part-time residence and for their children's formal education.[9] For such planters, the city of Salvador was supposed to intellectually represent the entire captaincy (or province) of Bahia, thereby automatically causing the Recôncavo, the "interior," to be regarded as culturally marginal.

The overwhelming "blackness" in the population of Salvador undoubtedly resulted from the long history of African slavery in Salvador and Bahia, but African slavery had not been introduced into Bahia until the mid-sixteenth century, when the colony's agro-export economy began to expand rapidly with the large-scale cultivation of sugar crops. Neither at the time of their "discovery" of Brazil (1500) nor immediately thereafter had Portuguese colonists found in Bahia the golden kingdom of *El Dorado* they had expected. Therefore their earliest commercial activities were limited to the cutting and exporting of logs from brazilwood (*pau brasil*) trees. The red dye extracted from the brazilwood was highly valued in Europe, especially at the French court. The Portuguese colonists increasingly turned to the indigenous population, namely the Tupinambás and the Tupiniquins, for dyewood logs, manioc flour, and labor. The Portuguese called these indigenous populations *gentios* (gentiles) or *negros da terra* (blacks of the land). These Portuguese terms reflect Portugal's historical experience of the slave trade and the institution of slavery in Portugal and the Atlantic Islands. By the time of Portuguese colonization of South America, the term *negro* had become almost synonymous with "slave" in the Portuguese language and was used in contrast to the description of African slaves as *negros de Guiné* (blacks from Guinea). Such parallel terminology as *negros da terra* and *negros de Guiné* suggests that the Portuguese perceived both the legally free indigenous population of Portuguese America and enslaved Africans as sources of slave labor.[10]

The barter system started to shift to chattel slavery in the 1530s with the introduction of the donatary system, which granted property rights to Portuguese noblemen. The donataries, with the obligations to develop their grants by settling colonists and establishing a secure economic basis, made new demands on indigenous populations. Barter could never supply enough labor for the cultivation of the new commercial crop, namely sugar, and the Portuguese began to enslave Indians to secure labor.[11] Whereas the Portuguese Crown made a distinction between "good" and "bad" Indians and permitted the colonists to take slaves obtained in "just wars," the Jesuits and eventually other religious orders were allowed to create *aldeias* (missionary villages), where the indigenous population were to be converted to be available for useful activities such as subsistence agriculture and work in the cane fields. From 1540 to 1570, Indian slavery was most commonly observed on sugar plantations on the coast of Brazil, and particularly in Bahia.[12]

It was the cultivation of sugar that led to the colony's prosperity in the sixteenth and seventeenth centuries. We are not certain exactly when sugar was introduced to Brazil, but as early as the 1530s and 1540s, sugar agriculture was established on a firm basis.[13] Fortunately, the fertile black and red *massapé* soil, together with abundant rain, made the Bahian Recôncavo ideal for large-scale sugar cultivation. As a result, the wealth of the colony was concentrated in the hands of a landed aristocracy of Bahian sugar planters and merchants.[14]

Cultivation of sugar in a plantation regime requires a large labor force. Indigenous labor was essential for the colony's growth in the sixteenth century, but could not meet the colonists' increasingly inexhaustible demands for labor on sugar plantations.[15] The Portuguese procured an alternative labor supply by extending African slavery from the Atlantic islands to Portuguese America. Africa became the source of labor for the sugar plantations of Bahia, and enslaved people were imported en masse from Guinea to Salvador as early as the 1570s. Under the very harsh working conditions, there was a high mortality rate, which made necessary a constant replenishment of the labor force with slaves from Africa.[16] During the seventeenth century, Bahia absorbed almost all human cargoes from Angola.

During the eighteenth century, the major slave source for Bahia shifted from Angola to West Africa, a change that was attributed to the fall of Brazilian sugar in the world market, as well as the emergence of a new local economy in central Brazil. By the end of the seventeenth century, Brazilian sugar had lost its predominance in the world market. Brazil's sugar production fell from 2.5 million *arrôbas* in 1730 to 1.4 million *arrôbas* in 1776. In terms of the share of the world sugar market, this represented a decrease from one-third to less than one-tenth. By 1787, according to one Englishman's estimate, Brazil's share had gone down further, to 7 percent.[17] At the same time, within the colony the discoveries of alluvial gold (1690s and subsequently) and diamonds (1728) in Minas Gerais shifted the center of prosperity from the sugar-producing Northeast (Bahia and Pernambuco) to the Central-South. In 1763, in recognition of the economic and strategic importance of the South, the Brazilian capital was transferred from Salvador to Rio de Janeiro, which had emerged as the main port of entry for Angolan slaves, whose final destination was the gold-bearing regions of Minas Gerais, Goiás, and Matto Grosso. This, coupled with changing conditions within Africa, prompted Bahia (and Pernambuco) to turn to the Gold Coast, whose demand for Brazilian tobacco was increasing. Bahia continued to be the dominant producer and supplier of tobacco, and Bahian tobacco became an important article of the slave trade.[18] By 1790, Brazil's sugar had begun to recover on the world market. The major export centers of sugar remained Pernambuco (plus Paraíba), Bahia (and the subordinate captaincy of Sergipe), and Rio de Janeiro, but sugar was also becoming a major crop in São Paulo.[19] In 1791, a slave uprising in Saint Domingue, which was the largest sugar producer in the world, grew into what has come to be known as the Haitian Revolution. During the ensuing war for independence, Saint Domingue was virtually eliminated from the market, and, as a result, sugar prices rose dramatically. To meet the vast demand for sugar, Europeans turned to the traditional suppliers, such as Brazil, as well as new ones. The Bahian sugar economy expanded enormously during the following decades.[20] The level of exports of Bahian sugar increased by 54.6 percent between 1757 and 1798, and advanced another 9.3 percent during the following decade. Since approximately one-tenth of the sugar produced in Bahia was locally consumed, yearly production rose from nearly 360,000 *arrôbas* in 1759 to 880,000 *arrôbas* by about 1807.[21] As the result of the recovery of the sugar industry, the total population of Bahia, which had rapidly decreased from 288,848 in about 1776 to 193,598 in 1780, recovered to 247,000 by 1799.[22]

The major suppliers of slaves to Bahia during the resurgence of Brazilian sugar in the last decades of the eighteenth century were the Bight of Benin and the Bight of Biafra of West Africa, although limited numbers of slaves continued to be imported from other parts of Africa.[23] The newly imported slaves, who were from different regions of West Africa, arrived in Bahia on vessels of Brazilian ownership. This was a reflection of important changes that took place after 1793 in the organization of the transatlantic slave trade, which affected the slave population in Bahia. First, French and Dutch were driven from the high seas as a consequence of war in Europe. After 1807, British and U.S. ships also withdrew from the slave trade, which left only the Portuguese to operate in the Bight of Benin. Spanish ships also purchased slaves in the Bight of Benin by the end of the first decade of the nineteenth century, but most of these slaves went to Cuba. After 1807, British pressure to end the transatlantic slave trade made it difficult for other countries to operate between Africa and Bahia. Consequently Brazilians did most of the transatlantic slave trade from Africa to Brazil during the sugar resurgence.[24]

The transfer of the Portuguese court from Lisbon to Rio de Janeiro (1808) exercised a significant influence on the transatlantic slave trade to Brazil; Great Britain exerted ever-greater pressure to abolish the slave trade to Brazil. Slaves who had been captured while on a slave ship en route to Brazil were called *africanos livres* (free Africans) or *emancipados* (the emancipated). Upon landing in Brazil, they were *de jure* "liberated" by the British-Brazilian Mixed Commission in Rio de Janeiro on the basis of the treaties of 1817 and 1826, and by the Brazilian authorities by the terms of the law of November 7, 1831, which finally banned the slave trade.[25] Although legally free, "free Africans" were *de facto* used in virtually the same way as slaves. Most were forced to work on public projects, for charitable institutions such as the Santa Casa da Misericórdia, and in army garrisons and naval arsenals. Many were also hired out to individuals, until this practice was forbidden after 1850.[26] The decree of 1831 appears to have been only temporarily effective. The total number of slaves imported from Africa to Brazil decreased dramatically from 43,000 in 1830 to 3,500 in 1831, but it rapidly regained previous levels. The number of imported slaves for the period 1836–1840 (240,600) nearly matched that for 1826–1830 (250,200). In sum, a substantial number of Africans continued to be imported into Brazil and sold as slaves until the end of the transatlantic slave trade in 1851.[27]

Enactment of the anti–slave trade law of 1831 had a crucial impact on African slavery in the city of Salvador; slaves were no longer taken directly into the port of Salvador. Slave ships from Africa unloaded their illegal cargoes clandestinely on the myriad of islands of the Bay of All Saints or, later, at the mouth of the Rio d'Una. The west side of the island of Itaparica became the main depot from which Africans were shipped farther in a clandestine coastal trade or taken directly to the slave market of Salvador.[28] The number of enslaved Africans imported into Bahia for the period 1811 to 1830 was 142,300. Surprisingly, over the next two decades (1831–1850), imports still amounted to 98,600. However, examination of the distribution of these slave imports for each year and by decades does demonstrate that the law effectively decreased the number of Africans imported into Bahia. (The single exception to this trend is a period between 1846 and 1850, when 45,000 slaves were imported.) The number of newly arrived Africans suddenly dropped from 7,000 in 1830 to 1,000 in 1831.[29] Since the plantations of the Bahian Recôncavo demanded a constant number of slaves for the agricultural labor force, there are reasons to believe that the city of Salvador accepted a lower percentage of new arrivals after 1831. Few documents trace the exact change in numbers, but, not surprisingly, baptismal registers of Santo Antônio parish for the period from 1808 to 1869 show that the number of baptized African-born slaves was already drastically declining in the 1830s.[30]

The anti–slave trade bill became law (known as the Queirós Law) on September 4, 1850; in 1851, the transatlantic slave trade was formally abolished, after which fewer and fewer slaves continued to be imported to Bahia, as well as to Brazil as a whole.[31] The effective termination of the transatlantic slave trade was to promote the rapid decline of slavery in Brazil.

Urban Slavery in Nineteenth-Century Salvador: Slaveholding Patterns and the Decline of Slavery

Urban slavery had prevailed in the city of Salvador for more than two centuries by the turn of the nineteenth century. Salvador thus matured fully as a "slave society," in which, according to the definition of the late Sir Moses I. Finley, slavery was established as the most dominant institution, both socioeconomically and culturally.[32] The distinctive patterns of urban slavery and slaveholding had been well established in Salvador.[33]

Sex Ratios among the Urban Slave Population

One of the major characteristics of urban slavery in Salvador is found in the sex balance among the slave population. As is well known by now, throughout the transatlantic slave trade from Africa to the New World, males consistently outnumbered females by at least a ratio of 2:1.[34] This was in response to the vast demand for male labor on plantations in the Americas, based on the Europeans' gender perception of manual labor as male, but it was also a reflection of the local demands for female slaves in sub-Saharan Africa.[35] According to David Eltis's calculation, 64.1 percent of slaves imported to Bahia for the period 1811–1850 were males.[36] Despite this sex imbalance among African-born slaves imported to Bahia, the urban slave population in nineteenth-century Salvador was nearly balanced by sex for both African-born and Brazilian-born, with females even slightly outnumbering males. Among slaves purchased and sold in Sé parish for the period 1838–1888, male-female ratios were 48:52 for African-born, and 47:53 for Brazilian-born.[37] Male-female ratios in the slave population were 44:56 in the surviving censuses of 1855 and 49:51 in the first national census taken in 1872.[38] The city contrasted with rural plantation areas, such as the Bahian Recôncavo, which recorded a much higher proportion of male slaves as field hands on the sugar plantations. For example, six Bahian *engenhos* (sugar plantations) in 1816 showed 275 males for every 100 females.[39]

Sex balance in the urban slave population is mainly attributable to the fact that the city demanded abundant female domestic slaves; almost every free household owned or rented at least one slave woman as a domestic. Among all slaves registered in their owners' inventories, which the historian Maria José de Souza Andrade studied for the period 1811–1888, 19.5 percent of males and 74.1 percent of females were domestic servants.[40] I consulted 370 inventories of slave owners registered in Salvador for 1808–1888; 27.1 percent of men were shown as engaged in domestic activities for the period 1808–1849 and 20.9 percent for 1850–1888, whereas 76.6 percent (1808–1849) and 63.1 percent (1850–1888) of slave women were indicated as domestics.[41]

The high demands for female domestic slaves in urban slavery were well reflected in the varying slave prices. Regardless of sex, the prices of skilled domestic slaves were higher than those of field hands. For instance, in Pilar parish from 1850 to 1888, the average slave prices of domestic slaves were 882$096 *réis* for men and 772$915 *réis* for women, considerably higher than those of field hands, which were 685$071 *réis* for men and 615$319 *réis* for women.[42] Even more importantly, the prices of female domestic slaves were much higher than those of male field slaves, despite the fact that men were more expensive than women in the same occupational category. In the city, where slave women were often used in skilled domestic services, their prices increased and occasionally exceeded those of male slaves. Brazilian-born women, who usually had acquired more domestic skills than African-born women, often cost more than their male counterparts, as clearly demonstrated by the data on the prices of slaves in Sé parish for the period 1838–

1888.[43] By contrast, in plantation slavery, in which gang labor was the basis for a slave system where physical strength was the fundamental criterion for slave labor, male slave prices were usually higher than those of female slaves.[44]

The Scale of Urban Slaveholding

Urban slaveholding took place on a much smaller scale than on the plantations. For instance, in 370 inventories of slave owners registered in Salvador for 1808–1888, 86.2 percent (319 individuals) owned no more than ten slaves. When further broken down, the figures are even more revealing: 16.4 percent owned only one slave; 13.5 percent owned two slaves; and 17.3 percent owned three slaves.[45] According to João José Reis, who used the same source for the period 1811–1850, among 395 individuals who registered inventories, 67.1 percent (256 individuals) owned only one to ten slaves, whereas 13.2 percent (342 individuals) did not own any slaves.[46] In nineteenth-century Salvador, every household with the financial means owned or rented at least one slave woman as a maid-for-all-service. There were exemptions from payment of taxes on slaves unless the number of slaves for the service of a single person exceeded two; for a married couple, four; for a big family, six; and where all slaves were under the age of fifteen.[47] Larger households not infrequently included slaves born as the owners' illegitimate children. Often there was a slave hierarchy, with special maids called *mucamas* (*mucumbas*) at the top. The *mucamas,* who were often mulattoes, and might be mistresses or common-law wives of the owners, served as supervisors of other slaves, washerwomen, cooks, housekeepers, and wet nurses (*amas de leite*) for the owners' legitimate children.[48]

The small scale of urban slaveholding was partly attributable to the critical limitations of space in urban households. Furthermore, even for those families who owned only a few slaves, not all slaves of the same owner could lodge under the same roof. In fact, many urban slaves, except for small numbers of full-time, live-in female domestics available for all services in the household, were live-out slaves who often rented the *lojas* (basements, or cellars under the house) with other slaves of the same sex (but often of different owners), or with ex-slaves, often in the same occupations as slaves.[49] In Salvador, where no racially segregated section originally existed, a slave lived side-by-side with, and in the same building as, other tenants who could be whites, free-born people of color, and ex-slaves.

Wage Earning

Urban slavery in Salvador was also characterized by its wage-earning (*ganho*) system, characterized as a "means of subsistence" for the owner. In 1848, the British Vice-Consul James Wetherell described slavery in Salvador as follows:

> A Brazilian has slaves, he sends them out to work at different trades—to cultivate the land, to sell vegetables, to hire as servants, as boatmen, & c.—in fact employs them in every way that servants or workmen are required. The master directs the slave to pay him at the rate of, it may be, about one shilling a day; this frequently is the case, and all the slave can raise above that sum which his master demands, belongs to himself. In the process of time those who are industrious raise sufficient money to pay the price their master values them at, and when such is the case, the slave can claim his freedom.[50]

The German travelers Jonathan B. von Spix and Carl Friedrich P. von Martius stated in the late 1810s that each wage-earning slave (*escravo de ganho*) was obliged to return the daily wage of 240 *réis* to his or her owner.[51] According to another source, in the first third of the nineteenth century, it was customary for the wage-earning slave to pay the owner one *pataca* (320 *réis*) per day or six *patacas* on Saturday, although there was no standard sum or wage authorized by the Bahian authorities.[52] In fact, among 194 African-born ex-slave women who resided in Santana parish in 1849, every one of nine washerwomen earned the smallest amount of 320 *réis* a day, while others with specific occupational skills earned much more.[53] These data may confirm that one *pataca* was an unofficial but widely determined minimum daily wage for unskilled laborers.

Slaves themselves, as another British traveler, Alexander Marjoribanks, observed in both Salvador and Rio de Janeiro in the mid-nineteenth century, applied this wage-earning system of urban slavery.[54] To earn extra cash, they "hired their time out" on a part-time basis in a variety of urban occupations, such as peddlers of both sexes, male porters and transporters in work gangs, and female market-stall keepers.[55] This practice should not be interpreted as suggesting that slavery in the city was less harsh than plantation slavery. The owner punished the slave terribly should the slave fail to return to the owner the wage that the owner and slave had mutually agreed upon. But the wage-earning system of urban slavery at least enabled the enterprising slave to accumulate enough money eventually to purchase freedom, even though it took many years. This also led slaves of both sexes in the city to be usually multifunctional. A female domestic might also peddle cooked foods after work and/or involuntarily or voluntarily engage in prostitution. A male sedan chair carrier (*carregador de cadeira*) might also work in his owner's vegetable garden in the suburbs of the city. Although notarial records, such as inventories and registers of purchases and sales of slaves, usually mentioned the primary or official use of slaves, many urban slaves had more than one occupation or function.[56]

Decline of Urban Slavery in Salvador in the 1840s: From "Slave Society" to "Slave-owning Society"

The above-mentioned distinctive characteristics of urban slavery and slaveholding began to change, and some even disappeared, by the mid-nineteenth century. By 1840, Salvador had been ousted by São Paulo from her position as the second most important commercial city of Brazil; the economic boom in Bahia of the late colonial and early imperial period had already given way to a deep recession. It was in the 1840s that the interprovincial slave trade started on a large scale, after the slave trade was banned in Brazil in 1831. As a result, according to the British official James Bandinel, in Brazil a newly arrived slave in 1840 cost four times more than had been the case in 1821.[57] By the mid-nineteenth century, free labor had replaced slave labor to a great extent in Salvador, as well as in other major Brazilian cities, whereas slaves were increasingly concentrated in the coffee regions through the interprovincial slave trade.[58] Slaves in Salvador, particularly males, were transferred en masse as agricultural laborers to rural regions, especially the booming coffee plantations of the Southeast (Minas Gerais, Rio de Janeiro, and São Paulo).[59] Interestingly, there was greater likelihood that urban slaves in Salvador would be sold to the internal slave trade than would plantation slaves from the Recôncavo. This was because urban slavery in Brazil was "an escape valve for further remunerative slave activity in the face of cyclical export stagnation," as in mainland British America. When the demand for slave labor declined in export-oriented rural-based activities, the growing excess in the labor supply in plantations and mining was transferred, rented, or sold for urban activities. Once new export cycles came into being, there was a significant transfer of urban slaves back to rural-based activities.[60] This is what took place in Salvador in the 1840s with the transfer of urban slaves to the booming coffee plantations in the Southeast.

The historian Herbert S. Klein, comparing the data on slaves transferred to Rio de Janeiro in 1852 with the national census data of 1872, demonstrates that skilled and more urbanized slaves, such as male artisans and female domestics, predominated among those being transported in the interprovincial slave trade. Among the 1,835 slaves who were exported from the province of Bahia in 1854, 836 were from urban centers, 583 had been in agricultural labor, and 416 were of unknown occupation. According to Klein's 1852 data for Rio de Janeiro, two-thirds of such slaves were Brazilian-born, and 73 percent were aged between 15 and 40. He asserts that, given the equal costs of transportation, highly priced slaves were more likely to be preferred as commodities for the internal slave trade.[61]

It is in this socioeconomic context of the 1840s that urban slavery in Salvador began to decline rapidly, which can be characterized as a crucial structural transformation, namely a transition from a "slave society" to a "slave-owning society," in Finley's definition. He maintains that "[i]f the economic and political elite depended primarily on slave labor for basic production, then one may speak of a slave society."[62] Hence, a slave-owning society is defined as the one that owned slaves and used slave labor but did not rely on slaves as the main labor force. Such a structural transformation of the larger society took two notable manifestations in Salvador: a decline in the proportion of the slave population and the larger society's shared perceptions of slaveholding.

The numerical strength of the slave population was a most important factor in defining the nature of the slaveholding society.[63] Before the 1840s, the enslaved population had been a numerical majority in the whole population of Salvador, and slaves were employed in every major economic activity of the port city. The slave proportion of the population in Salvador declined rapidly, from 42 percent in 1835 to 26 percent in 1855.[64] Thus, we may conclude that before or around the mid-nineteenth century, free labor replaced slave labor to a considerable degree.

The change in the form of labor simultaneously also took place at a cultural and ideological level. In a "slave society," slaveholding did not simply mean the predominant use of slave labor, but it also carried status or social prestige for the individual slave owner. This explains why in a "slave society" those, including ex-slaves or sometimes even slaves themselves, who did not own any other form of property owned slaves.[65] Once the slave society transformed itself into a slave-owning society, slaves were reduced to becoming either part of the labor force or commodities to trade. Therefore, in response to the prospering internal slave trade starting in the early 1840s, many owners in Salvador chose to sell their slaves to turn a quick profit. Even after the mid-nineteenth century, the elite in Salvador continued to own slaves and use slave labor, but the urban society no longer depended on the institution of slavery, either economically or culturally. Thus, the transformation of a slave society into a slave-owning society signifies that slavery was not as important a cultural institution for free urban residents in Salvador after the 1840s as before.

Slave prices in Salvador showed a rapid rise at mid-century, after the interprovincial slave trade started to take place, based on the assumption that inflation does not significantly distort the raw data. For instance, among the slaves purchased and sold in Sé parish for 1838–1888, average slave prices started to escalate in the 1850s, reached their peak in the period 1858–1862, and started to drop quickly.[66] This price movement was largely reflected in average prices for self-purchase: they rose sharply at mid-century, reached their peak in 1861–1862, but quickly dropped later in the 1860s.[67]

This overall movement of slave prices in Salvador corresponds to that recorded in the major plantation areas of the Americas (the U.S. South, Cuba, and Brazil), where slave prices increased rapidly during the 1850s and declined slightly in the early 1860s. Slave prices in the mid-1860s remained consistently and substantially above those for the years before 1850, as Manuel Moreno Fraginals, Herbert S. Klein, and Stanley L. Engerman demonstrate. This price movement is attributable to the importance of slave production for the expanding consumer markets in Europe and the United States in the 1850s.[68] Therefore, we may conclude that the movement of slave prices in nineteenth-century Salvador did reflect changes in the world economy, although we cannot deny the interprovincial slave trade's effect as a contributing factor to, as well as its secondary effect on, rising slave prices in local markets.

The data on slave prices in Sé parish for the period 1838–1888 reveal differentiation by sex. The average price for an adult male rose from 431$538 *réis* (1848–1852) to 753$750 *réis* (1853–1857), and then to 1:069$040 *réis* (1858–1862) for African-born; and from 442$941 *réis* (1848–1852) to 944$964 *réis* (1853–1857), and then to 935$830 *réis* (1858–1862) for Brazilian-born.[69] By contrast, the average price for an adult female did not go up as much as that for her male counterpart. The average price for an African-born adult female rose from 395$029 *réis* (1848–1852) to 671$849 *réis* (1853–1857), but then fell to 600$581 *réis* (1858–1862), whereas that for a Brazilian-born adult female rose from 493$571 *réis* (1848–1852) to 766$763 *réis* (1853–1857), and then to 994$964 *réis* (1858–1862).[70] This differentiation by sex in slave price increases is attributable to higher demands for male slaves in the interprovincial slave trade. Klein's study reveals a higher proportion of males among slaves transported in the internal slave trade than among the general slave population. For instance, the male-female ratio among slaves transported to Rio de Janeiro in 1852 was 2:1, whereas sex ratios among the nonmigratory slave population were 126 males to 100 females in the province of São Paulo (1836), 145 males to 100 females in the city of Rio de Janeiro (1849), and 151 males to 100 females in the province of Rio de Janeiro (1850).[71]

Around mid-century, when slave prices began to rise, the percentage of paid manumissions in every category of the manumitted (male/female and African-born/Brazilian-born) increased, whereas that of unpaid manumissions decreased.[72] These data on nineteenth-century Salvador concur with the overall manumission data in nineteenth-century Brazil analyzed by Thomas W. Merrick and Douglas H. Graham.[73] This significant change in the general patterns of manumission in Salvador correlates with the important transformation of urban Bahian society from a slave society to a slave-owning society, which took place in the 1840s. This structural transformation involved cultural and ideological changes. As long as slaveholding itself symbolized individual social status and prestige in society, many slave owners preferred to manumit some slaves whom they usually favored, such as Brazilian-born slaves and women and children, without payment, often unconditionally, noting in the manumission letters their appreciation of the slaves' "good services." By so doing, a slave owner made a public gesture of generosity or humanity, which would, in return, enhance the owner's prestige as a Christian. But, after the 1840s, due to the aforementioned structural change, slaveholding was no longer regarded as a status symbol. Once the price of slaves rose, slave owners were much more open to the idea of making profits through sales of their human commodities and to acceptance of cash for self-purchase of their freedom.

Free labor became the norm in the 1840s. The interprovincial slave trade, which expanded rapidly at mid-century, transferred large numbers of young male urban slaves from Salvador to the coffee-booming Southeast. This had an impact on slaveholding patterns in Salvador. While the enslaved African-born population continued to age, young Brazilian-born male slaves were highly valued for sale to the interprovincial slave trade. The urban slave population in Salvador began to experience an imbalance in terms of sex. The use of slaves was reduced to almost exclusively the domestic domain, where female servants were most needed. The familiar figures of street slaves of both sexes gradually disappeared from daily life in Salvador.

During the last decades of the slave regime, Salvador kept a larger part of the urban slave population of both sexes as domestics. Among the slaves registered in legal records for purchase and sale in Sé parish for the period 1861–1888, 66.3 percent of males (492 individuals) and 81.5 percent of females (626 individuals) were domestics.[74] Domestic slaves of both sexes appeared frequently for sale, purchase, and hire in the slave advertisements of contemporary Bahian newspapers.[75]

Categories for People of African Descent in Nineteenth-Century Salvador

The population of African descent in nineteenth-century Salvador was divided into two categories regarding the place of birth: African-born and Brazilian-born; and three categories in terms of legal status: slave (*escravo*), ex-slave (*forro* or *liberto*), and free-born (*livre*).

All people of African birth, with the exception of a small number of "free Africans" or the "emancipated" after the enactment of the decree of 1831, were brought to Salvador as slaves during the slavery regime. The Brazilian elite always preferred to import new slaves from Africa rather than reproduce the existing slave population. As a result, as long as the massive influx of human cargoes from Africa continued, the majority of Salvador's slave population remained African-born. Hence, for the first four decades of the nineteenth century, slaves constituted around 40 percent of the whole population of Salvador, and two-thirds of the slave population were African-born. In Salvador, at least during the early nineteenth century, *prêto* (black) meant African-born, either enslaved or freed, and *negro* (black) referred to an African-born slave, and neither of them was applied to the Brazilian-born population.

The term *forro* (freed) was originally the generic word for ex-slave, regardless of how the slave acquired freedom, but in colonial Brazil, the term *forro* did not always refer to ex-slave; it was used broadly and somewhat confusingly. In the sixteenth century, for instance, *indios forros* were not only ex-slaves but also the indigenous population who were not enslaved but under Portuguese control, especially, though not exclusively, that of the Jesuits.[76] Until around the end of the eighteenth century, *forro* referred to all legally free people of color, both free-born and ex-slave, without any clear distinction. For instance, in eighteenth-century Brazil, colored militia regiments were composed of the legally free population of African descent, both free-born and freed, under the same term *forro*; there is no document left regarding whether the African-born population was included or not.[77] On the other hand, the term "liberated" (*liberto*) came to carry a new meaning, which originated from the British antislavery movement during the first decades of the nineteenth century. It became a part of the official language in Brazil, and later in the 1840s dominated common usage among the ex-slave population for self-identification.[78] In nineteenth-century Salvador, *forro* and *liberto* were used interchangeably, except that a child born to a slave woman and baptized as legally free was always called *forro*, never *liberto*. During the colonial period and the nineteenth century, the city of Salvador witnessed the significant presence of the ex-slave population. No matter how small a percentage they constituted, it is important to note that slaves were manumitted with much greater frequency in the cities than in the rural, agricultural areas; an urban environment was much more conducive to the opportunities of freedom.

The term *livre* was used to clarify the legal status of the Brazilian-born individual of color, and was not used to refer to the status of any white person; the combination of *branco livre* (free-born white) is never found in historical documents. To whites, being called *livre* must have been offensive, as was also the case of the antebellum U.S. South, where the term "free-born" referred only to free-born people of color, to distinguish them from slaves and former slaves.

In nineteenth-century Salvador, in notarial records and other official documents, the Brazilian-born population of African descent, either slave, ex-slave, or free-born, were divided into several categories of color (*côr*), such as *crioulo* (black); *pardo* (mulatto); *mulato* (mulatto with pejorative connotation); *cabra* (mulatto, often darker-skinned); and *mestiço* (mixed-breed in general, but hardly used in the nineteenth century). The term *caboclo* referred to a person of Indian-European ancestry, but the city of Salvador included a very small *caboclo* population, unlike the rural regions of Bahia.

Part One
To Be African-Born and Enslaved, circa 1808–1831

There are no paths in water. No signposts.
There is no return. To a land trampled by the
muddy boots of others. To a people encouraged to war among themselves. To a father consumed with guilt. You are beyond. Broken-off,
like limbs from a tree. But not lost, for you
carry within your bodies the seed of new trees.
Sinking your roots into different soil.
                        —Caryl Phillips, *Crossing the River*

2 The Creation of New Identity, 1808–1831

An African-born individual's creation of new identity began to take place at the very moment of enslavement in the homeland of Africa. Many of these enslaved people were captives of warfare, pawns, victims of kidnapping, or captives for the services of oracles. Some parents, because of debts, laziness, and insubordination, even sold their own children.[1] Whatever the reasons, when those people lost their freedom, they were forced to give up their original identities, which were closely associated with their being freeborn and belonging to their own families, lineages, and larger local groups. They were soon sold by local slavers/merchants into the hand of European slave merchants, who shipped them from ports on the coast of Africa, where they often had to wait together for days or months for slave ships to show up. These people were loaded as human cargoes onto slave ships; they forcibly endured the long, terrible hardship of the Middle Passage, which many of their fellow passengers could not survive; and after a passage of a month or even longer they eventually arrived as commodities for trade in the New World.

This chapter examines processes by which African-born enslaved men and women of diverse ethnic origins created their new ethnic and gender identities at the workplace. Our special emphasis will be placed on critical tensions between attempts by the powerful to categorize/label the powerless for the sake of slave control and the latter's meticulous manipulations of such imposed categories/labels for the purpose of their daily survival of New World slavery.

Enslavement and the Imposition of New "Cards of Identity"

Being sold into the transatlantic slave trade did not merely mean the deprivation of one's original identities, but also the imposition of two new "cards of identity" by power holders on all enslaved human beings. One was a Portuguese/Christian name given at baptism, and the other was an African "nation" (*nação*).

Enslaved individuals of African birth were all forced to incorporate themselves into a New World slave system in a double sense: as human commodities in a labor system, and also as pagans who had to be converted into the new religious faith of Christianity. The State and the Church were essentially inseparable from each other in establishing the institution of African slavery in Portugal and its overseas colonies; the Portuguese had sought to justify the trade in slaves and the institution of slavery on the grounds of conversion to Christianity and the salvation of souls that would otherwise have been lost.[2] Therefore every African-born slave was theoretically obliged to be baptized as a Catholic before or upon arrival in Brazil, whereas Brazilian-born slaves were baptized at birth.

Henry Koster, who resided in northern Brazil as a sugar planter during the first decades of the nineteenth century, gave us a good description of the baptismal ceremony of the enslaved Africans:

> The Africans who are imported from Angola are baptized in lots before they leave their own shores, and on their arrival in Brazil they are to learn the doctrines of the church, and the duties of the religion in which they have entered. These bear the mark of the royal crown upon their breasts, which denotes that they have undergone the ceremony of baptism, and likewise that the king's duty has been paid upon them. The slaves which are imported from other parts of the coast of Africa, arrive in Brazil unbaptized, and before the ceremony of making them Christians can be performed upon them, they must be taught certain prayers, for the acquirement of which one year is allowed to the master, before he is obliged to present the slave at the parish-church. This law is not always strictly adhered to as to time, but it is never evaded altogether.[3]

In Angola, on the day before embarkation, slaves were usually assembled in a church, or perhaps in the main square of the port, to be baptized. As a prelude to the following ceremony, a Catholic priest walked among the slaves, assigned a Christian name to each, and handed the individual a paper with the name written on it.[4] As the anthropologist Jack Goody elucidates, the renaming of slaves was nothing new: "such new names served to cut the individuals off from their kinsfolk, their society, from humanity itself and at the same time emphasized their servile status."[5] Goody continues: "However the renaming was not in itself sufficient, the new name had to be written down and handed to the individual. . . . The paper is intended to convey information to the slave's purchaser in the New World. But at the same time it provides a card of identity, *a card to change an identity,* which at one level affects the change it purports to record."[6] Thus each Portuguese/Christian name came to symbolize the individual's lost identity through enslavement.

The other card of identity, namely an African "nation," was given to enslaved individuals of African birth collectively but functioned to divide them into a limited number of categories. The African "nation" was a legacy inherited from the European custom of identifying slaves in Africa by "nationalities," regardless of their specific places of origin or ethnic affiliations. Henry Koster mentioned that African-born slaves in Brazil were "known under the *names* of Angola, Congo, Rebolo, Anjico, Gabon, and Mozambique."[7] These names were African "nations" that European slave traders in Africa imposed on enslaved individuals to reduce them to a limited number of categories, before forced departure for the New World. But it fitted into the European scheme, where people had such identities.

According to Philip D. Curtin, such "nations"/"nationalities" can be broadly divided into two group labels. The first was the name of the port from which slaves were shipped. For example, the term "Mina" was originally applied to a slave shipped from the old Portuguese fort of El Mina on the Gold Coast, but its usage was extended in the nineteenth century to mean anyone from West Africa. The other was the ethnic or linguistic term, which was identified with a much larger group. For example, "Nagô," which had originally referred to a subgroup of the northern Yoruba, was broadly applied to all Yoruba-speaking peoples. Furthermore, some "nationalities" were loosely linked to geographical regions of origin, such as "Congo" and "Angola."[8] It should be added that some "nations"/"nationalities" in Africa were originally the group names by which they were known to other ethnic groups. The Yoruba called the Nupe "Tapa." The Yoruba were known to the Ewe (Gêge) as "Nagô." Such group labels for reference by others, of course, did not necessarily correspond to exact ethnic group boundaries.

European colonists identified these "nations" with certain physical types and cultural heritages, and expressed preferences for the one over the other when it came to the purchase of plantation labor for the Americas. Such stereotyping and perceived qualities, or lack of them, were reflected in higher or lower prices of such slaves.[9] These characterizations of slave types had been present in colonial Brazil and survived throughout the nineteenth century. Visiting Salvador in 1803, the British merchant Thomas Lindley characterized slaves from Angola and Benguela as "a sturdy kind of negroes, docile to a degree, and very active and lively."[10] Koster described "Angolas" as the best slaves because of their great attachment, fidelity, and honesty, whereas "Minas" were "represented as possessing great firmness of mind and body, and ferociousness of disposition."[11] The German travelers J. B. von Spix and C. F. P. von Martius noted that those from Congo and Angola were suited for domestic service because of their docility and language skills.[12]

Thus, with the imposition of these two new cards of identity, both of which signified their new social and legal status as slaves, women and men of African birth were forced to learn to perceive themselves as the absolute powerless in the New World. However, they were not entirely receptive to such labels/categories. Instead, as we shall discuss, they took an active involvement in the creation of their new identities.

The Creation of Ethnic Identity

Enslaved people of African birth in Salvador gradually adopted such group labels/categories as African "nations" to create and re-create their ethnic identities, through the Middle Passage experience and in the process of being incorporated into New World slave systems.[13] In this sense, the association of those who were transported on the same ship and called one another *malungos* (shipmates) was a part of this process of constructing and reconstructing ethnic groups. Koster mentioned that the term *malungo* was much regarded among African-born slaves and that these individuals showed "much attachment" to their *malungos,* as great as to their wives and children.[14] One of the participants in the Malê revolt (1835), a Nagô slave who was called Matheos in Portuguese but whose African name was Dadá, testified that two other participants, Belchior and Gaspar da Silva, were his *malungos.*[15]

Historian Paul E. Lovejoy suggests that in the case of early nineteenth-century Salvador such "shipmates formed allegiances, and the ethnic backgrounds of slaves further consolidated these ties" since they were originally from the same geographical area of Africa and arrived in Salvador on the same Portuguese-Brazilian ships.[16] As Mintz and Price discuss, this "shipmate" relationship was of a dyadic (two-person) nature between individuals of the same sex, partly because of the general policy of keeping men and women separate on a slave ship. Mintz and Price conclude that among the population of African descent in the New World these same-sex dyadic ties that were derived from the Middle Passage experience "became a major principle of social organization and continued for decades or even for centuries to shape ongoing social relations" and that "the development of these social bonds, even before the Africans set foot in the New World, already announced the birth of new societies based on new kinds of principles."[17]

Enslaved people of African birth, who had begun to develop such same-sex dyadic ties with one another on slave ships, were eventually brought into the port of Salvador. Interestingly, Salvador, the oldest port city of Brazil, did not develop such a commercially organized, large-scale slave market as the Valongo, a long winding street that runs from the sea, located at the northern edge of the newer port city of Rio de Janeiro. On the Valongo of Rio de Janeiro, almost every house was a large warehouse, where the slaves were deposited and customers came to purchase them, and each house was sometimes filled with three or four hundred slaves of all ages and both sexes.[18] Perhaps the geographical features of the port of Salvador hampered the establishment of a large slave market. Instead of one main street, many streets of Salvador served the function of a slave market. The British merchant Thomas Lindley observed the streets and squares of Salvador in 1803 being "thronged with groups of human beings, exposed for sale at the doors of different merchants to whom they belong, five slave ships having arrived within the last three days."[19] There were numerous small houses on various streets of the city that functioned as slave markets. Such houses were particularly concentrated on Rua Nova do Comércio of the lower city, as well as Baixa dos Sapateiros street,[20] near the Black Church of Our Lady of the Rosary (Igreja de Nossa Senhora do Rosário dos Homens Prêtos) in the Pelourinho (which means pillory), an old public square where owners brought their slaves for public whipping, in accordance with laws and regulations.[21] This public square, located at the administrative center of the upper city, had become identified with a *pelourinho*, which stood at the center of this busy square always crowded with street slaves.[22]

Upon arrival in Salvador, many slaves were traded individually on the streets. Slave merchants stood with their slaves for sale at busy street corners of the commercial districts, and touted their wares by yelling to passersby. Others even peddled their human commodities around residential districts. Slaves were most commonly sold and purchased one by one on the streets. This practice continued despite the edict of the municipal council forbidding it: "Those who sell and purchase slaves must do so only in shops situated in houses or stores. The penalty is 30$000 *réis* and eight days imprisonment."[23] Slaves in the city of Salvador thus saw other slaves being sold and purchased on the street, and had the opportunity to learn how this business of trading in slaves worked. Some may have made a single purchase of a new arrival at a cheaper price for investment, whereas others got involved in the business themselves.

Unlike the case of plantation slavery, in urban slavery in Salvador, the majority of slaves worked and even lived outside their owners' houses. The slaves constantly faced the danger of kidnapping; slaves were often stolen and subsequently resold on the streets. On July 22, 1830, for instance, a Portuguese man, a resident of the suburban parish of Brotas, was found guilty of having sold slaves who had been kidnapped in the city.[24] On May 20, 1834, when the police inspected a house in the Barroquinha of São Pedro Velho parish, they found two slaves who had been kidnapped and hidden by the Portuguese Francisco Antônio da Fonseca. These slaves were a newly arrived Nagô slave boy owned by José Barboza Madureira and an African-born woman, also Nagô, a slave of Domingos Jorcome Ferreira.[25] In and around the port city of Recife of Pernambuco during the early nineteenth century, the Brazilian historian Marcus J. M. de Carvalho documented fascinating cases in which slaves actually bargained with their prospective owners on the condition of being kidnapped,[26] but there are no such documented cases in the city of Salvador. Yet, there was indeed a thriving trade in kidnapped slaves from Salvador to the ports of southern Brazil.[27] Not only whites but many of African descent, including African-born and enslaved, were engaged in this interprovincial slave trade. In November 1831, in Rua do Passo parish, two *prêtos,* José Francisco and a certain Bonfim, the latter the slave of Domingo Ferreira Bastos, were imprisoned for having kidnapped and sold a *prêta* named Vitória, who was a slave of Bento Martins da Costa.[28] On July 19, 1831, in Vitória parish, a *crioulo,* Luíz Xavier, sold a *prêta,* Joanna. Joanna proved to be the slave of Antônio Diego de Sá Barreto, and the municipal police arrested Luís and his accomplice, a *prêto* by the name of João.[29] Thus, survival in the urban slave society entailed, among other things, escaping the danger of being kidnapped and resold, and avoiding falling victim to other urban crimes.

Daily interactions among urban slaves on the streets transcended the boundaries of both ownership and geography. This makes a very sharp contrast to plantation slavery, in which each plantation functioned as a virtually independent entity for human interactions under an organized labor system. Urban slavery gave slaves considerable latitude to move as wage-earners. Newly arrived African-born slaves continued to receive a minimum amount of guidance or occupational training from their owners. They were usually hired out without any special occupational training in domestic service or craft skills, or even comprehension of the Portuguese language. Much of this their Brazilian-born counterparts generally learned from birth. Among slaves registered in their owners' inventories for the period 1808–1849, all of the men whose primary occupations were transportation or porterage were African-born. They were even more noticeable in fieldwork and as full-time wage-earners than their Brazilian-born counterparts, many of whom were engaged in artisanal occupations and domestic work. Among slave women, one-fifth of the African-born were hired out as wage-earners on a full-time basis, whereas the majority of the Brazilian-born were primarily domestic servants. By contrast, very few Brazilian-born slaves of either sex were engaged in full-time wage earning.[30]

As discussed in chapter 1, urban households did not require large-scale slaveholding. Their needs were limited to full-time domestic servants, many of whom could also be engaged in part-time wage earning in the streets. Thus, slaveholding in the city largely took the form of cash earning. People may have purchased African-born slaves for personal service but found hiring them out on a full-time or part-time basis could be income enhancing. For those new arrivals who did not comprehend the Portuguese language or Luso-Brazilian culture, it was especially important to associate with other slaves who at least spoke the same language in order to enter an urban slave system.

In Salvador, many slave women and men were hired out for wage-earning activities on the street without the direct supervision of owners. For the enslaved individual, every street of Salvador, which was ill-paved with irregular, sharp, and large stones, was the workplace.[31] Slaves of both sexes worked barefoot, suffering from the annoying *bicho da pé,* a tiny insect that easily penetrated the skin of their feet.[32] For those slaves, the street served as the most important meeting place on a daily basis. Whenever African-born slaves encountered other African-born slaves on the street, all tried to distinguish "their people" from others by superficial physical features, as well as facial marks received at their initiation rites in Africa.[33] James Wetherell observed:

> Most of the blacks have their faces marked in a peculiar manner with scars or cicatrices, and each nation or tribe differs in some respect from another. The most numerous, the Nago blacks, for their national mark have three small cuts in the centre of the forehead. The Benguela have 5, 7, or 11 small *nodules* of flesh in the centre of the forehead, forming a line

of *warts* from the roots of the hair to the nose. A very difficult and painful mask to produce, I shall imagine. The cuts, being so much simpler, appear to be more generally adopted. . . .[34]

Small wonder that new arrivals from Africa could be easily distinguished by others from those who had lived in Brazil for many years and were therefore fairly acculturated, since the former's external appearance and cultural behaviors were not Luso-Brazilianized. However, even among the latter, the ethnic affiliation of the individual could be identified by phenotypical, behavioral, and cultural traits; the African-born population were keenly conscious of ethnic diversity among themselves.

If a stranger on the street appeared to be from a certain ethnic group of Africa, another individual would talk to the stranger in their native language, or might greet the person in terms and actions appropriate to their native culture to express mutual respect. Even when chained with other slaves in the same work gang, slaves would not pass by their fellow persons without making some friendly gesture. This was described by outsiders and foreign visitors as the "politeness of blacks." Wetherell observed this trait in 1842: "The Blacks seem naturally polite; they never pass without saluting by removing their hats, and when they meet, they crack the two first fingers of the right hand, each taking hold of the other's hand for the purpose, in the same way as if they were going to shake hands. If a black woman passes a man seated, with whom she is acquainted, he not only takes off his hat but rises from his seat."[35] Wetherell also noted cultural continuity among Africans in Salvador: African-born people paid special respect by kneeling before those who had been "princes" in their homelands.[36] When they met their people on the street, they used the special terms of salutations, such as "Selamat" ("I congratulate you on your safety"), "Teijibeen" ("I hope you are well"), "Ogirai" ("Good morning"), and "Occuginio" ("I hope you have risen in health"), none of which Wetherell identified with a specific African language.[37] In New World slavery, differences of status and some hierarchical orders originating from within native African cultures were also stressed, modified, and maintained among the African-born slave population of diverse ethnic origins, as well as in relation to the larger society. The American James Henderson observed in 1821 that the slaves in Salvador, assembling in a plaza of the upper city on Sundays and holidays, "frequently selected one from amongst the rest who was dignified with the title of chief, and received all the homage bestowed upon a chief in their home country."[38] Henderson stated further that a friend of his, passing through the plaza, had seen slaves conducting "the ceremony of executing, or putting to death, white men, which were represented by effigies dressed for the purpose; this was intended for the amusement of their chief."[39] Activities such as this are patent substantiation of persisting African cultural characteristics and therefore refute the notion that the experience of the Middle Passage left Africans devoid of humanity and common sense.

In Salvador, many of the African-born population continued to communicate with one another in their native languages in their daily lives.[40] In 1814, after a major slave uprising took place, slave owners sent a petition to the governor of Bahia (1810–1818), D. Marcos de Noronha, Count of Arcos, in which they noted: "Finally, *negros* crowd at night into the streets as before; they freely converse in their own languages; and they continuously use whistles and other passwords. They even talk openly in our language which they have come to understand."[41] While discussing the diversity of the enslaved African-born population and their native languages, which was supposed to lessen the danger of a slave revolt, J. B. von Spix and C. F. P. von Martius noted in the late 1810s that slaves in Salvador understood one another at least by means of certain expressions despite the fact that they lived distant from one another. They interpreted many African languages as having great similarities to one another and as forming an extreme contrast to those of the indigenous populations.[42] Of course, we do not know exactly to what degree these foreign travelers' statements were valid. Diverse African languages, none of which bore any resemblance to any European languages, could have sounded similar to those German travelers, who may have been struck, above all, by the superficial "racial" homogeneity of the large enslaved population in Salvador, as "blacks." The Bahian historian Nina Rodrigues believes that the Gêge (Ewe) language was used throughout the eighteenth century and until at least the middle of the nineteenth century. Tapa and Hausa were spoken during the entire nineteenth century. Above all, Nagô continued to be a *língua geral* (general language) among the African-born population, even in the early twentieth century.[43] As late as the late 1930s, the American sociologist Donald Pierson stated that he had heard Nagô spoken in Salvador and had met people whose command of Nagô was comparable to their command of Portuguese.[44]

Furthermore, the African-born population also commonly referred to one another by their African names, not by their Christian/Portuguese names given at Catholic baptism before or upon arrival in Brazil, by which they were widely known in the larger society.[45] Their usage of their African names may also suggest a shared attitude toward the larger society. African names had specific meanings in their native African languages, and their continued usage in the New World could be essential for African-born peoples' (re)creation of ethnic identity. On the other hand, Portuguese names officially bestowed on slaves by their owners were devoid of any symbolic significance and could have been viewed by their fellow enslaved individuals as tantamount to so many numbers. This is clear evidence that these enslaved people did not lose their African identities, although those identities were submerged in the New World.

Ethnicity in New World slavery was not simply a duplicate of ethnicity in their homelands of Africa. Franklin W. Knight and Margaret E. Crahan are accurate in stating that "Specific ethnic identifications did not necessarily indicate the retention of the formerly associated ethnic culture. . . . Representative ethnic cultures survived, but without necessarily reflecting closely the basic original mix of the African locality and religion."[46] Ethnicity needs to be perceived as "a process of interaction between 'objective category' and 'subjective identity' within a variety of social environments."[47]

In the case of Salvador, at his trial after the Malê revolt of 1835, one Nagô defendant, the slave Antônio, whose profession was a chair carrier, testified in court as follows: "[W]e all are Nagôs, but each of us has his/her own homeland [*terra*]."[48] This statement is worth noting, being uttered as it is in the context of his self-defense as Nagô, the African "nation" that represented the majority of participants in the uprising. Antônio identified his "nation" as Egba and referred to the slave José of the same owner as Oyo. Another Nagô slave, José, testified that he was from the Jabú "nation" (Ijebu), whereas the Nagô woman Edum was identified as Nagô-Ba (Egba).[49] These statements exemplify the creation of ethnic identity in New World slavery. Those who were from the same African language group, but from different lineages and/or subdivisions of an ethnic group associated with one another, often under the label of an African "nation."

These people sought and continuously created and re-created the common ethnic symbols that they could share among themselves, as well as some hierarchic order, perhaps based on their African lineage systems but in relation to the larger society. Yet coming to share a specific ethnic identity in common under New World slavery does not really mean that all such individuals belonged to the same ethnic group or took collective actions as members of the same ethnic group. As J. C. Mitchell clarifies, we should distinguish between "'ethnicity' as a construct of perceptual or cognitive phenomena on the one hand, and the 'ethnic groups' as a construct of behavior phenomena on the other."[50]

The Creation of Gender Identity

Enslaved people of African birth started to cultivate their gender identities during the Middle Passage. We have already discussed that on slave ships men and women were separated from each other, that therefore shipmate relationships called *malungos* were same-sex dyadic ties, and that such relationships played an important role in connecting enslaved peoples of African birth in New World slavery. Unlike the case of plantation slavery, in which men largely outnumbered women and sex did not critically determine the work an individual slave had to perform as a field hand, such same-sex, dyadic ties as *malungos* might well be maintained rather easily and were even strengthened for the creation of gender identity in Salvador, because of the unique nature of New World urban slavery. As discussed in chapter 1, the slave population in Salvador was balanced by sex, mainly because of the city's high demands for female domestic slaves. African-born slave women were physically as "visible" in the public sphere as their male counterparts. At the same time, one's sex as a slave critically determined the types of work and activities in which one had to and/or wanted to engage, which fostered the African-born people's creation of gender identity in urban slavery.

The historian Jacqueline Jones, in her study of the U.S. South, discusses the gender division of labor under slavery: "[T]he more freedom the slaves had in determining their own activities, the more clearly emerged a distinct division of labor between the sexes."[51] Her statement would equally apply to the case of the enslaved population of African birth in nineteenth-century Salvador. It is true that one's sex primarily determined how one would be used as an urban slave, but the flexible labor arrangements in urban slavery gave much freedom for the African-born population to (re)define gender relations and create new gender identity.

In the city of Salvador, enslaved men of African birth were used as porters and transporters who worked in gangs. These male work gangs were often composed of slave men who shared the same "nation" and who usually did not belong to the same owner because of the small scale of urban slaveholding. Such male associations at work appear to have been voluntary and may be interpreted as a notable manifestation of a collective ethnic identity among African-born slave men, but the associations could have been initially devised as an effective labor arrangement by slave owners who intended to make the best profits by hiring out newly arrived African-born slave men to the streets. Relatively acculturated slave men of African birth with sufficient occupational skills could train newly arrived male slaves in the same African languages. This arrangement did not threaten slave owners because those slaves did not belong to the same owner.

In every busy street of Salvador, at any time of the day, there was the sight of two slave men carrying a hammock or sedan chair on their shoulders. Sedan chairs for wealthy people consisted of "a cane arm-chair, with a foot-board and a canopy covered with leather; curtains, generally of moreen, with gilt bordering and lined with cotton or linen, are contrived to draw round, or open at pleasure; and the whole is slung by the top to a single pole, by which two negroes carry it at a quick pace upon their shoulders, changing occasionally from right to left."[52] Whereas, depending on the social status of the occupant, carriers of sedan chairs might be in uniform, male porters were nearly naked, dressed only in the scantiest pair of casse cotton drawers. They carried small things on the heads, but large objects were slung between two poles which were carried on the shoulders.[53] James C. Fletcher and Daniel P. Kidder described these male street gangs (1839) as follows:

> Immense numbers of tall, athletic negroes are seen moving in pairs or gangs of four, six, or eight, with their loads suspended between them on heavy poles. Numbers more of their fellows are seen sitting upon their poles, braiding straw, or lying about the alleys and corners of the streets asleep, reminding one of black snakes coiled up in the sunshine. The sleepers generally have some sentinel ready to call them when they are wanted for business, and at the given signal they rouse up, like the elephant to his burden.[54]

As they moved with their heavy burdens, they sang a kind of chorus, which consisted of "one of the blacks chanting a remark on anything he sees, and the others come in with a chorus of ridiculous description, which is seldom varied, however much the recitative solo part may."[55] Each grouping of these street male workers was obliged to have a captain or leader, who organized the work, set the fees, and took responsibility for payment of municipal taxes and licenses for his group.[56]

Slave men played a crucial role in communication between Salvador and the Bahian Recôncavo, which was very difficult even after the turn of the nineteenth century. The roads were no better than "mule-tracks," and all merchandise was carried in small packages by horses and mules. There were hardly any direct routes to any destination in the countryside, and the conveyance often took hundreds of extra miles. Carriage by road was thus very costly and laborious.[57] Sugar planters and their families spent part of the year in their houses in the upper city of Salvador, and when they went to the city some slaves from their rural properties who served as porters and domestic servants always accompanied them. The Bahian Recôncavo has several major rivers: São Francisco, Vermelho, Joannes, Jucuipe, Pojuca, Guassú, Paraguassú, and Serigy, which played an important role for the daily transportation of people and things throughout the nineteenth century. Slave men were employed as canoeists on the rivers for the transport of passengers. Slave paddlers propelled canoes while singing a monotonous chorus, even sometimes raising the paddles completely out of water and striking the flat part of them with their hands, keeping time.[58]

Slave men also transported agricultural products by water to the city. The Bay of All Saints and the São Francisco River were the two great, distinct market zones of Bahia.[59] The urban inhabitants of Salvador depended on the Recôncavo for their daily diet. For instance, Itaparica, whose principal product was sugar, supplied Salvador with poultry, vegetables, and fruit.[60] Every day, numerous country boats, launches, sailing boats, and other types of vessels crossed the bay laden with produce for consumption in the city. Canoes arrived from places twenty to thirty leagues away from Salvador.[61] James Wetherell described in 1848 the arrival of a *barca* in the city as follows:

> Upon a barca reaching the city, a scene of confusion ensues, boats put off with market women to besiege with the new arrival, large crates of fowls are borne off by the fortunate purchasers, ananas [*sic*] and oranges are piled in golden heaps, the shore boats are quickly laden with cabbages, yams, sugar cane, pumpkins, or melons. each [*sic*] freighter hastening to her market-stand to make the best of her bargains by retailing. The barca then draws near the quay to discharge the heavier part of her cargo, puncheons of spirit, cattle, or empty packages sent down to be returned filled with European productions.[62]

Yams, manioc flour, corn, rice, and many other vegetables, as well as tobacco, wood, coral, fish, and even cattle were thus constantly brought from the Recôncavo to Salvador by water by slave men.[63] Chewing tobacco was very popular among the population of African descent in the city.[64]

Male stevedores, most of whom were hired-out African-born slaves, were the most common figures among workers of African descent in the port of Salvador. They used large wooden carts for the conveyance of sugar to the place of shipment.[65] These manual laborers also carried heavy loads on their heads, or on dollies, from ships to waterfront warehouses and from warehouses to the commercial district of the lower city.

At the harbor, slave men moved commodities and people in canoes and lighters from ship to shore. Besides small sailing vessels, one of the most common vessels was the *falúa,* with two masts, each with a large sail, manned by four to eight slave oarsmen, and with a covered stern to protect customers from the sun.[66] It was also the role of slave men to bring newly arrived slaves ashore for auction in the slave markets.

Many male slaves engaged in fishing in Salvador, which was chronically short of meat but endowed with an abundant and varied supply of fish from the bay. Fish was sold at a high price, particularly during Lent.[67] On the sandy beach, slaves were employed to catch shellfish, oysters, mussels, and turtles.[68] Every morning, in the bay near Rio Vermelho parish, slave fishermen manned forty to fifty launches in search of whales. These launches had one large lugsail and were very fast. Every launch was composed of ten crewmen: eight oarsmen, one patron, and one harpooner. According to the observation by the British traveler Robert Elwes (1848), the crew of a whale-fishing launch was "often dressed in costume; one crew in red, red woolen shirts, red trousers and red caps, another in blue, and & c." Whales were brought into the warehouse called *armação,* where they were processed for food and oil.[69]

African-born slave men also engaged in larger-scale marine activities. These ranged from the coastal trade between Brazilian cities to the transatlantic slave trade. A considerable number of men of African descent chose to engage in transatlantic trade, developed networks exclusively among men, and, as a result, made a significant contribution to the transatlantic communication among peoples of African descent.[70] In the case of men of African birth, their ethnic origins and backgrounds seem to have been an advantage for their profession as slave traders. Those who served as canoeists, oarsmen, or sailors were generally African-born, many working also as wage-earning slaves. Captains of slave ships hired slaves as cooks, cabin boys, seamen, and barber-surgeons.

Many slave men of African birth were also trained in various artisanal skills, because of the lack of skilled free labor. Such enslaved men were used as carpenters, joiners, masons, pavers, printers, sign and ornamental painters, carriage and cabinet makers, coopers, sculptors in stone and carvers of saintly images in wood, silversmiths, lamp makers, jewelers, and lithographers. Nearly a quarter of the male slaves listed in their owners' inventories for the years 1811–1888 were artisans.[71] As the historian Lyman Johnson points out, in many colonial Latin American cities, purchasing a slave to train him as an artisan guaranteed a master artisan a profitable return on his investment. Since the artisan as slave owner turned a profit on the difference between the cost of the slave's subsistence and the value of his production, the owner's profit increased as the slave's skills improved. Furthermore, sales by a slave artisan provided the owner with a profitable supplement to his regular business activities.[72] The use of slave labor also gave a master artisan a greater degree of control over his workshop.[73] In accordance with the degree of skill, slave artisans were classified in their owners' inventories as *mestre* (master), *official* (skilled), and *apprendiz* (apprentice).[74] The British traveler Thomas Ewbank stated that a vicar in the city of Rio de Janeiro had mentioned a slave who was a first-rate workman in Bahia.[75] Many such skilled slave craftsmen were hired out by their owners.

The variety of street peddling and vending by slaves was not exclusive in terms of gender; both men and women were widely engaged in daily peddling and door-to-door vending. Some, such as butchers' slaves who sold fresh meat by peddling, were ordered by their owners to do so on a full-time or part-time basis. Others hired themselves out on Sundays, holidays, or late in the evening after their obligatory work as domestic servants or field hands. Urban slaves used their free time to grow vegetables in their owner's gardens and in provision gardens attached to suburban plantations, or to cook foodstuffs in their owner's kitchens and on the streets, or to engage in prostitution as part-time hustlers. Should they be successful as vendors, owners might send them out as full-time peddlers. Street peddlers offered for sale whatever they could carry in a basket or tray on their heads: various vegetables, fresh or cooked foodstuffs, oranges, limes, and tropical fruits, cakes and candies, eggs, sugar canes, bundles of firewood, and even shoes and children's toys.[76] These street peddlers, most of whom were African-born, visited every house, calling out each item's name in rhythmic chants. The residents of Salvador were also supplied with water from fountains by these slave peddlers. J. B. von Spix and C. F. P. von Martius mentioned in the late 1810s that the fountain of Campo de São Pedro was regarded as the best in Salvador.[77] Water was carried from the fountains in jars or small barrels, generally on the shoulders of men, on mules, or in carts, and sold to every household at a modest price.[78]

Despite this prevailing practice of street vending by slaves of both sexes, marketing in the city and all aspects of petty commerce were virtually monopolized by African-born women. African-born women's marketing activities were prevalent in Salvador at least by the beginning of the 1830s.[79] Mary C. Karasch points out elite perceptions in colonial and nineteenth-century Latin America of "those who sold groceries and liquor as lower in status, especially if they sold to the poor and enslaved."[80] In the British Caribbean, which was described as where "[n]egroes are the only market people" and "[n]o body else dreams of selling provisions," slave marketing activities might be divided into two categories: one was carried out by itinerant slave peddlers, usually favored women who sold such household products as beeswax candles, seeds, and vegetables from the manager's large garden; and the other by slaves who bartered or sold their own commodities.[81] In cities, slave women were generally in a much better position than their male counterparts in terms of market participation, since the former could sell on the street what they cooked as domestics in the kitchen of their owner's house. "House" and "street" thus formed a continuous, single living space for slave women.[82] Unlike their male counterparts, many slave women simultaneously belonged to two different social/cultural spheres: the slave owner's household and the street.[83] This may explain the prevailing dominance of women in the internal market system in the cities of the Third World, where poor women usually work as domestic servants.[84] Furthermore, men did not wish to engage in such a "woman's job" as street vending, which was not valued in their community. The anthropologist Marisol de la Cadena states in her case study of a contemporary "Indian" community near Cuzco: "Prevailing male view holds that the sale of products is not work because it is done 'sitting down.' For them this labor is secondary and deviant—the fruit of masculine work."[85]

African-born slave women were prominent as *quitandeiras* in nineteenth-century Salvador. The term *quitandeira* referred to women who sold items at their own market stalls (*quitandas* or *vendas*) on the street or in the markets. In Salvador the daily green-market located on the beach was well supplied with tropical fruits and vegetables, which were brought from the nearby coast by slave men in small launches or boats. The market was filled at an early hour of the morning with coconuts, plantains, oranges, melons, jacks, papayas, guavas, mangoes, and tamarinds, as well as yams, manioc, peas, beans, and cucumbers.[86] According to a Bahian historian and professor of Greek named Luís dos Santos Vilhena, during the eighteenth century market stalls were concentrated in three places in the city: the waterfront of Conceição da Praia parish, the square of Terreiro de Jesus located on the street now called Nova in Sé parish, and outside the St. Benedict monastery of Santana parish.[87]

Most market-stall keepers and market vendors (*mercadejas*) were women, especially those of African birth. Wetherell described market women in Salvador (1848) as follows:

> Amongst heaps of fruit, vegetables, & c., shaded by mats, which are some of them formed into something like huts, in others only propped up by sticks, are seated the black market women. They are dressed in highly characteristic but picturesque dresses of many diversified colours, but all of the same fashion. Some have their infant children slung across their backs with the "Panno da Costa" (coast cloth shawl), others with heavy baskets of fruit and edibles on their heads. Little children, whose only article of clothing consists of bracelets, ear-rings, and a band round the body of coral heads, squatted on flat wooden dishes, like Indian gods.[88]

Market-stall keepers and market women sold a diversity of commodities: cooked ethnic dishes such as fried cake of cooked beans called *acarajé* of West African origin (*akara* in Dahomey), *carurú* (shrimp and okra stew), and *vatapá* (fish-based paste), candies, cakes, fruits, vegetables, *mingão* (pap), half-salted meat, pork fat, and whale bone.[89] Fresh meat was very expensive and usually sold on wooden platters and trays on the streets, despite the fact that the municipal council prohibited such sales on penalty of 30$000 *réis* or eight days of imprisonment (1847).[90]

African-born slave women virtually monopolized commodities at the market. Fishermen did not sell to just anybody, even if they could afford the highest prices. Instead fishermen had only their relatives as customers. Vegetable and fruit growers directly delivered their produce to the market women.[91] At the market, exclusively women sold fish. There was a commercial relationship between market-stall women and male workers of African descent at the whaling station in the suburban parish of Rio Vermelho. After extracting oil from the whales, the male workers sold whale meat to the market-stall women, who cooked it and sold it on the streets.[92] Wetherell stated (1847) that blubber was brought to market already cooked, wrapped in banana leaves.[93] These women sold fresh, salted, and dried fish from their stalls, for example, outside the St. Benedict monastery or in the square in front of Barroquinha.[94] While there is no written documentation to support the assertion, we can assume that women developed their own commercial associations as independent entrepreneurs. These were not the domain of specific ethnic groups, but ethnic considerations did become a factor in distribution networks, such as for fish, and determined locations of stalls in markets and on the streets. Newcomers underwent an informal apprenticeship as peddlers or assistants to established market-stall women, and later might be assisted by others with the practical experience, networking, skills, and even capital to install their market stalls.

Sharing another special gathering place further strengthened association among African-born slave women: the river and public fountains for laundry, which were exclusively for women. Slave women carried heavy laundry in barrels or in bundles on their heads to a stream or fountain in the neighborhood. One district in Salvador where laundresses gathered is still called "Barris" (barrels) after the number of barrels sunk into the marshy ground to form wells of water. The laundresses, who were half-naked or entirely naked at work, washed the clothes by beating them against large stones with great force. The fruit of a tree or horse dung was used in lieu of soap. After washing, they spread the clothes in the sun to dry. Throughout these busy operations in the open air, these women talked to one another at the top of their voices, while their little children sprawled about playing, protected from the sun's heat by a cover made of a propped-up mat.[95] After the laundresses returned the clean laundry to the owners' houses, they or other female domestics known as *engomadeiras,* who specialized in starching and ironing, would continue the arduous process of bringing the final product to perfection.

Such opportunities for association among African-born slave women played critical roles not only for distributing and sharing information but also in breeding a sense of collective identity. An individual's daily engagement in gossiping was essential for him or her to become and remain a member of a community.[96] African-born slave women were most likely to create and develop a much stronger collective gender identity, beyond ethnic identity, in New World urban slavery than their male counterparts.

Conclusion

At the time of enslavement in the Old World, African-born women and men were officially deprived of their original identities as free, and the powerful imposed the two new cards of identity as enslaved in the New World: Portuguese/Christian names and African "nations." But it does not mean that all such enslaved people of African birth were entirely passive or receptive to the larger society's labeling/categorization of them for the sake of slave control; they continued to communicate among themselves in some of their native languages and identify themselves and refer to one another by their originally given African names.

The enslaved population of African birth soon managed to find certain effective ways to manipulate such labels as African "nations" for their own benefit in an urban slave society. The urban slave population was composed of diverse ethnic groups, and therefore they were quite heterogeneous. When they came into contact as strangers they also needed to categorize one another in urban slavery and chose to adopt African "nations" for categorization. Categorization is always a two-way process; in differentiating others, one is also defining oneself. Epstein maintains that "ethnic categories always have a dual aspect: they are at one and the same time both 'objective,' that is external to, or independent of, the actor, and 'subjective,' that is internal to the actor, a perception of the self."[97] Through this dialectic process the enslaved population of African birth created their ethnic identities in the New World.

But the creation of ethnic identity did not really embrace men and women of African birth exactly in the same way; gender divided people who shared the same ethnic identity in Salvador. The uniqueness of urban slave systems, wage earning in particular, enabled the enslaved population of African birth to create and develop distinctive gender identities at the workplace. African-born slave men fostered and reinforced their gender identity by sharing the same ethnic identity with those of the same "nation" in work groups. By contrast, slave women created their own gender identity, which oftentimes transcended divergent ethnic identity among the urban slave population of African birth.

3 The Representation of Identity, 1808–1831

The enslaved population of African birth in Salvador, who shared the same cruel "fate" of enslavement in Africa and the hardships of the Middle Passage, soon began to get connected with one another as they were being incorporated into urban slave systems in the New World. Oftentimes their interpersonal connections were the clear reflection of sharing common ethnic and/or gender identities. Sharing of the same identity clearly stimulated and encouraged the enslaved African-born population to form groups, establish voluntary associations, or rebel militantly against the power systems, for instance.

This chapter will investigate the representation of ethnic and gender identities in a collective form: daily gatherings and groupings; mating, consensual unions, and fictive kinship; voluntary associations; and flights and uprisings.

Daily Gatherings and Groupings:
Cantos, Batuques, and Candomblé

African slaves occupied the urban public space of Salvador in accordance with their collective ethnic identities. Those who came to share the same ethnic identity tended to visit and stay at a specific meeting place, namely a street corner called *canto*. On work days, the *cantos* functioned as meeting places for wage-earning slaves. At these meeting places, while seated on low stools with three legs, waiting to be summoned by regular and casual customers, slaves made straw hats, small baskets, iron chains for parrots, birdcages, and bead bracelets and polished leather or repaired umbrellas, usually made of yellow cotton cloth, which African-born slaves carried wherever they went.[1]

The *cantos*, which generally took names from their locations, such as the street or square, existed all over the city and represented specific ethnic groupings. The contemporary historian Nina Rodrigues located the *cantos* in Salvador. For instance, in the lower city, the *cantos* of Rua do Comércio and Rua das Princesas were exclusively for Nagôs. In the upper city, *cantos* of Nagôs included those of Rua da Ajuda, Largo da Piedade, and Ladeira de São Bento. In the *canto* of Campo Grande, up from the Forte de São Pedro, Nagôs also gathered, but not exclusively, since three or four Gêges were included in the group. Hausas had a *canto* between Arcos de Santa Barbosa and the Hotel of the Nations. Minas tended to congregate in the *canto* of São Raimondo on Rua das Mercês. These *canto* locations were exclusively for men, as gender identity was also clearly manifested in the *cantos*. African-born women gathered in *cantos* on Rua da Vala near São Miguel, on Rua da Guadelupe, on Rua da Cabeça, in the Largo Dois de Junho, and on the Ladeira do Boqueirão of Santo Antônio parish.[2] According to Nina Rodrigues's observations, *cantos* for women generally manifested less of collective ethnic identities than those of men.[3] Considering the fact that slave women of African birth developed a common gender identity at the workplace across ethnic boundaries, as discussed in chapter 2, Rodrigues seems to have been correct in pointing out gender differentiation in African-born slaves' participation in *cantos*.

Ethnic identity collectively shared by male African-born slaves gathered at a *canto* was strengthened by the presence of a few itinerant barber-surgeons of African birth who accompanied the canto. These African-born men cut the hair of male street slaves and performed rudimentary medical procedures.[4] Wetherell described the barber-surgeon in Salvador (1848) as "not only expert at shaving and hair-cutting, but draws teeth and bleeds with leeches, besides being musicians; thus whilst the master is performing any of the operations of his profession, his companions will endeavor to soothe the soul, or drown the cries of pain, as the case may be."[5] Some owned their own barbershops, but many others with less capital and probably with only rudimentary skills as medical practitioners peddled their services not only at the *cantos* but in the squares or streets as ambulatory barbers.

These barber-surgeons were also employed as musicians for religious holidays in the city. For instance, for the "Day of the Kings," musicians with guitars, drums, and other musical instruments roamed the streets in groups, going from house to house throughout the night.[6] They also played music in bands for the arrivals and departures of European merchant ships, as Thomas Lindley observed in 1802:

These musicians were entirely black, and are trained by the different barber-surgeons of the city, who are of the same colour, and have been itinerant musicians from time immemorial: they always command a full band ready for service; and a variety of young learners whose discordant tones are hatefully grating as you pass where they are practicing. Numerous as these swarthy sons of harmony are, they find constant employment: not only as above mentioned, but also at the entrance of the churches on celebration of festivals; where they sit playing lively pieces, regardless of the solemnities going forward within.[7]

These barber-surgeons/musicians contributed to communication networks as messengers between those who belonged to the same *canto* as well as among the overall African-born slave population beyond ethnic boundaries.

Interestingly, the *cantos* did not include female medical practitioners, despite the fact that in Salvador people of African descent virtually monopolized the rudimentary medical professions, as barber-surgeons if males and as midwives if females, throughout the slavery regime.[8] In contrast to male barber-surgeons, many of whom were African-born and enslaved, the art of midwifery in colonial Brazil was limited to free Brazilian-born women of African descent, who acquired their professional knowledge and skills largely from Luso-Brazilian society.[9] Once again, we see an interesting contrast by gender. Whereas men's rudimentary medical knowledge and practice among the population of African descent strongly relied on knowledge more or less directly derived from Africa, women widely depended on Brazilian-born women of African descent for one of their most important life events, namely reproduction.

Another representation of collective ethnic identity was "African" drum dances called *batuques,* which were a prominent feature of the street scene in Salvador.[10] On Sundays and holidays and at night after work, the African-born population gathered for such drum dances, singing in their native languages, dancing, and attending festivals related to their native African religions.[11] According to Albert J. Raboteau, in West African religions the vibrant pattern of music is interwoven with the ritual experience; dancing, drumming, and singing play a constant and integral part in the worship of gods and the ancestors.[12] In Salvador, the practice of *batuque* was divided by African "nations," and those who identified themselves with the same "nation" seemingly had their own gathering place for *batuques* on the streets.[13] For instance, in 1814, official correspondence from the governor of Bahia to the Portuguese royal court in Rio de Janeiro observed that "in Rio de Janeiro, 10,000 or 12,000 *negros* dance according to their nations but all together in the Campo de Santana, whereas here in Bahia [Salvador], one hundred Nagôs dance in the Largo do Teatro, fifty Gêges in the Piedade, eighty Hausas in the Rua de João Pereira, and thus it is throughout all over the city."[14]

This correspondence gives us an interesting contrast between Salvador and the other major port city, Rio de Janeiro, in which various ethnic groups shared the same space. Salvador's longer history of importing African-born slaves of diverse ethnic backgrounds directly though the transatlantic slave trade and incorporating them in urban slavery may have fostered the creation of stronger ethnic identities among the urban slave population, who therefore collectively claimed and occupied their own separate ethnic territories in accordance with their shared identities.[15] Thus ethnic groupings and groups were formed, and these people made the funerals of their people the occasion for *batuque*, probably in accordance with their own traditions and customs.[16]

Over time African-born slaves and their descendants had their African religions syncretized with Roman Catholicism and developed their own unique form of religion called *candomblé*. In addition to several well-known *terreiros* (temple grounds or sacred meeting places) of *candomblé*, in which leaders were officially given the title *pai de santo* (father of the saint) or *mãe de santo* (mother of the saint), small *candomblé* houses (*casas de candomblé*) were dispersed all over the city.[17] These were usually modest homes in working-class neighborhoods, and even the basements of such houses, but they turned out to be special gathering places for religious festivals in the neighborhood. Even on an ordinary day, a neighbor would drop by to ask for fortune-telling or to make wishes. Each *candomblé* house came to function as the African-born population's neighborhood center, where information could be exchanged. Each of these houses allegedly had its own African "nation" as its ethnic identity, and many were identified as Nagô-Gêge.[18] Needless to say, slave owners were very attentive and even nervous, particularly about their slaves' cultural-religious associations with the *batuques* and, by extension, *candomblé*. Their major concern was that such congregations of slaves signified a degree of loss of control by owners. Owners tried to control any opportunity for slaves to develop associations that might lead to rebellion. But owners' concern was no less attributable to their fear of the power of pagan (or what were to them strange) religions and a spiritual force and cohesion which they could not understand.[19]

As a result of the daily ethnic gatherings and groupings by the African-born enslaved population on the streets, communication networks developed along ethnic lines throughout the city. Many African-born kinsfolk, who had been separated from one another and transported to Salvador as slaves, managed, through opportunities for congregation provided by such groups, to be reunited and resumed their relationships. Some, such as mother and infant child(ren), had been enslaved and shipped together, but others looked for their enslaved parents, children, siblings, and other kinsfolk in Salvador, or possibly even ran into them in the streets.

Let us take three examples from the wills of ex-slaves. The first is the African-born ex-slave Joana Fernandes. She and her son João Sararis were enslaved in Africa, baptized as Roman Catholics in Lisbon, and shipped together to Salvador, where they were sold to different owners. They later somehow succeeded in being reunited, and in her will the mother named her son as her executor, as well as her heir.[20] The second example is Maria do Bonfim, an African-born ex-slave, whose specific "nation" was not mentioned in her will. She had neither married nor borne any children in Salvador, but had given birth to a son in her homeland, before being enslaved. Her son had also been enslaved, transported to Salvador, and lived with the Portuguese name of Joaquim do Nascimento. He had left Salvador for the port of Whydah. Maria do Bonfim found her siblings in Salvador: a brother named Caetano de Miranda, and two sisters, named Maria de Jesus and Maria das Moroas.[21] The third is Domingas de Salles. Because of her enslavement, she had left her daughter in Africa and had been transported to Salvador, where she eventually married Joaquim de Salles, an ex-slave of the same owner, and by whom she had a son named Manuel da Cruz, who died at five years of age. Sometime during this process, Domingas got acquainted with an African-born ex–slave woman named Justina Maria Luísa and in her will of June 8, 1842, recognized Justina as the daughter she had left behind in Africa.[22] No wonder these resumed kinship relationships in turn fostered and strengthened the creation of collective ethnic identity by the enslaved African-born population.

Mating, Consensual Unions, and Fictive Kinship[23]

The African-born population, particularly those who had not yet spent many years in the New World and were therefore relatively unacculturated and unassimilated, naturally sought out their partners from among those who shared the same ethnic identity. As discussed in chapter 1, the urban slave population in Salvador was balanced by sex, unlike most cases of New World plantation slavery but like the case of most cities of Latin America and the Caribbean. Therefore, theoretically, urban slaves had at least no demographic constraints on mating. While the small scale of urban slaveholding made it difficult for a slave to find a suitable partner from among the slaves owned by the same owner, urban slaves' daily gatherings and groupings gave them abundant opportunities to meet prospective partners who shared the same ethnic identity. A. J. R. Russell-Wood suggests that slaves may have avoided choosing a partner of the same ownership because by doing so they avoided both being subject to the whims of a single owner,[24] but we do not know if that was really the case in urban slavery; most urban slaves were hired out to the streets for all sorts of urban occupations, where they could mingle freely with one another regardless. For instance, a Hausa slave man named Francisco had mated and developed a relationship with a slave woman named Silvana, also a Hausa, who was owned by another owner named João de Campos. Francisco and Silvana produced two daughters, Fermiana and Fermina, who were inevitably born into slavery because of the legal status of their enslaved mother, Silvana. Perhaps at the time of his self-purchase, Francisco adopted his ex-owner's family name, da Rocha, as his own. As an ex-slave, Francisco da Rocha resided in Pilar parish when he registered his will in Salvador on March 10, 1830. His will states that Silvana lived as a freedwoman across from the cathedral but does not tell if he continued to maintain his relationship with her; Francisco chose as executor of his will not Silvana but Antônio Pereira de Almeida, who was his godfather. Francisco da Rocha never contracted marriage. His older daughter Florinda, fourteen or fifteen years of age at the time he made his will, had been sold to a male worker in a town of the Bahian Recôncavo, called Nazaré das Farinhas ("Nazareth of the flours"), named after its major product, manioc flour (*farinha*). In his will, Francisco expected Florinda to purchase her freedom from proceeds of the sale of the possessions he was to leave to her, and named her as his heiress. He did not make any provision in his will for his younger daughter Fermina because he had no knowledge of her whereabouts, except that she had been sold to Rio de Janeiro.[25]

We have no way of knowing how strongly the sharing of the same ethnic identity could unite African-born slaves as longtime partners, because of the critical limitations of existent historical data on their mating and consensual unions. First of all, both census records and parish marriage registers are of very little use. As illustrated by the case of Francisco da Rocha, the urban slave population in Salvador rarely contracted church marriage.[26]

This is attributable to various social and cultural factors: the high cost of a church marriage, which slaves could barely afford; slave owners' reluctance to allow their slaves to marry; slaves', especially African-born slaves', unwillingness to accept Catholic marriage;[27] and general lack of marriages among the poor, namely non–property owners.[28] Secondly, neither household records nor slave owners' inventories reveal slave unions on paper; slave partners seldom co-resided.

Probably the only available data that enable us to trace the African-born people's choices of partners based on collective ethnic identity are African-born ex-slaves' wills. Among the 325 of them who registered their wills in Salvador during the nineteenth century, 74 were married with African-born spouses; 23 shared the same African "nations," only 7 were of different "nations," and the rest (44 cases) did not identify the "nations" of either of such African-born spouses.[29] Regardless of the limited quality and quantity of these data, they imply that among the African-born population in urban slavery, sharing the same ethnic identity was a key determinant in choosing partners and forming consensual unions, and in some cases ultimately contracting marriages at the church, usually only after both partners had gained legal freedom.[30]

Most newly arrived African-born slaves were baptized as adults, at the time of their purchase, unless they had been converted to Catholicism before landing in Brazil. Godparenthood usually was established at the time of baptism, and nearly 95 percent of African-born slaves baptized in Santo Antônio parish between 1809 and 1869, regardless of gender, were baptized only with godfathers, the majority of whom (more than 60 percent) were free-born men.[31] The owners of newly arrived African-born slaves made the selection of godparents, and used two strategies to control their slaves. For African-born slaves baptized with African-born godparents, it was common for godparents to be of the same "nation," but usually those godchildren and their godparents were under different ownership, or the godparents were ex-slaves.[32] Baptizing new arrivals with godparents of the same "nation" who had already been exposed to New World slavery and Luso-Brazilian culture to a great degree, and who would instruct or supervise their godchildren at the workplace, would certainly promote the smooth and rapid integration of newly arrived slaves into the work force. Yet owners were afraid that too strong a solidarity might develop if both godparents and godchildren were under the same ownership. So slave owners chose slaves of different "nations" as godparents of new arrivals in those cases where godparents and godchildren had the same owner. African-born slaves under the same ownership served as godparents only when they were not of the same "nation" as their godchildren.[33] Of course, African-born slaves, particularly men, took advantage of their owners' strategies involving the issues of ethnic identity and used the opportunity for the development of their collective ethnic identity at the workplace, which became a good foundation for solidarity when taking various collective actions against the slave systems.

Voluntary Associations: Savings Associations and Lay Sodalities

Savings Associations

Male African slaves created and developed much stronger collective ethnic identities than did their female counterparts. Their solidarity resulted in the formation of unique savings associations, called *juntas* (unions), and *caixas de empréstimo* (boxes of loan) for making loans. No primary data on *juntas* are extant, since, according to the contemporary historian Manoel Querino, nothing about their activities was written down.[34] We may attribute this to general illiteracy among the African-born population, as well as to the major characteristic of the *juntas* as secret societies. Each *junta* had a leader chosen from among the most respected members. The leader had a wooden stick for each member of the *junta,* and recorded the transactions with cuts on the stick. Another person was appointed as a treasurer, who kept the collected money, invested it in mortgages, and loaned it at interest for the betterment of the association. Every Sunday, members of the same *junta* met to make payments in copper coins and to discuss the question of loans. If a member needed a loan, he was entitled to withdraw a sum of money at a specified rate of interest. The loan was sometimes used for self-purchase by the member.[35] One of the very few references to such *juntas* comes in the will (1878) of African-born freedman Marcos Gasper, who had been treasurer of the "Junta dos Africanos."[36] French traveler Joseph Arthur de Gobineau, the Count of Gobineau, made another reference, in 1869, to a savings association among Mina slaves.[37]

Black Lay Sodalities

Black lay sodalities functioned as a very special type of voluntary association for the enslaved population of African birth and their descendants during the slavery regime.[38] Slave men and women held the memberships of black sodalities equally; lay sodalities did not limit their memberships in terms of gender and admitted both men and women almost equally.[39] Every African-born slave was obliged to be baptized as a Roman Catholic before or upon arrival in Brazil. Conversion to Christianity immediately gave enslaved peoples of African birth equal spiritual rights with the prosperous white laity in the eyes of God; it allowed them to marry in church, to attend mass, and to receive confirmation in the faith by visiting bishops. African-born slaves were also free to participate in various religious celebrations in honor of Christian saints. Most importantly, such newly converted Christians were entitled to acquire a membership in lay sodalities, which guaranteed a decent Christian funeral and the saying of masses for the deceased. Despite the spiritual equality that all enslaved Africans and their descendants shared with the well-to-do white laity, in reality the latter never accepted the former into their white lay sodalities as their fellow members. Many white sodalities, especially the prestigious Santa Casa da Misercórdia (Holy House of Mercy), which itself owned a number of slaves, limited membership to whites.[40] Mulatto sodalities, which came into being later than black sodalities, accepted and welcomed whites but excluded both the African-born and the Brazilian-born black populations (see chapter 6). Therefore, lay sodalities were inevitably divided by race. African-born slaves, being denied the membership to all white (and later also mulatto) sodalities, had to establish lay sodalities of their own with their priorities and agendas. In a black sodality, most members were enslaved individuals who not only were desperately poor but also were human commodities owned by others. Black sodalities were naturally badly off and did not own their independent churches or even chapels; white sodalities with their own chapels sometimes allowed black sodalities to build altars for their patron saints and to hold ceremonies in honor of their saints.

The enslaved population of African birth had obviously sought the formation of lay sodalities for their own needs; in 1789 the presence of at least seventeen black sodalities was recorded in Salvador.[41] Unlike the case of the aforementioned *juntas,* namely savings associations for slave men that functioned as secret societies, all black lay sodalities were officially recognized by the larger society; every lay sodality, either black, mulatto, or white, established in Portuguese America was required to have its statutes approved by the archbishop and by the Portuguese Crown. No matter how strongly African-born slaves had initially reacted against forced conversion to Christianity, they soon found it beneficial to belong to lay sodalities for their daily survival in slave society.

One unique function of black lay sodalities was as emancipation societies. The statutes of black sodalities stipulated the provision of loans from emancipation funds for their slave members. Once the slave obtained freedom, he or she was obliged to return the money to the sodality, so that another slave member could use the loan.[42] Yet it seems that such manumission funds in black sodalities were never in active use, at least in the case of Salvador.[43] It is possible that slaves did not mention the loan of manumission funds from sodalities in notarized documents. It is even more likely that the archbishop rarely approved of the petition from black sodalities regarding the loan of their manumission funds. Whatever the case, it would seem most important for black sodalities to be officially equipped with manumission funds. Their ideological, not necessarily practical, readiness to take actions for the freedom of slave members could appeal not only to the slave population but also to whites and mulattoes who wanted to be good Christians by lending a hand to the needy.

The formation and development of black lay sodalities in Salvador inevitably reflected the African-born slave population's historical creation of ethnic identities; first, "Angolan" sodalities came into being, and later slaves originally from West Africa established their own sodalities.

The oldest black sodalities in Salvador were not established until the last decades of the seventeenth century; the intensive influx of slaves from Angola, many of whom shared the same ethnicity, had not resulted in the immediate establishment of lay sodalities. Many black sodalities had been formed but quickly dissolved absent official approval; the dominant society had successfully hampered the enslaved population in establishing their own lay sodalities. The first approved black sodality was finally established in 1685, mainly by slaves from Angola and their descendants, as the sodality of Our Lady of the Rosary (irmandade de Nossa Senhora do Rosário) in Conceição da Praia parish. The archbishop eventually approved the statutes of 1686 in 1702. The black sodality of Our Lady of the Rosary in Conceição da Praia parish was soon followed by another: the black sodality of Saint Anthony of Catagerona (irmandade de Santo Antônio de Catagero) in the chapel of São Pedro parish in 1699, which was also established by Angolans and their descendants. At the beginning of the eighteenth century, members of the black sodality of Our Lady of the Rosary in Conceição da Praia parish left their parish church because of insults they had received as *prêtos*

(African-born slaves) from the white sodalities housed at the same church.[44] From 1703 until 1726, they constructed their own church at the present location in the Pelourinho by working at night, on Sundays, and on holidays, while a famous white painter offered them help for the plan and construction of the church. They moved the image of their patron saint to the new church in the Pelourinho.[45] Thus this black sodality has been called the black sodality of Our Lady of the Rosary in the Pelourinho.

Ethnic identity was represented clearly in the governing of these two oldest "Angolan" sodalities; only Angolans and *crioulos* were accepted and equally represented on the governing body of both of these black sodalities. Office positions alternated between Angolans and *crioulos;* whenever the former held an office, a comparable post went to the latter.[46] This might have been at least initially a device for the offspring of Angolan-born members to participate in the sodalities with their parents and kinsfolk, so that the sodalities might represent the interests of such people of Angolan descent. Since the larger society did not have any specific term to define Brazilian-born people of Angolan descent, they were broadly described as *crioulos,* together with those of non-Angolan origin. Such ambiguity of description may have subsequently encouraged some of the general *crioulo* population, not only those of Angolan descent, to join the "Angolan" sodalities. We are not sure whether these sodalities were eager to be exclusively "Angolan" or not, but whatever the case, the strong representation of *crioulos* on the governing body certainly suggests that the successful establishment of the oldest black sodalities near the end of the seventeenth century had something to do with the creolization of the urban slave population. Black sodalities relied on their *crioulo* members, who were born in Brazil, baptized at birth, and much better integrated into the larger society, with sufficient understanding of Luso-Brazilian culture and the Portuguese language, as intermediaries. In the last decade of the seventeenth century, with the significant presence of the *crioulo* population, the African-born slave population in Salvador finally found it possible to have their black sodalities approved by the larger society.

West African slaves started to arrive in Salvador around the end of the seventeenth century, and many of them joined in the existent "Angolan" sodalities. As a result, the new members of the black sodality of Our Lady of the Rosary in the Pelourinho for the period from 1722 to 1786 were predominantly enslaved, and Brazilian-born only slightly outnumbered African-born. Among the African-born members, West Africans (48.3 percent) outnumbered Angolans (29.0 percent).[47] Nevertheless, *crioulos* outnumbered

Africans. The percentage of West Africans among the new members of African birth continued to grow; for the period from 1798 to 1865, 73.7 percent of the African-born were from West Africa, while Angolans constituted only 20.5 percent.[48] Despite the prominence of West African members, maintaining a collective ethnic identity as "Angolan" continued to be important for the members of the black sodality of Our Lady of the Rosary in the Pelourinho. In 1786, the sodality asked the queen of Portugal, Dona Maria, for permission to wear masks and to dance while singing in the "Angolan language" during festivals of Our Lady of the Rosary, on the grounds that this had been done in other Christian countries.[49]

In the late eighteenth century, slaves from West Africa also established their own black sodalities. Formation of these new black sodalities during the eighteenth century reflected the creation of new ethnic identity by West African slaves in Salvador. The sodality of Good Jesus of the Necessity and Redemption (irmandade de Sr. Bom Jesus das Necessidades e Redempção) in the Corpo Santo Church was established by Gêges (Ewes) in 1752. The sodality of Our Lady of the Good Death (irmandade de Nossa Senhora da Boa Morte) in the Barroquinha Church was established by Nagôs (Oyo-Yorubas).[50]

As stated earlier, black sodalities did not discriminate against women in their memberships; both women and men held memberships of black sodalities, almost equally. This is attributable to the fact that many slave women of African birth worked as market women in the city and were capable of earning more cash than their male counterparts, who worked as porters and transporters.[51] Such women members of African birth could have made a significant financial contribution to black sodalities. Nonetheless, women were not allowed to hold offices in some black sodalities. For instance, while no slaves of either sex were entitled to become officeholders, the statutes of the black sodality of the Rosary in the Pelourinho (both in 1698 and in 1820) stipulated that women were excluded from the governing body "because of the condition of their sex."[52]

Black sodalities were not exclusive in their memberships, either regarding ethnicity and gender or in terms of race; they allowed, and in fact even welcomed, well-to-do white and mulatto members because of the potential for bequests from them. Indeed, black sodalities were never exclusively black. Furthermore, the offices of treasurer and scribe of black sodalities were often reserved for white members, who usually paid higher entrance fees and annual dues, because of the alleged illiteracy and poverty of their black members. This custom was abolished only around the end of the eighteenth century, by which time more and more black members had become literate.[53] Russell-Wood maintains that prosperous whites paid dues to be members of several sodalities, including black sodalities, all of which, by statute, guaranteed the attendance of all members at their funerals; ostentatious display at a funeral was an indication of the deceased's socioeconomic standing in colonial Brazil.[54] British vice-consul James Wetherell stated that in Salvador a "curious custom exists at the funerals if the deceased has been a member of one of the Irmandades [lay sodalities] or clubs; most of the members attend the funeral procession, and both the corpse and the attendant brothers are habited in the peculiar dress of their order."[55] For instance, in the 1830s, wealthy Portuguese merchant José Coelho Maia belonged to seven sodalities, including the mulatto sodality of Our Lady of Guadalupe. During the same decade, Portuguese bricklayer Manoel Antônio da Costa Rodrigues belonged to eight sodalities, including two black sodalities: the sodality of Our Lord of Martyrs (irmandade de Nosso Senhor dos Mar-tírios) in the Barroquinha church; and the sodality of Saint Benedict in the church of Conceição da Praia parish.[56] Obviously, white members did not mind having blacks attend their funerals. Perhaps black members stood in the same line where the deceased's slaves did, which could appear as if the deceased had owned many more slaves. Of course, others joined black sodalities simply out of Christian charity to help the needy, including slaves. Some became members of black sodalities out of curiosity about their slaves' activities and/or black culture, or out of their inevitable concern for slave control.

Black sodalities chose to be devoted to the cult of specific Christian patron saints, often for the purpose of worshiping African gods and goddesses; in disguise of Catholicism and Christian saints, enslaved African peoples in colonial Brazil attempted to maintain their own African religious rites and customs, and to create and re-create their collective ethnic identity. Many black sodalities in Salvador were devoted to the cult of Our Lady of the Rosary (Nossa Senhora do Rosário). Roger Bastide maintains that the veneration of Our Lady of the Rosary, initiated by Saint Dominic, had fallen into disuse and was revived only when the Dominicans started to send their first missionaries to Africa, which explains why it took root in and spread among enslaved Africans.[57] Later, Africans in Brazil may have found a way to identify the Rosary with the African goddess Yemanjá. In Brazil, Our Lady of the Rosary was sometimes painted with a black face and hands.[58] Black sodalities of Our Lady of the Rosary annually crowned African "kings" and "queens" in their religious festivals. Henry Koster, a British planter who lived in northern Brazil during the early decades of the nineteenth century, wrote: "[T]he Brazilian Kings of Congo worship Our Lady of the Rosary, and are dressed in the dress of white men; they and their subjects dance, it is true, after the manner of their country; but to these festivals are admitted African negroes of other nations, creole blacks, and mulattoes, all of whom dance after the same manner; and these dances are now as much the national dances of Brazil as they are of Africa."[59] Another most popular patron saint of color was Saint Benedict the Moor (São Benedito), who had been known as a miracle worker immediately after his death in 1589, although his cult remained marginal in orthodox Roman Catholicism until 1743, and he was canonized only in 1807.[60] The black sodality of Saint Benedict in Saint Francis Monastery maintained the highest popularity in Salvador. Saint Ephigenia and Saint Elesbão are also saints of color.[61] Saints worshiped by the African-born population in Salvador included St. Barbara, St. John, Sts. Cosme and Damaio, St. Jerome, St. Anthony, St. Lazarus, St. Roque, St. Ann, Our Lady of the Conception, Our Lady of the Candles and, above all, Our Lord of Good Ending.[62] According to Albert J. Raboteau, Ibeji (in Yoruba), the spirit of twins, is syncretized with the twin saints Cosme and Damaio, and correlations are also found between Ogun, the god of iron and war, and St. John the Baptist; Oshun, the African Aphrodite of voluptuous beauty, and the Virgin of Bobre; and Shopana, lord of smallpox and St. Lazarus.[63] Over time such identification of African gods and goddesses with Christian saints and accompanying religious festivals by African-born slaves resulted in dynamic syncretisms between African religions and Roman Catholicism, most notably in *candomblé*. The backyard of the Barroquinha Church, in which the black sodality of Our Lady of Good Death was established by Nagôs, functioned as a place for *candomblé* festivals of Nagô origin for many years until the church fell into ruin in the late twentieth century because of financial problems.[64]

Black sodalities were relatively free to bury the dead, in the name of Catholicism, with non-Christian rituals, especially in the case of the black sodality of Our Lady of the Rosary in the Pelourinho, which had an independent church of its own. In the backyard of the church there was a cemetery for the burial of their sodality members, as in any other church in colonial Brazil. However small the cemetery, it was indeed used for the burial of slaves who were members of the sodality. Having an independent cemetery associated with their independent church guaranteed slave members a decent burial on church property. In Salvador at least as late as the first decades of the eighteenth century, it was not uncommon for African-born individuals to be buried in a non-Catholic mode.[65] Burial rites have been very important in West African religions, because of the powerful position of ancestors. Ancestors, both those who passed away a long time ago and those of more recent memory, are revered as founders of villages and kinship groups throughout West Africa, where funeral ceremonies are long, complex, and expensive.[66] Therefore, in Salvador, the sites of such burials served as very important gathering places for the African-born population on spiritual occasions, through which they reaffirmed their collective ethnic identity.[67]

While the individual's ethnic identity did not always determine his/her membership in a specific black sodality, collective ethnic identity continued to be a critical factor for the association. It was expressed and maintained by a black sodality through its worship of African gods and goddesses in the disguise of Christian saints, its modified practice of African burial rituals, and its continued use of African languages. Ironically, such an emphasis on collective ethnic identity observed in black sodalities resulted in preserving and reinforcing ethnic divisions among the enslaved African-born population, as long as the transatlantic slave trade continued to bring enslaved Africans to the city of Salvador.

Flights and Uprisings

Ethnic identity was collectively manifested in the frequent incidence of the slave flights and uprisings that took place in Salvador and the Bahian Recôncavo during the first decades of the nineteenth century.[68] British traveler George Gardner, expressing a commonly held view, stated in 1836 that the slaves in Bahia were "more difficult to manage than those of any other part of Brazil, and more frequent attempts at revolt have taken place there than elsewhere." Gardner ascribed this "rebellious" character of Bahian slaves to their shared ethnicity: the "Gold Coast" of West Africa.[69] During the sugar resurgence in the last decade of the eighteenth century, an increasing number of slaves continued to be imported from Africa to Bahia, and its major component was those from the Bights of Benin and Biafra of West Africa. The variety of sources from which slaves were drawn reflected the colonists' attempts to offset the disruption stemming from West African internal civil and religious conflicts, called *jihad* in Arabic, and to take advantage of increased numbers of war captives sold into slavery. Usman da Fodio launched a campaign with the help of the Muslim Fulani to take control of the Hausa Kingdom. Oyo collapsed in the 1820s and 1830s, and

Dahomey and various Yoruba warlords fought among themselves through-out the nineteenth century. The Oyo nobility had relied on Muslim military slaves, who became involved in Oyo politics. The important split of the Oyo Empire took place in 1817. Many more slaves came onto the market between 1818 and 1823 as subject provinces struggled for autonomy. By the early 1830s, when the Oyo capital was destroyed, a new Islamic empire was built in the savannah. As a result, a large number of war captives were disposed of by way of the slave trade to Bahia.[70] It is hard to ascertain to what degree slave uprisings in Bahia can be interpreted as an extension of the *jihads* of West Africa. True, many such individuals had been the captives of the *jihads* and therefore had been exposed to Islam in West Africa, but their degree of con-version and devotion to the religion of Islam varied. Islam in West Africa might not have provided them with strong religious faith in the same God but, as Jack Goody elucidates, the written religion of Islam, whose text was written in Arabic, could have given its adherents literacy and could have functioned as the universal means of communication among them.[71]

From the early colonial period there had been increasing formation of small fugitive slave communities, called at first *mocambos* and by the eigh-teenth century *quilombos*,[72] in relative proximity to plantations and towns and even within urban areas.[73] Urban slaves had constantly run away from Salvador to the suburbs of the city, such as Soledade, Forte de São Pedro, Agua de Meninos, Itapoam, Barra, and Rio Vermelho, and as far as Rio Joanes in the Recôncavo.[74] Often bush captains (*capitães de mato*), who were usually free men of color, were hired to search for runaways in the bush.[75] These fugitive slave communities were usually conveniently situated near the city, towns, and plantations on which they could depend and prey. The *mocambo* economy was parasitic; those fugitive slaves lived on highway theft, cattle rustling, raiding, and extortion.[76]

Slave flight gained prominence in the Bahian Recôncavo around the be-ginning of the era of the resurgence of Brazilian sugar fortunes in the 1790s and the early 1800s.[77] In March 1807, the Bahian authorities found that two *quilombos* had been formed near the villages of Nossa Senhora dos Marés and Cabula within two leagues of the city center. On March 29, the gover-nor of Bahia, João de Saldanha da Gama, the Count of Ponte, sent a troop of eighty soldiers who, on the following day, destroyed the *quilombos* and arrested seventy-eight slaves and ex-slaves.[78] On April 7, the Count of Ponte reported to the Portuguese overseas council that there had been numerous *quilombos* in the suburbs of Salvador and within the surrounding bush. Ac-cording to his statement, these maroon communities were "organized by industrious charlatans, and attracted credulous, vagrants, the superstitious, robbers, criminals, and the sick."[79] In these *quilombos,* people were free to "perform dances, wear capricious clothes, practice false medicine, recite blessings and fanatical prayers, eat, and entertain themselves with the most scandalous acts offensive to all of the laws and public tranquility."[80] This was the prelude to the slave uprisings of 1807–1831. Interestingly, prior to 1807 no organized slave uprisings had been recorded either in Salvador or in Bahia, in which the slave population was largely engaged.

The first uprising by African-born slaves was planned to take place on the evening of the 28th of May, 1807. The plotters were thirteen African-born slaves, all of whom were allegedly Hausas. This had been carefully planned on the assumption that many residents of Salvador would be out of town, because the 29th of May marked the religious festival of Corpus Christi. The participants intended to set fire to the customhouse and to a chapel in Naz-aré, a suburban district of Salvador, and then to escape to Africa by seizing ships in the port. It seems to have been symbolically important to the rebels, who were relatively new arrivals from Africa, to destroy the chapel that they saw as a manifestation of Catholicism, the religion of slave owners. The rebels had intended to be armed with bows, arrows, pistols, and rifles. But, on the 22nd, an unidentified slave leaked these plans to the authorities.[81] All the rebels were arrested just before the uprising. The leader was a slave named Antônio, resident of Rua do Corpo Santo. His occupation as trader enabled him to be in regular contact with Hausa slaves in the Recôncavo. He was known by the title of "ambassador" and was assisted by "captains," each assigned to a different district of the city. Antônio and his principal lieutenant, Balthazar, also a slave living on Rua do Corpo Santo, were sentenced to death. The other plotters received 150 lashes each in the public square. After this plot, the Count of Ponte not only prohibited *batuques,* but also placed restrictions on the physical movement of slaves and ex-slaves. The Count of Ponte became conscious of slaves' African birth, especially their ethnic origin, as a lethal threat to the larger society and, in his letter dated June 16, 1807, noted that in 1806 Bahia had imported 8,037 slaves from Costa da Mina, and that these were more rebellious than those from East Africa.[82]

The following year of 1808 witnessed the brief stopover of the Portuguese court in Salvador on their way to the colonial capital of Rio de Janeiro. We do not know the enslaved population's general reaction to this historical event, except through the short but interesting account by the British traveler James Henderson. According to Henderson, the visit of the Crown Prince to Salvador led the slaves of African birth to challenge the right of the governor of Bahia to inflict the statutory 150 lashes, now that "the Lord of the land (Dom da Terra)" had arrived. The slaves expressed their feelings in the following saying: "The Lord of the land arrived, the rule of 150 lashes over."[83] As soon as the royal family departed, the Count of Ponte posted the following lines all over the city and its suburbs: "The Lord of the land has passed, the rule of 150 lashes remains."[84] Of course, we have no way of knowing if this event actually took place; it might be an oral tradition because Henderson only recorded it in 1821. Yet, this story still tells us how conscious the enslaved population was of political changes and the power structure of the colonial society; after all, the governor of Bahia was an agent of the king, and not the embodiment of real power as was the king of Portugal. In this story, the common punishment of 150 lashes for slaves was used as a symbol of the harsh reality of slavery.

Rapid commercial expansion resulting from the transition from mercantilism to free trade (1808) aggravated Bahia's longtime problem: food shortage. From the beginning of the seventeenth century, the municipal council had passed various regulations to ensure an adequate supply of manioc flour to the population of Salvador and slaves of the Recôncavo. Manioc was a crop that merchants, planters, and even humble farmers disregarded in their quest for high profits derived from sugar and tobacco. Larger allotments of land were used for agro-export commodities, such as sugar, tobacco, and cotton. Subsistence production, particularly of manioc and beans, continued to decline drastically, despite the fact that the population was growing rapidly. As a result, the price of basic commodities rose sharply, and the material conditions for the slave population deteriorated. Bahia resorted to importation of food and clothing from the other provinces and from abroad, which contributed to drastic inflation through the first third of the nineteenth century.[85] These socioeconomic factors could have contributed to the frequent uprisings among the ever-starving enslaved population in Salvador (and Bahia) from 1808 to 1830.

The last days of 1808 and the first week of the New Year witnessed two separate incidents involving slave flight and the formation of a *quilombo* in the Recôncavo. The first started on December 26, 1808, when unknown numbers of slaves escaped from some sugar plantations, especially in and near the town of Nazaré das Farinhas. Within two days, they formed a *quilombo* in Riacho da Prata, located nine leagues from Salvador. On January 4, 1809, slaves, whose number was estimated at between two hundred and three hundred, fled from the city to join the *quilombo*. At some three leagues from Salvador, they began to engage in "robberies, acts of arson, assaults, ferments, and all evil things." On January 6, the Bahian governor sent troops to defeat these rebels. The troops not only killed many rebels but also took as prisoners eighty-three males and twelve females. Others escaped into the woods.[86] After these two slave uprisings of 1807 and 1809, the Bahian authorities began to pay close attention to a specific African "nation," Hausa, as the group most threatening to slave control.[87]

The uprising of 1814, involving many urban slaves, occurred in Itapoam. Located only two leagues north of the city, Itapoam was an area inhabited predominantly by fisherfolk, who were principally people of African descent engaged in whale fishery.[88] Once again, the majority of rebels were Hausas.[89] This uprising was planned to occur on an evening of *semana santa* (holy week), when the whole population of the city was occupied by numerous processions, such as that of the Penitentiary Disciplinants and the festival of Judas Iscariot.[90] On the 27th of February, some two hundred slaves from Salvador and from sugar plantations in the Recôncavo converged outside Itapoam. At about four o'clock in the morning of the 28th, they began to attack the *armação* (warehouse and processing plant for whale products) and the home of the future president of Bahia, Manoel Ignácio da Cunha Menezes, and killed his foreman and family members. They liberated his slaves, who joined the uprising. Then the rebels burned down the *engenhos* of João Vaz de Carvalho and Francisco Lourenço Helclano, liberated more slaves, and proceeded to the village of Itapoam, where they continued on their rampage of arson and killed "whites and *pardos*." The rebels' plans called for them to leave this area and march into the Recôncavo, but the Bahian troops tracked them down. After a one-hour bloody battle in the region of Santo Amaro de Itapiranga near the Rio de Joanes, the rebels suffered defeat by six o'clock in the evening on the 28th. At least fifty-six rebels lost their lives in combat. The authorities arrested and imprisoned thirty-one in Salvador and apprehended eight others later at various places in the Recôncavo. They hanged four slaves in public, and deported a further twelve to the ports of Angola, Benguela, and Mozambique.[91]

In response to a recommendation from the royal court in Rio de Janeiro dated March 14, 1814, the new governor of Bahia (1810–1818), D. Marcos de Noronha, Count of Arcos, increased the number of police in Salvador and ordered the police to impose more severe restrictions on slaves. The Count of Arcos also reissued regulations prohibiting *negros* from carrying arms as well as an edict that ordered punishment by 150 lashes of any slave who was out on the street after nine o'clock at night without an owner's pass. Furthermore, he issued a new regulation prohibiting slaves from gathering in groups larger than four persons without their owners' supervision.[92] The Count of Arcos took a much more liberal view of slaves' gatherings than had the Count of Ponte. In his decree of April 10, 1814, the Count of Arcos stated:

> The dances *negros* are accustomed to performing to the sound of dissonant and rattling instruments in the streets and public squares are totally prohibited. . . . Acknowledging, however, that many slaveowners understand their needs and try to diminish the horrors of slavery by permitting their slaves from time to time to divert themselves and forget for some hours their sad condition, and acknowledging also that all civilized cities in the world permit public entertainment even for the lowest classes of the nation, there will be no prohibition on slaves assembling at the two public squares of Graça and Barbalho to dance until the sound of Ave Maria, after which they must return to the houses of their owners.[93]

The Count of Arcos did not regard the *batuques* as the reason for the uprising of 1814. In his letter to the Portuguese court in Rio de Janeiro, the governor referred to the maltreatment of slaves and the shortage of meat and beans in their diet. In his view, preserving the *batuques* among slaves of diverse "nations" that were supposed to be hostile to one another promoted "disunion" among the slave population and robbed them of that unity of purpose essential to a successful uprising.[94]

Bahian slave owners did not agree with the Count of Arcos in his view of the *batuques* and insisted that the only way to control the slave population was with the threat and application of rigorous punishment. In their petition to the governor, slave owners noted that "they know and speak of the fatal success of the island of Santo Domingo and other revolutionary discourses and assert that by the day of St. John [São João] no white nor *mulatto* will remain alive."[95] In response to this petition, the Count of Arcos prohibited the use of firearms in that year's festivals on St. John's Day or Midsummer Eve (June 24).[96] St. John's Eve, which, among other festivals, was celebrated by bonfires, was an occasion when the enslaved could establish godparentage relationships despite the Church's consistent attempts to limit the practice; by joining hands and leaping over a bonfire together, people became "coparents of the fig tree (*compadres da figueira*)."[97] Aware of the conflicting views on slave control between the Count of Arcos and slave owners, the rebels elected Arcos their "prince" during the uprising of 1814.[98]

Despite the Count of Arcos's assertion that the Bahian slave population was engaged in revolutionary discourses, in the case of slave uprisings for the period 1807–1830 there is no historical document written by slaves themselves. Therefore, it is uncertain to what degree the occurrence of the Haitian Revolution or any other uprising or revolt in other parts of the New World influenced these slave uprisings in nineteenth-century Salvador, as Bahian planters and slave owners were convinced.[99]

The next slave uprising took place on the 12th of February, 1816 in the regions of Santo Amaro and São Francisco do Conde. This too was scheduled to coincide with a religious festival. Around thirty armed rebels, most of whom were Hausa slaves, burned down several *engenhos* and killed a number of people. This uprising lasted four days. This was the last slave uprising during the colonial era in Bahia, and the last Hausa-dominated uprising.[100]

During the war of independence, slaves in Bahia rebelled only on a small scale. These rebellions occurred in agricultural regions, such as in the village of São Mateus (February 1822), on the island of Itaparica (June 13, 1822), and in the *quilombo* of Pirajá (November 12, 1822), but had no impact beyond these immediate regions.

On August 25, 1826, the tobacco-producing Recôncavo town of Cachoeira suffered a large slave insurrection led by a Nagô slave who proclaimed himself "King." In December 1826, more than one hundred slaves converged on the *quilombo* of Urubú, located in the region of Pirajá. Urubú was established as a center for the clandestine practice of *candomblé*, and later became a refuge for runaway slaves. They began to attack a nearby village on the 15th of the same month. It took several days for the Bahian authorities to defeat the rebels.[101]

Again in Cachoeira, on April 22, 1827, slaves of the Engenho da Victória, whose owner was the merchant Pedro Rodrigues Bandeira, together with those from three nearby sugar plantations, rebelled and killed the foreman and his brother. Thirty slaves were arrested. Pierre Verger's research shows that around this time the word "Nagô-Malê" began to appear in police records.[102] According to Verger, *malê* originates from *iamle*, the Yoruba term for Muslim.[103] It suggests that the Bahian authorities had become aware of the association of the African "nation," Nagô, and the religion of Islam.

During the evening of March 11, 1828, slaves fled from Salvador into the bush of Pirajá to be united with those from *engenhos* in Cabrito and Cabula. On the following morning, they began to set fire to the *engenhos* of this area and proceeded to attack the buildings of the former Bahian president, Manoel Ignácio da Cunha Menezes, and Francisco Lourenço Helclano, both of whom had been victims of the uprising of 1814. Some eighteen other slaves, predominantly *negros novos* (newly arrived African-born slaves), joined the uprising. After a bloody battle, twenty slaves were killed and at least five, including two female slaves, were taken as prisoners to Salvador. All five prisoners were Nagôs. Throughout the 1820s, however, urban slaves in Salvador do not seem to have had a major role in the frequent uprisings in Bahia.[104]

The uprising of 1830 occurred in the center of the city of Salvador. On the 10th of April, around seven o'clock in the morning, a group of eighteen to twenty slaves who were identified as wage-earners (*negros de ganho*) attacked the hardware store of Francisco José Tupinambá, located on Rua da Fonte das Pedras in the lower city. They wounded the owner and his employee and took twelve swords and five long-knives. After breaking into two more hardware stores to obtain additional arms, they proceeded to Rua de Julião, also in the lower city, to attack the slave market of Wenceslau Miguel de Almeida. The armed insurgents freed over one hundred newly arrived slaves and wounded some eighteen others who refused to join the uprising. Once the rebels, who now numbered over one hundred, arrived in sight of the police station of Soledade, they were defeated by troops and civilians. Police investigation revealed that the mission of this uprising was to obtain weapons for a larger revolt planned for the 13th of April, 1830. The leaders of this uprising were identified as Nagôs.[105]

In the first three decades of the nineteenth century, the enslaved African-born population in Salvador frequently rebelled against the larger society. On many of these occasions, slaves carefully timed their uprisings for the times when the city residents were preoccupied by religious festivals. Women had virtually no participation in these slave uprisings. In each of these uprisings, most of the participants seem to have been drawn from a specific "nation": Hausa prior to 1816 and Nagô thereafter. As Schwartz points out, this change in the representation of ethnic identities among the participants took place in accordance with the changing composition of newly arrived African-born slaves. Although Nagô was the most prominent African "nation" in Salvador throughout the nineteenth century, Hausa constituted the majority of new arrivals from West Africa in the first decade of the nineteenth century because of the political turmoil within Hausaland. Nagô slaves did not arrive in Bahia in substantial numbers until after 1815.[106]

The slave uprisings from 1807 to 1830 also reflected the development of collective ethnic identity across the urban-rural geographic boundaries among the African-born male slave population who often worked in groups. This is partly attributable to the physical mobility enjoyed by African-born male urban slaves, such as chair carriers who accompanied their owners from their plantations in the Recôncavo to their urban residences in Salvador, suburban field workers who regularly came to the city to sell their agricultural products, and oarsmen and sailors who transported people and goods by rivers and by sea between Salvador and the Recôncavo towns.

Conclusion

Ethnic identities were clearly manifested in the African-born population's daily groupings and voluntary associations and in their participation in slave uprisings, as well as in their choice of partners for consensual unions and of their children's godparents. At the same time, distinctive gender identities effectively undermined the further development of collective ethnic identities. African-born slave men, who worked as porters, transporters, and artisans, tended to be strongly united by sharing the same ethnic identity, which was reflected in the formation of unique voluntary associations, as well as in the incidence of slave flights and uprisings. By contrast, African-born slave women, who became successful in marketing in the city, oftentimes chose to separate themselves from their male counterparts who shared the same ethnic identity, and formed their own groupings and associations beyond ethnic identities. Yet African-born slave women were structurally hampered from establishing official power because of their gender; they were not eligible for holding offices in black sodalities while participating equally with male members, for instance.

Through the process of being integrated quickly into urban slave systems and being assimilated gradually into Luso-Brazilian culture, the African-born population got connected with one another in urban slavery by sharing ethnic and gender identities. Yet that does not mean that the creation of identity in the New World embraced all the enslaved African-born population strongly enough to unite them as a group or community. The majority of them had been free in the Old World, and they knew what freedom meant. Their willingness to gain freedom often divided their solidarity. As long as opportunities existed in urban slavery for the individual pursuit of freedom, the African-born slave men and women were strongly motivated to recover their lost freedom in the New World, and for that purpose they also found effective ways to utilize their ethnic and gender identities. How did they (re)create their identities upon gaining freedom? How did their identities change over time? That will be our major focus in Part II.

Part Two
To Be African-Born and Freed, circa 1808–1880

The man who emigrated—my grandfather—
carried within him the memory of home, the
former world, the place where he was once
"real." It tore at him, that memory, and yet it
kept him anchored: he knew where his home
was, knew that he had lost it. The son of that
man—my father—believed he could make the
new place home. The task was probably impossible, but it kept him occupied.

> —David Mura,
> *Turning Japanese: Memories of a Sansei*

4 The Re-creation of Identity, 1808–1831

Most enslaved Africans in the New World had something important in common, which was the experiences and memories of freedom in the Old World; they had been born free in their homelands of Africa and therefore had once taken freedom for granted, no matter how varied their individual experiences were. Such enslaved people knew "what it was to be free, before they were enslaved; they were captives who could remember freedom."[1] For whatever reasons, other human beings, including their parents and other kinsfolk, betrayed their trust, denied their humanity, and reduced them to chattels, to be traded as mere commodities. The physical and emotional trauma of enslavement and the excruciating horror of the Middle Passage scarred their sense of self-worth, damaged their dignities, and wounded their souls. They remembered what freedom had once meant to them, and they constructed and reconstructed their individual notions of freedom in their daily experiences of oppression and exploitation in New World slavery. They learned in a very hard way that other human beings, even their parents and siblings, were able to deprive them of their freedom, which they had once taken for granted. Naturally these enslaved people desperately sought the recovery of their lost freedom in the New World.

This chapter will examine the African-born population's re-creation of identity as ex-slaves during the period in which the Atlantic slave trade continued to bring abundant enslaved labor into the port of Salvador. We shall first discuss how the African-born population obtained their "letters of liberty" (*cartas de alforria*) in urban slavery—since slave owners rarely manumitted their African-born slaves without payment, the slaves had to seek self-purchase—and how some African women and men manipulated their ethnic identities in their individual pursuits of freedom in manumission. We will also question whether gender differentiated their experiences. Then we shall scrutinize the special character of the "freedom" that African-born ex-slaves could obtain. African-born ex-slaves usually kept the same occupations they had formerly acquired as slaves. These jobs were ones that the white population could not fill because of the shortage of free labor or did not want to engage in because of the lack of prestige, such as transportation or craftsmanship, or those that only the African-born population could do well because of their ethnic backgrounds coupled with their multilinguistic skills, such as the slave trade. Thus legal freedom did not change their occupations. African-born ex-slaves naturally distinguished themselves from their enslaved counterparts and made every effort to appear to be "free" by adopting family names and taking up the elite's values and distinctive behavior patterns, such as slaveholding and multi-membership in lay sodalities. Yet, no matter how hard they tried to prove themselves as free people— to themselves as well as to others—their cultural otherness derived from their foreign birth hampered them from being fully accepted or integrated into the larger society as free. After all, all of their otherness would remain in the larger society's perceptions of them regardless of their newly acquired legally "free" status.

Although this chapter focuses on the period from 1808 to 1831 for our discussions of the re-creation of identity by the African-born ex-slave population, the data of the manumission of African-born slaves that I use in this chapter covers the entire period of 1808 to 1888, which is essential for the purpose of contextualizing our arguments.

Manumission and the Manipulation of Ethnic Identity[2]

"The slave can oblige his master to manumit him, by tendering to him the sum for which he was first purchased, or the price for which he might be sold, if that price is higher than what the slave was worth at the time he was first bought."[3] British planter Henry Koster's well-known assertion (1817) on the alleged legal rights of slaves in Brazil became the basis for Frank Tannenbaum's (1947) and Stanley Elkins's (1959) views. It spurred a debate during the 1960s among U.S. historians, primarily regarding the alleged "softness" and "hardness" of slavery in a comparative perspective. In reality, the prevailing practice of self-purchase by slaves in Brazil had no basis in law, except in small numbers and on special occasions. Until the Free Womb Law was enacted in 1871, no slave owner in Brazil was bound by any legal obligation to liberate slaves who claimed their right to buy themselves out of slavery by offering a sum equivalent to their asserted values.[4] Koster himself reported malfunctions of the laws:

[T]he master sometimes does refuse to manumit a valuable slave; and no appeal is made by the sufferer, owing to the state of law in that country, which renders it almost impossible for the slave to gain the hearing; and likewise this acquiescence in the injustice of the master proceeds from the dread, that if he was not to succeed he would be punished, and that his life might be rendered more miserable than it was before.[5]

Koster even questioned the basis for such legal rights.[6]

In fact, self-purchase was a widespread practice only under customary law; no owner had a legal obligation to come to terms with a slave who was willing to purchase freedom. Thus, as the Brazilian anthropologist Manuela Carneiro da Cunha puts it: "[T]he law was not silent—it was *silenced*."[7] Only the owner could grant freedom to a slave; the State maintained the widely prevailing practice of self-purchase as a common law. This created a hierarchy of subordination and personal dependence of slaves on individual owners even for those gaining their freedom legally. Not only did such private control of manumission maintain the subjection of slaves as a system, but it also successfully produced a group of ex-slaves as dependent laborers.[8] Thus, in the practice of manumission, power was exercised over slaves in extremely personalized forms; without having any official apparatus that could protect their common-law rights in manumission, a slave who aspired to gain freedom had to maneuver carefully in developing a personal relationship with the owner who might give the slave easier access to the path for freedom. Regardless of the wide prevalence of manumission, the accumulation of sufficient capital to fully cover the price of one's own value as a commodity could not free the slave from slavery without the owner's consent. In other words, any slave who was eager to be manumitted had to behave well in the eyes of the owner; the slave had to know his or her "place" and walk a thin line in the ongoing relationship with the owner. Freedom was possible only with the consent of the owner, who would continue to exercise power over ex-slaves. Over time such highly personalized owner-slave relations in the practice of manumission seem to have contributed greatly to the establishment of distinctive patterns of race relations in Brazil, which are characterized by patronage and clientage.

In Salvador during the first three decades of the nineteenth century, African-born slaves outnumbered Brazilian-born slaves at least by the ratio of 2:1, but the former were by no means favored over the latter by the larger society in the practice of manumission. Brazilian-born ex-slaves always outnumbered their African-born counterparts throughout the nineteenth century.[9] In urban slavery in Salvador, gender did not determine one's opportunity to gain freedom among the African-born population. The male-female ratio among the African-born ex-slaves was nearly equal, with a ratio of 47:53. By contrast, among the manumitted of Brazilian birth, women outnumbered men by two to one, as we shall discuss in chapter 6.[10] Neither did ethnicity become a crucial factor affecting the opportunities for individual slaves of African birth to gain freedom by manumission. The geographic and ethnic distribution of African-born ex-slaves in Salvador between 1808 and 1884 agrees with that of African-born slaves purchased and sold in Sé parish for 1838–1848 and 1852–1888, as well as of slaves of African birth registered in their owners' inventories, which I consulted for 1808–1849 and 1850–1888.[11] It makes a sharp contrast to the mining towns of Minas Gerais, where twice as many slaves from "Costa da Mina" were freed as slaves from the Congo-Angola region. This is attributable not to specific ethnicity but to advanced mining technology, which had been developed in the Costa da Mina region of West Africa; Kathleen Joan Higgins suggests that those slaves from Mina had more experience in mining and were successful in accumulating quantities of gold sufficient to buy slaves themselves.[12] Such technological advantage demonstrated by a specific (ethnic or regional) group of African-born slaves in their pursuit of freedom was not seen in the case of urban slavery in nineteenth-century Salvador.

African-born slaves, who had been born free in their homelands, often planned and participated in slave uprisings. They remained the cultural "other" in the larger society's view mainly due to their continuing usage of their native languages, with the relatively limited acquisition of Portuguese, as well as their distinctively "exotic" cultural behaviors, which were perceived as dangerous to the maintenance of social order. African-born slaves' undeniably ostensible otherness provoked a great amount of suspicion in slave owners, and it impeded them from cultivating and developing interpersonal and paternalistic relationships with their owners in the same manner as their Brazilian-born counterparts could with little trouble.

Thus African-born slaves of both sexes did (or could) not benefit from the practice of unpaid manumission as frequently as did their Brazilian-born counterparts (46.1 percent for African-born and 74.1 percent for Brazilian-born for the period 1808–1844; and 48.0 percent for African-born and 65.0 percent for Brazilian-born for the period 1851–1888). Therefore, for African-born slaves, regardless of gender and ethnicity, the most prevalent path to legal freedom by manumission was through paid manumission; half of the manumitted of African birth paid for their own freedom (47.6 percent for males and 52.8 percent for females for 1808–1842; 63.3 percent for males and 51.1 percent for females for 1851–1884). By way of contrast, a much smaller percentage of Brazilian-born slaves (17.8 percent for men and 21.4 per cent for women for 1808–1842; 28.9 percent for men and 24.5 percent for women for 1851–1884) were manumitted by self-purchase.[13]

Having learned that self-purchase was possibly the only means available to them, African-born slaves were forced to devise their own strategies and tactics. Was it even possible for them to accumulate enough capital for self-purchase, first of all? How could a slave and the owner come up with a mutually agreeable price for the former's self-purchase? And how did the slave pay the price for freedom? African-born slaves were desperate to free themselves from New World slavery and were very eager to utilize all that might work to their advantage. Small wonder that for the purpose of exploitation some African-born slaves did definitely look for the even more powerless than themselves, namely newly arrived African-born slaves, whose market values were much lower than theirs and who did not comprehend the Portuguese language and lacked familiarity with Luso-Brazilian culture.

Aspiring to self-purchase and possessing good knowledge of his or her own occupational skills and capacities, the slave had to make a realistic assessment of how to achieve the goal. First, the slave had to know how much it would cost. The price of freedom did not necessarily correlate with the commercial value of an individual slave; price for self-purchase was determined situationally, often based on the slave's capacity to skillfully negotiate with the owner, who retained and exercised the absolute power over the former.[14] Chances were that, because of their cultural alienation from the larger society, as well as even from each other, and their lack of interpersonal ties with their owners, African-born slaves were easily forced to pay much more for self-purchase than their Brazilian counterparts of the same sex with comparable ages, qualifications, and occupational skills, but there is no way of proving this point. Unfortunately, the data on slave prices in Sé parish for 1838–1888 and my sample of manumission letters in Salvador for 1808–1884 are not compatible enough for us to make valid generalizations on a possible correlation between the slave's commercial value and the price actually paid for self-purchase. Yet, based on the existing data in hand, no matter how limited they are in terms of both quality and quantity, we are able to attempt to speculate on some general tendencies. On the one hand, we certainly take note of a clear parallel between slave prices and prices for freedom among African-born slaves by gender; men were more expensive than women, and they also paid more for self-purchase. In the data on slave prices in Sé parish for 1838–1888, African-born males were usually more expensive than African-born females.[15] Letters of liberty also indicate that, with the exception of the years 1871–1872, male ex-slaves of African birth indeed paid more for self-purchase than did their female counterparts.[16] On the other hand, among slave women, when the given data are divided by birthplace, African-born were generally forced to pay higher prices for their freedom than their Brazilian-born counterparts, despite the fact that the latter, many of whom were skilled domestics, usually cost more than the former, who had fewer skills in domestic service.

When a slave came up with a proposal for self-purchase, the owner would definitely attempt to raise the price of freedom as high as possible, knowing well that the slave had the capacity to pay more than his/her price as a commodity. This is especially the case for African-born slave women, many of whom became successful entrepreneurs in informal markets of the city, as discussed in chapter 2, and could easily earn much higher wages than skilled domestic slave women. This point is supported strongly by the data on daily wages earned by African-born ex-slaves (133 men and 197 women) who lived in Santana parish in 1849; successful market women earned much more than skilled domestic servants. The average daily wage of eighty-nine market women (*mercadejas*) was 805 *réis,* and that of twenty-eight female market-stall keepers (*quitandeiras*) was 981 *réis.* Thirteen women in business (*negócio*) earned a higher average daily wage of 1$283 *réis.* By contrast, a female domestic servant with special skills as a laundress (nine individuals) earned only 320 *réis* a day.[17] Thus, market women earned much higher wages and could indeed afford to pay more for self-purchase than could skilled female domestics.

How could the slave accumulate sufficient cash and eventually make a payment to the owner for self-purchase? After all, the slave, who was property, had no property rights. Whatever a slave "owned" legally belonged to his or her owner and could be taken away at any moment if the owner had not previously consented to the slave's owning property. It is very likely that the slave, who was hired out to the street every day on a full- or part-time basis, saved cash little by little in complete secrecy from the owner, as well as from fellow slaves, who might just steal it if there was any chance. The slave could not be too careful about it. There were no authorities a slave could appeal to if savings mysteriously disappeared. Some could eventually manage to come up with sufficient savings in cash for self-purchase; in fact, it was most common that the slave made a payment by cash. But cash payment was not always the case. An example found among the ex-slaves' wills is payment by real estate. A Nagô ex–slave woman named Gertrudes Maria do Espírito Santo obtained her freedom with the payment of her value to her owner, Silveiro da Silva, and his wife Joana da Silva, with a house located on Rua do Genipapeiro of Santana parish, which she owned among a few others.[18] Although it was not officially recorded in nineteenth-century Salvador, some slaves purchased freedom not only with real estate but also with cattle in Paraíba from 1850 to 1888.[19]

The most extreme form of payment was with another enslaved person (or two persons, albeit rarely) through substitution, or "trade-in."[20] Let us take one example first. A Nagô slave man named Francisco obtained his letter of liberty on May 14, 1852, by paying his owner the equivalent of 700$000 *réis*, the price of his freedom. Instead of paying cash, Francisco substituted another male slave called João, whom he, Francisco, owned. João was also Nagô and subsequently took Francisco's place working on a small boat known as an *alvarenga*, which is a lighter used for ferrying goods between ship and shore.[21] To our disappointment, Francisco's letter of liberty does not tell how he had accumulated enough money to purchase João, nor how Francisco had come to own his own slave, albeit temporarily, presumably with the permission of his owner. Francisco, employed in an urban occupation, possibly for many years, negotiated with his owner to arrive at a mutually agreed upon price for João, a price equivalent to what the owner was demanding for Francisco's freedom, and the owner agreed to accept João in lieu of cash payment. Interestingly, Francisco provided his owner with a substitute slave not only of the same sex, but also a Nagô, the same ethnicity as himself.

In my sample of 3,516 letters of liberty for nineteenth-century Salvador, there are a total of 35 recorded cases of substitution, including the aforementioned one of Francisco. These cases of self-purchase transactions through substitution constitute only one percent of the total number of letters of liberty, and 2.63 percent of self-purchases (1,332), for the period 1808–1884. The number and percentages are certainly small, but it is important to note that substitution did exist as a special form of self-purchase and that its practice by the enslaved population was officially acknowledged and recorded in notarial records. The scrutiny of substitution will enable us to discuss a fascinating aspect of the re-creation of identity by the African-born population.

In nineteenth-century Salvador, the slave's gender did not determine the practice of substitution; women and men were equally represented among those who purchased freedom by substitution. The 35 ex-slaves who obtained freedom through substitution numbered 17 males and 18 females. On the other hand, it seems that substitution was predominantly an "African" phenomenon; the 35 ex-slaves were composed of 24 African-born of diverse ethnic origins (13 males and 11 females); 3 Brazilian-born (1 male and 2 females); and 8 persons without any indication as to origin or color (3 males and 5 females).[22] Also, substitution took place when the transatlantic slave trade was intact and therefore newly arrived African-born slaves were available for sale; with one exception, which took place in 1861, all cases of substitution occurred between 1808 and 1852.

In the practice of substitution, one-to-one replacement was common; in only two cases were two slaves of the same gender substituted for one person to be freed.[23] The common phrase used in cases of substitution was "the slave gave another slave in his/her place," but specific occupations were mentioned in four letters, including the letter of Francisco.[24] The slave to be freed usually chose a substitute slave of the same sex (29 cases out of 35). In three cases the ex-slave provided not only a substitute but also cash to make up the gap between the price of the ex-slave and the lower price of the substitute. One example illustrates such a negotiated settlement between a slave and an owner. An African-born slave man named Ventura, whose "nation" was Mina and whose occupation was a bricklayer, paid 300$000 *réis* to his owner: 200$000 *réis* represented by the value of another African-born slave man named Torcano, who was of the same occupation and whose "nation" was "gentio da Costa" (gentile from the coast), and 100$000 *réis* in cash.[25]

Certain naming practices in the procedure of substitution reveal a fascinating aspect of identity politics for the enslaved; the African-born population was well aware of how they could play with their identity for their benefit. In two cases the slave to be freed and his/her substitute shared the same Christian/Portuguese name.[26] As discussed in chapter 2, the African-born population in Salvador often identified themselves, and referred to one another, by their original African names, whereas their Christian/Portuguese names, given at baptism, were employed by their owners and the non-African-born population in general; such new names represented their continued enslavement in the New World, not their personhood in the Old World. Therefore, the slave might well intentionally name the substitute with the same Catholic/Portuguese name to show others his or her legal ownership of the substitute, while at the same time using the original African name when communicating with the substitute slave in their native language.

Few letters of liberty tell us how a slave obtained a substitute, as in the case of Francisco, and only two letters state who supplied the substitute. A slave woman, Josefa, received her substitute slave, named Rita, from her niece Marcelina Maria da Conceição. In the other case a *crioula* slave, Barnardeira, obtained her letter of liberty by providing her owner with another female slave, named Rola, African-born and Nagô, who had belonged to Barnardeira's mother, Felicidade, also still enslaved but under different ownership. In both cases, a kinswoman who herself had become a slave owner made a significant financial contribution to the manumission of a slave woman.[27]

One wonders how some slaves and ex-slaves in Salvador could manage to obtain and own newly arrived African-born slaves. For rural Bahia, Stuart B. Schwartz presents interesting testimony made before the probate judge of São Francisco do Conde in 1836 which suggests that it was indeed possible even for slaves in Salvador and other parts of Bahia to purchase newly enslaved human commodities in Africa. A *crioula* slave, Luciana Maria da Conceição, wanted to purchase a slave as a dowry for her granddaughter. For that purpose, she sent her money to a friend, who went to Africa and acquired a Nagô woman who was to be named Jeronima at baptism. Jeronima was subsequently delivered to Luciana as her slave at Engenho Cahipe. Despite her initial motivation, Luciana changed her mind; she kept Jeronima as her own personal slave and sent her to the city for wage earning, while Luciana herself continued to work as a slave on the plantation.[28] We do not have the ending to this story. It is noteworthy that while working on a plantation Luciana could manage to save enough money to purchase another slave. One should not be amazed at the fact that this slave woman, who remained enslaved herself, wanted her granddaughter to own a slave woman as a dowry. We wonder if Luciana was finally freed, possibly by the accumulated earnings of her own slave Jeronima or by substituting Jeronima for herself. We do not even know if Luciana made the effort to gain her own freedom. But this example does serve to illustrate how agents, possibly African-born ex-slaves, traveled to Africa on a regular basis to trade in slaves and to make them available at reasonably inexpensive prices to buyers such as Luciana in Salvador.[29]

Newly arrived Africans were usually chosen as substitute slaves because their prices were less than those for skilled Brazilian-born slaves and also acculturated African-born slaves.[30] This explains why the practice of substitution virtually disappeared with the termination of the transatlantic slave trade (1851). Twenty-five letters declare that substitute slaves were African-born and/or new arrivals; the other ten letters do not provide information as to the slaves' place of birth or "nation." With the consent of his or her own owner, a slave purchased the substitute, acculturated and trained that slave in special occupational skills, and finally "traded in" the slave in exchange for freedom.

As the case of Francisco illustrates, some slaves purchased as their substitute slaves of the same "nation." Of nineteen cases in which both the slave and the substitute were identified, the replacements for six Nagô slaves were also Nagô. This could be attributed to the law of probability because individuals defined as Nagô comprised one-third of African-born ex-slaves. But studies on manumission in colonial and imperial Brazil by Schwartz, Karasch, and Higgins also note the coincidence of "nation" between the slave and the substitute, thereby confirming that this coincidence was not confined to any specific ethnicity.[31]

We conclude that substitution was an expedience attractive to both owner and slave. Karasch is correct in stating that "[o]wners willingly accepted these 'trade-ins,' for they did not have to acculturate them, and they solved the problem of capital depreciation. In place of an aging African woman, they might receive a teenage boy with years of service in the future."[32] For the slave, the financial advantage of purchasing a new African-born slave for much less than he or she would need to accumulate for self-purchase was offset by the consideration that the slave had to take time to acculturate the new slave before the latter was a viable replacement. Some slaves, in their capacity as slave owners, may have worked side by side with their own slaves, or sent them out onto the street as wage-earning slaves to earn money for several years, before finally offering them as substitutes for themselves. In this context, purchasing a substitute who shared the same ethnicity made sense. This eased the problem of instructing the new arrival, who did not understand the Portuguese language or Luso-Brazilian culture. The sharing of the same ethnicity between the ex-slave and the substitute was no mere coincidence, as Schwartz and Karasch imply. Rather it reflected the creation of ethnic identity in New World slavery, in which enslaved individuals of African birth struggled to survive on a daily basis. Cognition and behavior are different phenomena; sharing the same ethnic identity does not mean that such individuals would automatically create ethnic group solidarity and/or behave as members of the same ethnic group.

The practice of substitution was not exclusive to Salvador but, from what we have learned from preceding studies on manumission, seems to have been mainly used in an urban environment, such as the port cities of Salvador and Rio de Janeiro and the mining towns of Minas Gerais.[33] Substitution was less prevalent in agricultural regions, such as Paraty, Paraíba, or even the Bahian Recôncavo.[34] This should not be taken to imply that substitution was an exclusively urban phenomenon, but substitution rarely occurred in rural agricultural areas because of the plantation slave system and the relative lack of socioeconomic mobility of slaves who were field hands. In one exception at the beginning of the nineteenth century, Henry Koster observed a similar practice on a sugar plantation of the Benedictines in Jaguaribe in Pernambuco. More than one hundred slaves, all Brazilian-born, belonged to this plantation, whose overseer was a male mulatto slave. He first purchased the freedom of his mulatto wife, who had been owned by the Order, and then their children's freedom. Subsequently, he offered the friars, in exchange for his own freedom, two African-born slaves whom he owned. The friars refused to accept his proposal on the grounds that the estate could not be properly managed without him.[35]

Substitution as a form of self-purchase was unique to Brazil, as far as New World slavery is concerned. The origin of substitution as self-purchase goes back to Roman times. In imperial Rome, which constituted an urban slave society, there was a special feature of some slaves' condition, called the *peculium,* which was a fund of money controlled by slaves themselves. The slave could use it for investments or, ultimately, for self-purchase. Furthermore, slaves could use the *peculium* to purchase other slaves to stand in for them (*vicarius/vicaria*). The *peculium* was usually reserved for urban skilled slaves, not for rural workers.[36] Among many studies on manumission outside of Brazil, the only example I have found of substitution is of a Mandingo slave in Port-of-Spain, Trinidad, in 1830, very close to the date of abolition in 1834. The Muslim preacher named John Mohammed Bath purchased a slave as a substitute for himself as a "colonial negro" of the British government, since the government had declined to accept Bath's money for his self-purchase. The urban Mandingo community, whose members were Muslims, used part of its considerable economic assets to function as an emancipation society. As in the case of nineteenth-century Salvador, some Mandingos in Trinidad became slave owners. Carl Campbell interprets the retention of African names as evidence of their determination to "return" to Africa, but does not address the process of substitution in terms of ethnicity and ethnic identity in New World slavery. Campbell's implicit assumption is that the Mandingos, who shared a strong ethnic identity, owned non-Mandingo slaves, and some of them "traded in" non-Mandingos for their own freedom.[37]

The African-born population's re-creation of identity as ex-slaves started to take place while they were still enslaved but at the very moment when they became determined to recover their lost freedom. Such highly motivated individuals of African birth found some interesting ways to manipulate their ethnic identities for self-purchase, as the case of substitution clearly illustrates.

To Be an Ex-Slave of African Birth: Neither Enslaved nor Free

The acquisition of a manumission letter by self-purchase did not totally end the African-born individual's desperate struggles for freedom. The letter of liberty was a legal document for transfer of property (the slave) from the former owner to the new owner, namely the slave himself or herself, and this had to be formally registered and publicly notarized before a notary (*tabalião*). Once this formality was completed, the ex-slave was legally free. It was the ex-slave's awesome responsibility to preserve the original letter of liberty; loss or inability to produce it on demand would make the ex-slave vulnerable to re-enslavement.

Freedom, of course, did not alter much of the external appearance of African-born ex-slaves; they could not be easily distinguished from their enslaved counterparts, who constituted the majority of the African-born population. Whether enslaved or freed, most had been born free in Africa, and their shared cultural otherness distinguished them from the Brazilian-born population of African descent. There were only a few visible signs of their newly acquired free status. First, ex-slave street laborers who worked in gangs, as porters, transporters, and artisans were not chained at the ankle or neck. Second, ex-slaves were entitled to wear shoes; the British lady Maria Graham describes shoes as the "mark of freedom" in her travel journal.[38] Perhaps with their shoes on, African-born slaves of both sexes continued to work with their co-workers of African birth, both slaves and ex-slaves, side by side, and were engaged in the same occupations as when they had been enslaved. Their jobs could have been stigmatized by association with slavery, and the free-born population may not have wished to take them up. But it was African-born people's unique occupational skills that enabled them to earn extra money as slaves and to purchase their freedom in the end. African-born ex-slaves usually continued to be engaged in the same occupations, in which they could fully utilize their ethnic backgrounds and/or take full advantage of the enslaved population of African birth.

Gender determined the African-born individual's experiences to a considerable degree. As discussed in chapter 2, African-born women were most prominent in the informal market of the city and gained a substantial amount of financial power; as examined earlier in this chapter, their marketing skills enabled them to purchase freedom with cash, usually with the payment of more than their commercial value as slaves. Among the African-born ex-slave population, women continued to dominate the urban informal market. For instance, in 1846, in Conceição da Praia parish, nearly 90 percent of market-stall keepers among 331 African-born ex-slaves were females. Likewise, among 207 African-born ex-slaves in Santana parish in 1849, 92.7 percent of market persons and 87.5 percent of market-stall keepers were women.[39]

As for men of African birth, skilled artisans made up an important portion of the male ex-slave population. Among the African-born freedmen who lived in Conceição da Praia parish in 1846, 15 out of 96 men were artisans.[40] In Santana parish in 1849, African-born ex-slave artisans (who numbered 25 out of the total number of 133) earned an average daily wage of 962 réis, which is significantly higher than that of chair carriers (794 réis), as well as of those who were classified as wage-earners (793 réis).[41] Because of the better economic opportunity enjoyed by slave and ex-slave artisans, the number of free artisans of African descent gradually grew in colonial and early nineteenth-century Salvador, and their increasing financial power eventually enabled the establishment, at the mid-nineteenth century, of an unusual voluntary association called the Society for the Protection of the Needy, which we shall discuss extensively in chapter 7.

Among male skilled artisans, barber-surgeons occupied a unique position and constituted a significant part of the African-born male ex-slave population. Despite the fact that full-time slave barber-surgeons were only about one percent of the whole male slave population, barber-surgeons constituted a significantly larger part of the ex-slave population.[42] Six barber-surgeons represented 6.3 percent of the African-born freedmen in Conceição da Praia parish (1843), whereas five ex-slave barber-surgeons (3.8 percent of the total African-born ex-slave population) earned the highest daily wage, 1$384 réis, of all wages in Santana parish (1849).[43] Among the wills of ex-slaves, two ex-slave testators of African birth identified their professions as barber-surgeon.[44] One of them, Bernardino da Sena, made his will in the 1820s despite the fact that he was in perfect health. He intended to "return" to Africa to live there until his death; he chose to take passage by being employed as a barber-surgeon on the ship *Gerna Marina*, owned by Alves da Cruz Rios.[45] Another ex-slave originally from Angola, Antônio José da Silva, earned the wage of 1$000 *réis* a month as a sailor on a smack owned by Francisco José Vieira, who resided both in Angola and in Rio de Janeiro, and whose ship's master was José Gomes da Rocha. The smack was engaged in the slave trade from Angola to Pernambuco.[46]

Some African-born freedmen, in fact, became slavers themselves. Such was the case of the Hausa freedman named Francisco da Rocha (see chapter 3). Francisco made no mention of his ex-owner's occupation or his own previous occupation as a slave, but it is possible that Francisco had worked as a sailor or hired out as a wage-earning slave on a ship to West Africa. Francisco's Hausa origin, together with his bilingual skills, may have facilitated his entry into the slave business in Salvador, where there were many slave traders who were themselves of African descent. Later his ethnic origins, coupled with his linguistic abilities, may have helped Francisco to establish good business relationships with local slavers and merchants in the ports of West Africa. Francisco had a business contract with Manoel José de Almeida, resident of Salvador, for the supply of slaves; Francisco ordered Manoel to arrange for the transportation of slaves from Costa da Mina, and Francisco was to receive 6:500$000 *réis* for having sold four slaves. Luís Marques, overseer of the schooner *Esperança*, owed Francisco 85$000 *réis*, the remainder to be paid on the sale of one newly arrived slave boy, one female slave, three barrels of olive oil, and one sack of pepper. From this voyage Francisco brought back as cargo slaves for various persons. He also did business with a *prêto*, Bernardino da Sena, in Salvador, and arranged two assignments for José da Costa de Miranda, which resulted in three slaves. Francisco owed to the African-born ex-slave Angelo 13$000 *réis*, which Francisco had received from Angelo to employ Angelo in Costa da Mina, although such employment did not materialize.[47] Thus Francisco da Rocha had developed extensive business networks in Salvador with business partners, employees on ships, and his customers, among whom were the freeborn population of African descent and ex-slaves. The port city of Salvador gave Francisco the opportunity to decide for himself to engage in the slave trade with Africa.

The British traveler Robert Walsh in Rio de Janeiro had noted the involvement of former slaves of African birth in the transatlantic slave trade in 1828. "There has been such a range for acquiring this sort of property," he wrote, "that negroes themselves who had obtained their freedom, frequently sent ventures to Africa to purchase their countrymen, who were brought back to them in exchange for the beads and looking-glasses which they sent out."[48] There were many African-born "Brazilian" merchants and slavers in the late eighteenth and early nineteenth centuries who returned to reside in West African ports, such as Agoué, Porto-Novo, Badagry, Popo, Lagos, or Abéokuta, at least for a part of the year.[49]

As a result of transatlantic trade in which African-born male slaves and ex-slaves played an important role, communication networks developed between Salvador and various parts of Africa from which not only men but also women benefited greatly. Some maintained contact with their kins-folk in Africa, sent their Brazilian-born children to them, or themselves emigrated to Africa after having been freed.[50] Maria Antônia, an Angolan woman, was manumitted unconditionally by her owner, Bernardo Silva Mello, solely because of her "good services." She gave birth to a *pardo* son named Raphael Fortunato da Silva, who embarked for Costa da Mina in 1830. She did not even know whether he was alive or not, although she named him as her primary heir; as such he was to inherit two-thirds of her possessions.[51] The free-born *crioula* woman Jeronima Maria da Conceição was the child of the Gêge woman Anna Joaquina and Bernardino José Bar-bosa, both of whom were dead. Jeronima had been raised in the house of a businessman who lived in the lower city, José Alves Cruz dos Rios, and his wife, and later married an African-born man named André da Conceição da França. They had a son, Manoel, who died at age nine months. Then André went alone to the coast of Africa. Jeronima named her former owner as executor of her will and her sister, Joanna Francisca, as her heiress.[52]

The Re-creation of Identity as "Free"

Upon gaining freedom against all the odds, African-born ex-slaves immediately adopted family names. For an ex-slave, having a last name, which symbolized the status of being legally free, was very important to re-store human dignity.[53] In nineteenth-century Salvador, as in many other parts of the Americas, ex-slaves usually adopted the last names, either in full or in part, of their ex-owners.[54] This is also the case of the Bahian Recôn-cavo. For instance, at the Jesuit-owned Engenho Santana of Ilhéus in 1752, all slaves were listed with family names, since the Jesuit administration had assigned family names or asked the slaves to select them in order to regu-larize family life among slaves. Among 108 slaves whose family names could be easily established, more than 70 percent bore the names of administra-tors of the estate.[55] At least in the city of Salvador, the naming custom ap-pears to have been practiced on the initiative of the ex-slaves and does not seem to have been used by ex-owners to identify or control slaves. So common were some first names, such as José or Maria, among different owners' slaves, some of whom often worked together as wage-earners, that it was necessary to differentiate between them. Maria, for example, became known as Sr. Santana's Maria. Therefore, it was convenient for ex-slaves to adopt their owners' surnames, by which they had been commonly known for many years, as their own formal surnames upon being freed.

Furthermore, African-born ex-slaves were very eager to be perceived as free by the larger society. Therefore they mimicked the white elite and took up their distinctive behaviors and attitudes, most notably slaveholding and multi-membership in lay sodalities.

The majority of African-born ex-slaves could not afford to own slaves or any other forms of property. They had made every effort to purchase freedom, but that does not mean that all of these people found it possible to escape from poverty and successfully become property owners. For instance, 79.7 percent of African-born ex-slaves (263 out of 330) who resided in Santana parish (1849) and 89.9 percent of them (186 out of 207) in Conceião da Praia parish (1846) did not own a single slave. But when some of the African-born ex-slave population—naturally a very small percentage—did become successful enough to own property, they usually chose to invest their money in slaveholding; after all, Salvador in the early nineteenth century was a slave society, in which only slaveholding could make a person a member of the society. Some ex-slaves (36 for Santana and 17 for Conceião da Praia), both men and women, actually owned more than one slave, and one African-born ex-slave in Conceião da Praia parish owned nineteen slaves.[56] The wills of African-born ex-slaves support this point very clearly; usually only property owners registered their wills for the sake of inheritance. For instance, among the 261 African-born ex-slaves who registered their wills between 1790 and 1850, slave owners constituted the majority: 72.3 percent for men (81 out of 112), and 82.9 percent for women (122 out of 147).[57] Slaveholding was certainly a norm among African-born ex-slave property owners who could afford it.

Many such ex-slave property owners of African birth simultaneously owned both African-born slaves, including those who shared the "nations" with them, and *crias,* namely Brazilian-born slaves raised in their owners' households. Interestingly, those ex-slave property owners of African birth treated each group differently; they favored the Brazilian-born slaves over their African-born counterparts.[58] This "double standard" is readily apparent from those owners' wills. Whereas many Brazilian-born slaves were liberated unconditionally on their owner's death and even were occasionally named as heirs to an owner's estate, many African-born slaves—including those of the same "nations" as their owners'—were usually *coartado*, that is, obliged to pay a fixed price to the heirs for their freedom within a limited period of time after the death of the owner.[59] A Nagô ex-slave might have instructed his or her Nagô slaves in their common language and demonstrated their shared cultural behaviors, but this did not necessarily mean that the owner favored the slave who shared the owner's ethnicity.

The property-owning African-born ex-slave population also held multiple memberships in black lay sodalities; they adopted an ostentatious attitude they had observed in the white laity's participation in lay sodalities, not only in their own white sodalities, which limited memberships only to whites, but also in mulatto ones, which did not allow African-born people and *crioulos* to join them, and even black sodalities, as discussed in chapter 3. In the late colonial period and the early nineteenth century, holding the multi-membership of sodalities was a common practice among well-to-do African-born ex-slaves, many of whom were slave owners themselves. For instance, among the 159 wills of ex-slaves (63 men and 96 women) registered in Salvador for the early nineteenth century, nearly half were members of one or more sodalities, and a third were affiliated with more than one sodality.[60]

A good example is Ana Maria do Carmo, an African-born woman originally from Costa da Mina, who registered her will on July 4, 1811. Ana Maria do Carmo was an ex-slave of the Reverend Luís de Sousa, who had liberated her on payment of 84$000 *réis*. She herself owned three African-born female slaves (Antônia, Maria, and Rosa), all also from Costa da Mina, and had limited assets in the form of gold, furniture, and used clothes. She had no children by her late husband Manoel Martins de Miranda da Cruz, or by anybody else, so she ordered that her property was to be inherited by José Maria do Carmo, who had been her slave but had been liberated. Ana Maria do Carmo declared in her will that the habit of Saint Francis should be her shroud, that the vicar of her parish should officiate at the funeral service, and that her cortège was to be accompanied by sixteen priests. Her burial was to be in the church of her sodality of Our Lady of the Rosary in the Pelourinho, where she had held the office of judge. Ana Maria was also a member of the sodality of Our Lady of the Rosary in the church of Santo Antônio parish. On the day of her death, the executor of her will was to say twelve masses for her soul, and another twelve masses for the saint of her name, each at the fee of 320 *réis*. She also left an additional 3$000 *réis* for masses to be said for her former owner, for twelve masses for the soul of her late husband, and for another twelve masses for her soul, each for the fee of 320 *réis*. Her funeral was to be accompanied by sixteen members of the sodalities to which she had belonged, and each of them would be given alms of 40 *réis* for such participation.[61]

An extreme example was the case of the African-born freedman Maximiano de Freitas Henrique. He had been a judge of the black sodality of Our Lady of the Rosary in the Pelourinho and a treasurer of the black sodality of Good Jesus of Redemption (Sr. Bom Jesus da Redempção), and served on the advisory boards of the black sodality of Saint Ephigenia in the Carmelite monastery and the black sodality of Saint Benedict in the same convent. He was also a member of the black sodality of Our Lady of the Rosary on Rua de João Pereira and of the black sodality of Jesus, Mary, and Joseph (Jesus Maria José), whose sect was the Carmelite monastery. In his will, he stipulated burial in the Franciscan monastery, accompanied by all members of the black sodalities of which he was a member.[62]

We have to emphasize the cruel reality that freedom did not change the larger society's perceptions of African-born ex-slaves; no matter how affluent African-born ex-slaves became, their wealth never enabled them to hold memberships in either white or mulatto lay sodalities; they were entitled to belong to black sodalities only. Their multi-membership in black sodalities carried prestige and signified their superior position as well-to-do ex-slaves only among the population of African descent; it did not make a significant appeal to the larger society as long as such ex-slaves' extended participation was confined to black sodalities. Freedom could never "whiten" African-born ex-slaves.

Conclusion

Enslaved Africans, most of whom had been born free in the Old World and remembered what freedom had meant, made all possible attempts to regain freedom from New World slavery. Their desperate efforts resulted in the prevailing practice of substitution as a form of self-purchase, through which slaves themselves became slave owners, rather than helping other slaves gain freedom; their shared experiences of enslavement (and exploitation) did not necessarily help the enslaved (and the exploited) develop a collective identity as enslaved Africans in the New World, with which they would have acted as a group against the institution of slavery. Realizing that self-purchase was virtually their only means to gain freedom, African-born slaves had to use and manipulate anything available that could work to their advantage, such as their shared ethnicity with new arrivals.

After many years of hard work, some African-born ex-slaves surely gained what they had yearned for: the recovery of their lost freedom, but it was not the same freedom that most of them had experienced as free-born in the Old World. They immediately recognized the limitations of their regained freedom and struggled to become "free" in a slave society. Sadly, they always ended up identifying themselves as ex-slaves only by distinguishing themselves from the enslaved population.

5 The Convergence of Identity, 1831–1880

Upon regaining freedom by self-purchase, African-born women and men, who had learned how to utilize their ethnicities to their advantage, expected to be treated as equals with the white elite, but they immediately learned that their regained freedom had lethal limitations: their freedom had been fatally damaged and permanently crippled. African-born ex-slaves learned the white elite's distinctive values and attitudes, imitated their behaviors, but nothing could elevate their ex-slave status to that of the free-born. As ex-slaves, they continued to wonder how to deal with their own otherness. They did not see it in terms of race; instead they tended to ascribe the limitations of their freedom to their African birth, which was associated most notably with their imperfect acquisition of the Portuguese language and their insufficient understanding of Luso-Brazilian culture. It made their naturalization impossible and therefore kept them from gaining equal legal rights as Brazilian citizens.

This chapter discusses the processes by which African-born ex-slaves, as early as the 1830s, came to develop a newly convergent ethnic identity as African-born. It fostered the formation of a distinctive ethnic community on both sides of the Atlantic Ocean after the mid-nineteenth century: as "African-born" in Salvador and as "Brazilian" back in Africa.

The Creation of African-Born (*Africano*) Identity

The African-born ex-slave population started to converge their diverse ethnic identities into a broader one during the 1830s, in response to the larger society's changing perceptions of them. The Bahian authorities had become more and more alert to and suspicious of the activities of the African-born population after a series of slave uprisings took place between 1807 and 1830. The law of 1830 prohibited people of African birth, both slaves and ex-slaves, from traveling freely. They were obliged to be in possession of passports (*pasaportes*) whenever they went beyond "the city, villages, settlement, or plantation and region" where they resided, whether for reason of business or for any other purpose. Whereas the passport for a slave had to be signed by the owner, an ex-slave had to obtain the passport from the criminal judge residing in his or her locality. Passports indicated the name of the person, destinations, and permitted period of travel. Without it, any African-born ex-slave was liable to imprisonment for eight days for transgression of the law.[1]

Furthermore, the decree of 1831 changed an important part of the landscape of the port city of Salvador, in whose busy streets newly arrived slaves had been most commonly traded because of the absence of a central slave market. With the enactment of the decree, African-born slaves were no longer taken directly into the port of Salvador from slave ships. Yet, the illegal slave trade continued to take place on a large scale from Africa to Brazil, including the province of Bahia. Although no statistical data are available to trace the numbers of illegally imported African-born slaves who were brought into the city of Salvador, we may assume that Salvador might have received fewer and fewer African-born slaves after 1831, due to the continuing demands for slaves as plantation labor in the Recôncavo. As discussed in chapter 1, slaves still constituted 42.0 percent of the whole population of Salvador in 1835, but the proportion declined to 26.1 percent by 1855. Yet African-born slaves continued to outnumber the Brazilian-born slave population until mid-century. For instance, 56.2 percent of slaves purchased and sold in Sé parish for 1838–1848 were African-born, while among the slaves (1,170 individuals) registered in 154 inventories of their owners for 1808–1849, 67 percent were African-born.[2] João José Reis estimates that in 1835 African-born slaves constituted 63 percent of the enslaved population of Salvador.[3]

During the 1830s Salvador remained an urban slave society, while among the African-born population diverse ethnic identities could no longer be revitalized on a daily basis in the absence of infusions of newly arrived African slaves of diverse ethnic origins. Regardless of the freedom they had ultimately regained, the urban African-born ex-slave population began to identify themselves more and more with African-born slaves as African-born, beyond legal distinctions, whereas their distinctive gender identities continued to differentiate individual experiences, as a well-organized uprising in Salvador on January 24–25, 1835 clearly showed.

This armed uprising has been long known as the Malê (African Muslim) revolt, because of the allegedly prominent role of Muslims among the participants.[4] It was originally planned for dawn on the day of Nossa Senhora da Guia (Our Lady of Guidance), Sunday, January 25, which came after the festival of Senhor do Bonfim (the Lord of the Good Ending). On this day, it was the custom of many residents of Salvador to leave the city to attend the church of Bonfim, located at the northern edge of the city, a church noted for its miracles and, as such, a place of pilgrimage, and later to spend the night on Itapagipe peninsula.[5] And dawn was the time of the day when slaves left their owners' houses to fetch water, so many of them could join the uprising without arousing suspicion.[6] The rebels, all of whom were wage-earners in the city, were to set fire to several places in the city simultaneously to distract the police and the troops. They were then to be joined by slaves coming by water from Santo Amaro, a town of the Recôncavo. On the evening of the 24th of January, however, the revolt was denounced to the authorities.

Unlike the previous aborted slave uprisings between 1807 and 1830 (as discussed in chapter 3), in the case of the Malê revolt there are police records and court testimonies detailing the circumstances and the personalities involved in this denunciation, and the story is worth telling at length here.

Prominent was the role of two African-born freedwomen, both Nagô. One was named Guilhermina Roza de Souza, resident of Vitória parish in the house of her former owner, Firmiano Joaquim de Souza Velho. Guilhermina heard of the uprising from the father of her children, Domingos Furtunato, a Nagô freedman. Domingos was a former slave of Furtunato Jozé da Cunha, who had lived in the lower city. On the 24th, Domingos overheard some *negro* boatmen (*negros de saveiros*) talking of the impending arrival of some *negros* in Salvador on the 25th. They were to join with the leader Aruna, or Uahuna, who had already arrived some days before, and to take over the city with other *negros* on the following day. Their intent was "to kill whites, *cabras,* and *crioulos,* as well as those *negros* of another faction or group (*banda*) who did not wish to join the uprising; the *pardos* would be spared for use as lackeys and slaves." Domingos wanted to alert his ex-owner, who was living in Pilar parish, to this impending danger, by asking somebody to write a note for him to this effect. While Guilhermina was standing at the window of her house digesting this news, she heard a couple of Nagôs saying that those *negros* who were to rebel with the help of those from Santo Amaro should go to the public fountains in the lower city to fetch water at dawn. Guilhermina went to tell her own ex-owner and, on her way home, encountered her *comadre* (comother), Sabina da Cruz, also a Nagô freedwoman of José Manoel Gonçalves, resident of Itapagipe. Sabina was searching for a certain white man to warn her ex-owner that many *ne-*

gros had been gathering on Rua da Guadalupe and that firearms were being distributed.[7]

Around four o'clock in the morning on the 24th, Sabina had quarreled with the father of her children, Victoriano, also Nagô, who was known by his African name of Sule. After spending the day vending in the lower city, she returned to her house to find everything inside a mess. Convinced that Victoriano was the culprit because of their quarrel in the morning, she began to search for him by going from house to house of his acquaintances. In one such house on Rua da Guadalupe, *negros* from Santo Amaro were gathered. In the corridor of the house, Sabina saw many Nagôs assembling and heard them talking in the language of Nagô. She was scared and did not go further to enter the room where the meeting was taking place. But she did catch a glimpse of a Nagô-Bá (Yoruba from the kingdom of Egba) woman, whose African name was Edum, leaving the room. Sabina did not know her name in Portuguese, the language of "the white's land" (*terra de branco*). Edum carried her baby on her back in a shawl, and Sabina recognized her immediately because Edum had bought some yams from Sabina earlier on the same day. Sabina learned from Edum that Sule was in the meeting room but would not come out until the following morning, when the men were scheduled to "take over the land (*terra*)." The yams Edum had bought from Sabina were for Aruna, the leader, who was now inside the room, armed and well-prepared, together with a lot of people. In response to Sabina's statement that all of them would be the possessors not of the land (*terra*) but of a whip-lashing (*senhor de surra*) on the following day, Edum told her to wait and see until the next day. Among others in the room, Sabina recognized only a male slave whose African name was Honomonin, and whose owner was the baker, Pedro, resident of Pilar parish. The slave Honomonin was rented out to Sabina's *negro* neighbor, Belchior de Silva Cunha. Terrified by what she had seen and heard, Sabina fled and ran to report the momentous events to her comother (*comadre*) Guilhermina. This was the information that Guilhermina took to the authorities.[8]

This short story, which I have reconstructed mainly based on the few African-born ex–slave women's court testimonies, raises some interesting points. First, the participants of the Malê revolt regarded as their enemies not only the whites but also all of the Brazilian-born population of African descent regardless of color, and even other ethnic groups among African-born. As discussed in chapter 2, the African-born population in Salvador identified themselves and were referred to by others by their original African names. Gossip and rumor circulated quickly, often through the instrument of African languages and thus within ethnic boundaries. Second, in the court records of the Malê revolt, Salvador and/or Bahia was characterized as "the white's land" in distinction to Africa as "our land."[9] This we-they dichotomy indicated that the African-born population began to develop a convergent ethnic identity as African-born in opposition to the white elite in Salvador after having spent a number of years in the New World. Third, this story reveals the existence of associations among women of African birth. The two Nagô freedwomen, Guilhermina and Sabina, were related to each other by fictive kinship as comothers, and seem to have developed communication networks and commercial associations with other women of African birth who were engaged in the informal market of the city. The market was the place where symbolically important commodities, such as yams, were brought by water from the Recôncavo, and were used for *candomblé* rituals and traded by such women of African birth. It is significant that the Nagô-Bá woman Edum bought the yams from Sabina for the leader Aruna. These yams may have been intended for use in a ritual in celebration of the prospective uprising.

With the denunciation by the two African-born freedwomen, the police immediately began to investigate and increased patrols in the city. Around one o'clock in the morning on the 25th, a group of patrols searched a two-storied house located on the Ladeira da Praça. The first floor was occupied by the *pardo* tailor Domingos Martin de Sá; his *parda* companion Joaquina da Santa Anna; their infant child; and a Nagô slave, Ignácio, whom Domingos owned. Domingos rented the basement to two African-born freedmen, Manoel the caulker, who was Nagô, and Aprigio the bread peddler and chair carrier, who was Nagô-Oyo. With the information from a neighbor that a number of *negros* had gathered in this basement, the troops broke into the place, from which some sixty rebels came out shouting and shooting. They easily overcame the small group of police in front of the house and proceeded to the municipal jail. Here they hoped to rescue the African-born Muslim slave Pacífico, who had been held prisoner because of his owner's debt to the Carmelites. After failing to invade the jail, they attacked the guards of the governor's palace and injured some of them. In this, they were joined by another group of rebels. The rebels proceeded southward, and more people joined them on their way to Rua da Vitória. After an unsuccessful attack on the fortress of São Pedro, they headed back to Vitória, where they were united with another group who had been waiting at the convent of Mercês. They returned downtown, appeared on Rua da Ajuda, and proceeded to Largo do Palácio, where they failed once again to breach the jail. The final battle between the rebels and the Municipal Cavalry took place in Agua de Meninos, which was one and a half miles away from the Bonfim Church. After about fifteen minutes of fighting, the rebels were defeated. Unaware that the uprising was already over, between six and seven o'clock in the morning of the 25th, six armed slaves of João Francisco Ratis set fire to their owner's house and attempted to reach Agua de Meninos, but all were killed.[10]

It is difficult to ascertain exactly how many people participated in this revolt. Howard Prince estimates the number at between 400 and 500.[11] After an immediate and rigorous search and investigation of the houses of African-born slaves and ex-slaves, the police arrested a total of 326 individuals. Of these, 284 were brought to trial.[12] These participants in the revolt seemingly included many slaves owned by British and other foreign merchants who lived in the wealthiest residential district of Vitória parish. Of the 160 slaves who were incriminated, 50 were owned by foreigners. The owners of 45 slaves were British. The police were particularly suspicious about a potential British anti-slavery agenda behind the revolt, but there was no basis for their suspicion.[13] British merchants, who were Protestants, were presumably less concerned with the commitment of their charges to the Catholic faith, and on many occasions British owners, in fact, did claim "British privilege" for runaways.[14] The local white population of Salvador resented the British privilege and charged the British with "inciting their own slaves to insurrection and preparing them to emulate the horrors of Saint Domingue."[15]

On the one hand, there are remarkable similarities between the Malê revolt and the earlier slave uprisings (chapter 3). First, very few of the Brazilian-born population of African descent participated. Second, the Malê revolt was a predominantly male phenomenon; the proportion of women who participated in the revolt was very small (less than 10 percent). In contrast with their male counterparts, African-born slave women of diverse ethnic backgrounds, many of whom worked together as market women on the street, associated with one another and therefore developed a distinctive gender identity beyond ethnicity (see chapter 2).[16] The prominent absence of women from the revolt may also be attributable to the prevalent matri-local family among the urban African-born population in the early nineteenth century. We should remember that the denunciation of the Malê revolt in 1835 to the police was by two Nagô ex–slave women who were co-mothers, both of whose common-law spouses of African birth participated in the revolt. Third, as in the slave uprisings in the 1820s and 1830, Nagôs predominated (68.1 percent of all defendants).[17] The court records of the revolt show that many non-Nagô individuals of African birth defended themselves by referring to their respective "nations" and use of different languages. For instance, the Hausa freedman Narcizo Pinheiro, whose occupation was peddler of cloth on the street, was arrested with two other Hausa freedmen who shared the same house with him on Rua da Oração. In court, Narcizo declared that since he did not comprehend the Nagô language he could not have known that the Nagôs had been planning to revolt, nor had he himself been one of the rebels. He continued: "[E]very day at the time of Ave Maria I was at home, and did not go out after that. Some days in the morning I saw various *negros* enter the house of Belchior and Gaspar da Silva, but I did not know why. I just ignored them."[18]

On the other hand, the Malê revolt was different from the uprisings of the African-born population in the earlier period in the following three aspects. First, the revolt was not really a slave uprising; ex-slaves were prominent and comprised 41.4 percent of the defendants. The Malê revolt manifests the creation of a collective identity, beyond distinction of legal status, as people of African birth.[19] Second, the Malê revolt involved African-born ex-slaves of diverse "nations." African-born slaves and ex-slaves, who had already spent many years in Brazil and had gained a relatively good sense of Luso-Brazilian culture, joined forces to rebel against the larger society. The majority of slave participants (81.8 percent) were identified as Nagô, which is a representative composite of the enslaved population of African birth, as had been the case of the slave uprisings from 1807 to 1830, but it suggests that, as in the preceding cases, sharing the same ethnic identity continued to be a determinant factor for the enslaved African-born population in taking collective actions against power holders. By contrast, ex-slaves were composed of diverse West African "nations": Nagô (48.6 percent); Hausa (19.5 percent); Tapa (6.4 percent); and Gêge (5.5 percent).[20] This supports the point made in chapter 4 that African-born ex-slaves had created a collective ex-slave identity beyond diverse ethnic identities, but we should take special note that despite their regained freedom those African-born ex-slaves joined African-born slaves for this uprising in 1835. Third, Islam played important roles in this specific uprising. This was apparent from the rebels' desperate attempts to rescue the highly respected African-born Muslim slave Pacífico (Lucian by his African name or Biali by his Arabic name) from jail. His presence itself seems to have been very important among the population of African birth. Despite the fact that Pacífico himself had not been involved in the uprising, he was later sentenced to six hundred lashes.[21]

In the Malê revolt, the rebels wore Muslim-style clothes with protective good-luck charms and papers.[22] Other Muslim teachers who were found guilty during the court hearings on this revolt included Aluna, the Nagô slave who was a water seller and whose owner had recently gone to live on a plantation in Santo Amaro; the Nagô freedman Victoriano (or Sule), an itinerant vendor of cloth; and the Tapa slave Luís.[23] During the intensive investigation that followed, the police seized papers and books written in Arabic, as well as ritual garments, banners, and rings. They also found evidence of sheep having been sacrificed in the houses of many rebels, including in the basement sublet to Manoel and Aprigio. "Father" Manoel was also a Muslim preacher.[24]

The Malê revolt in Salvador, however, should not be interpreted as an Islamic holy war (*jihad*) against Christianity, as the French sociologist Roger Bastide has maintained in his *The African Religions in Brazil,* and most recently Paul E. Lovejoy has suggested in his diasporic interpretation of New World slavery.[25] Nor was it a reflection of any political or religious situation in West Africa, nor a "nativistic" movement with religious millenarian overtones, as scholars including Nina Rodrigues and Howard Prince have suggested.[26] Then, what were the roles of Islam in the Malê revolt? May we interpret Islam not as a religion but as an ethnic identity that was created in New World slavery and that bound the rebels of West African birth together, as João José Reis has suggested?[27]

Some of the papers in Arabic seized by the police had been written by highly literate Muslims, probably educated in their homelands of Africa, and contained instructions to the insurgents coming from Vitória parish to "seize the country, kill all the whites, and go to a meeting place where they would be joined by others from the Recôncavo," but many participants had only copies of single verses from the Koran, perhaps written by barely literate people who became adherents of Islam after being transported to Brazil.[28] Probably, for some of those who were not even necessarily believers in the religion of Islam, there was the belief that by carrying the sacred passages from the Koran in Arabic they would be protected from the bullets of police and soldiers. According to the anthropologist Mariane Ferme, who studies gender among the present-day Mende of West Africa, many West Africans who are not Muslims by religion, nor literate in Arabic, believe documents in Arabic to be imbued with strong sacred powers.[29] The leaders planned the revolt and committed their plans to paper in Arabic, whereas many of the participants, who were Nagôs, communicated verbally with one another in Nagô. That this would be their usual practice was clearly illustrated by the story of the denunciation by the two African-born ex–slave women. This raises the question of why the insurgents chose to use the Arabic language, which had been closely identified with the religion of Islam, in their written planning of the revolt. Was the motivation solely that Arabic could be useful as a secret code for communication among those African-born men?

Jack Goody's theoretical monograph on the Malê revolt, albeit largely based on secondary sources, discusses the significance of the written religion of Islam in this particular revolt. First, the fact that writing was employed in the uprising to make secret arrangements by means of letters suggests that the superior planning was related to literacy. Sharing the common written language of Arabic enabled a careful planning of a revolt that possibly recruited several hundred people. Secondly, the words from the Koran were not simply a matter of magical power or material protection but of religious faith. Thirdly, the written religion of Islam seems to have functioned as an ideological foundation for the rebels. The notion of "death to the whites," which appeared not only in the Malê revolt but also in some of the earlier uprisings, was also characteristic of many recent uprisings in West Africa, where the word *nasala* for "white" is derived from the Arabic form of Nazarene, Christian. Therefore, according to Goody, ethnic and even racial definitions were dominated by religious overtones.[30] Thus the Malê revolt took on anti-Christian forms and characters. Furthermore, Goody, citing Eugene D. Genovese's seminal work entitled *From Rebellion to Revolution* (1979),[31] discusses the importance of literacy in major New World slave uprisings during the Age of Revolution in general and maintains that the results of Islam's commitment to literacy were particularly marked in the Malê revolt.[32] In contrast to an oral religion, which specifies a population boundary, a written religion is defined in relation to a text to which reference is made. Consequently, the written religion is by definition capable of crossing ethnic boundaries and of recruiting adherents, as in the case of the Malê revolt, on a non-ethnic basis and of overcoming the ethnic divisions among the African-born population in Salvador.[33] Thus, the written religion of Islam could have provided a solid religious foundation that enabled some of the African-born population in the New World to join together in the name of their own god, Allah, beyond ethnic divisions, to rebel against the larger society whose full members believed in another god, namely Jesus Christ; people of African birth and their owners or ex-owners in Salvador did not belong to the same religious community. Such religious separation of slaves from slave owners must have been the key factor in the relative success of the Malê revolt, because of which, according to Genovese, "Bahia had come close to becoming another Haiti."[34]

In the Malê revolt of 1835, in contrast to the preceding slave uprisings from 1807 to 1830, we do not find among the enslaved male African-born population ethnic identities developed strongly enough to transcend geographical urban/rural borders in Bahia. Whereas the majority of the slave rebels were Nagôs, the revolt also involved African-born freedmen of diverse West African "nations." The participants in the revolt were in almost equal numbers slaves and ex-slaves, many of whom had already spent many years in Brazil and had gained a relatively good sense of Luso-Brazilian culture. The aim of the participants in the Malê revolt had been to rebel against the larger society, which was composed of the white elite and Brazilian-born people of African descent. To this end, they employed the Arabic language as the means of communication for this very special event and, more importantly, used the written religion of Islam as a shared symbol of their collective (if temporary) African-born male identity.

The Malê revolt had an enormous impact on the larger society's perceptions of the African-born population in general; they came to be viewed as the most decisive obstacle to social order in slave society. In the first three decades of the nineteenth century, slave owners had been most apprehensive of African-born slaves, whom they classified by specific "nations," such as Hausa for the earlier periods and, later, Nagô, who were regarded as most prone to rebellion. After the Malê revolt, in which both slaves and ex-slaves of diverse African "nations" participated, the larger society began to rapidly develop fear and suspicion of all the African-born population. People of African birth, both enslaved and freed, thus came to be viewed as the most dangerous threats to public security.[35]

As a result, the Legislative Assembly of the province of Bahia, being confused and terrified, wrote to the General Legislative Assembly in Rio de Janeiro suggesting establishment of a Brazilian colony, to which African-born ex-slaves could be repatriated in any port on the coast of Africa. They cited the case of the British colony of Sierra Leone, to which maroon slaves had been sent from Jamaica. The imperial government of Brazil sent a consul-general, Lieutenant E. A. da Veiga, to Luanda to pursue this possibility, but his residency was denied by the Portuguese authorities.[36]

The provincial assembly of Bahia also issued a new law (Law no. 8) on May 5, 1835 to control the African-born population by severely restricting their legal rights.[37] African-born ex-slaves became obliged to pay a head tax of 10$000 *réis* annually.[38] They were no longer allowed to acquire any form of property.[39] Of course, many ignored these regulations and acquired property such as real estate and slaves, but registered it in the names of their Brazilian-born children, kinsfolk, or even slaves or ex-slaves they had raised in the household as *crias*. For example, the African-born freedman Joaquim de São José, who purchased his second wife, the African-born slave named Maria do Bonfim and her four children, registered ownership of his wife and children in the name of his legitimate daughter Veríssima Maria José, born to the late Rosa Barbosa, an African-born freedwoman who had been his first wife.[40] Furthermore, Article 18 of the same law prohibited any real estate owner, renter, sublessee, agent, or administrator from renting or leasing houses to African-born ex-slaves, as well as to slaves. Penalty for infringement was 100$000 *réis*.[41]

On May 27, 1835, within a month following the passage of Law no. 8, the provincial assembly passed another law to establish the office of foreman in charge of wage-earners (*ganhadores*) in the city of Salvador. The law defined wage-earners as those engaged in the practice of wage-earning, both by land and sea, whether they were slaves or ex-slaves. Each foreman was paid his salary by the wage-earners in his work gang. All wage-earners were obliged to register their homes, the districts in which their homes were located, the names of owners in the case of slaves, their qualification, and the type of service in which they were gainfully employed. This registration was to be renewed monthly. Any individual who was employed in the service of wage earning without registration was liable to a fine of 10$000 *réis*.[42] Although this law does not specify sex of wage-earners, apparently it refers exclusively to men who worked in gangs as wage-earners, such as porters, stevedores, and sailors. Furthermore, throughout most of the early nineteenth century, virtually all male wage-earners were of African birth, whether enslaved or freed. For instance, the 370 inventories of slave owners I consulted do not include a single slave wage-earner of Brazilian birth for 1808–1849.[43] Well aware of this fact, the municipal council established this law to strengthen their legal control of the African-born population.

The provincial law of 1842 also obliged African-born ex-slaves to claim annually to reside in Bahia. Each had to register his or her name, "nation," marital status, age, and present address, along with the year of manumission. The richness of such sources can be gauged by the following example: "On September 12, 1842, in this Secretariat of Police, in the presence of a judge of the court of appeals and Antônio Simoes da Silva, police chief of the province, Antônio Xavier de Jesus, an African-born freedman, Nagô, thirty years of age, married to Felicidade Francisca Fernandes, an African-born freedwoman, also Nagô, and who lived from his business dealings, declared his residence to be in Cais das Ananas, and that he had been liberated in the year of 1835. He presented the document certifying that he had paid the head tax as stipulated in Article 8 of the provincial law for 1842–1843. He obtained a residency permit for one year."[44]

On November 2, 1850, the president of the province of Bahia issued another new decree applicable to the African-born population. It prohibited boatmen of African birth from plying at the quayside and within the harbor of Salvador, as this service was henceforth the exclusive prerogative of the Brazilian-born population. The British consul, Edward Porter, reported that about 750 African-born ex-slaves were thus thrown out of employment as boatmen and that the decree—ostensibly issued for the purpose of "encouraging national labor"—in fact was intended to "gradually induce the white population to engage in out-door labour."[45]

With the establishment of a series of new laws restricting the legal status and upward social mobility of the African-born population, particularly men, the Bahian authorities undertook the reduction of a dangerous component of the African-born ex-slave population by deporting them to Africa. Already in August and September of the year of the Malê revolt (1835), rumors of a possible insurrection were circulated in Salvador. Panicked and distracted, the Bahian police soon imprisoned 300 to 400 African-born ex-slaves. Of these, 148 were expelled in a Brazilian schooner on November 12, 1835, to the port of Whydah in West Africa. On the 5th of the same month, there were further deportations to Africa.[46] Interestingly, this forced deportation of African-born ex-slaves to Africa stimulated voluntary departure for their homelands in Africa by many other African-born ex-slaves, who were under severe daily supervision by a police force that continued to harass them without cause. Individually, these African-born ex-slaves took passage on Brazilian or Portuguese ships which sailed regularly between Salvador and the Bight of Benin. Among such emigrants were Antônio da Costa and João Monteiro, who had become wealthy slave traders. On January 25, 1836, these two well-to-do freedmen chartered the English schooner *Nimrod* so that they and 160 other African-born ex-slaves could emigrate to Africa. Under the British flag, these African-born passengers were well protected from patrols, which might have otherwise suspected that the *Nimrod* was engaged in the clandestine slave trade. The *Nimrod* dropped passengers at the ports of Arriba Athuna, Agoué, Aunim (Lagos), and Minas Pequenas.

Other African-born ex–slave men and women soon followed this successful example of group emigration from Salvador.[47] Passports were issued to

422 African-born in 1835 and to 329 in 1836. The percentage of African-born among the total number of people to whom passports were issued was 33 percent and 59 percent, respectively.[48]

The Bahian authorities welcomed and encouraged African-born ex-slaves' repatriation movements to Africa as much as possible. Law no. 420 of June 7, 1851 exempted from the aforementioned head tax of 10$000 *réis* those African-born ex-slaves who volunteered to leave Brazil forever within three months of the enactment of the law, on the condition that they would never return.[49] At the same time the elite continued to impose more and more economic pressure on the African-born ex-slave population. That same year of 1851 witnessed the establishment of new annual taxes on various licenses issued to African-born ex-slaves, or "free Africans": 20$000 *réis* to buy and sell merchandise; 6$000 *réis* to carry chairs (*cadeiras*); 30$000 *réis* on sailing vessels known as *saveiros;* and 20$000 *réis* on boats used for disembarkation of people and cargo.[50] No doubt, these legal regulations at mid-century that discriminated against the African-born population because of their foreign status motivated people of African birth living in Salvador to consider the option of emigrating to Africa.

This large-scale emigration of African-born ex-slaves to Africa seems to have been largely limited to Salvador and Bahia.[51] One of the few cases outside Salvador is reported by the Americans the Reverend James C. Fletcher and the Reverend Daniel P. Kidder in the city of Rio de Janeiro. In 1851, sixty Mina ex-slaves paid four thousand dollars as passage money to leave for Badagry on the Bight of Benin, and they arrived there safely. The following year, a deputation of eight or ten Mina ex-slaves waited for a delegation from the English Society of Friends. They had money for their passages, but wanted to be assured that the coast was free of slavers.[52] Probably the large-scale migration of African-born ex-slaves and their families from Salvador to Africa was partly attributable to Bahia's depressed agro-export economy. This contrasted with the coffee-booming Southeast (Rio de Janeiro and São Paulo), where even those of African birth could find better economic opportunities. In 1865, the French traveler Joseph Arthur de Gobineau, the Count of Gobineau, while observing the return of Mina ex-slaves to Africa, noted that some ex-slaves left Salvador for Rio de Janeiro, where oftentimes they would make a small fortune.[53]

By mid-century, African-born emigrants from Brazil, mainly from Salvador, together with Luso-African slave traders, their former servants, and slave ship captains, had settled in the major coastal towns of the Bight of Benin such as Agoué, Whydah, Porto Novo, and Lagos.[54] The British ex-military officer John Duncan, visiting Whydah in 1845, observed that the residents of this coastal town included many who had obtained freedom by purchase, and others who had arrived as servants or slaves of slave dealers who had come from Brazil. The owners in their wills had manumitted these slaves at the owners' deaths.[55] Duncan also observed that in the countryside ten or twelve miles distant from Whydah, many places were well cultivated by "people returned from the Brazils." These people had originated from Foolah and Eya, had been enslaved, and had been transported at the age of twenty to twenty-four years to the port of Badagry, from where they had been shipped to Brazil.[56]

These coastal towns accepted "returnees" not only from Brazil but also from other parts of the world. African-born ex-slaves who emigrated from Cuba were later to join "Brazilians."[57] They were also to be joined by Africans (mostly Yorubas) who had been captured on slave ships and emancipated in Sierra Leone by the action of the Royal Navy, but who returned to the Bight of Benin and chose to settle in these towns. These people who moved from Sierra Leone were commonly called Saros.[58] African-born ex-slaves who emigrated from Salvador came into contact with the ex-slave returnees from Cuba and with the Saros, as well as with the indigenous population of West Africa, and they created their own ethnic identity, which separated them from others.

The Development of Collective African-Born Identity, ca. 1851–1880

The African-born population in Salvador quickly developed their new ethnic identity as African-born after the mid-nineteenth century. The year 1851 marked the official termination of the transatlantic slave trade, and after that date notarial records no longer indicate specific African "nations" for the African-born population, as had hitherto been the case. In manumission letters, the percentage of African-born ex-slaves who were identified by "nations" declined from 83 percent for 1808–1842 to less than half (48.8 percent) for 1851–1884.[59] This change is also apparent not only in legal registers of slaves in Sé parish and inventories of slave owners, but also in wills of ex-slaves and parish records of baptism and marriage.[60] Specification of African "nations" probably mattered less after the mid-nineteenth century than it had previously, either for official use in records or for the African-born population themselves; it had already been two decades since the port of Salvador stopped importing new arrivals directly, and the African-born ex-slave population had gone through a substantial amount of acculturation. As we have discussed, their newly converged "African-born" identity, at least among men, played an important role in their choice of participation in the Malê revolt.

Legal freedom was a key factor in African-born ex-slaves' choice of holy matrimony. One example is the African-born ex-slave Gonçalo de Sousa, who purchased his freedom from his owner, the priest Luís de Sousa, for the price of 120$000 *réis*. By June 25, 1842, when Gonçalo made his will, he had married Ana Maria do Sacramento, by whom he had no children. However, as a bachelor, Gonçalo had fathered three natural children. The first two, Gonçalo de Sousa and Maria de Sousa, were by a *cabra* woman named Maria das Neves, whose legal status was free-born or ex-slave. The mother of the third and last, Martiniana, was an African-born woman (*prêta*) named Mariana, who was probably Gonçalo's own slave. Martiniana was baptized as an ex-slave (*forra*), and her father registered her manumission letter at the notarial office in 1834. Before his death in 1845, Gonçalo named as executors of his will, in order of preference, first his wife's son Francisco José Moreira, secondly his wife, Ana Maria, and thirdly his son, Gonçalo de Sousa. Whereas he named Ana Maria as his "universal heiress," he appointed her son, his stepson Francisco, as guardian of his second daughter, Martiniana, who was in her early teens.[61]

In the case of the union between an ex-slave and a slave, they usually waited to contract marriage until the latter attained the status of an ex-slave, so that their future children would be born free. This was usually the case of a freedman and a slave woman, and the former often contributed money for the latter's self-purchase. The wills of ex-slaves include six such cases.[62] The manumission letters do not describe the relationship between the slave woman and the non-kinsman who paid for her freedom.[63] Some ex-slave husbands liberated their wives' slave children fathered by other men before their marriage. Such was the case of Sebastião Alves da Rocha, an ex-slave originally from Angola. Sebastião purchased the freedom of his fiancée, Maria Pedro, who was a slave of José Joaquim Pires, also from Angola, in order to marry her. Each had a child by other partners before marriage. After they married, Sebastião also purchased the freedom of Maria's daughter, Ana, from the same owner. But neither Sebastião nor Maria had enough money to pay the price for Ana, namely 400$000 *réis*. Sebastião borrowed 300$000 *réis* from Manoel Fernandes Suenpira, and a legal document to this effect was notarized. After the death of his wife Maria, Sebastião lived with his own son, of the same name, a bricklayer in Santana parish. Sebastião the son had been born of a *prêta*, Laurença, then a slave, and had been baptized by Sebastião the father as his son. Whereas Sebastião the elder instituted his son as his heir, he not only made it clear that Ana had no right to inherit any of his property, but also insisted that she still owed him 303$200 *réis,* namely the total amount of the loan of 300$000 *réis,* interest of 200 *réis,* and notarial fee of 3$000 *réis,* since Ana had never returned any amount of money to him.[64]

Since a child born of a slave woman was automatically the property of the mother's owner, mother and child frequently shared the same surname as ex-slaves of the same owner. Despite the fact that they never shared the same family names with their children born to slave women, many fathers recognized the consanguinity of their natural children and left money in their wills for such children to purchase their freedom if they were still enslaved, and legitimized them as their heirs in those cases where they were already legally free. Recognition of paternity was most important to patrilineal inheritance.

There are two interesting wills made by freedmen in which the testator officially rejected his paternity of a child who was recognized by others as his natural offspring. The first case is Bento Dias Coelho, a bachelor ex-slave from Costa da Mina. In his will registered on May 2, 1816, Bento left 16$000 *réis* to the *crioulo* Bernardino, since Bernardino claimed that he was the son of Bento. However, Bento insisted that he did not recognize Bernardino as his son, but that he left the money to him because of his "conscience."[65] As we shall discuss later, until 1847 Brazilian law offered ample means in a situation such as that of Bernardino to prove patrilineal succession. Bernardino or his mother's family could easily have established Bento's paternity in court. Perhaps it was recognition of such popular awareness of the facts of the case, and not his conscience, which led Bento to leave the money to Bernardino.

The second case is the African-born freedman Ronvaldo de Cerqueira. Ronvaldo refused to recognize Clemente de Cerqueira Pinto as his son, although Clemente was born of his first wife, Maria Rosa de Conceição, after their marriage. In his will of August 16, 1873, Ronvaldo confidently asserted his opinion that Maria had been already pregnant by another man at the time of their marriage. After Maria's death, Ronvaldo remarried, choosing Felicidade Maria da Conceição as his second wife. He named his second wife as the "universal heiress" of the property that he had bought with her money after their marriage.[66] Since this occurred after the enactment of the succession law of 1847, Clemente was denied the right of patrilineal inheritance.

In the case of common-law conjugal unions between ex-slaves and/or free-born people of African descent, natural children always took the father's surname, as would legitimate children. Some unmarried parents surely made their natural children share their fathers' surnames, by which paternity could be widely recognized and which would become useful in justifying any subsequent claim to patrilineal inheritance. This custom of taking natural fathers' surnames is exemplified by the case of Narcesa Francisca de Oliveira, a *crioula* ex–slave woman. She had three legitimate children by Anselmo Lopes: Theodoro, João Feliciano, and Francisca Maria. After her husband's death, she bore four natural sons: José Gonsalves Ramos, Gonsalo Ramos, Domingos Gonsalves Ramos, and Vicente Ferreira Ramos. They shared their common surname, Ramos, with their natural father, Narcesa's lover or common-law spouse.[67]

Fathers often shared their first names with sons, whereas mothers and daughters rarely shared the same first name. Naming a son after his father is a common practice in any patrilineal society, but in the context of nineteenth-century Salvador, where common-law marriages among slaves did not always imply co-residence of partners and where children were usually raised by mothers, this naming practice helped children born as slaves to maintain father-son relationships in those cases in which the father and mother ended their relationship. Despite strong matrilocality among the population of African descent, their intergenerational kinship relationships extended bilaterally, while fathers' recognition of consanguinity was evidenced in their naming practices.

Both grandmothers and grandfathers recognized their ties to their slave grandchildren, paid cash for their purchase of freedom, left property or money to them, and even named them as their heirs. For instance, the African-born ex-slave Valentino Paschoal left half of his property to his wife, Maria Espírito Santo Pires, also an African-born ex-slave, and the rest to his still enslaved granddaughter, Belimira, for her freedom. Belimira was one of the four children of his natural daughter, whom Valentino had had by a slave woman.[68] Although parent-child relationships seem to have extended bilaterally, it is likely that matrilineal ties survived in the long run with much greater frequency than patrilineal ones; many more grandmothers than grandfathers referred to their grandchildren in their wills. Maria de Araújo Ribeiro, an ex–slave woman from Costa da Mina who died on October 3, 1815, named her granddaughter, Anna Florencia de Almeida, as the heiress of two-thirds of her property, and left the rest to her little great-granddaughter, named Anna, daughter of Anna Florencia and her husband,

Sergeant-Major Luís Gonsaga de Barros. Maria appointed her son-in-law as executor of her will.[69]

In nineteenth-century Salvador, ex-slaves' accounts of how they viewed holy matrimony and the institution of marriage have not been documented. The few exceptions are some ex-slaves' brief references to their own marriages in their wills, but only in terms of inheritance. The Gêge ex–slave woman Joana Maria da Conceição had been separated from her husband, the African-born freedman Antônio da Costa, resident of Ladeira de Santa Tereza. When she made her will on July 28, 1842, she clarified that she and her spouse each had total control over their respective property. Therefore, she did not leave any of her property to her husband.[70] This is the only will I have found in which a married couple were separated from each other.[71] Another example is the African-born ex-slave José Alves Matheos, who was married to Justina Maria do Nascimento, whose legal status, place of birth, and color were not stated. In his will, dated December 16, 1867, he left his house to his wife to live in with her sister Martinha, her son Eugério, her family, and her goddaughter (*afilhada*) Martinha, on the condition that his wife lived "as a widow and in a chaste manner."[72] Thus, by controlling her rights of inheritance, knowing that she would need the house to take care of her own family, José Alves Matheos tried to prevent his wife from remarrying or even having a relationship with another man.

Most common-law conjugal unions among ex-slaves were monogamous and lasted for many years. After the mid-nineteenth century, many wills of African-born ex-slaves mentioned the names of their common-law spouses (*companheiros* or *companheiras*), also African-born ex-slaves, who often served as executors of their wills. Through their longtime monogamous unions, some common-law couples had several natural children between them.[73]

Polygamous unions were exceptional. One example is afforded by the African-born freedman Antônio de Almeida, who fathered natural children by different women. A bachelor, he fathered three children by the African-born freedwoman Esperança Bages: Cosma, Martiano, and Paulina. He also had one daughter, named Maria Laurença, by Justina Baptista do Reis, an African-born freedwoman. When he registered his will in 1869, he was living with the African-born freedwoman Maria Antônia Guimarães.[74]

After mid-century, African-born ex-slaves started to contract marriages very late in life, sometimes even on the deathbed of one of the spouses. The 763 listings in the marriage register of Conceição da Praia parish over forty-six years (1843–1888) include eighteen male and fifteen female African-born ex-slaves. Fifteen marriages were registered between African-born ex-slave spouses, but often with partners of both sexes aged anywhere from their forties through their eighties, and only after many years of common-law conjugal union.[75] The wills of ex-slaves include four cases of deathbed marriages. One example is the old African-born ex-slave Rafaina Rosa Friandes, who married João de Oliveira Sampaio, also an African-born ex-slave, on June 25, 1863, since she had no expectation of surviving a serious illness. They had lived in an "illicit" union for many years. She died, as a married woman, on August 13, 1863. After her death, her husband married another African-born ex–slave woman, Marcolina Porfina Vianna, and passed away on May 19, 1867.[76] This raises the question of why such deathbed marriages became more prevalent after the 1850s and whether such marriages were solely among African-born ex-slaves.

Historian Linda Lewin's study of traditional Brazilian succession law reveals that such a change in marriage patterns did not take place exclusively among ex-slaves who made wills leaving bequests, but was widespread among all property owners who had natural offspring. With Law no. 463 of September 2, 1847, Brazilian legislators rewrote the rules of patrilineal succession for natural offspring. Paternal "recognition" conferred succession rights on natural offspring, and equal rights continued to be presumed to exist for all appropriately recognized natural children until 1917, but the legal definition of paternal recognition did change over time. Until 1847, civil law construed proper recognition of paternity to include not only notarized declarations and those inserted in wills but also common knowledge. The law of 1847 drastically restricted the procedural opportunities for fathers to declare paternity of natural offspring. Furthermore, it ended a natural offspring's opportunity to establish kinship in court for the purpose of paternal succession. On the other hand, by the same law, natural offspring automatically gained succession rights by virtue of their parents' subsequent marriage.[77] This explains why, in the later part of the nineteenth century, property-owning ex-slaves contracted marriages very late in their lives.

In the late nineteenth century, when specific "nations" of African-born were no longer mentioned in baptismal records, mothers and their coparents were often African-born.[78] In the manumission letters, one male and six female Brazilian-born slaves (1808–1842) and two male and seven female Brazilian-born slaves (1851–1884) were manumitted with payments from their godparents.[79] Unfortunately, the manumission letters usually mentioned only the names of godparents, and only one of the sixteen godparents for Brazilian-born slaves at baptism was identified as a Nagô freedman.[80] Yet these data at least suggest that slave mothers chose as godparents those who could later afford to pay for a slave child's freedom.

In some wills of ex-slaves, their godparents (*padrinhos* and *madrinhas*) or coparents (*compadres* and *comadres*) were named as executors, whereas testators left money or property to their godchildren.[81] By the terms *afilhados* and *afilhadas,* they were usually referring to godchildren, but sometimes they included younger people to whom they were emotionally tied as quasi-kinsfolk, but without the relationship, such as their coparents' children or ex-owners' children, being recognized by formal Catholic rituals. For instance, Pedro Pires Monção, a *crioulo* ex-slave, named as executors of his will his godmother, Maria Francisca Rodrigues Seixas, resident of Quinze Mistérios and, secondly, his *crioula* wife, Bernardina Rodrigues Seixas (a daughter of the late Gêge woman Maria Thereza) together with his godfather, José Pereira da Silva. Pedro was determined to grant a letter of liberty to the *prêta* Thereza, one of his slaves and his *afilhada,* a year after his death.[82] Another example is the will of Matheos da Silva Guimarães, originally from Costa da Mina, who had married the late Joaquina da Silva Vasconcellos, also from Costa da Mina, but had no children by her. As executors of his will he named in descending order of preference his *compadres,* Joaquim de Santa Ana Lima and João Luís Ferreira, and his *comadre,* Bernardina Joaquina das Neves. His *compadre* Joaquim de Santa Ana Lima was also the godfather of his Gêge slave woman Antônia, who was to be freed because of her "good services" upon the death of her owner and was to be his heiress.[83]

Unfortunately, the legal status or color of a godparent, coparent, or godchild was not often mentioned in wills of ex-slaves. Researching of these wills in chronological sequence does suggest an interesting evolution in the changing patterns of fictive kinship networking among people of African descent. Just after mid-century, African-born ex-slaves, who were often coparents, began to establish relationships with one another as debtors and creditors. This practice, clearly revealed through their wills, suggests that coparenthood came to function as a solid base for establishing economic relationships among African-born ex-slaves, who began to develop a common collective identity after the termination of the Atlantic slave trade.[84] Occasionally, a person of financial means had several creditors and debtors concurrently, some of whom were his or her coparents. It is not clear whether fictive kinship networks as coparents were developed on the basis of a prior debt-credit relationship or vice versa, but these two kinds of relationships overlapped each other to a great degree and did strengthen individual ties among African-born ex-slaves.

Furthermore, in the late nineteenth century, African-born ex-slaves started to establish a pattern of naming as the executors of their wills those who were identified as African-born ex-slaves, including their kinsfolk and fictive kinsfolk. Some executors of wills were also heirs. Among the 325 wills of ex-slaves (159 for 1808–1849 and 166 for 1850–1888), 15 fall into this category, and all were registered after mid-century.[85] One example was an African-born freedwoman, Maria Roza Pereira, who registered her will on the 18th of June, 1867, and died less than three months later. She had been baptized in Santo Antônio parish and was an ex-slave of Severo José Pereira, who had liberated her unconditionally for her "good services." Maria Rosa was the widow of Francisco de Santana. She had neither legitimate nor natural children. As executors of her will she named first Henriqueta Joaquina do Bomfim, the widow of Benedicto Fernandes Galiga; secondly, Lucrecia Luisina; and thirdly, her nephew, Manoel Luisino. Each was African-born and an ex-slave. Maria Rosa owned a house at Rua do Genipapeiro. She had loaned 500$000 *réis* to her nephew Manoel for his self-purchase. In her will, she waived repayment of 200$000 *réis,* but requested Manoel to return the remainder to the executor of her will, since these funds were to cover the cost of her bequests. She left to Oliva, a daughter of Cora, an African-born woman, 50$000 *réis;* to her goddaughter Joana, an African-born slave owned by a baker on Rua de São Miguel, 50$000 *réis;* and to her niece Damiana, daughter of Rosa, 25$000 *réis.* Maria Rosa also left 50$000 *réis* to Lucrecia Geisina, an African-born freedwoman, who had taken care of her during her illness. Finally, she named as her heiress Henriqueta, an African-born freedwoman and the first executor of her will.[86]

Another example is the African-born barber-surgeon José Domingos dos Santos, whose "nation" was Nagô. José was an ex-slave of Lourenço Domingos dos Santos, also a barber-surgeon. His ex-owner had been a resident of Rua do Cais Dourado (Pilar parish), where José still resided. In his will of April 14, 1859, José named as executors of his will three African-born ex-slaves, all of them barber-surgeons and barbershop owners: Simão Bento de Cabalho, resident of Rua do Cais Dourado of Pilar parish; Manoel Antônio Guimarães, resident of Rua de Dom José of Sé parish; and Antônio Marcelino d'Almeida, resident of Rua de Dom José of Sé parish.[87] This is one of those rare cases in which the occupations of the testator and of all the executors were indicated in the will.

The evidence overwhelmingly supports the hypothesis that in the late nineteenth century, the African-born ex-slave population, which included longtime common-law ex-slave spouses, started to develop actual and fictive kinship networks among themselves, and that these came to function as a base for economic relationships.[88]

The Creation of "Brazilian" Identity Back "Home"

After the mid-nineteenth century, African-born ex-slaves who returned to Africa started to create Brazilian identity in Lagos, West Africa. Throughout the nineteenth century, the port of Lagos maintained the strongest commercial relations with Salvador, particularly for the trade of slaves in exchange for Bahian tobacco. After mid-century, the slave trade declined but was replaced by trading in palm oil (used to manufacture candles and soup, and as a lubricant) and oil made from the kernel of the palm nut (a raw material for margarine). Salvador's African-born population continued to import great amounts of cotton cloth, called *pano da costa,* and kola nuts from Lagos, as well as diverse ritual objects.[89] After the establishment of the British colony of Lagos in 1850, many African-born ex-slaves from Salvador began to settle in this colony, rather than leaving for their own specific homelands, as had formerly been the case. In Lagos, the Pax Britannica, instituted in 1851, protected their legally free status so that they were in no danger of re-enslavement.[90] Lagos also gave these immigrants good economic opportunities.

Lagos, as a common destination, was likely to be gradually identified with their shared image of "Africa" in the minds of the African-born population in Salvador. In the 1850s and 1860s, African-born ex-slaves often took great pride in publicizing their emigration to Africa in the classified advertisements of local newspapers, such as *Diário da Bahia* and *Jornal da Bahia,* before embarkation in Salvador. Examples are "Pedro Antônio Felicimo de Santana, an African-born ex-slave, his Brazilian-born son Eleodorio, and Felicidade, an African-born freedwoman, will go back to the coast of Africa (Costa da Africa)"; "Salvador Ramos das Neves will go back to the coast of Africa, taking his family, Maria Luisa da Conceição, his daughter Tecla Maria das Mercez, their former slaves of Brazilian birth (*crias forros*), Camila and Guimarães, and Dona Maria Bareto, João Maria Porciana and Maria Izabel"; and "Tito and Antônia, African-born ex-slaves, will leave for the coast of Africa with their *crioulo* sons, Luiz and Acurcio."[91] The destination of such emigrants was never more specific than the "coast of Africa (Costa da Africa)," perhaps because the specific name of the town to which they were headed, such as Lagos, did not matter to them. To such emigrants, of paramount importance was to "go back" to the symbolically reconstructed Africa as an image far removed from reality. Ironically, because of such advertisements, some prospective emigrants who had not yet fully met the payments for their self-purchase found that their owners refused to release them from bondage, and thus they were not able to take passage for Africa.[92]

Emigration to Africa usually took place as a family unit, which included Brazilian-born children. Emigration kept the immediate family together but sometimes separated kinsfolk on both sides of the Atlantic Ocean. This was the case of the African-born freedwoman Luiza Francisca Gonçalves, who had married Antônio Gonçalo, by whom she had six legitimate children (Joaquim, José, Raimundo, Manoel, Severiano, and Carolina). When the time came for her to make her will on September 4, 1864, her husband and all of their children were already dead, so Luísa named as her "common heirs" the children of her three sisters and her two Brazilian-born former slaves. Her nephews and nieces included the African-born children of Atipé, named Armado and Margarida, who were already back on the coast of Africa.[93]

Once they settled in the colony of Lagos, these African-born immigrants from Salvador, both Catholics and Muslims, separated themselves from the indigenous population and immigrants from other regions, such as the Saro, and contracted church marriages among themselves.

A male Muslim teacher, resident of the British colony of Lagos in what is now Nigeria in West Africa, registered his will in the city of Salvador with the date of March 9, 1877. His name was Victoriano Maria, and he was a native of Iguinem on the coast of Africa and the son of the African woman Omalia. Probably in the early nineteenth century, Victoriano Maria was imported to Salvador as a slave. This resulted in separation from his mother, whom he knew only by her African name. Somehow he had managed to keep in contact with her, so that he learned of her death. In Salvador, he fathered a natural son, Theodoro, who later fathered a boy named Manoel Theodoro de Aleluia, thereby making Victoriano a grandfather. After gaining his manumission letter, Victoriano returned to Africa, leaving behind in Salvador his son and grandson, with whom he continued to communicate across the Atlantic. In Lagos, Victoriano married three wives under Islamic law. His wives all bore Portuguese names: Constança Joaquina do Sacramento, Lourença Catarina Chaves, and Catarina Maria da Conceição. These three marriages in Lagos did not result in any children. Victoriano became a man of means in Lagos. In his will, he left all his possessions in Lagos, including two houses, to his three wives in Lagos and 200$000 *réis* to his grandson in Salvador.[94] His will does not provide any more information on his wives, but it is assumed that they were also African-born immigrants from Salvador. Despite his baptism as a Roman Catholic at the time of his enslavement and a superficial forced conversion to Christianity, Victoriano emphasized in his will that he "had been living and would die in the faith of the law of Muhammed." He was not the only African-born person in Salvador whose religious faith was Islam. This makes all the more impressive the fact that, among the 325 wills of ex-slaves I consulted, no other person publicly declared his or her Islamic faith in an official document.

Victoriano Maria and other "Brazilians" who settled down in Lagos preserved Portuguese language and Brazilian customs, built schools and Catholic churches in the Luso-Brazilian style, and observed religious holidays and festivals, such as that of Our Lady of the Good Ending (Nossa Senhora do Bonfim), the counterpart of Our Lord of the Good Ending, which was most popular in Salvador. They also built a Brazilian cemetery so that they could be buried together in a common place, in contrast to the local custom of burials within the homes. In "Brazilian" schools, instruction was in Portuguese as their first language, and in English as their second. On the other hand, their African identity encouraged them to abandon Portuguese family names, which they had adopted from their former owners upon being freed in Brazil, and to take Yoruba family names.[95]

In December 1853, there were already some 130 families of these immigrants in Lagos.[96] The population of Brazilians in Lagos rose to 4,000 in 1868, but this immigration movement of African-born Brazilians gradually declined after 1870.[97] This coincides with the period during which there was a decrease in the number of references to specific places of birth in manumission letters granted to ex-slaves in Salvador. After 1870, there was also a rapid increase in the percentage of ex-slaves whose identifications in the manumission letters did not include places of birth.[98] The decrease in numbers of African-born ex-slaves and their families emigrating to Africa after 1870 was related to the decrease in the proportion of African-born people in the overall population of African descent. This led to the transformation of self-identities among peoples of African descent, most of whom were by now Brazilian-born. By 1881, the population of Brazilians in Lagos decreased to 2,723 among a total population of 37,452, but emigration of African-born ex-slaves from Salvador to Lagos continued until the end of the century. The anthropologist Manuela Carneiro da Cunha estimates the total number of these emigrants at nearly 8,000.[99]

After the abolition of slavery in Brazil (May 13, 1888), some Brazilian immigrants in Lagos went back to Salvador or sent back their African-born children.[100] Thus, family networks developed on both continents. Brazilians of African descent on either side of the Atlantic were in constant contact. In June 1972, historian J. Michael Turner interviewed the president and some members of the Lagos Brazilian Descendants Society at their monthly meeting held at the Casa de Agua, home of the president. They talked to Turner about their memories of parents and relatives who had returned to West Africa.[101]

Among people of African descent in Salvador, "Africa," both as a symbol and as reality, has remained important until the present day and is constantly evoked in *candomblé,* carnival, and other cultural-religious activities throughout the year. Even today on the streets of Salvador a passerby will hear people of African descent talking about their kinsfolk in Africa. The memories of Africa have been constantly reinterpreted and revitalized in the context of their daily activities.

Conclusion

During the 1830s the African-born population began to create a convergent African-born identity beyond diverse ethnic identities. The re-creation of ethnic identity was manifested in the occurrence of the Malê revolt in 1835. Islam emerged as a common symbol shared by the participants of African birth, both enslaved and freed, and as such transcended ethnic divisions; the written religion of Islam was closely associated and identified with literacy in Arabic, which enabled cross-ethnic communication and the creation of an African-born identity.

After mid-century, when identifications for the population of African birth in notarial and legal records gradually converged from specific African "nations" to African-born, a significant change was observed in African-born ex-slave families. African-born ex-slaves, who constituted a minority among the population of African descent, began to adopt Luso-Brazilian patterns of conjugal unions characterized by co-residence of partners, yet without contracting holy matrimony. Unlike the previous situation, where slaves formed conjugal unions but such common-law couples did not live in the same households, now African-born ex-slave partners coresided. As a result, their Brazilian-born children were raised in a double-headed household. They had their newborn natural children baptized with godparents who were also African-born ex-slaves. This led to greater stability of urban families and stronger emotional bonds among the ex-slave population of African birth.

Yet, it should be emphasized that these changes in family and kinship among African-born ex-slaves were not merely the result of their legally free status. These changes certainly involved a change in their self-identities, which occurred when the African-born population, both slave and freed, started to merge their identification by specific "nations" into a common identity as African-born. Property-owning African-born ex-slaves started to name as executors of their wills those who were identified also as African-born ex-slaves, including their actual and fictive kinsfolk. African-born ex-slaves, who were often coparents, also began to deal with one another as debtors and creditors. These financial relations were frequent enough to be regarded not merely as sporadic circumstances, but to form a pattern of behavior. Coparenthood had come to function as a solid base for African-born ex-slaves. Thus, the African-born population in this period became bound together through kinship and fictive kinship, and also through the sharing of a broader and convergent ethnic identity as African-born.

The development of family and kinship networks among African-born ex-slaves coincided with their new "return" movement to Africa. The family unit often provided the context for such decision making. After the Malê revolt of 1835, the Bahian authorities continued to impose more legal restrictions on the African-born population in general, which spurred many African-born ex-slaves to immigrate to West African towns. Once the British colony was established in Lagos, African-born common-law spouses of diverse ethnic origins, with their Brazilian-born children, started to return, often in a family unit, to this common destination, where their legally free status would be protected by the Pax Britannica. For such emigrants, Lagos came to symbolize Africa. It was as African-born, not as Nagôs or Gêges, that they returned, and as such no longer did they feel the need to return to their original homelands. In Lagos, African-born immigrants from Salvador separated themselves from other inhabitants to develop their Brazilian identity. It should be noted that their decisions at this stage were predominantly family oriented. This contrasted with the individuality of decision making and participation by individual males in the preceding slave uprisings in Bahia in the first half of the nineteenth century. In Lagos, these immigrants from Salvador geographically separated themselves from the local population and other inhabitants, including returnees from other parts of the New World, and identified themselves as Brazilians. Thus a Brazilian community came into being in Lagos. The Brazilians in Lagos contracted church marriages among themselves and preserved the Portuguese language and Luso-Brazilian culture. On the other hand, their new African-born identity encouraged them to abandon Portuguese family names and replace them with Yoruba names.

After 1870, emigration of African-born ex-slaves to Africa gradually declined. This was related to the quick decrease in numbers of the African-born population in Salvador, but also attributable to their own changing identities. The rapid reduction in statements as to birthplace in manumission letters after 1870 probably means that the birthplace no longer mattered for individual self-purchase. During the last decade of slavery, African-born male ex-slaves outnumbered their female counterparts by the ratio of 3:2, whereas the percentage of women among Brazilian-born ex-slaves reached new heights because of the high demand for young male workers.[102] Owners were more willing to manumit slave men of African birth, who had worked as field hands and transporters throughout their lives and were now ill, handicapped, and aging, whereas owners could still squeeze labor as domestics from African-born slave women around the same age.

After the mid-nineteenth century, "Africa" was no longer a trans-ethnic label or category simply imposed by the larger society for the purpose of slave control; it became a common destination shared by African-born ex-slaves of diverse ethnic origins. After having spent many years in Salvador, their differences in ethnicity and ethnic identity started to be overcome by their commonness as African-born in contrast to Brazilian-born, especially once the slave trade was banned in 1831. Individual memories of their respective homelands in Africa had been reconstructed and changed over time and were to be replaced by the singular image of Africa as their common homeland, which was largely an imaginary creation among the African-born population through their experiences of New World slavery. Thus African-born ex-slaves created a new collective identity as African-born in Salvador and as Brazilians in Lagos. They formed a community with the common symbol of Africa or African birth, which led them to seek "true" belonging in Africa, where they were once again to be classified as "outsiders" by indigenous populations. It may be one of life's ironies that in a sense, they remained outsiders despite their voluntary relocation after they gained legal freedoms. This unchanged outsider-ness was the hallmark of African slavery in the New World.

In Part I (chapters 1 and 2) and Part II (chapters 3 and 4), we have so far discussed the creation of identity by the African-born population in slavery and freedom: the creation of new ethnic and gender identities; collective representations of such identities in urban slavery; the emergence of ex-slave identity among the African-born population; and the creation of African-born identity in Salvador and of Brazilian identity in Lagos of West Africa after the termination of the transatlantic slave trade. Our next question is: In contrast to the African-born population, most of whom were born free in the Old World and all of whom were brought to the New World as slaves, how differently did the Brazilian-born population of African descent create their identities in slavery and freedom? This will be the subject of Part III.

Part Three
To Be Brazilian-Born, circa 1808–1888

Yet this vacuum is not new to her. It has an
edge; somewhere in the bottom lid is the
distance. She has seen it lurking in the eyes
of all white people. So. The distance must be
for her, her blackness. All things in her are
flux and anticipation. But her blackness that
accounts for, that creates, the vacuum edged
with distance in white eyes.

—Toni Morrison, *The Bluest Eye*

6 The Creation of Disparate Identity, 1808–1851

The Brazilian-born slave population in Salvador created their identities in a quite different way than did their African-born counterparts. They had never been legally free; they were born into slavery in Brazil. Naturally they created a different notion of freedom from that of the African-born population. As Sidney W. Mintz elucidates: "The slaves who were born into slavery may have known about 'being free' as their parents told them of it. But they also knew of 'freedom' as defined by the colonial societies in which they lived."[1] Brazilian-born slaves did not identify themselves with the African-born population; the larger society always favored the former over the latter. As a result, for instance, very few Brazilian-born slaves participated in the frequent slave uprisings of the first decades of the nineteenth century (see chapter 3).

This chapter, by focusing on the period from 1808 to 1851, when Brazilian-born were outnumbered by African-born among the slave population in Salvador, examines historical processes by which the Brazilian-born population of African descent created their disparate identities in accordance with color distinctions in slavery and freedom. We shall also discuss how the free-born *crioulo* population started to express a newly emergent collective racial identity by establishing new lay sodalities of their own.

Born as Slaves in Brazil: Kinship and Fictive Kinship

A high illegitimacy rate among Brazilian-born slaves resulted from the rare incidence of church marriage among the urban slave population (see chapter 3). Records of births for Penha parish (1844) in Salvador show that only 4 out of 26 slave children were legitimate.[2] Among 679 Brazilian-born slaves (354 men and 325 women) baptized in Santo Antônio parish, who were registered between 1808 and 1869, only 8 males and 10 females were registered as legitimate.[3]

Even those Brazilian-born slave children whose parents were unmarried benefited from the presence of strong kinship ties, especially with their slave mothers, unlike the case of the African-born population. Since a child born to a slave woman was automatically the property of the mother's owner, regardless of the legal status of the father, a slave child was raised by his or her mother in the household of their owner without the constant presence of the father, who was usually under a different ownership. Strong mother-child ties among the Brazilian-born slave population were fostered and strengthened by the owners' practice of selling, purchasing, and manumitting the slave mother and her child together.

Mother and child(ren) were especially often sold and purchased together in the case of a child still being in infancy or early childhood. Among 2,608 listings in the legal register of slaves purchased and sold in Sé parish during the period 1838–1888, 131 (5 percent) fall into the category of mother-child(ren) sales. By contrast, in only four documents were fathers and sons sold and purchased together.[4] To our surprise, only one whole slave family, all of whose members were Brazilian-born, was transferred without separation. This family was composed of parents and their two children: the 30-year-old father (*crioulo*), the 22-year-old mother (*cabra*); their 8-year-old son (*crioulo*), and 2-year-old daughter (*cabra*).[5] Needless to say, this common practice of purchase and sale of child and mother together did not derive from any humanitarian consideration on the part of owners about not breaking up mother-child ties. Raising an infant slave with a very low sale price was a costly business, especially in the absence of the mother. Poor nutrition and unsanitary conditions contributed to a high infant mortality rate. For these reasons, people were reluctant to sell or purchase infant slaves. For the same reasons, mother and Brazilian-born child(ren) were occasionally manumitted together, often unconditionally, and in "appreciation" by the owner of the mother's "good services." Sixty-three out of the 3,516 manumission letters for the years 1808–1884 describe mother-child manumission in appreciation of the mother's good services.[6] Two-thirds of these cases were unconditional and gratis manumissions, because of the mother's good services. One exceptional case is the unconditional liberation of a whole Brazilian-born slave family: Gormano, *pardo,* the father; Maria Magarida, the mother; and their children Rodrigo (*crioulo*), Ferigrino, Felsarda, and Maria (all *cabras*).[7] Only two slave children were officially recorded as their owner's illegitimate children. Both *mulattos,* born to the same owner by his slave woman Marcelina, were manumitted.[8] We suspect there were numerous cases in which their biological fathers, who owned their mothers, manumitted slave children.

Their mothers manumitted Brazilian-born children with the payment of money with greater frequency than their fathers. Among 3,516 manumission letters for the period 1808–1884, fifty-five cases of Brazilian-born children were paid for by mothers (thirteen slaves, nineteen ex-slaves, and twenty-three with no indication of legal status). By contrast, only eleven fathers (one ex-slave and ten without any identification of legal distinction) paid money for their children's freedom.[9] Some of the mothers themselves were still enslaved when their children were manumitted. The mother and child(ren) were usually owned by the same owner, so that the slave mother was in a good position to negotiate her infant child's price for freedom and schedule of payments with an owner who was concerned about the cost of raising the child. Some Brazilian-born slave children were manumitted with the assistance of their mothers' spouses. An example is the case of Pedro, son of the African-born ex–slave woman Luduvina Rebelo, resident of Rua da Saldanha. She had had this son by another man before her marriage to Manuel Alves da Silva. There was no offspring of her marriage to Manuel. Luduvina, together with Manuel, got her son freed at age ten. After Pedro obtained his letter of liberty, Luduvina asked Manuel to teach his stepson Pedro his skills as a carpenter, and both gave every assistance to Pedro until he reached adulthood. In her will Luduvina insisted that her son had no right to inherit any of the couple's property.[10] One possible explanation is that her husband had made most of their common property and had somebody else, probably his own child by another woman, in mind to inherit it.

Brazilian-born slaves' intergenerational kinship relationships developed bilaterally only with fathers' recognition of consanguinity. This has been already illustrated by the manumission of child slaves paid by their fathers.[11] Such was the case of Bernardino da Sena, an African-born freedman originally from Costa da Mina, who had been a slave of the Franciscans for more than twenty-five years, until he substituted another slave of a value equal to that stipulated for purchase of his own freedom. He never married, but as a bachelor fathered a son named José Maria Vilela by Luduvina Proza, an African-born woman from Agomê, who was a slave of Colonel Manoel José Vilela de Carvalho. Bernardino paid 200$000 *réis* to the same owner to get his slave son freed.[12] One extraordinary case is that of the Nagô freedman Tomé de França, resident of Pilar parish. He had four different companions, perhaps at different times, all African-born (Esperança Pinto, Ignez Maria do Bomfim, Maria do Pilar, and Catharina), all of whom were slaves at the time of the relationship and each of whom bore Tomé a child: Maria da Piedade (19 years of age at manumission), Ventura da França (11 years of age at manumission), Juliana da França (7 years of age at manumission), and José da França (less than 8 months at manumission). Tomé de França not only liberated these African-born mothers and his Brazilian-born *crioulo* children but also, in his will of December 26, 1868, declared all of these children legitimate and named them as his heirs.[13] Having been manumitted, his children obtained the legal right to succeed as his testamentary heirs. No slave had the legal capacity to accept or reject an inheritance before the Free Womb Law of 1871.[14]

In urban slavery in Salvador, African-born enslaved fathers often shared their first names with sons of Brazilian birth, whereas mothers and daughters rarely shared first names. Naming a son after his father is a common practice in any patrilineal society, but in the context of nineteenth-century Salvador, where common-law unions among slaves did not always accompany the coresidence of partners and children were usually raised by mothers, this naming practice helped children born as slaves to maintain father-son relationships in those cases in which the father and mother were to end their relationship. Bilateral kinship relationships developed with the recognition of consanguinity by fathers, and this was evidenced in their naming practices.

Brazilian-born slaves could also receive financial support from their grandparents. Some grandparents paid cash to purchase their grandchildren's freedom, some left property or money to them, and some named their grandchildren as their heirs. The African-born freedman Victoriano Maria, who lived in the colony of Lagos as a professional Muslim teacher, left some money to his son's son in his will registered in Salvador (see chapter 5).[15] Another African-born ex-slave named Valentino Paschoal left half of his property to his wife, Maria Espírito Santo Pires, also an African-born ex-slave, and the rest to his still enslaved granddaughter, Belimira, for her freedom. Belimira was one of the four children of his daughter, whom Valentino had had by a slave woman.[16]

Although parent-child relationships seem to have extended bilaterally, it is likely that matrilineal ties survived in the long run with much greater frequency than patrilineal ones; many more grandmothers referred to their grandchildren in their wills than did grandfathers. Maria de Araújo Ribeiro, an ex–slave woman from Costa da Mina, who died on October 3, 1815, named her granddaughter, Anna Florencia de Almeida, as the heiress of two-thirds of her property and left the rest to her little great-granddaughter named Anna, daughter of Anna Florencia and her husband, Sergeant-Major Luís Gonsaga de Barros. Maria appointed her son-in-law as executor of her will.[17]

Brazilian-born slaves benefited from their fictive kinship as another source of financial support. During the early nineteenth century, nearly 90 percent of Brazilian-born slaves of both sexes were baptized only with godfathers, most of whom were free-born, as in the case of African-born slaves for the same period.[18] One naturally suspects that some of the godfathers may very well have been the fathers of the Brazilian-born slave children, but unfortunately their relationships were not mentioned in baptismal records. In the early nineteenth century, Brazilian-born slave children were sometimes baptized with African-born godfathers, who shared the same "nation" with their slave mothers, who were also of African birth.[19] Brazilian-born slave children could have benefited from their mothers' ethnic networks. Some godfathers indeed paid for the manumission of Brazilian-born slaves; sixteen godparents (seven for the years 1808–1842 and nine for 1851–1884) paid money to purchase the freedom of Brazilian-born slaves.[20] By contrast, only three godfathers contributed to the manumission of three African-born slaves, all women, for the years 1808–1884.[21] This suggests that slave parents, mothers in particular, could have chosen as their children's godparents those who might be able to afford to pay for the freedom of their godchildren, or in cases where they had no right to choose their children's godparents, they could have at least successfully developed good relationships with their coparents for their children's sake.

The Pursuit of Freedom in Manumission

The practice of manumission greatly favored Brazilian-born over African-born: Brazilian-born slaves were manumitted more frequently than their African-born counterparts throughout the nineteenth century (see chapter 3).[22] Even during the first three decades of the nineteenth century, when the African-born slave population largely outnumbered their Brazilian-born counterparts by two to one, the larger society always favored the latter over the former in the practice of manumission.[23] Brazilian-born slaves benefited from the practice of both unconditionally and conditionally unpaid manumission. The individual slave's birthplace determined to a great degree the experiences with manumission; Brazilian-born had a much better chance to gain freedom than African-born.

In many cases, Brazilian-born slaves were granted freedom unconditionally for such reasons as "good services," "fidelity and obedience," "love of God," and "love of raising the slave." As Stuart B. Schwartz points out, these were not real motives for manumission but usually a kind of necessary "precondition" or minimum requirement.[24] In most cases of conditional unpaid manumission, the owners obliged their ex-slaves to "accompany and serve" them (or sometimes their spouses, children, or siblings) until the death of the latter. Those thus manumitted conditionally, who were now named *agregados* (dependents in households), continued to work for their former owners in the same way as formerly when they had been slaves.[25] Despite their legally free status, these Brazilian-born ex-slaves remained totally subject to other people's power. Owner-slave relations were thus maintained with little modification after the slave gained freedom.

The most common path to freedom for Brazilian-born slaves was unpaid manumission, either unconditional or conditional, and not manumission by self-purchase as in the case of their African-born counterparts. But this does not mean that their individual experiences in manumission were monolithic or homogeneous; all Brazilian-born slaves were not treated equally in the practice of manumission. Most importantly, gender, age, and skin color determined the individual's chance in manumission. Interestingly, two-thirds of Brazilian-born ex-slaves were women, most of whom had developed strong and/or intimate interpersonal relationships with their owners and their families as domestics, some of whom were forced to become their owner's mistresses. As for age, children were favored over adult slaves in the practice of manumission.[26] Thirty percent of Brazilian-born ex-slaves in Salvador for 1808–1884 were classified as children.[27] This is a much higher percentage than among the slave population of Brazilian birth, as illustrated by the adult-child ratio of 85:15 among slaves purchased and sold in Sé parish for the period 1838–1888.[28] In combination of gender and age in the practice of manumission, women comprised nearly 60 percent of Brazilian-born adult ex-slaves and 70 percent of Brazilian-born child ex-slaves. Furthermore, some newly born and child slaves were baptized as *forros* on the grounds that the owner was grateful to the slave's mother, also a slave under the same ownership.[29] In only one of these cases did the owner become his slave's godfather in order to "benefit him [the slave]."[30] As long as "cheaper" human commodities were continuously supplied from Africa, owners in Brazil usually preferred to manumit Brazilian-born slaves at birth and during childhood unconditionally and without payment. Because of the high risk of infant and child mortality, raising them was much more costly than purchasing newly arrived African-born adult slaves.[31]

Skin color also determined the Brazilian-born slave's experiences in the practice of manumission. Mulatto slaves had a better chance of manumission than their black counterparts; lighter skin color gave the slave a great advantage; the *crioulo*-mulatto ratios for Brazilian-born ex-slaves were 64:36 for 1808–1842 and 63:37 for 1851–1884.[32] Brazilian-born slaves purchased and sold in Sé parish suggest higher percentages of *crioulos,* namely 75.2 percent for 1838–1848 and 67.4 percent for 1852–1888.[33] Slaves registered in the 370 inventories from Salvador show an even higher percentage of *crioulos:* 89.3 percent for 1808–1849 and 78.2 percent for 1850–1888.[34] Mulatto slaves, regardless of gender and age, evidently had easier access to freedom than did their *crioulo* counterparts, but this tendency is most clearly observed in the case of female child slaves.[35] There is no doubt that some of these mulatto slave girls were their owners' illegitimate children by slave women; their biological fathers might have manumitted them out of affection, although they would still have been raised by their mothers in the same household, as quasi-slave domestic servants.

A further factor weighed by owners was economic. Male slave children were valued as capital more highly than their female counterparts and thus were more worthy of an owner's investment of time and money; for those with good occupational skills, slave men were usually more highly valued in monetary terms than were slave women.

The manumission of the Brazilian-born slave population constantly produced a specific group of the newly manumitted, who were characterized as predominantly female, child/young, and mulatto, and many of whom were to be easily and smoothly incorporated into domestic servitude, in which they were legally free but in a situation that was not very different from slavery. The rest, namely male, adult, and black, who were supposedly much more suitable for plantation slave labor and who constituted the majority of the Brazilian-born population, were forced to remain in slavery for use in all sorts of manual labor, and later as human commodities for the interprovincial slave trade with the coffee-booming Southeast. Thus the racial/gender hierarchy among the Brazilian-born slave population was preserved and strengthened with a sufficient supply of slave labor force for the maintenance of the urban slave society.

From the early colonial period, the free Brazilian-born population of African descent had expanded through recruitment, through manumission, and through reproduction, with a lower child mortality rate than that of the slave population. Free people of African descent created and re-created disparate identities over the years, most importantly in accordance with color and gender.

The Creation of Identity in Freedom

The Brazilian-born population of African descent, either enslaved, freed, or free-born, had always been divided into various categories of color since the early colonial period. In nineteenth-century Salvador, color functioned as a clear index of the individual's social status, particularly in the case of holy matrimony. Marriage never had been a norm for the general populace in Salvador, but marriage rates among the legally free population were certainly much higher than among slaves, who rarely contracted church marriages. Slave status was the most crucial obstacle to church matrimony, and ex-slaves certainly enjoyed marrying with much greater frequency than the enslaved population. This is well exemplified by the case of property-owning African-born ex-slaves, who married their longtime common-law spouses after gaining freedom but late in their lives, often on their deathbed, obviously for the sake of inheritance (see chapter 5). Marriage registers in Penha parish and Conceição da Praia parish clearly suggest the correlation between marriage and color. Being lighter-skinned meant being better off, socioeconomically; one could afford more easily the cost of a church marriage. Also, when marriage was contracted, it was largely endogamous: marriage partners were chosen within the same categories of legal distinction (free-born, freed, or slave) and place of birth (Brazilian-born or African-born), as well as of color (white, *crioulo, pardo,* or *cabra*).[36] These data for marriage in nineteenth-century Salvador concur with demographic studies for the overall population of Brazil conducted by Thomas W. Merrick and Douglas H. Graham: marriage rates certainly reflected "a distinct racial hierarchy."[37] This suggests that marriage functioned as an important institution to strengthen pre-existing group solidarity, not to develop new networks across group boundaries.[38] Such endogamous tendencies are a clear reflection of the ways in which the population of African descent created their identities in relation to the larger society's perceptions of race and color.

Interracial marriage rarely took place, at least officially; color determined one's choice of marriage partner. When interracial marriages did occur, they were most frequently between white men and Brazilian-born mulatto (*pardo* or *cabra*) women of legally free status. For instance, the complete census data of 6,194 residents for São Pedro Velho parish in 1835 include no case of interracial marriage.[39] Interracial unions usually occurred in the form of concubinage. Such is the case of the African-born freedwoman Faustina Maria dos Prazeres, who never married. She purchased her freedom for 100$000 *réis* from her owner, Rita Maria dos Prazeres, and then as a concubine of Captain Cristóvão da Rocha Pinto, Faustina Maria bore three daughters, respectively named Julia, Claudiana, and Maria da Penha. In his will Captain Rocha Pinto recognized their daughters as well as his other children as his heirs. After his death, Julia also passed away, so that three *crioulo* slaves of minor age (Raimunda, Ardeza, and Calistato), whom her father had given to Julia during his life, passed into the possession of Faustina Maria, who liberated all three slaves in her will dated July 7, 1840. Faustina Maria left her property to her two surviving daughters as her legal heiresses, and she appointed as executor of her will the grandfather of her daughters, Captain-Major Cristóvão da Rocha Pinto, Sr.[40]

For the free Brazilian-born population, color was a "symbol of social status," in the words of the anthropologist Verena Martinez-Alier (a.k.a. Stolcke) in her study of nineteenth-century Cuba.[41] Those who were categorized by others and/or identified themselves as the same color formed an endogamous group for the sake of marriage as a social institution, at least temporarily.[42] On the one hand, marriage across color boundaries may have brought dishonor to the family of a spouse who married down, as in the case of nineteenth-century Cuba.[43] On the other hand, in Brazil, which never established "legal colors" for the prevention of interracial marriage, the individual could have more freedom to officially change his or her color to match the socioeconomic status of the spouse, particularly in the case where he or she would move up on the social ladder by means of marriage. Therefore, statistical evidence for the prevalence of marriage within the same color category does not necessarily suggest that color was an absolute determinant for the official choice of marriage partners. The significance of one's individual color may have been regarded (and overlooked or dismissed) as a personal preference among the free population of African descent. But the lighter skin of the *pardo* or *cabra* definitely gave that population a great advantage in manumission, and furthermore various awesome benefits for upward social mobility in a racially stratified society, benefits which the dark-skinned population could not possibly expect. Naturally the mulatto population preferred to separate itself from the black population. It tended to comprise a rather exclusive, homogeneous social group or stratum and created a distinctive identity in freedom.

From the early colonial period, mulattoes (*pardos*), who were often born free or had a much better chance for freedom in manumission, had refused to identify themselves with "blacks," namely the African-born and *crioulo* populations. Mulatto women and men established and developed their own lay sodalities, which came into being later than black sodalities. Mulatto sodalities accepted and welcomed white members, as their black counterparts did, but did not allow either slaves (both African-born and Brazilian-born), African-born ex-slaves, or *crioulos,* either free or slaves, to be members. Mulatto sodalities were often dedicated to Our Lady of the Liberation (Nossa Senhora do Livramento), Our Lady of Succor (Nossa Senhora do Amparo), Our Lady of Conception (Nossa Senhora do Conceição), and Our Lady of Guadalupe (Nossa Senhora do Guadalupe). During the colonial period mulattoes had established the sodality of Our Jesus of the Cross (irmandade de Nosso Senhor Jesus da Cruz) in the Church of Palma; the sodality of Our Lord the Good Jesus of Patience (irmandade do Nosso Senhor Bom Jesus da Paciência); and the sodality of Our Lady of Conception of Boqueirão (irmandade da Nossa Senhora da Conceição do Boqueirão), both in the church of São Pedro parish.[44]

The free mulatto population's creation of identity was reflected in certain collective actions that they took during the Age of Revolution. They had become receptive to the ideas of the Enlightenment and initiated an insurrectionary plot generally known as the Tailors' Revolt (Conspiração dos Alfaiates).[45] This event started on August 12, 1798, when the urban residents in Salvador awoke to a proclamation posted on a church door, calling for liberty, freedom, and independence. The police arrested forty-six men from Salvador and the Recôncavo. Among thirty-two participants, all men, brought to trial, twenty-three were *pardos* (twelve free men and nine slaves), and ten were whites. Only one man was African-born: a newly arrived slave from Costa da Mina. Seven free men and four slaves were tailors by occupation, which is the reason why this conspiracy has become known as the Tailors' Revolt, or the Conspiracy of the Tailors.[46] The Bahian authorities accused four free *pardos* as chief conspiratory plotters: Luís Gonzaga dos Birgens, soldier; João de Deus Nascimento, tailor; Lucas Dantas d'Amorim Torres, soldier; and Manuel Faustino dos Antos Lira, tailor, all of whom were executed. The authorities prosecuted four white upper-class intellectuals, three of whom were members of a secret Masonic society, the Knights of the

Light, which had been established on July 14, 1797.[47] Contemporary documentation shows that the idea of "liberty," derived from the Age of Revolution, was critical in spurring participants to collective rebellion, but that their motivations varied from one individual to the next.[48]

Most of the participants in the Tailors' Revolt were "elite" Brazilian-born people of African descent, as generally observed in slave uprisings in other parts of the New World.[49] But unlike the other cases, many were free-born; the Tailors' Revolt was allegedly plotted mainly by free *pardo* artisans. The ideas of the revolutionary era prevailed only among a specific group of free light-skinned men who were skilled artisans, and these people utilized the new concept of "liberty" to take collective political actions.[50] We should emphasize that no women participated in the Tailors' Revolt, either. It was an entirely male phenomenon, as in the case of all the slave uprisings in Bahia. There existed a limited amount of upward social mobility for the free population of African descent, albeit only for men, regardless of color; small numbers of free men of African descent, mostly those of Brazilian birth, found an opportunity in a military career to move up on a social ladder, only within the well-defined parameters. In colonial and imperial Brazil, military service depended on the free poor, who were predominantly those of African descent, particularly in the case of Salvador; the army was perceived as an assembly of the poor, the ignorant, and the lazy. The social status of soldiers, who were poorly and irregularly paid, was only slightly higher than that of slaves.[51] Most soldiers remained poor but, as Joan E. Menzar discusses in the case of the Northeast for 1830–1875, military service in colonial and imperial Brazil responded to social differences among the free poor, and the army accentuated such divisions as those between the honorable and the dishonorable, the worker and the vagrant, and the free and the slave.[52] The rank and file were predominantly poor, since a large number of men were exempt from military service by virtue of their occupation and status.[53]

In colonial Brazil, colored militia regiments had come into existence in all major Brazilian cities by the eighteenth century. As in the case of mulatto sodalities, urban mulatto regiments were usually formed at a later date than those of blacks.[54] Free soldiers of African descent in Salvador were furthermore divided into separate militia regiments by color distinction. By the late eighteenth century, Salvador had established four militia regiments organized by color and occupation: two white regiments (one for leading merchants and another for less wealthy whites); the "henriques" (named after Henrique Dias, the black hero of the war against the Dutch from 1645 to 1654), enlisting free *crioulos;* and the free mulatto regiment. In the first decades of the nineteenth century, the militia had been reorganized into six regiments but with the same division by color. The six regiments were the following: one company of mounted gentlemen, forming the government of honor; one squadron of flying artillery; two regiments of whites, almost all tradespeople; one regiment of mulattoes; one of free blacks, whose number totaled 4,000 in the early 1820s.[55] Thus, as in the case of black and lay sodalities, free blacks and mulattoes had to belong to separate regiments by color.

Furthermore, there was an irreconcilable cleavage of identity among the "free black" men in the same regiment. Schwartz documents a very interesting petition made by *crioulos* in Bahia in 1775: The black militia regiment of Bahia complained that African-born ex–slave men were appointed to posts of commands, against the usual practice in Bahia and Pernambuco. The *crioulo* supplicants claimed that African-born people were "suspect in their faith and orthodoxy and were capital enemies of the whites against whom they often plotted rebellion," while identifying themselves as "loyal servants of the Crown who had proven their value on many occasions." Interestingly, the governor of Bahia responded to this petition by pointing out that the exclusion of African-born was not due to any royal order but rather to the practice of the regiment.[56] We have no way of knowing to what degree African-born ex-slaves were recruited for the free black regiment, but this particular petition made by the *crioulo* men clearly suggests that there had been clear divisions in identity among the free "black" men who belonged to the same regiment because of the same color. *Crioulos* did not identify themselves with African-born ex-slaves, although, as "blacks," people of African birth and the *crioulo* population had established and developed the prominent form of voluntary associations together: black lay sodalities.

The presence of the free black regiments functioned by design for the maintenance of the existing social structure based on color hierarchy by incorporating free black men into the power systems with only a very limited amount of upward social mobility. The free black men were forced to locate themselves close to the bottom of the larger society, albeit at least not at the very bottom of it, which was occupied solely by the slave population.

The Emergence of a New Free-Born Black (*Crioulo Livre*) Identity

Demographic changes among the population of African descent in Salvador progressed gradually once the slave trade was officially banned in

Brazil (1831). The proportion of the free Brazilian-born population of African descent began to expand. With their increasing financial power, the free-born male *crioulo* population created a collective identity and established and developed new sodalities of their own around the same time the laity's participation in sodalities began to decline rapidly.

The "Disappearance" of Black Lay Sodalities

Black sodalities virtually "disappeared" from the sociocultural scenery in Brazil during the nineteenth century, as several historians of Brazil have already noted. The disappearance took place when the general laity's active participation in lay sodalities declined rapidly because of the secularization process of Luso-Brazilian culture; during the nineteenth century the Church itself became a less decisive factor, with the diminishing importance of lay sodalities whose origins lie in medieval Europe.[57]

In fact, in the case of Salvador, regardless of race, gender, or color, the general free laity's participation in lay sodalities declined sharply before the mid-nineteenth century. At the beginning of the nineteenth century, for instance, nearly a hundred lay sodalities, either white or black, existed and functioned in Salvador, and more than 85 percent of the free-born residents of both sexes who registered their wills in Salvador held memberships in lay sodalities.[58] But this percentage decreased rapidly during the late nineteenth century: 20 percent of men and 24.2 percent of women were members of lay sodalities for 1851–1854; and only 19.3 percent men and 8.4 percent women for 1878–1885.[59] The wills of African-born ex-slaves demonstrate the same disposition in their memberships of black sodalities; among the 166 wills of ex-slaves I consulted, very few ex-slaves of either sex (94 males and 72 females) who registered their wills between 1850 and 1888 were members of even a single sodality.[60] The number of black sodalities mentioned in their wills also decreased from twenty (1808–1849) to eleven (1850–1888).[61] As a result, for instance, in the year 1862, the black sodality of the Rosary in the Pelourinho, while still holding 1,412 members (825 males and 587 females), accepted only 8 new members (3 males and 5 females), and lost 4 members through death.[62]

The major reason for the aforementioned change in the laity's participation in sodalities is that long-prevailing Baroque religious values were losing ground in nineteenth-century Brazil. Indeed, around 1850, the form of registered wills in Salvador became more abbreviated, and their statements became simplified and more straightforward, which is attributable to the ongoing secularization process of Luso-Brazilian culture. No longer did Luso-Brazilian culture place importance on formal participation in religious festivals and other ceremonial activities under the name of a specific patron saint. Neither did ostentatious display at a funeral, which required attendance of fellow sodality members, serve as an indication of the deceased's social status, as had hitherto been the case for the preceding centuries. No matter how important church burials might still be for sodality members, after the middle of the nineteenth century no lay sodality in Salvador was entitled to bury any of its members within its church. After the prevalence of yellow fever in Salvador in the year of 1849, burials within churches were strictly prohibited; people had to be buried in one of three cemeteries at a short distance from the city.[63]

Interestingly, despite the above-mentioned secularization of Luso-Brazilian culture, increasing religiosity was noted in Salvador at around the same time. It was clearly manifested in the rapid penetration of lay Christianity in the form of Marian devotion among the Brazilian-born slave population. The cult of the Virgin Mary and its miraculous manifestations have always been extremely popular over the centuries in the Iberian Peninsula and in Portuguese and Spanish overseas colonies, according to C. R. Boxer. This cult was not limited to the poor and lowly, but was common to all ranks and conditions.[64] In Brazil, Marianism, which defined women's roles in the family, and veneration of the Virgin Mary were of unparalleled importance and far exceeded devotion to any single saint.[65] In 1848, for instance, James Wetherell noted that there were niches in the walls at many street corners of Salvador, and in these were offerings by the faithful under statues to the Virgin Mary.[66]

In Salvador, during the first four decades of the nineteenth century, the Virgin Mary (Nossa Senhora) was not recorded as godmother in baptismal records for either African-born adult slaves or Brazilian-born child slaves. But in the late 1840s, the custom of invoking the Virgin Mary as godmother started to prevail for baptism of the Brazilian-born slave population in Salvador. For the period 1848–1849, 470 baptismal records in Santo Antônio parish reveal that forty Brazilian-born infant slaves (nineteen boys and twenty-one girls), as well as two African-born slave women, were baptized with the Virgin Mary as their godmother. For the years 1858–1859 and 1868–1869, there were thirty-eight Brazilian-born slaves (twenty boys and eighteen girls) for whom the Virgin Mary was named godmother. Many of these godchildren were baptized with human godfathers, but others did not have any godfathers.[67] Being baptized and having the Virgin Mary as god-mother has possessed spiritual meaning for the population of African descent, perhaps as well as for whites. There is a contemporary dimension to this practice, in that the custom prevails today among people of color and whites alike of baptizing new-born babies and choosing the Virgin Mary as their godmother.[68]

Invoking the Virgin Mary as godmother for baptism has been a common Catholic religious practice that derives from early medieval Europe.[69] Through the Virgin Mary as a mediator, the faithful could reach God/Christ.[70] God and Christ were more feared than loved; the former was a remote and brooding eminence, whereas the latter was represented either as a child or sacrificed on the cross—images that referred to plague and judgment. By contrast, Mary was a beloved intercessor who worked to deflect or soften the harsh judgment of a stern God.[71] Thus, by having the Virgin Mary as godmother as well as having the name of Mary, a lay person's soul was connected with God/Christ, and that soul might eventually be saved. In medieval Europe lay Christian practices came into being such as selecting the Virgin Mary or a local female patron saint as godmother, choosing multiple sets of godparents, and having the officiating priest serve as sponsor at baptism.[72] In the mid-sixteenth century the Council of Trent finally prohibited these lay Catholic practices, which had occurred in the Iberian world over centuries. Yet these practices were slow to disappear and continued to exist in the Iberian Peninsula and in Brazil, especially in the baptism of slaves or among the lower class.[73] Secularization of Luso-Brazilian culture led to the reemergence of such lay Catholic customs among the general populace in Salvador during the early years of the nineteenth century. Probably many slave owners forced their slaves to practice the same Christian customs, but there is no doubt that in the 1840s slaves and the free population of African descent, many of whom were Brazilian-born, began to accept them in their own search for a Christian faith.[74]

In Salvador, lay Christianity penetrated the population of African descent after the 1830s, when the influx of new arrivals from Africa started to drop drastically. The Brazilian-born population of African descent, both slave and legally free, more easily accepted Luso-Brazilian culture and social norms. The population of African descent, including slaves, began to find more and more symbolic meanings in lay Christianity, which had reemerged among the general laity in Salvador, in relation to the secularization of Luso-Brazilian culture. It is no coincidence that the lay Christian practice of in-

voking the Virgin Mary as godmother became prevalent among the population of African descent when the laity's participation in sodalities began
to disappear rapidly.

The Establishment of New Black Sodalities

The black laity's rapidly declining participation in black sodalities,
however, is by no means the end of the story for black sodalities in Salvador.
In the late colonial period, *crioulos* had established sodalities dedicated to
Good Jesus of Martyrs (Senhor Bom Jesus dos Martírios), and venerated
Saint Benedict in all churches in Salvador.[75] But, of course, most of those
crioulos were slaves, and their sodalities were inclusive in terms of race, ethnicity, gender, and birthplace, as in the case of "African" black sodalities.
The *crioulo* population did not just give up this special form of voluntary
associations, which their enslaved ancestors had sought after and skillfully
elaborated for their specific needs and priorities; free-born blacks of Brazilian birth (*crioulos livres*) established and developed two new black sodalities
with a much more exclusive character than had hitherto been the case.

A new *crioulo* sodality came into being at a meeting in the chapel of Our
Lady of the Rosary in the Church of the Quinze Mistérios of Santo Antônio
parish on September 16, 1832. It was named the sodality of Our Lady of
Solitude and Support of the Needy (irmandade de Nossa Senhora da Soledade Amparo dos Desvalidos). The founder and judge was Manoel Victor Serra, a free-born *crioulo* man whose occupation was wage earning. The
other founding members, all of whom were free-born *crioulo* men, included
officers Manoel da Conceição (cabinet maker), as treasurer; Luís Teixeira
Gomes (bricklayer), as scribe; José de Nascimento, as procurator; José Maria
Vitela, as a member of the administrative committee. Other founding members were Gregório M. Bahia (cabinet maker), Ignácio de Jesus, Bernabé Al-
vano dos Santos, Bernardino S. de Souza (bricklayer), Pedro Fortunato de
Farias (bricklayer), Gregório de Nascimento (carter), Balthazar dos Réis
(cabinet maker), Manoel Sacramento Conceição Roza (cabinet maker),
Teotonio de Souza (vinegar maker), Francisco José Repino (caulker), Daniel
Correia (wage-earner of the canto of Pilar parish), Roberto Tavares (water
carrier), José Fernandes do Ó (bacon seller), and Manoel Martins (worker
at the Lenha wharf). There was no woman among all the officeholders. The
sodality placed its safe box in the keeping of the vicar of Santo Antônio
parish, the Reverend Joaquim José de Sant'Anna. The three different keys to
this safe box were kept in the hands of the above-mentioned judge, trea-

surer, and scribe.[76] In August 1832, the founder of the sodality, Manoel Victor Serra, proposed the creation of a lottery, with printed tickets of 320 *réis*, as a potential financial source for the sodality. His proposal was approved, and the lottery was named "Loteria Nossa Senhora da Soledade."[77] Unfortunately, we have no way of knowing the composition of the membership of the *crioulo* sodality of Our Lady of Solitude and Support of the Needy; the statutes and the other primary documents of the sodality, which were housed in the Church of Quinze Mistérios, have been lost, and failure to maintain the church has eliminated any hope of finding them.

The *crioulo* sodality of Our Lady of Solitude and Support of the Needy did not just "disappear" during the 1840s; instead it survived this critical decade and even thrived with the financial power of the members. This particular sodality continued to function at the chapel in Quinze Mistérios Church during the 1830s and 1840s; then on December 17, 1848, its headquarters were transferred to the black church of Our Lady of the Rosary in the Pelourinho. This new free-born *crioulo* sodality was to transform itself into a new type of mutual-aid "black" association named the Society for the Protection of the Needy (Sociedade Protetora dos Desvalidos), as we shall discuss in chapter 7.

Another new sodality of free-born *crioulos* came into being in December 1843 in Agua de Meninos of Pilar parish. This was named the sodality of Saint Francis of Paula of Free-Born *Crioulos* Born in the Empire of Brazil (irmandade do Glorioso São Francisco de Paula de crioulos livres nascidos no Imperio do Brasil).

The prologue to its statutes tells us an interesting "history" of this sodality. The Reverend Father Antônio Borges Monteiro was in the habit of taking his walks to visit the house of an elderly friend to converse with him for a couple of hours every afternoon. One day, Father Monteiro found a tin veronica bearing the image of Saint Francis of Paula. He picked it up and locked it in a drawer at home, but three days later he again found the same veronica in the same place. Recognizing a miracle, he bought the house of his friend and ordered an area cleared where there was a fugitive slave community (*quilombo*) and bush and weeds. Father Monteiro made use of all of his financial resources in building a chapel. He stipulated that the chapel be dedicated to Saint Francis of Paula and placed the image of St. Francis, which he ordered to be made, in the *capela-mor* (primary chapel). At his death, he left all of the possessions that he had inherited from his parents to establish the patrimony for the chapel and to provide for the upkeep of the veneration of the saint. He named as his executor Theotonio de Amorim

Falção, and in one of the clauses of his will, Father Monteiro declared himself as the Father Founder. He ordered his executor to make his godchild, named Francisco de Paula Borges Monteiro, responsible for the chapel, to apply his endowment to its administration, and to let him be the chaplain. In another clause of his will the Father Founder ordered that if, some day, one or more priests of the order of Saint Francis of Paula were to appear in Salvador, his executor or the aforesaid godchild was to let the priest or priests maintain the chapel. This would nullify the provision charging his godchild with this responsibility. However, the executor died in 1819 without seeing Father Monteiro's wishes brought to fruition. The chapel was abandoned until, in 1843, some *crioulos* appeared. Wishing to venerate Saint Francis of Paula and support the chapel, they requested that the archbishop grant permission for them to adopt the chapel as the seat of their new sodality.[78]

We have noted that Agua de Meninos had formerly been a place of refuge for fugitive slaves. It was also there that African-born slaves and ex-slaves had engaged in their final battle with the municipal troops in the Malê revolt of 1835 (chapter 5). This story or oral tradition may be symbolically important in considering the establishment of a free-born *crioulo* sodality, since they chose the chapel built in the place where a *quilombo* had once been formed and which was to become the battlefield for the last stage of the Malê revolt.[79] As for the governing body of this *crioulo* sodality, whereas no limitation was placed on slave status, officeholders had to be *crioulos*. The charitable activities of the sodality were directed toward assisting the indigent in general by creating a mutual insurance society (*monte pio*).[80] The mutual insurance society was governed by a board composed of a director and six brothers, which acted independently of the governing body (*mesa*) of the sodality. Only male members who were in good standing and whom the scribe of the sodality recommended were allowed to participate in the mutual insurance society. Dues were 25$000 *réis*, which could be paid in monthly installments of 500 *réis* over four years. The first month's contribution was deposited by the board in an account in the Caixa Económica da Provincia. Minimum capital of 400$000 *réis* was to be established and placed on loan, principally to the elderly and the sick who could not provide for themselves. Wives and children were entitled to receive financial assistance in those cases where the death of a husband would result in destitution for the survivors.[81]

Although the membership was not exclusive in terms of legal status, color, or gender, this new sodality clearly represented the interests of the free-born *crioulo* population. The establishment of a mutual insurance society within the sodality represented husbands' concern for their wives and children. Among the free *crioulo* population, family had become an important institution, in which gender roles were redefined and gender identities were re-created to a degree. Yet many such couples were not united by church matrimony; they were merely common-law spouses.[82]

Conclusion

In the eyes of the larger society, the "otherness" of Brazilian-born slaves was not determined culturally but merely in terms of race. By being born into slavery in Brazil they naturally shared with their owners the same language (Portuguese) and the same Luso-Brazilian culture. Whereas they had never been free and therefore did not have a clear notion what freedom meant, Brazilian-born slaves had a much easier access to freedom than their African-born counterparts. First of all, Brazilian-born slaves had their parents, other kinsfolk, and sometimes godparents who could pay cash for the purchase of their freedom or negotiate with their owners for freedom. Furthermore, rather than struggling for the opportunity of self-purchase, Brazilian-born slaves usually chose to maneuver in their interpersonal relationships with their owners so that they could be manumitted without payment, although it might well mean that they would have to remain in quasi-slavery servitude under the absolute domination of their former owners despite their legally free status. The practice of manumission greatly favored women, mulattoes, and children among the Brazilian-born population.

The Brazilian-born population of African descent by no means shared a single, homogeneous identity among themselves; they had been always divided by color, and the mulatto population had separated themselves from the *crioulo* population, most of whom remained enslaved. During the late 1830s and 1840s, when the urban Bahian society was quickly transforming itself from slave society to slave-owning society, the *crioulo* population became more and more receptive to Luso-Brazilian culture, which was rapidly secularizing itself with the laity's declining participation in sodalities and the penetration of lay Christianity. This is when the free-born *crioulo* population established two new sodalities that covered their new needs. With their new financial resources, they started to create a collective identity based on their memories of the glorious history of their enslaved ancestors, while (re)defining gender identities in the new framework of double-headed households.

7 The Labyrinth of Identity, 1851–1888

With the official termination of the transatlantic slave trade in 1851, the institution of slavery started to decline gradually nationwide, while the booming interprovincial slave trade continued to move the still active yet predominantly Brazilian-born slave population from the Northeast to the coffee-producing Southeast. By the mid-nineteenth century the urban slave population in Salvador had already diminished to no more than one-third of the whole population of color.[1] During the late nineteenth century, Brazilian-born slaves substantially outnumbered their African-born counterparts: by a ratio of 64:36 among those purchased and sold in Sé parish for the years 1851–1884 and by a ratio of 58:42 among slaves registered in the 370 inventories of slave owners.[2]

The free Brazilian-born population had come to dominate among the urban population of African descent in Salvador by the turn of the 1870s. In 1872, when the first national census was taken for Brazil, the free population of color constituted 57.3 percent of the whole population of Salvador. By contrast, the slave population had decreased to only 11.6 percent of the whole population, and they constituted less than a quarter of the whole population of color in the city.[3] The hitherto prominent figures of male street slaves as chair carriers had already disappeared from the streets of Salvador. In the last two decades of the slavery regime, urban slaves were employed mainly as artisans if males and as domestics if females.

This chapter will discuss the creation of racial identity by focusing on the expanding Brazilian-born population of African descent from the mid-nineteenth century until the year of abolition. In order to do so, we shall first discuss how the notion of freedom changed after the mid-nineteenth century, and how and why the terminology of color changed in the last few decades of the nineteenth century. Our emphasis will be placed on a unique mutual-aid association named the Society for the Protection of the Needy and on its members' creation of racial and gender identities during the last few decades of the slavery regime.

The Changing Notion of Freedom

The notion of freedom in Brazil changed rapidly during the late nineteenth century. First of all, being under the strong influence of Great Britain, Brazilian abolitionist movements advanced quickly and intensified during the last few decades of the slavery regime.[4] Naturally, abolitionism had much more success in the urban centers, where free labor had already made progress.[5] In Salvador, abolitionist societies were established in the 1850s and 1860s, and they contributed money for manumission, but only to Brazilian-born slaves and mainly to infant and child slaves. In my sample of manumission letters, for instance, twelve men and twelve women, all Brazilian-born, were manumitted with payments of money for the years from 1851 to 1884, from such abolitionist societies as the Society of June the 2nd (Sociedade de Dois de Junho), September the 7th Liberating Society (Sociedade Libertadora Sete de Setembro), Commercial Association (Associação Comercial), Commercial Abolitionist Society (Sociedade Abolitionista Comercial), Masonic Felicity Beneficiary Society (Sociedade Maçonica Felicidade Beneficiencia), Fraternal Society of Sergipe (Sociedade Fraternidade Sergipana), Rocini Philharmonic Society (Sociedade Filarmonica Rocini), Terpriano Philharmonic Society (Sociedade Filarmonica Terpriano), and Bahian Liberating Society (Sociedade Libertadora Bahiana).[6] These abolitionist societies not only contributed money to the slaves' self-purchase but also filed criminal lawsuits against slave owners who mistreated their slaves. For instance, the Bahian Liberating Society filed legal papers with the date of January 3, 1887 for the case of the 30-year-old Brazilian-born slave Silvestre, resident of the *engenho* Agua Comprida, against the slave named Ana d'Argolo.[7]

Brazil's involvement with international warfare resulted in the emancipation of small numbers of male slaves but did not improve the slave population's official opportunities of freedom. During the Paraguayan War (1865–1870), the Brazilian government was willing to buy the freedom of slaves who agreed to serve in the military; their owners had to agree to emancipate such slaves. In Bahia, the owner was paid the price of 1:400$000 *réis* per slave but only 400$000 *réis* in cash and the rest in public bonds. Also, Brazilian citizens who were called for military service were allowed to free slaves and enlist them as substitutes. The province of Bahia officially sent a total of some 1,800 ex–slave men to the war. According to Barbara Trosko, this number probably represents only slaves who were bought and freed by the government, and does not include slaves who went to war as replacements for the upper classes or as volunteers or runaways.[8]

Most importantly, the Free Womb Law (*Lei do Ventre Livre*) of September 28, 1871, widely known as the Rio Branco Law, declared legally free the newborn children of slave women, but only on the condition that the owners took care of the children until the age of eight. Although the "free" children, or *ingênuos*, were obliged to work in a state of quasi-slavery until the age of twenty-one, this law resulted in a large *ingênuos* population; the number of *ingênuos* in Brazil expanded quickly and amounted to 439,831, according to the report by the Imperial Government as of June 30, 1888. The Free Womb Law also established an official emancipation fund to be used for the annual manumission of slaves in all provinces. For the first time in Brazilian history, slaves were granted the legal right, with the consent of owners, to have savings (*peculio*). Slaves were entitled to purchase freedom if they could present an amount equal to their "value." The law also freed slaves owned by the state, including those of the imperial family, and slaves in unclaimed inheritances or abandoned by their owners.[9]

With the enactment of the Free Womb Law, slaves in Brazil became legally eligible for self-purchase. Now that more and more slave owners were willing to manumit their slaves for monetary payment, some slaves in Salvador managed to negotiate with their owners for monthly payments for self-purchase. Such were three Brazilian-born slaves who were freed in 1871 on condition they make monthly payments: Romana, 29-year-old *crioula*, daughter of Virginia, Angola, with 6$000 *réis* a month; Martinho, *crioulo*, with 10$000 *réis* a month; Marcelino, 26-year-old *crioulo*, son of the Angolan slave woman, 10$000 *réis* a month.[10] Other slaves made an effective use of public deposits for their savings. For instance, the slave woman Eduarda paid 500$000 *réis*, which she had saved in the public deposit, to eventually obtain her letter of liberty with the date of March 20, 1883.[11]

The urban slave population in Salvador soon became keenly aware of their newly granted legal rights and indeed fought for them in court. In 1872, a *parda* slave woman, Augusta, represented by her owner, Domingos João José de Almeida Costa, a resident of Santana parish, filed a criminal law suit against a free-born *crioulo* man, Carlos Hermes da Purificação, charging that he had deceived her with intent to steal 600$000 *réis*. Augusta had saved this large amount of money in her account in the public deposit of the Caixa Econômica (Public Saving Bank) to purchase her own freedom. Carlos had been having an affair with Augusta's sister, Ubaldina Anna de Conceição, slave of Major Joaquim Domingos Lopes. One day, Carlos heard from Ubaldina of Augusta's large nest egg and began to scheme to take it from her. First, Carlos proposed marriage to Ubaldina, and they became engaged. The new fiancé made up the fake story that the September the 7th Liberating Society (Sociedade Libertadora Sete de Setembro), a Bahian abolitionist society, would pay some money toward Ubaldina's freedom, but that amount of money would not be enough. But if Augusta were to withdraw her savings and loan that money to Carlos, this sum together with the money from the abolitionist society would be enough for Carlos to purchase Ubaldina's freedom. Carlos begged Augusta to do so for her sister's sake. Augusta was finally persuaded to do as he asked for her sister's happiness. Ten months passed after Carlos had taken the money and disappeared. Augusta reported the matter to the police, and they quickly arrested Carlos. Of course, the money would never be regained by the poor slave woman Augusta.[12]

The Free Womb Law completely broke the social ideology of urban slavery in Brazil. As Brazilian historian Sidney Chalhoub discusses in his study of the manumission of slaves in the city of Rio de Janeiro during the nineteenth century, especially in urban areas of Brazil the ideology of manumission was an "essential aspect of work-discipline under bondage." For, before the Free Womb Law, owners and slaves "did abide and live according to the assumption that each owner's exclusive power to decide his slave's access to freedom was a key organizing principle of daily social relations."[13] With the enactment of the law that "humanized" the human chattel, the owner became unable to discipline a slave for work and to exercise absolute power over the slave. The U.S. historian Sandra Lauderdale Graham, utilizing court records and focusing on female slave prostitution in the city of Rio de Janeiro, also demonstrates that, with the enactment of the Free Womb Law, Brazilian officials prosecuted the owners of slave prostitutes and removed their slave property in the city's campaign to eliminate forced prostitution in general.[14] Lauderdale Graham reports a case in which a slave woman named Honorata found allies among her clients for her charges against her widowed mistress, Maria Elenteira. Three of Honorata's clients, a retired sergeant and two casual laborers, all Brazilian citizens, collaborated in court and testified that Honorata had been forced to engage in prostitution.[15]

The Free Womb Law made another important change among the urban slave population of Salvador. Now that any child born to a slave mother was legally declared free-born, some common-law slave spouses chose to contract church matrimony. In the national census of 1872, those who had been married (registered as married as well as widowed) constitute 14.8 percent of men and 12.5 percent of women among slaves; these figures are much lower than the 35.3 per cent of men and 17.0 per cent of women among the legally free population (both free-born and freed).[16] However, considering that there were virtually no slave marriages reported for the previous years (zero, at least until 1855), this is still a remarkable increase. The percentage of married slaves in Salvador was even higher than that for the overall Brazilian slave population (8 percent),[17] and the percentage of married slave women (12.5 percent) had grown close to those in Bahia (14.9 percent).[18] The percentages of the married among the population of African descent in Brazil furthermore rose significantly after the abolition of slavery: from 14 percent for men (slaves, 8 percent; free, 20 percent) and 15 percent for women (slaves, 8 percent; free, 21 percent) in 1872, to 24 percent for men and 25 percent for women in 1890. These increased percentages suggest that slave status was indeed a critical obstacle for church marriage and that legally free status created more opportunity for ex-slaves to contract matrimony. However, the change in the percentages is also attributable to a tendency in the 1890 census to classify coresidence of ex-slave common-law spouses as marriages.[19] It was in the very year of 1890 that civil marriage was finally recognized as legal in Brazil so that consensual unions without holy matrimony might be counted as marriages.

Changes in the Terminology of Color

The Brazilian-born population of African decent had been always labeled/categorized and divided by color distinctions, but in the early 1870s the official usage of multiple color distinctions started to change. Unlike the preceding local censuses of Salvador, and despite the common distinctions of color in colonial and imperial Brazil, the first national census of 1872 divided the legally free Brazilian-born population of African descent into only two dichotomous categories of color: *prêto* (black) and *pardo* (brown). At least in this new classification for census taking, the *pardo* population in the city of Salvador outnumbered *prêtos* by 2:1 among the entire population of African descent. This is attributable to the rapid growth of the free *pardo* population, which constituted more than 70 percent of the free population of African descent. The *pardo* population had grown also among the slave population, but nearly two-thirds of slaves were still classified by the color of *prêto*.[20] Of course, we do not know exactly how the census taker identified an individual's color, but most likely census taking relied largely on self-declaration, at least by legally free individuals. It is worth emphasizing that the majority of the Brazilian-born free population of African descent identified themselves as *pardos,* declining to be regarded as *prêtos;* being identified and/or classified as *prêto* generally indicated being socioeconomically close to slave status. But it does not mean that all of the self-declared "mulatto" population was regarded as such, and not as blacks, by the larger society. Since there existed no subjective criterion for the identification of the individual's color, people tended to self-identify with the color the larger society preferred. Therefore, based on their legally free status, free people of African descent in nineteenth-century Salvador were likely to choose *pardo* over *prêto* as their color, beyond visible skin colors and other ostensible phenotypes.[21]

By the beginning of the 1870s, the folk terminology of color in Salvador also had begun to change to a considerable degree. The term *crioulo,* which specified Brazilian birth and the color black, had disappeared.[22] Of course, now that the majority of the population of African descent in Salvador was Brazilian-born, there was not really a point in specifying the individual's birthplace. For the same reason, the term *prêto,* which no longer referred specifically to African-born, either enslaved or freed, began to refer merely to the skin color of black.[23] At the same time, the term *negro,* which had referred to the enslaved African-born and had mainly been used in official correspondence and documents (but not in any notarial records), gradually came to identify the general black population, regardless of birthplace or legal status. Of course, the word *negro* would have been taken as offensive when it was used to address people who did not identify themselves as blacks. For instance, on April 8, 1872, a self-identified white man, Aristides Ricardo de Santana, a typographer, native of Salvador and resident in São Pedro parish, filed criminal charges against Dr. Eloy Martins de Souza and his son Braulio Soares Martins de Souza, residents of Vitória parish, and against João Tavares da Silva Godinho, native of Portugal, as their accomplice, for their having publicly shouted at Santana and called him a *negro.*[24]

One may now wonder how free Brazilian-born "blacks" came to identify themselves in a changing context during the last decades of the slavery regime. The Society for the Protection of the Needy provides an exemplary case for our discussions.

The Creation of Racial Identity: The Society for the Protection of the Needy

The black sodality of Our Lady of Solitude and Support of the Needy, which had been established in 1832 as one of the two new free-born *crioulo* sodalities (see chapter 6), transformed itself in the year of 1851 into a new type of mutual-aid association named the Society for the Protection of the Needy (Sociedade Protectora dos Desvalidos). Interestingly, this historically significant transformation of the *crioulo* sodality took place in the very same year that the transatlantic slave trade was officially terminated, although we will never know whether the officeholders of the Society indeed chose the timing or it was merely coincidental.

The Society for the Protection of the Needy has maintained strong ties with the black church of Our Lady of the Rosary in the Pelourinho from the transfer of the headquarters of its predecessor, the black sodality of Our Lady of Solitude and Support of the Needy, to the church on December 17, 1848 until the present day. On May 10, 1868 the Society eventually moved out of the church, because of disagreements with the black sodality of Our Lady of the Rosary over use of the church, and rented a place of its own on Rua do Bispo. The Society has been located since 1877 at Cruzeiro de São Francisco, no. 17, near the Church of Saint Francis, but has continued to have strong ties with the black church of Our Lady of the Rosary in the Pelourinho.[25] Until today the majority of the members of the Society for the Protection of the Needy have also been members of or associated with the black sodality of Our Lady of the Rosary in the Pelourinho. For instance, Sr. Aloisío Conceição Rocha, the former treasurer and longtime member of the Society, has a cousin (Padre Rocha) who is the priest of the black church of Our Lady of the Rosary in the Pelourinho.[26]

It was on August 26, 1873 that the statutes of the Society for the Protection of the Needy were finally approved by the governor of the state of Bahia. While there was no restriction on the number of members, the Society limited its membership to "all Brazilian citizens whose color is black (*prêto*), who have sufficient income for subsistence, and who are neither under the age of eighteen nor over fifty." A member was to pay 15$000 *réis* as an entrance fee, and 1$000 *réis* in monthly dues.[27] Small wonder the statutes of the Society did not employ the term *crioulo*, which had already disappeared from the folk terminology of color by the turn of the 1870s. It is especially noteworthy that the term *negro*, which used to refer to both African birth and the enslaved status, was not used, either; instead the term *prêto*, which had come to refer to color in the official terminology, as in the case of censuses, was chosen to separate themselves from the majority of free people of African descent, who preferred to identify themselves as *pardos*. Furthermore, unlike the case of all black lay sodalities in Salvador, the Society for the Protection of the Needy surely did not depend on well-to-do whites financially, nor even allow them to become members. Obviously exclusion of well-to-do whites who could have made additional contributions from the membership cost every member much higher entrance and monthly fees, but it seems to have been worth creating a racially exclusive voluntary association that represented their own specific interests.

Whites were not the only group that the Society for the Protection of the Needy excluded from its membership; it did not allow either mulattoes or people of African birth to join. What do these seemingly strict exclusions mean? Why did the members of the Society for the Protection of the Needy choose to identify themselves as those whose color was "black" (*prêto*)? As we discussed earlier in this chapter, being perceived as "black" was almost synonymous with being a slave in nineteenth-century Salvador. Therefore many of the free Brazilian-born population of African descent, particularly those who attained a higher socioeconomic standing with specific occupational skills, naturally wanted to identify themselves not as "blacks" but "browns" in the case of census taking. True, ostensible skin color indeed mattered for one's social standing, and the individual choice of color was largely limited by a person's phenotype, although one's self-identification did not always correspond with the larger society's perception of the person's color. Having a lighter skin color was a great advantage in Brazilian society, and preference for it was widely prevalent among the Brazilian-born population of African descent, either slave or free. In 1855, for instance, James Wetherell reported in Salvador that among the "Creole blacks," a child who was whiter than his or her mother was looked upon with pride.[28] It is very likely that the special emphasis of the Society for the Protection of the Needy on the color "black" in its membership represented some free-born blacks' collective racial frustrations, caused by the larger society's unchanged perceptions of blackness, regardless of their newly acquired socioeconomic positions (and financial resources). Such individuals of African descent would be tolerated individually by the larger society as self-identified "browns," in accordance with their class positions, but the meanings of collective blackness would never change; despite their individual social color of "brown," they would continued to be treated as "blacks" on many occasions because of their race. Forming their own "black" association, whose membership was exclusive by race and class, they thought to be their effective means to (re)define their blackness in their own terms, not in the view of the white dominant society, thereby creating a new racial identity at a collective level.

The establishment and successful development of the Society for the Protection of the Needy signifies the emergence of a collective racial consciousness among some of the Brazilian-born population of African descent after the mid-nineteenth century. Represented among the membership were a variety of artisans and other skilled urban workers such as musicians and barber-surgeons, but there were no domestic servants, who were very poorly paid.[29] Furthermore, the Society restricted the age of members from eighteen to fifty, when male workers could be professionally most productive. The Society for the Protection of the Needy was a new type of mutual-aid association exclusively for men who were socioeconomically stable, with specified occupational skills. Unlike the case of lay sodalities, the Society did not provide any funeral services or any other charitable activities for members.

The exclusive character of the Society for the Protection of the Needy was also very noticeable in its treatment of women and children. The statutes obliged every member to "accompany the entrance of his wife, mother, and children; otherwise, he would be fined 1$000 *réis*."[30] Here we see the same kind of concern about family as in the mutual insurance society established within the new free-born *crioulo* sodality of Saint Francis of Paula (established in 1842), as discussed in chapter 6. Women were not entitled to hold memberships in the Society for the Protection of the Needy and were included only marginally, in the same way children were, and they were regarded as an "appendix," either as the wife or mother of a full member, who had to be a "black" male. It may suggest reconstruction of gender relations among the free-born population of African descent in the late nineteenth century. Unlike slave women, especially those of African birth, who engaged in the informal market in the city, most free Brazilian-born women of African descent worked as full-time domestic servants in their employers' houses, while living with their common-law husbands and children. The Society for the Protection of the Needy represented the interests of the free "black" household that was headed by a man who held a stable employment with his artisanal skills. This may suggest that, after mid-century, not only among African-born ex-slaves, as seen in their "return" movement to Africa (chapter 5), but also among other groups of people of African descent, the family had become a much more important institution in individual decision making. This contrasts with slave uprisings and the Malê revolt in the early nineteenth century, in which participation was largely limited to men (chapters 3 and 4).

With rare exceptions, the Society for the Protection of the Needy did not accept women as full members until around 1950.[31] Present-day officeholders of the Society, who are longtime members, insist that the Society did not discriminate against women as regular members, and ascribe the absence of women's formal participation to their "historical lack of socio-political consciousness," since "most of them were domestic servants." Of course, being domestic servants does not necessarily indicate women's lack of any collective sociopolitical consciousness. The present-day officeholders' statement on gender roles in the late nineteenth century does reflect much of patriarchalism prevalent in Brazilian culture. Yet it may enable us to consider reconstruction of gender relations among the population of African descent after about the mid-nineteenth century. Whereas young male slaves continued to be sold into the interprovincial slave trade, the city constantly demanded female domestic servants. Unlike slave women, especially those of African birth, maids were not hired out to the street for wage earning. Free Brazilian-born women of African descent were full-time domestic servants in their employers' households, and they had to devote their spare time to taking care of their spouses and/or children at home. Women became more limited in their daily mobility, and no longer moved beyond the boundary between the "house" and the "street" as freely as before, as discussed in the case of African-born slave women in chapter 2. Among the free-born population of African descent, the urban space may have come to be divided largely by gender into two distinctive spheres: the "street" for men, and the "house" for women.

The Society for the Protection of the Needy has attempted to participate in local politics, with mixed results. For instance, a longtime member became a perennial candidate for election to the city council. Committed to developing its collective racial consciousness, the Society has been very eloquent on the strong presence of racism in present Bahian society, which is still often denied by many Bahian intellectuals. Unlike the situation during the late nineteenth century, when it excluded the African-born population from its membership and was proud to be a voluntary association exclusively for "black" Brazilian citizens, the present-day Society for the Protection of the Needy has been promoting Africanism among the present population of African descent in Salvador by welcoming ambassadors and other visitors from African countries. One older member of the Society traveled to Angola in the early 1980s. Granted that Afro-Brazil in general has been developing an extremely complicated and ambiguous relationship with continental Africa, the Society's new "Pro-Africa" agenda has been perceived by a younger generation of Afro-Brazilian activists as a "redoubt for an older generation not on the frontline of protest." But at the same time,

African ambassadors and other international visitors are "more likely to be 'taken' to the Society's premises."[32] In fact, the president and a few other longtime members of the Society, based on the "international" nature of their association, asked the author, a Japanese national, to make connections with the Japanese government and major foundations for the financial support of the Society.

The Society for the Protection of the Needy has remained a predominantly black male association, although its current membership is officially open to any Brazilian citizen, regardless of race, color, or gender.[33] Despite the continuing success of their "black" association, the members of the present-day Society for the Protection of the Needy continue to struggle to identify themselves as blacks (*negros*). While they are very proud of their own unique association, they cannot help but reveal their feelings of being caught between their collective self-assertion as "blacks" and the larger society's perception of them as "blacks" based on their phenotypes. One day during my frequent visits to the headquarters of the Society for the Protection of the Needy in 1989, I was told by several longtime members, including the president, that the criterion for membership during the late nineteenth century had been the "color of the gums." They had to be "black," because those with "pink-colored" gums were regarded as mixed, not blacks. The elderly officeholders eagerly showed me their "pink-colored" gums and told me that they would not have been qualified for membership back in the nineteenth century; they would have been *mestiços* (mixed).[34] Needless to say, this "racial" criterion is by no means correct, but this story reveals the members' ambiguous "black" identity. They virtually insisted that at least during the nineteenth century they would not have been naturally classified as "blacks," who were not favored in the larger society and constituted a lower social stratum than the mulatto population; and even today they may well change their social color to "mulatto" because of their education and higher class standing than the masses. On a separate occasion for an informal chat, one of these longtime members, in front of a few other members, insisted on the presence of strong racism in present-day Salvador, and told me that whenever he made friends with a white man, he was always addressed as a *negro* by his friend, despite the fact that they shared the same socioeconomic standing. In other words, the members of the Society insist that they have become "blacks" by choice; but they are by no means naturally "black" in accordance with the larger society's pejorative perception of race. We should not fail to note that those who choose to identify themselves as "blacks" generally distance themselves from the poor majority, who are by all means labeled as "blacks" by the larger society, not only for their phenotypes, but also for their poverty, and who do not always identify themselves as such.

Conclusion

The terminology of color in Salvador changed in relation to the rapid decline of the institution of slavery, opportunities for freedom, disappearance of the aging population of African birth, and expansion of the free Brazilian-born population of African descent. In the last two decades of the slavery regime in Brazil, the meanings of color were redefined in the new context of free labor.

All in all, color is indeed a legacy of African/black slavery in present-day Salvador, as well as in all of Brazil, where color distinctions indicate not only visible differences in physical appearance derived from non-European ancestry, but also individual socioeconomic standings. In short, color in Brazil is a labeling/categorization of the individual by others (i.e., Brazilian society's view), mainly based on phenotype or ostensible "genetic" characteristics, such as skin color, hair, lips, and nose, which do not imply any exact genealogy or ancestry. In order to clarify this point, Daphne Patai, in her book *Brazilian Women Speak: Contemporary Life Stories* (1988), transcribes her conversation with two sisters in their early thirties, both of whom are highly educated feminists. The sisters were born to the same father and mother in a racially mixed family in the city of Rio de Janeiro. Because of the family's long history of miscegenation, the sisters happened to inherit different sets of physical features: the older sister Alma is completely "white" in appearance, while the younger sister Júlia's phenotype is regarded as "black." Alma and Júlia have been treated accordingly by the larger society and even within the family, which has created racial cleavages between the two sisters.[35] These terms of color are, of course, a representation of Brazilian culture and are ambiguous even within Brazilian culture, as Patai points out.[36]

Interestingly, this color label attached to the individual is changeable to a considerable degree according to the person's socioeconomic status. In his Pulitzer Prize–winning book, *Neither Black nor White: Slavery and Race Relations in Brazil and the United States* (1971), Carl N. Degler observes that in Brazil, where there is no definite line between blacks and whites because of the existence of the large mulatto population, it is possible for the individual of color to raise his or her socioeconomic status and therefore eventually to change (whiten) his or her social color.[37] In short, the color by which one is labeled by others is the indication of one's socioeconomic position within the racially stratified society and in relation to others with different physical characteristics. Individuals of color, whose self-perceptions are inevitably limited by the larger society's view, maneuver to manipulate social classification for the creation of racial identity. This sociocultural mechanism to determine one's racial identity with public affirmation is well exemplified by the anthropologist Virginia R. Domínguez in her provocative book, *White by Definition: Social Classification in Creole Louisiana* (1986).[38]

Generally speaking, being perceived as "black" in Brazil means being located at the lowest edge of the socioeconomic ladder, with relatively little formal schooling. Color continues to carry social stigmas resulting from the long history of African/black slavery in Brazil.[39] People of African descent, both individually and collectively, continue to suffer from the dishonor of having ancestors who had been enslaved, and are forced to fight various forms of prejudice and discrimination. Two U.S. journalists published in 1994 an illuminating episode in a Dallas newspaper article focusing on the issue of race in Brazil. In 1993 Daniel Sacramento ran for city council of Salvador; his platform was to improve jobs, housing, and security for "blacks." His sister, who is a professor of sociology at the Federal University of Bahia and campaigned for him, remembers a typical remark from a woman after entreaties to vote for him: "I am not voting for him. He is black," despite the fact she herself is phenotypically black, at least in the eyes of those two U.S. journalists.[40] We, of course, do not know if this woman, as well as other prospective voters who gave a similar response to the candidacy of Mr. Sacramento, would identify herself as black. She is very unlikely to do so since she is literate and aware of her voting power, which means she is well above the poor majority. In Brazil, to be black means to be poor; it carries a connotation that goes beyond indicating merely that this individual has different phenotypical characteristics derived from African ancestry.[41] In Salvador, as well as in the entire nation of Brazil, it may well be that blackness is still largely "dissembled and hidden"[42] and is perceivable only to those who seek to see it.

The creation of a collective racial identity by the members of the Society for the Protection of the Needy in Salvador during the late nineteenth century exemplifies the omnipresent nature of the short-lived *movimento negro,* or black movement, which modern Brazilian history has repeatedly witnessed. The *movimento negro,* which began with the Frente Negra Brasileira (Brazilian Black Front) first established in the city of São Paulo (1931–1937), has evolved over the years through more prominent incarnations, such as the Teatro Experimental do Negro (TEN; Black Experimental Theater) of the 1940s and 1950s, "Black Soul" of the 1970s, and the Movimento Negro Unificado (United Black Movement) of the 1980s and 1990s.[43] The *movimento negro* is an umbrella label that includes various kinds of political empowerment movements by various groups of Afro-Brazilians that have taken place in different locations at different times over the years.[44] In this long process of social mobilization, Afro-Brazilian activists have had to construct the *negro* as a new political subject; the *negro* has come to be defined as a socially constructed category that encompasses different colors and embraces the shared African ethnicity for the sake of political empowerment.[45] Although the term *negro* has been thus employed in all of these movements as the "signified/signifier of a race-conscious subject (equivalent to African-American)," there has been no clear consensus on the definition of the *negro* even among the Afro-Brazilian activists.[46] At the same time the leadership of the *movimento negro* has been predominantly middle-class, which George Reid Andrews, in his monograph titled *Blacks and Whites in São Paulo, Brazil, 1888–1988* (1991), notes as "class exclusivity" in the case of the city of São Paulo during the twentieth century. Andrews has documented middle-class Afro-Brazilians' various political attempts to set themselves apart from poor and working-class Afro-Brazilians, many of whom have refused to identity themselves as *negros* (blacks).[47]

The same kind of alleged "class exclusivity" has been observed in the commercial success of the new biweekly Brazilian magazine *Raça Brasil* (Brazil Race). In 1994 the first issue of *Raça Brasil* sold out immediately at every newsstand in southern Brazilian cities. This made a sensational headline, and the magazine soon received international attention. *Raça Brasil* has been modeled after the U.S. magazine *Ebony,* and it advocates the beauty of "blackness," which is represented in their unique hair, body, dress codes, sexuality, and so on. We should not fail to note that *Raça Brasil* has been "criticized for its advertisements on skin lightness and light-skin models," as in the case of their U.S. counterpart *Ebony*.[48] But, of course, *Raça Brasil* cannot escape Brazilian realities and customs, which persistently negate blackness and encourage individuals of color to change their "colors" in accordance with their better socioeconomic standings. The magazine has survived financially to this day, with the support of urban middle-class Afro-Brazilians, who have desired to give positive affirmations to their collective blackness, while at an individual level being strongly tempted to shed their race through "whitening." In fact, many of these white-collar Afro-Brazilian readers are lighter-skinned, and most of them would rather pass as mulattoes in the larger society.[49] On the other hand, the poor majority, all of whom are naturally darker-skinned, largely lack a collective racial consciousness and identity, while overlooking/denying the presence of prevalent racial prejudice and discrimination against peoples of color in Brazilian society.[50] Only with sufficient financial resources have Afro-Brazilians been able to make attempts to create a positive black identity, albeit by inevitably excluding the poor majority. In other words, class has been used by such Afro-Brazilian activists as a shared springboard for the creation of a collective racial identity. Ironically this is exactly the same mechanism, albeit with the opposite effect, as in an old, yet very popular, Brazilian saying: "Money whitens [color]." Money gives an individual the power to choose his or her color, even as black.

But, sadly, the story does not end here. As long as whiteness signifies power and blackness is identified with poverty, many of the self-declared Brazilian "blacks" find themselves being caught between their politically constructed racial identity and the individual social "color." Such internal dilemmas have been making every *movimento negro* extremely fragile and vulnerable, with the critical lack of a long-lasting group racial solidarity. In Brazil, class and color have been closely intertwined with each other; middle-class Afro-Brazilians have been allowed to pass individually as mulattoes or even whites in Brazilian society, thereby making blackness associated forever with poverty only.

Afro-Brazilians have created and re-created their distinctive identities over the years from the beginning of the slavery regime until the present day. And identity, either individual or collective, is indeed a choice in relation to others. But, whichever color (black, mulatto, or white) Afro-Brazilians collectively choose as their common racial identity, as long as the mechanism remains the same for the exclusion of the lower-class and underclass Afro-Brazilian masses, they continue to be caught within their own labyrinth of identity. They may utilize their financial resources to create a collective racial identity only by distinguishing and isolating themselves from the poor Afro-Brazilian majority, who deny their blackness and lack collective racial consciousness. Sadly, Afro-Brazilians' movements for collective political empowerment have been demonstrating their fatal limitations, which derive from the ambiguity of race, fluidity of color categories, and negative connotations of blackness, all of which have been prevalent in Brazilian culture over the years.

Conclusion

Slavery surely changed individuals as well as communities. But this study of slavery in the major Atlantic port city of Salvador, Brazil, during the nineteenth century reveals complex patterns of change in identity. Slavery profoundly changed perceptions of ethnicity, gender, and race.

To this day people of African descent have always predominantly populated Salvador. This is attributable to the long history of large-scale urban slavery in combination with the continuing massive influx of African-born slaves to Salvador that lasted from the late sixteenth century to the mid-nineteenth century. During the nineteenth century, many international travelers from Europe and North America, undoubtedly all whites, took special note of the visible prominence of the large black population in the city and described them as a people who naturally shared the same collective identity. But such an ostensible homogeneity in the eyes of outsiders was oftentimes quite misleading. All those who were categorized by others under a single label/category did not always share the same identity; individual actors of African decent in nineteenth-century Salvador created and re-created distinctive ethnic, gender, and racial identities in relation to political, socioeconomic, and cultural changes in the larger society.

The Creation of Ethnic Identity

Enslaved Africans created their ethnic identities in the context of New World urban slavery. For the first several decades of the nineteenth century, two-thirds of the slave population in Salvador was African-born, with diverse ethnic backgrounds. Such enslaved peoples of African birth were labeled/categorized by the larger society for the purpose of slave control; they were reduced into a certain number of African "nations," which did not always correspond to their original ethnic identifications back in continental Africa. The enslaved African-born population was quick to learn how to manipulate these labels/categories of African "nations" for the creation of ethnic identity. Although they were known in the slave society by their newly given Portuguese/Christian names, among themselves the

African-born population continued to speak their native African languages, while identifying themselves and referring to one another by their original African names.

Sharing of the same ethnicity became a solid foundation for the African-born population's daily gatherings and groupings on the streets. Ethnic identity functioned as a determinant factor in the African-born slave's choice of a partner or in parents' choice of their Brazilian-born child's god-parent(s) for baptism. It was also well represented in the establishment and formation of voluntary associations, as well as in the frequent occurrence of slave flights and uprisings.

Already by the mid-1830s, the African-born enslaved population's diverse ethnic identities began to converge into a broader ethnic identity, based on their common place of birth, Africa. This significant transformation of diverse ethnic identities manifested itself in the course of the Malê revolt (1835), in which several hundred African-born men, both slaves and ex-slaves, were united under the common symbols of Islam and their Yoruba ethnicity. The larger society started to perceive the population of African birth as a most serious obstacle to social order. In the late 1830s, as a result of societal pressures and in the face of new legislation that limited the status of the African-born ex-slave population, more and more of that population voluntarily emigrated, typically in a family unit (common-law spouses of African birth and their Brazilian-born children), to Africa, sometimes to their original hometowns. At the mid-nineteenth century, the very same year that the transatlantic slave trade was officially terminated, African-born ex-slaves' repatriation movements from the New World (i.e., Salvador) to the Old World (i.e., Africa) converged into their collective settlement in the newly established British colony of Lagos, in what is the present-day Nigeria. In Lagos, such African-born "returnees" (and their Brazilian-born children) from Salvador separated themselves from the local, indigenous populations as well as from those of African birth who had returned from other parts of the New World, such as Cuba, and identified themselves as "Brazilians." Thus the creation of ethnic identity also took place back in the Old World.

All in all, in slavery and freedom, enslaved Africans did not identify themselves exclusively in terms of race, and their creation of identity in the New World took place primarily within the parameters of ethnicity as well as gender. By re-creating strong ethnic identities and maintaining various ethnic continuities with their original African cultures, the African-born population in Salvador demonstrated remarkable resilience against the odds of New World urban slavery.

The Creation of Gender Identity

Enslaved Africans' creation of distinctive gender identities undermined the further development of their collective ethnic identities. While the urban African-born slave population was balanced by sex, with women even slightly outnumbering men, such distinctive features of urban slavery in Salvador as wage earning and the small scale of slaveholding determined important ways by which the African-born population created their gender identities. African-born slave men under different ownerships were usually hired out to the streets to work in gangs as porters and transporters. Those who shared the same ethnicity were arranged to work in the same gang mainly for their owners' convenience, but that this had the unintended consequence of making a significant contribution to the strong combination of gender with ethnic identity among the male slave population of African birth, which developed beyond the geographical urban/rural boundaries, cannot be denied. By contrast, African-born slave women were widely engaged in the informal market of the city, associated with one another across ethnic boundaries, and developed their collective gender identity in common without sharing the same ethnic identity. Small wonder that few African-born slave women participated in ethnic slave uprisings, which were a predominantly male phenomenon. We also take note that African-born slave women, particularly in the case of market women, gained much more financial resources than many African-born slave men who worked as manual laborers on the streets. Their financial resources, for instance, enabled them to hold membership in black lay sodalities, although it still did not allow them to become officeholders. Within the context of New World slavery and in the specific case of Salvador, Bahia, the common pattern within which African-born partners formed temporary or long-lasting bonds with mates but did not coreside further strengthened African-born slave women as they (re)created their distinctive gender identity.

This creation of gender identity took a completely different form in the Brazilian-born slave population, born and raised exclusively within Luso-Brazilian culture. They created their gender identities often in their close, interpersonal relationships with their owners. Brazilian-born slaves were manumitted most often without payment, either conditionally or unconditionally, and Brazilian-born women were freed with much greater frequency than their male counterparts. Yet most of these Brazilian-born ex–slave women remained in their former owners' households, in which they continued to work as quasi-slave domestic servants. Unlike the case of African-born market women, Brazilian-born ex–slave women were unable to move much on the socioeconomic ladder on account of their financial resources.

With the expansion of the free-born *crioulo* (Brazilian-born black) population in accordance with the rapid destruction of urban slavery after the mid-nineteenth century, gender relations were redefined and gender identities were re-created within the new framework of a two-headed household now that common-law spouses coresided, with their children. Men became the household heads and breadwinners for their families, while women, who worked as full-time domestic servants in their employers' households, had their gender roles re-created in relation to their domestic roles, largely as wives and mothers.

The Creation of Racial Identity

The Brazilian-born population of African descent separated themselves from their African-born counterparts and identified themselves primarily in terms of race, but this racialization does not mean that they all shared a single racial identity. For, either slave or legally free, they had always been divided into various color categories according to the individual's skin color and other phenotypes. As for the legally free population, color functioned as an index of one's socioeconomic status, for instance, for the choice of a marriage partner. Slave owners always preferred *pardos* (browns; mulattoes) over *crioulos* (blacks). Naturally the former had always had a much better chance in manumission and separated themselves from the latter, the majority of whom had always been slaves, and established their own mulatto sodalities that excluded blacks, namely the African-born and *crioulo* populations. Over time the free mulatto population came to constitute a distinct social stratum, and their racial identity was represented in the collective actions they took in the Tailors' Revolt in 1798. They had been strongly influenced by Enlightenment ideas in the conceptualization and the execution of the Revolt, which was an all-men event.

By contrast, the free *crioulo* population had been allowed to enjoy only a very limited amount of upward social mobility, most notably through military recruitment into the black regiments. As free black men, they were not located at the very bottom of the slave society, but as black men they were

very close to it. The presence of the black militia regiments in the slave society was designed to maintain the social order and hierarchy based on racial
slavery.

The creation of racial identity is exemplified by the development of the
Society for the Protection of the Needy during the last decades of the slavery
regime. The Society had been established in 1832 as one of the two new free-
born *crioulo* sodalities and subsequently transformed itself into a new type
of voluntary association in 1851. Its statutes were approved by the government of Bahia in 1873. The Society for the Protection of the Needy turned
out to be the first exclusively "black" voluntary association in Brazil that did
not extend membership to whites and mulattoes, nor was it open to the
African-born population, which had been disappearing in any case. The
statutes limited membership of the Society to male Brazilian citizens, aged
eighteen to fifty, whose skin color was *prêto* (black) and who possessed
the requisite means and, therefore, could afford to pay the relatively high
registration and membership fees. Interestingly, for self-identification they
avoided using the term *negro,* which referred to the general Brazilian-born
black population from the 1870s. Most of the members of the Society were
skilled artisans who could earn stable salaries; they did not include domestic
servants, who were poorly paid. With their newly emerging financial power,
these men chose not to change their color from "black" to "mulatto"; instead they (re)created their collective racial identity as "blacks" by separat-
ing themselves from the poor black majority. Only improved socioeconomic
standing made one's choice of color possible. As this creation of a "new"
identity shows, class exclusivity was a noticeable characteristic of Brazilian
racial identity then and now.

* * *

Individuals who appear to be homogeneous and undifferentiable to others, either as a group or community, or who are labeled by the larger society under a single category because of their ostensible shared sameness in
phenotype and/or color do not necessarily share a common identity. Individuals create and re-create their identities in relation to other people's perceptions and categorization of them, and the creation of identity invariably
takes place within the context of power relations.

In the New World, particularly in Brazil and in the antebellum American
South, African/black slavery developed and prevailed as a major socioeconomic institution, and, as a result, race and class have been intricately inter-

twined with each other in the establishment of power relations and structures and their maintenance. The face of power has been white because of the legacy of racial slavery, although the definition of whiteness varies from one culture to another. Nonetheless, all the non-white populations in the New World have been regarded as a social and political minority, and their minority status has been marked by their visible otherness.

In Brazil, African/black slavery prevailed and flourished as a national institution for the country's agro-export economy for more than three centuries. The non-white population had always been a majority in number from the early colonial period throughout the nineteenth century. In the case of nineteenth-century Salvador, which this book treats extensively, some 70 percent of the whole population was classified as people of color or non-white. The white elite had to establish some sophisticated mechanisms by which only they could recruit a select, elite group of the population of African descent as individuals, through the political practice of clientage and patronage, into the power systems and permit them, as mulattoes, not as blacks, to move up on a social ladder.[1] At the same time, the larger society divided the majority of the non-white population into various categories, such as "nations" (for African-born) and colors (for Brazilian-born), which effectively hampered them from creating a common collective ethnic/racial identity. This book has demonstrated that the creolization of the Afro-Brazilian population did not automatically result in the historical creation of a single, homogeneous racial/ethnic identity. Afro-Brazilians have manipulated various labels/categories in relation to their skin colors and other phenotypes, as well as their class positions, and have individually played politics of identity within their socio–racial/ethnic group designations.

By contrast, in the United States, slavery did not become a national institution; it evolved only regionally with the development of the plantation economy in the antebellum South, with a much smaller number of slave imports from Africa, approximately one-ninth as many as entered Brazil.[2] African Americans have always constituted a numerical minority, whose presence as a collective could not be perceived as a critical numerical threat to white supremacy in the colonial society. For the sake of social control, the larger society has lumped together all people of African ancestry and classified them as blacks by disregarding other ancestries they have also inherited, such as European, Native American, and Asian, although, as Melissa Nobles's study demonstrates, the official category of "mulatto" was not removed from the U.S. censuses until 1930.[3] In the United States, historically, having "one drop of blood" of an African ancestry automatically determined one's race as black, no matter how white one appeared to be. Individual variations in color and other phenotypes among African Americans have been treated mainly as a personal preference. In the late 1980s and early 1990s the U.S. society observed a crucial change in its racial categorization with the advancement of the multiracial movement; people increasingly questioned the long-standing, rigid racial categories solely based on single ancestors and raised many issues concerning multiracial identity.[4] While it became common for us to see in the United States the category of "others" for those who inherit more than one ancestry (and therefore are unable to identify themselves with one of the traditional rigid racial/ethnic categories), the rule of thumb has not changed at all. In the United States, African ancestry continues to play the central role in determining one's (either singular or multiple) racial identity.

* * *

Since the late fifteenth century, which was marked by the emergence of the Portuguese empire, the rapid expansion of world capitalism has moved, relocated, and marginalized a great number of people as a forced (enslaved and indentured) or voluntary (immigrant) labor force. As a result, world history has repeatedly witnessed the formation of various diaspora communities, these geographically diverged and culturally displaced peoples' creation of new identities as minorities in the larger societies, and their repatriation movements to their homelands in search of their "true" identities.[5] An example is the "emancipated Africans" in Sierra Leone, who migrated to Jamaica as indentured servants, and ultimately "returned" to Africa, as studied by historian Monica Schuler for the period 1846–1865.[6] Another example is reported by anthropologist George Gmelch in his collection of narratives by thirteen Barbadians who have "returned" from various places in England and North America.[7]

Around the mid-1980s, from Brazil, as well as from Peru, Argentina, and other Latin American countries, albeit on a much smaller scale, people of Japanese descent began to migrate on a large scale to Japan, whose booming economy demanded a massive manual labor force. Such labor movements of Japanese Brazilians to Japan have been called *dekassegui* in Brazil, and the term has been incorporated into the Brazilian Portuguese vocabulary. Many Japanese Brazilian migrant workers were white-collar workers in Brazil, often with college degrees, but chose to work as unskilled laborers in Japan.[8] Needless to say, their decision on this transnational labor migration from Brazil to Japan was made first and foremost for financial reasons; they could easily earn wages several times higher than when working in Brazil. But we should not fail to point out that at the same time Japanese Brazilians' labor migration to Japan demonstrates a striking resemblance to African-born ex-slaves' emigration from Salvador to West Africa. Japanese Brazilians, who have been categorized and identified as "Japanese" (*japonês/japonêsa*), with pejorative racial/ethnic biases and stereotypes despite their middle-class position in the larger society, had long romanticized Japan as their "homeland," regardless of their Brazilian birth and citizenship, and tended to identify themselves in ethnic terms as Japanese, not as Brazilians. In Japan, in June 1990, new laws were enacted to grant permanent residency to all non–Japanese citizens whose parents or grandparents were of Japanese nationality so that Japanese industry might attract and more readily obtain cheap labor from overseas. This change in labor laws contributed to the sudden great increase in the numbers of Japanese Brazilian migrant workers who left Brazil. Ironically, upon arrival in Japan, Japanese Brazilians, many of whom look exactly like Japanese, have been regarded as the "other" regardless of the shared Japanese ancestry because of their cultural differences and lack of language skills. Faced by ethnic prejudice and discrimination, Japanese Brazilian workers and their families have separated themselves from the Japanese and formed "Brazilian" communities.[9] Many have moved back to Brazil after having saved a substantial amount of money, which has been used typically for the purchase of real estate and business, but others continue to move back and forth between Brazil and Japan, still being unsure of their ambiguous Japanese Brazilian identity.[10] Clearly these Japanese Brazilians' "repatriation" to Japan constitutes a present-day, global-age counterpart to the historical experiences of African-born ex-slaves and their Brazilian-born children who took a passage from the city of Salvador to Africa and re-created their ethnic identity as Brazilians in Lagos during the late nineteenth century.[11]

This book has demonstrated that the creation of identity by enslaved Africans and their descendants in nineteenth-century Salvador, Brazil was, in fact, not unique to its specific time, space, and historical context. In our global age, with the expansion of global markets, people and commodities are circulating beyond national boundaries, and as a result we have been observing the rapid formation of seemingly homogeneous communities in the United States. This is exemplified by the rapid emergence of non-English-speaking "blacks" in Washington, D.C.; "Hispanics" in Miami,

Florida; and "Asians" in Atlanta, Georgia; all of whom, in reality, have been heterogeneous groups whose ethnic compositions continue to change as a result of the ongoing massive transnational migrations. It is no longer possible to study all the important issues of identity by confining our discussions to a specific national/racial/ethnic territory.[12] This case study on the population of African descent in a specific nineteenth-century Atlantic port city in Brazil clearly suggests intriguing leads for our understanding of identity in this global world, despite the fact that the verb "globalize" was not coined until 1944.[13] Thus my historical study is testimony to the fact that studies of the past can indeed help and promote a fuller understanding of the present. We are able to continue to learn from history how to perceive and work on many sociocultural "problems," including the important issues of identity in our global age.

* * *

We cannot deny that the Middle Passage and New World slavery dehumanized all enslaved Africans and their descendants to the most damaging degree. But all of their terrifying experiences did not necessarily result in "social death." As this book has illustrated at many points, peoples of African descent in nineteenth-century Salvador, Brazil demonstrated a remarkable degree of resilience, self-identity, and self-consciousness during the time of slavery. Their actions, hopes, and memories all indicate that Afro-Brazilians, individually or collectively, never lost a strong sense of who they were. That is one important dimension of the power of identity. Of course, Afro-Brazilians' struggle for freedom did not end with the abolition of slavery in 1888. The institution of racial slavery surely ended in legal terms, but racism and racial discrimination, which derived from the long history of slavery, have hampered Afro-Brazilians as a group from rising in the society. At the same time Brazilian society has always encouraged and allowed them to move up individually on a social ladder, albeit by changing their social color from "black" to "mulatto" or even "white." This resulted in the continuing critical divisions among the Afro-Brazilian population, which was reflected in a series of various short-lived black movements during the twentieth century. To be black has remained largely an individual choice for racial politics in Brazil. Afro-Brazilians, who chose to identify themselves as "black," have continued to fight rigorously for the creation and (re)affirmation of racial identity for their collective political empowerment.

Glossary

afilhado/ afilhada	godson/goddaughter
agregados	dependants in households
alforria	manumission
amas de leite	wet nurses
armação	warehouse and processing plant for whale products
arrôba	unit of weight; one *arrôba* is approximately 32 pounds
batuque	dance of African origin practiced by persons of African descent on the street after work and on weekends and holidays
candomblé	Afro-Brazilian religion resulted from West African religions' syncretism with Catholicism during the slavery regime
cabra	mulatto
caboclo	person of Euro-Indian ancestry
caixa	unit of weight; one *caixa* is around 40 *arrôba*
canto	street corner; in nineteenth-century Salvador, the street corner where African-born slaves and ex-slaves of the same nation gathered on the work day
companheiros, companheiras	common-law spouses
conto	Brazilian currency; one *conto* was equivalent to 1,000 *mil-réis,* and written 1:000$000 *réis*
copadre/ comadre	coparent
cria	Brazilian-born slave raised in his or her owner's household
crioulo	Brazilian-born black
emancipados	the emancipated
engenho	sugar mill; sugar plantation by extension
farinha	manioc flour
fazenda	plantation
forro/ forra	ex-slave
ganho	wage earning
ganhador/ ganhadora	wage-earner

irmandade	lay sodality
juntas	unions
liberto/liberta	ex-slave
livre	free-born
madrinha	godmother
malungos	shipmates
mercadejas	market vendors
mocambo	fugitive slave community
mulato/mulata	mulatto, often with pejorative connotations
negros novos	newly arrived African-born slaves
pardo/parda	mulatto
padrinho	godfather
pataca	320 *réis*
peculio	savings
pessoas de côr	persons of color
prêto/prêta	African-born black
quitanda	market stall
quitandeiro/quitandeira	market-stall keeper
quilombo	fugitive slave community
Recôncavo	hinterland of the city of Salvador (Bahian Recôncavo); the word's original meaning is cave, hole, and land surrounding a port or a city
real	former Brazilian currency, plural, *réis;* 1,000 *réis* is written 1$000 *réis,* and called *mil-réis*
terreiros	temple grounds or sacred meeting places
venda	market stall

Notes

Introduction

1.   On the notion of identity, see, for instance, A. L. Epstein, *Ethos and Identity: Three Studies in Ethnicity* (London: Tavistock Publications, 1978), pp. 100–101; Edmund Leach, *A Runaway World?* (London: British Broadcasting Corporation, 1968 [1967]), p. 34; Anita Jacobson-Widding, "Introduction," in Anita Jacobson-Widding, ed., *Identity: Personal and Socio-cultural* (Uppsala, Sweden: Acta Universitatis Upsaliensis, 1983), p. 13; Dorinne K. Kondo, *Crafting Selves: Power, Gender, and Discourses of Identity in a Japanese Workplace* (Chicago: University of Chicago Press, 1990), p. 48; and Richard Handler, "Is 'Identity' a Useful Cross-Cultural Concept?" in John R. Gills, ed., *Commemorations: The Politics of National Identity* (Princeton, N.J.: Princeton University Press, 1994).

2.   Historians have studied human behaviors and actions in the colonial setting, based on archival sources and other historical documents. Such is the case of historian Rhys Isaac's ethnographic method, named "action approach." By "translating" his historical data of colonial Virginian plantation society as "doings of particular people in particular circumstances," Isaac, as the "field ethnographer," leads us to a full understanding of society not as "primarily a material entity" but as "*a dynamic product* of the activities of its members—a product profoundly shaped by the *images* the participants have of their own and others' performances" (italics in original). See Rhys Isaac, "Ethnographical Method in History: An Action Approach," *Historical Methods* 13, no. 1 (1980): 43. See also Rhys Isaac, *The Transformation of Virginia 1740–1790* (Chapel Hill: University of North Carolina Press, 1982). Another excellent monograph on human behaviors is William B. Taylor, *Drinking, Homicide, and Rebellion in Colonial Mexican Villages* (Stanford, Calif.: Stanford University Press, 1979). Of course, we are well aware of the limitations, both quantitative and qualitative, of historical evidence on human behavior. As the historian Robert F. Berkhofer, Jr. states: "Since the historian can never see the real actions of his subjects, he must derive behavioral manifestations from the subjective documents he reads according to some theoretical scheme that postulates that relationship." See Robert F. Berkhofer, Jr., *A Behavioral Approach to Historical Analysis* (New York: Free Press; and London: Collier-Macmillan, 1969), p. 18.

3.   Dauril Alden, "Late Colonial Brazil, 1750–1808," in Leslie Bethell, ed., *Colonial Brazil* (Cambridge: Cambridge University Press, 1987), p. 289.

4. The population of the city of Rio de Janeiro in 1808 was 54,245, which doubled by 1822 and rapidly doubled again (222,313) by 1872. See Mary C. Karasch, *Slave Life in Rio de Janeiro 1808–1850* (Princeton, N.J.: Princeton University Press, 1987), p. 61; and Alden, "Late Colonial Brazil," p. 289.

5. Howard M. Prince, "Slave Rebellion in Bahia 1807–1835" (Ph.D. diss., Columbia University, 1972), pp. 15–16. *Conto* was a colonial and imperial Brazilian currency measurement. One *conto* was 1,000,000 *réis*. The *real* (plural *réis*) was the Brazilian currency of account. One *caixa* of sugar was around forty *arrôbas* (an *arrôba* is approximately 32 pounds).

6. Epstein, *Ethos and Identity,* p. 5.

7. J. Clyde Mitchell, "Tribe and Social Change in South Central Africa: A Situational Approach," *Journal of Asian and African Studies* 5 (1970): 85. On the concept of "situation" in social anthropology, see, for instance, Max Gluckman, "Analysis of the Social Situation in Modern Zululand," *Bantu Studies* 14 (1940): 1–30, 147–174.

8. Mitchell, "Tribe and Social Change," p. 85.

9. J. Clyde Mitchell, *The Kalela Dance: Aspects of Social Relationships among Urban Africans in Northern Rhodesia* (Manchester: Manchester University Press, 1956); idem, *Tribalism and the Plural Society* (London: Oxford University Press, 1960); idem, "Tribe and Social Change." Elizabeth Bott, A. L. Epstein, and J. C. Mitchell devised "network analysis" to examine the concrete networks developed by migrant workers and their families living in urban areas. Elizabeth Bott, *Family and Social Network: Roles, Norms, and External Relationships in Ordinary Urban Families* (London: Tavistock Publications, 1959); A. L. Epstein, "The Network and Urban Social Organization," *Rhodes-Livingstone Journal* 29 (1961): 29–62; J. C. Mitchell, ed., *Social Networks in Urban Situations* (Manchester: Manchester University Press, 1969). The Manchester School did not use or develop the term "ethnic group," or the concept of "ethnicity" in this earlier stage of their studies. On the school's studies of ethnicity, see Abner Cohen, *Custom and Politics in Urban Africa: A Study of Hausa Migrants in Yoruba Towns* (Berkeley and Los Angeles: University of California Press, 1969); idem, *Two-Dimensional Man: An Essay on the Anthropology of Power and Symbolism in Complex Society* (London: Routledge & Kegan Paul, 1974); Abner Cohen, ed., *Urban Ethnicity* (London: Tavistock Publications, 1974); and Epstein, *Ethos and Identity.* On the historical creation of ethnicity, see Eric Hobsbawm and Terence Ranger, eds., *The Invention of Tradition* (Cambridge: Cambridge University Press, 1983); Terence Ranger, *The Invention of Tribalism in Zimbabwe* (Gweru, Zimbabwe: Mambo Press, 1985); and Leroy Vail, ed., *The Creation of Tribalism in Southern Africa* (London: James Currey, 1989).

10. Mitchell, "Tribe and Social Change," pp. 88–89.

11. Ibid., p. 89.

12. E. P. Thompson, *The Making of the English Working Class* (New York: Vintage Books, 1966 [1963]).

13. Ibid., p. 9.

14. Ibid. My italics.

15. Herbert G. Gutman, *The Black Family in Slavery and Freedom, 1750–1925* (New York: Vintage Books, 1977 [1976]); Herbert G. Gutman, "Interview with Herbert Gutman," in Middle Atlantic Radical Historians' Association, Henry Abelove, et al., eds., *Visions of History* (New York: Pantheon Books, 1983), p. 211. Gutman states: "In other words, there had to be connectedness. The important discovery in the book, I think, is not that slaves lived in families that were frequently broken, but that the family could serve the slaves as a way of creating social and class connections far more important than the family. Call these connections what you will! Once you know such connections exist, then you can also find out when, why, and how they came together." Ibid., p. 211.

16. Gutman, *Black Family,* p. 3. He also states his book is "about a special aspect of working class history." See Gutman, "Interview with Herbert Gutman," p. 206.

17. Gutman, "Interview with Herbert Gutman," p. 205. See also Gutman, *Black Family,* p. 3. Gutman states: ". . . understanding nineteenth-century slave behavior and belief (the developed *class*) required a reexamination of the process by which Africans first became a social *class* in North America (the new *class*)" (my italics). See Gutman, "Interview with Herbert Gutman," p. 207. On Gutman's usage of the term "class," Ira Berlin states: "He [Gutman] used the term 'class' gingerly, preferring 'workers' and other synonyms precisely because 'class' analysis had been identified with a belief that economic structure determined behavior and belief. . . . Thompson's understanding of class as the precipitate of common experiences within a system of productive relations, and of class consciousness as the articulation of those experiences, was also Gutman's." See Ira Berlin, "Herbert G. Gutman and the American Working Class," in Herbert G. Gutman, *Power and Culture: Essays on the American Working Class,* ed. Ira Berlin (New York: Pantheon Books, 1987).

18. Sidney W. Mintz and Richard Price, *An Anthropological Approach to the Afro-American Past: A Caribbean Perspective* (Philadelphia: Institute for the Study of Human Issues, 1976). This book has been republished with a new preface as *The Birth of African-American Culture: An Anthropological Perspective* (Boston: Beacon Press, 1992).

19. Mintz and Price state: "An African heritage, widely shaped by the people imported into any new colony, will have to be defined in less concrete terms, by focusing more on values, and less on sociocultural forms, and even by attempting to identify unconscious 'grammatical' principles, which may underlie and shape behavioral response. To begin with, we would call for an examination of what Foster [George M. Foster] has called 'cognitive orientations,' on the one hand, basic assumptions about social relations (what values

motivate individuals, how one deals with others in social situations, and matters of interpersonal style), and, on the other, basic assumptions and expectations about the way the world functions phenomenologically (for instance, beliefs about causality, and how particular cases are revealed)." See Mintz and Price, *Birth of African-American Culture,* pp. 9–10; idem, *Anthropological Approach,* p. 5.

20. For the discussion of creolization in colonial British America, see T. H. Breen, "Creative Adaptations: Peoples and Cultures," in Jack P. Greene and J. R. Pole, eds., *Colonial British America: Essays in the New History of the Early Modern Era* (Baltimore: Johns Hopkins University Press, 1984); and Jack P. Greene, *Pursuits of Happiness: The Social Development of Early Modern British Colonies and the Formation of American Culture* (Chapel Hill: University of North Carolina Press, 1988), especially chapters 7 and 8.

21. Mintz and Price, *Birth of African-American Culture,* p. 14; Mintz and Price, *Anthropological Approach,* p. 7. Their italics. See Stephan Palmié's excellent critiques on this cultural creolization model: Stephan Palmié, "Slave Culture and the Culture of Slavery in North America: Some Remarks on Historiography and the Present State of Research," and "Ethnographic Processes and Cultural Transfer in Afro-American Slave Populations," both in Wolfgang Binder, ed., *Slavery in the Americas* (Würzburg: Köningshausen & Newman, 1993).

22. Stephan Palmié, "Spics or Spades? Racial Classification and Ethnic Conflict in Miami," *Amerikastudien/American Studies* 34 (1989): 211–221.

23. Anthony P. Cohen, *The Symbolic Construction of Community* (New York: Tavistock Publications, 1985), p. 12.

24. Suzanne Oboler, *Ethnic Labels, Latino Lives: Identity and the Politics of (Re)Presentation in the United States* (Minneapolis: University of Minnesota Press, 1995).

25. See, for instance, Thomas Skidmore, "Bi-racial U.S.A. vs. Multi-racial Brazil: Is the Contrast Still Valid?" *Journal of Latin American Studies* 25, no. 2 (1993): 373–386.

26. Sidney W. Mintz, "Defining Black and White," *Johns Hopkins Magazine* 46, no. 5 (1994): 10. His italics.

27. George Reid Andrews, Emília Viotti da Costa, and Franklin W. Knight, "George Reid Andrews, *Blacks and Whites in São Paulo, Brazil, 1888–1988* (Madison: University of Wisconsin Press, 1991). Introduction, Two Comments, and a Rejoinder by the Author," *Luso-Brazilian Review* 29, no. 2 (1992): 141–158, 146.

28. Sidney W. Mintz, "A Melting Pot—Sort of," *Johns Hopkins Magazine* 46, no. 4 (1994): 25. His italics.

29. David W. Cohen and Jack P. Greene, "Introduction," in David W. Cohen and Jack P. Greene, eds., *Neither Slave nor Free: The Freedmen of African Descent in the Slave Societies of the New World* (Baltimore: Johns Hopkins University Press, 1972), p. 7. Their assertion that everywhere else these color categories

"became increasingly vague and confused within a century of the beginnings of the slave societies" (ibid., p. 7) is obviously not correct.

30.   C. R. Boxer, *Race Relations in the Portuguese Colonial Empire 1415–1825* (Oxford: Clarendon Press, 1963), p. 120.

31.   A. J. R. Russell-Wood, "Colonial Brazil," in Cohen and Greene, eds., *Neither Slave nor Free,* pp. 84–85.

32.   George Reid Andrews, *Blacks and Whites in São Paulo, Brazil 1888–1988* (Madison: University of Wisconsin Press, 1991), p. 249.

33.   Joseph C. Miller, *Way of Death: Merchant Capitalism and the Angolan Slave Trade 1730–1830* (Madison: University of Wisconsin Press, 1988); Orlando Patterson, *Slavery and Social Death: A Comparative Study* (Cambridge, Mass.: Harvard University Press, 1982).

1. A "Capital of Africa" in Brazil

1.   The Jesuits were expelled from Brazil in 1759.

2.   James Henderson, *A History of the Brazil: Comprising its Geography, Commerce, Colonization, Aboriginal Inhabitants, & C. & C. & C.* (London: Longman, Hurt, Rees, Orme, and Brown, 1821), pp. 336–337; Robert Dundas, *Sketches of Brazil: Including New Views on Tropical and European Fever, With Remarks on a Premature Decay of the System Incident to Europeans on their Return from Hot Climates* (London: John Churchill, 1852), pp. 200–201; and Charles Frederick Hartt, *Geology and Physical Geography of Brazil* (Boston: Fields, Osgood, 1870), p. 334.

3.   Hartt, *Geology and Physical Geography,* p. 335. Hartt also stated that in 1867 a street to connect the two parts of the city was in the process of construction. See also George Gardner, *Travels in the Interior of Brazil Principally through the Northern Provinces and the Gold and Diamond Districts during the Years 1836–1841* (London: Milford House, 1987 [1846]), pp. 74–75; and L. F. de Tollenare, *Notas dominiais* (Recife: Governo de Estado de Pernambuco, 1979), p. 212. Nineteenth-century Salvador was composed of ten parishes: Sé, São Pedro Velho, Santana, Conceição da Praia, Vitória, Rua do Passo, Pilar, Santo Antônio, Brotas, and Penha, until a new parish, Maré, was created in 1870 by subdividing Penha parish. See Anna Amélia Vieira Nascimento, *Dez freguesias da cidade do Salvador: aspectos sociais e urbanos do século XIX* (Salvador: Fundação Cultural do Estado da Bahia, 1986), pp. 28–51.

4.   Robert Abé-Lallemant, *Reise durch Nord=Brasilien im Jahre 1859,* 2 vols. (Leipzig: F. D. Bradhaus, 1860), vol. 1, p. 10. I am indebted to Mrs. Hannelore Russell-Wood for the translation from the original text in German. The Portuguese translation is defective. See Robert Abé-Lallemant, *Viagem pelo norte do Brasil no ano de 1859,* trans. Eduardo de Lima Castro, 2 vols. (Rio de Janeiro: Instituto Nacional do Livro, 1961).

5.   See, for instance, Robert Walsh, *Notices of Brazil in 1818 and 1829,* 2 vols. (Lon-

don: Fredrick Westley and A. H. Davis, 1830), vol. 2, p. 182; Gardner, *Travels in the Interior of Brazil*, p. 78; Thomas Ewbank, *Life in Brazil: A Journal of a Visit to the Land of the Cocoa and the Palm* (New York: Harper & Brothers, 1856), p. 439; Robert Elwes, *A Sketcher's Tour round the World: Illustrations from Original Drawings by the Author* (London: Hurst and Blackett, 1854), p. 94; and Wilson Burgess, *Narrative of a Recent Visit to Brazil, to Present an Address on the Slave-Trade and Slavery, Issued by the Religious Society of Friends* (London: Edmund Marsh, 1853), p. 49.

6.   Thales de Azevedo, *Povoamento da cidade do Salvador* (São Paulo: Companhia Editora Nacional, 1955), pp. 191–193; Brasil, Diretoria Geral de Estatística, *Recenseamento da população de Imperio do Brasil a que procedeu no dia 1 de agosto de 1872* (Rio de Janeiro: Leuzinger, 1873–1876), pp. 508, 510.

7.   See Stuart B. Schwartz, *Sovereignty and Society in Colonial Brazil: The High Court of Bahia and Its Judges, 1609–1751* (Berkeley and Los Angeles: University of California Press, 1973).

8.   Stuart B. Schwartz, *Sugar Plantations in the Formation of Brazilian Society, Bahia, 1550–1835* (Cambridge: Cambridge University Press, 1985), p. 78.

9.   On sugar planters in Bahia, see Schwartz, *Sugar Plantations*, pp. 264–294. On the urban life of sugar planters and their families in nineteenth-century northern Brazil, see Gilberto Freyre, *The Mansions and the Shanties: The Making of Modern Brazil*, trans. and ed. Harriet de Onís (New York: Alfred A. Knopf, 1963).

10.   James Lockhart and Stuart B. Schwartz, *Early Latin America: A History of Colonial Spanish America and Brazil* (Cambridge: Cambridge University Press, 1983), p. 198; Schwartz, *Sugar Plantations*, p. 52; and Russell Menard and Stuart B. Schwartz, "Why African Slavery? Labor Force Transitions in Brazil, Mexico, and the Carolina Lowcountry," in Binder, ed. *Slavery in the Americas*, p. 95. See also Mário Maestri, "Consideração sobre o cativeiro do 'negro da terra' no Brasil quinhentista," *Estudos Ibero-Americanos* 16, no. 1/2 (1990): 197–210.

11.   Alexander Marchant, *From Barter to Slavery: The Economic Relations of Portuguese and Indians in the Settlement of Brazil, 1500–1580* (Baltimore: Johns Hopkins University Press, 1942); and Schwartz, *Sugar Plantations*, pp. 34–35.

12.   Schwartz, *Sugar Plantations*, pp. 35–37.

13.   Ibid., p. 16.

14.   On the sugar plantation society in Bahia, see Schwartz, *Sugar Plantations*. Also, on Bahian planters and merchants, see John W. Kennedy, "Bahian Elites, 1750–1822," *Hispanic American Historical Review* (hereafter *HAHR*) 53, no. 39 (1973): 415–439; Rae Jean Dell Flory, "Bahian Society in the Mid-Colonial Period: The Sugar Planters, Tobacco Growers, Merchants, and Artisans of Salvador and the Recôncavo" (Ph.D. diss., University of Texas at Austin, 1978); Rae Jean Dell Flory and David Grant Smith, "Bahian Merchants and Planters in the Seventeenth and Early Eighteenth Centuries," *HAHR* 58, no. 4 (1978): 571–

594; and Catherine Lugar, "The Merchant Community of Salvador, Bahia, 1780–1830" (Ph.D. diss., State University of New York at Stony Brook, 1980).

15. On Indians and Indian slavery in Brazil, see Marchant, *From Barter to Slavery*; Stuart B. Schwartz, "Indian Labor and New World Plantations: European Demands and Indian Responses in Northern Brazil," *American Historical Review* (hereafter *AHR*) 83, no. 3 (1978): 43–78; and John Hemming, *Red Gold: The Conquest of the Brazilian Indians* (Cambridge, Mass: Harvard University Press, 1978).

16. Schwartz, *Sugar Plantations,* chapter 3; and Robert Edgar Conrad, *World of Sorrow: The African Slave Trade to Brazil* (Baton Rouge: Louisiana State University Press, 1986), pp. 15–19.

17. Schwartz, *Sugar Plantations,* p. 422. One *arrôba* is approximately 32 pounds.

18. Alden, "Late Colonial Brazil," pp. 314–318; and David Eltis, *Economic Growth and the Ending of the Transatlantic Slave Trade* (New York: Oxford University Press, 1987), pp. 48–49.

19. Alden, "Late Colonial Brazil," p. 311.

20. Schwartz, *Sugar Plantations,* pp. 415–438.

21. Alden, "Late Colonial Brazil," p. 312.

22. Ibid., pp. 286–287, 289.

23. Joseph C. Miller, "Slave Prices in the Portuguese Southern Atlantic, 1600–1830," in Paul E. Lovejoy, ed., *Africans in Bondage: Studies in Slavery and Slave Trade* (Madison: University of Wisconsin Press, 1986), pp. 43–44. Various scholars, with mixed results, have attempted to periodize the slave trade. An early proponent was Luís Viana Filho, who identified four "cycles," namely the Guinea cycle in the sixteenth century; the Angola cycle in the seventeenth century; the Mina Coast and Bight of Benin cycle in the eighteenth century until 1815; the fourth and last phase, namely the period of clandestine slave trade, 1816–1851. See Luís Viana Filho, *O negro na Bahia,* 3rd ed. (Rio de Janeiro: Nova Fronteira, 1988), p. 38. The French scholar Pierre Verger also viewed the trade in cyclical terms, but developed these as follows: the Guinea cycle, during the second half of the sixteenth century; the Angola and Congo cycle in the seventeenth century; the Mina Coast cycle, during the first three quarters of the eighteenth century; the Bight of Benin cycle between 1770 and 1850, including the period of clandestine slave trade. See Pierre Verger, *Trade Relations between the Bight of Benin and Bahia from the 17th to 19th Century,* trans. Evelyn Crawford (Ibadan, Nigeria: Ibadan University Press, 1976), p. 1. This book is an English translation of Pierre Verger, *Flux e Reflux de la Traite des Negres entre le Golfe De Bénin et Bahia de Todos os Santos du Xvii au Xix Siècle,* 3 vols. (Paris: Mouton, 1968). A Portuguese translation was later published as Pierre Verger, *Fluxo e refluxo do tráfico de escravos entre o Golfo do Benin e a Bahia de Todos os Santos, dos séculos XVII a XIX,* trans. Tasso Gadzanis, 2nd ed. (São Paulo: Editora Corrupio, 1987). On Portuguese slave trade from Angola to Brazil, see Miller, *Way of Death.* On the transatlantic slave trade

in general, see Philip D. Curtin, *The Atlantic Slave Trade: A Census* (Madison: University of Wisconsin Press, 1969); and Joseph E. Inikori and Stanley L. Engerman, eds., *The Atlantic Slave Trade: Effects on Economics, Societies, and Peoples in Africa, the Americas, and Europe* (Durham, N.C.: Duke University Press, 1992). For the African side of the Atlantic slave trade, see a collection of narratives by West Africans in the eighteenth and nineteenth centuries edited by Philip D. Curtin, *Africa Remembered: Narratives by West Africans from the Era of the Slave Trade* (Madison: University of Wisconsin Press, 1967).

24. Paul E. Lovejoy, "Background to Rebellion: The Origins of Muslim Slaves in Bahia," *Slavery and Abolition* 15, no. 2 (1994): 154–155.

25. Leslie Bethell, *The Abolition of the Brazilian Slave Trade: Britain, Brazil and the Slave Trade Question 1807–1869* (Cambridge: Cambridge University Press, 1970), especially p. 137, note 2; Robert Edgar Conrad, "Neither Slave nor Free: The *Emancipados* of Brazil, 1818–1868," *HAHR* 53, no. 1 (1973): 50–70; and Conrad, *World of Sorrow*, chapter 3.

26. Arquivo Público do Estado da Bahia, Salvador, Brazil (hereafter APB), Seção Histórica, maços 1404–1406, 2896. On "free Africans," see James Bandinel, *Some Accounts of the Trade in Slaves from Africa as Connected with Europe and Africa* (London: Longman, Brown, 1862); W. D. Christie, *Notes on Brazilian Questions* (London: Macmillan, 1865); Conrad, *World of Sorrow*, chapter 7. On the employment of "free Africans" in Bahia, see, for example, "Fala de Francisco Gonçalves Martins" (1852), in *Fala receitada da Assembléia Legislativa (falas e relatorios dos presidentes em exercio da Provincia)* (Bahia, 1839–1889), pp. 27–28; APB, maço 2885, Relação dos africanos livres illicitamente importados no Imperio, apprehendidos e destribudos na Capital da Provincia da Bahia. On their employment at the Santa Casa da Misericórdia of Salvador, see Arquivo da Santa Casa da Misericórdia, Livros do assentamento dos africanos livres à serviço da Santa Casa, nos. 52–62, B2–200.

27. Eltis, *Economic Growth*, p. 244.

28. Ibid., p. 199.

29. Ibid., pp. 243–244.

30. I consulted baptismal records registered in Santo Antônio parish for two out of every ten years between 1809 and 1869. My data include 211 male and 202 female African-born adult slaves, and distribution is as follows: 44 males and 55 females (1809–1810); 80 males and 61 females (1818–1819); 80 males and 80 females (1828–1829); 2 males and 2 females (1838–1839); 4 females (1848–1849); and 5 males and 1 female (1858). After 1851, when the transatlantic slave trade to Brazil was officially terminated, there were only 6 African-born slaves baptized in Santo Antônio parish, and they appear to have gone unbaptized for at least eight years after arrival in Brazil. The number of baptisms of African-born slaves dropped drastically in the 1830s, a direct result of the virtual termination of the influx of slaves from Africa to Salvador in 1831. See Arquivo da Cúria Metropolitana de São Salvador da Bahia (hereafter ACMS), Livros de batizados, freguesia de Santo Antônio. These years are 1809–1810, 1828–

1829, 1838–1839, 1848–1849, 1858–1859, and 1868–1869. The irregularity in this sample, namely for 1809–1810, is because the data in 1808 were totally inadequate. Church archives of Salvador seem to have lost most of the registers for that year. It should be also emphasized regarding baptismal records that Santo Antônio parish is one of the few whose data were nearly complete among major parishes of Salvador in the nineteenth century. For instance, those of Sé are not acceptable, because of the physical deterioration of the registers.

31. Bethell, *Abolition of the Brazilian Slave Trade,* chapter 12. The number of slaves imported from Africa to Brazil for 1851–1855 amounted to 6,100 (3,300 for the South of Bahia; 1,900 for Bahia; and 900 for the North of Bahia). No more slaves were imported to either Bahia or the North of Bahia, but 300 slaves were still imported to the South of Bahia in 1856. Eltis, *Economic Growth,* p. 244. On the abolition of the transatlantic slave trade in general, see David Eltis and James Walvin, eds., *The Abolition of the Atlantic Slave Trade: Origins and Effects in Europe, Africa, and the Americas* (Madison: University of Wisconsin Press, 1981).

32. M. I. Finley, "Slavery," in *International Encyclopedia of the Social Sciences,* vol. 14 (New York: Macmillan and Free Press, 1968), p. 308.

33. Kátia de M. Queirós Mattoso and her former graduate students at the Federal University of Bahia have produced substantial research on urban slavery and urban society in Salvador during the nineteenth century. See Kátia de M. Queirós Mattoso, *Entre esclave au Brésil: XVIe–XIXe* (Paris: Hachette, 1979), which has been translated by Arthur Goldhammer as *To Be a Slave in Brazil, 1550–1888* (New Brunswick, N.J.: Rutgers University Press, 1986), and *Bahia, século XIX: uma província no império* (Rio de Janeiro: Editora Nova Fronteira, 1992); Maria Inês Côrtes de Oliveria, *O liberto: o seu mundo e os outros* (São Paulo: Corrupio, 1988); João Josè Reis, *Rebelião escrava no Brasil: a história do levante dos malês (1835),* 2nd ed. (São Paulo: Editora Brasiliense, 1987), which has been translated by Arthur Brakel as *Slave Rebellion in Brazil: The Muslim Uprising of 1835 in Bahia* (Baltimore: Johns Hopkins University Press, 1993); and Maria José de Souza Andrade, *A mão de obra escrava em Salvador 1811–1860* (São Paulo: Corrupio, 1988).

34. Curtin, *Atlantic Slave Trade,* pp. 19, 41–47; and Herbert S. Klein, "African Women in the Atlantic Slave Trade," in Claire C. Robertson and Martin A. Klein, eds., *Women and Slavery in Africa* (Madison: University of Wisconsin Press, 1983).

35. Claire C. Robertson and Martin A. Klein, "Women's Importance in African Slave Systems," in Robertson and Klein, eds., *Women and Slavery in Africa,* especially pp. 3–11; and William D. Phillips, Jr., *Slavery from Roman Times to the Early Transatlantic Trade* (Minneapolis: University of Minnesota Press, 1985), pp. 122–123.

36. Eltis, *Economic Growth,* p. 257.

37. Arquivo Municipal da Cidade do Salvador, Salvador, Brazil (hereafter AMCS), Livros de escrituras da compra e venda de escravos, freguesia da Sé, nos. 82.1–

82.20. Sé parish, which was founded in 1552 as the second oldest parish in Bahia, had the most important role as the administrative and ecclesiastical center, not only for the city, but also for the captaincy of Bahia. In about 1724, one quarter of the population of the city was concentrated in Sé, and in 1807, 21.8 percent of the population were residents of this parish located at the center of the city. See Schwartz, *Sugar Plantations*, p. 88; and Luís dos Santos Vilhena, *A Bahia no século XVIII*, vol. 2 (Bahia: Editora Itapuã, 1969), p. 460.

38. APB, Seção Histórica, maço 1549, caderno 2 (São Pedro Velho parish, quarteirão 15 [1855]); maço 1602 (Sé parish, quarteiroes 20, 21, 22, 23 [1855]); Santo Antônio parish, 1st district, quarteirão 18 [1855]; São Pedro Velho parish, quarteirão 1 [1855]; São Passo parish, quarteirão 6; maço 1605 (Santana parish, quarteirão 3 [1855]); San Antônio parish, 1st district, quarteirão 15 and 2nd district, quarteirão 11 [1855]; and Brasil, *Recenseamento da população*, p. 510.

39. Schwartz, *Sugar Plantations*, pp. 347–389.

40. Andrade, *A mãe de obra escrava*, pp. 129, 130.

41. APB, Seção Judiciária, Inventários da capital (1808–1888). The 370 inventories I consulted comprise 14 (registered for the period 1808–9); 30 (1810–19); 16 (1820–29); 37 (1830–39); 57 (1840–49); 88 (1850–59); 58 (1860–69); 42 (1860–69); and 28 (1880–88). Male-female ratios in these data are 2:1 among the African-born and 49:51 among the Brazilian-born for the period 1808–1849; and 59:41 among the African-born and 49:51 among the Brazilian-born for the period 1850–1888. Among the slaves of African birth, men largely outnumbered women. This is because the 370 inventories of slave owners include some owners of large-scale plantations of suburban Salvador, where the majority of the registered slaves were male field workers. For instance, the inventory of Pedro de Espirito Santo, registered in 1850, showed that he owned 126 slaves, of whom only 45 were women (APB, Inventário da capital, 04/1624/2093/01). Therefore I do not interpret these data derived from the inventories of slave owners as negating my discussion on balance by sex in urban slavery.

42. Maria Luiza Marcílio, "The Prices of Slaves in XIXth Century Brazil: A Quantitative Analysis of the Registration of Slave Sales in Bahia," *Studi in memoria di Federigo Melis*, vol. 5 (Paris: Giannini Editore, 1978), pp. 90, 92. In writing amounts of *réis*, the symbol used in the U.S. as a dollar sign ($) separates the thousands from the hundreds, as a comma does in writing U.S. dollar amounts.

43. AMCS, Livros de escrituras de compra e venda de escravos, freguesia da Sé.

44. Manuel Moreno Fraginals, Herbert S. Klein, and Stanley L. Engerman, "The Level and Structure of Slave Prices on Cuban Plantations in the Mid-Nineteenth Century: Some Comparative Perspectives," *AHR* 88, no. 5 (1983): 1201–1218, especially 1219–1223.

45. APB, Inventários da capital. Forty-two individuals (11.4%) owned 11–20 slaves. Nine owned 20–29 slaves, while the rest owned 39, 54, 57, and 126 slaves.

46. Reis, *Rebelião escrava*, p. 25.

47. APB, Seção Histórica, maço 1070-4, artigo 3 (December 7, 1832).

48. On slave wet-nurses in the city, see Robert Edgar Conrad, *Children of God's Fire: A Documentary History of Black Slavery in Brazil* (Princeton, N.J.: Princeton University Press, 1983), pp. 133–140.

49. Maria Graham briefly mentioned the *loja*. See Maria Dundas Graham, *Journal of a Voyage to Brazil and Residence There, during Part of the Years 1821, 1822, 1823* (New York: Frederick A. Praeger, 1969 [1824]), p. 149. The surviving census records of 1855, for instance, reveal the residence pattern among live-out urban slaves. See APB, maços 1549, 1602 and 1605.

50. James Wetherell, *Brazil: Stray Notes from Bahia: Being Extracts from Letters, &c., during a Residence of Fifteen Years*, ed. William Hadfield (Liverpool: Webb and Hunt, 1860), pp. 16–17.

51. Johann B. von Spix and Carl Friedrich P. von Martius, *Viagem pelo Brasil*, vol. 2, trans. Lúcia Furquim Lahmeyer, 2nd ed. (Rio de Janeiro: Impresa Nacional, 1938), p. 301.

52. Edison Carneiro, *Ladinos e crioulos* (Rio de Janeiro: Editôra Civilização Brasileira, 1964), p. 9.

53. APB, maço 2898, Relação dos africanos libertos existentes nesta freguesia, Santana, February 11, 1849.

54. Alexander Marjoribanks, *Travels in South and North America*, 5th ed. (London: Simpkin, Marshall, 1854), pp. 67–68.

55. On "hiring-out" and "hiring one's time out," see Richard C. Wade, *Slavery in the Cities: The South 1820–1860* (New York: Oxford University Press, 1964), pp. 38–40, 48–49.

56. APB, Inventários da capital; and Reis, *Rebelião escrava*, pp. 208–209. Karasch analyzes these diverse "functions" of urban slaves in early nineteenth-century Rio de Janeiro. See Mary C. Karasch, "From Porterage to Proprietorship: African Occupations in Rio de Janeiro, 1808–1850," in Stanley L. Engerman and Eugene D. Genovese, eds., *Race and Slavery in the Western Hemisphere: Quantitative Studies* (Princeton, N.J.: Princeton University Press, 1975); idem, "Suppliers, Sellers, Servants, and Slaves," in Louisa Schell Hoberman and Susan Migden Socolow, eds., *Cities and Society in Colonial Latin America* (Albuquerque: University of New Mexico Press, 1986); idem, *Slave Life*, chapter 7. See also Luiz Carlos Soares, "Os escravos de ganho no Rio de Janeiro do século XIX," *Revista Brasileira de História* 8, no. 16 (1988): 107–142.

57. Bandinel, *Some Accounts*, p. 288.

58. On the coffee plantations and labor in the Southeast, see Stanley J. Stein, *Vassouras, a Brazilian Coffee County, 1850–1900: The Role of Planter and Slave in a Plantation Society* (Princeton, N.J.: Princeton University Press, 1985 [1957]).

59. On the internal slave trade, see Herbert S. Klein, *The Middle Passage: Comparative Studies in the Atlantic Slave Trade* (Princeton, N.J.: Princeton University Press, 1978), chapter 5; and Conrad, *World of Sorrow*, chapter 8.

60. Thomas W. Merrick and Douglas H. Graham, *Population and Economic Devel-*

opment in Brazil: 1800 to the Present (Baltimore: Johns Hopkins University Press, 1979), pp. 50–52.

61. Klein, *Middle Passage,* pp. 102–105, 114.

62. Finley, "Slavery," p. 308. According to Finley, *genuine* slave societies include classical Greece (except Sparta) and Rome, the American South, and the Caribbean, whereas *slave-owning* societies are found in the ancient Near East (including Egypt), India, and China. See ibid., p. 306. His italics.

63. Finley emphasizes that it is not the absolute number or proportion of slaves, but rather their location and function that characterize a society that holds and uses slaves. He maintains: "It does not matter, in such situations, whether as many as three-fourths were not slaveowners, or whether slavery was not fairly widespread outside the elite in domestic or other nonproductive roles." See ibid., p. 308.

64. Philip D. Morgan, in his study on varying race relations in the first British Empire, employs the same definition of "slave societies" and "slaveowning societies": "In the former, some slaves exist; in the latter, slavery is *the* determinative institution. A slaveowning society may become a slave society, but only when a significant proportion of its population is enslaved (say, for argument's sake, more than 20 percent) and, more important, when slavery becomes central to the economic functioning of that society." Morgan does not tell how he has calculated 20 percent for the distinction. See Philip D. Morgan, "British Encounters with Africans and African-Americans, circa 1600–1780," in Bernard Bailyn and Philip D. Morgan, eds., *Strangers within the Realm: Cultural Margins of the First British Empire* (Chapel Hill: University of North Carolina Press, 1991), p. 163. His italics.

65. Among the 3,156 letters of liberty I consulted for this study, there were only 16 in which ex-owners declare that they themselves were African-born ex-slaves. See APB, Livros de notas and maço 135. This may be a reflection of the fact that a very small percentage of ex-slaves could become slave owners. For instance, 186 out of 207 (89.9%) African-born ex-slaves who resided in Conceição da Praia parish (1846) did not own a single slave. Likewise, 263 out of 331 (79.5%) African-born ex-slaves who resided in Santana parish (1849) were not slave owners. See APB, maço 6472, Arollomento dos africanos libertos . . . Conceição da Praia, 1846; ibid, maço 2898, Relação dos africanos libertos . . . Santana. On non–slave owners in colonial and imperial Brazil, see Iraci del Nero da Costa, *Arraia-miúda: um estudo sobre os não-proprietários de escravos no Brasil* (São Paulo: MGSP Editôres Ltda., 1992).

66. AMCS, Livros de escrituras de compra e venda de escravos, freguesia da Sé, nos. 82.1–82.20. The Municipal Archives of Salvador (AMCS) house numbers of legal documents concerning slaves registered in the parishes of the city. Among them, those for Sé parish have been preserved almost in their entirety. Maria Luiza Marcílio consulted the same type of slave sale registers (the total of 2,527) in Pilar parish of Salvador for 1838–1882. However, she analyzes only 544 cases of slaves who were either domestics or field hands, and without any

physical defects, registered for 1850–1882, and does not make any breakdown of the period. See Marcílio, "Prices of Slaves," pp. 83–97.

67. APB, Livros de notas and maço 2898.

68. Moreno Fraginals, Klein, and Engerman, "Level and Structure of Slave Prices," pp. 1207–1209.

69. APB, Livros de notas and maço 2898. In writing amounts of *réis*, the colon separates the millions from the thousands, as a comma does in writing U.S. dollar amounts.

70. AMCS, Livros de escrituras de compra e venda de escravos, freguesia da Sé.

71. Klein, *Middle Passage*, p. 101.

72. APB, Livros de notas and maço 135. On slave prices recorded in the inventories of slave owners in Salvador for 1811–1888, see Andrade, *A mão de obra escrava*, pp. 207–211.

73. Merrick and Graham maintain: "Approximately one out of every two freed slaves gained their freedom through self-purchase. This proportion grew (and gratis manumissions declined) during periods of rising slave prices." See Merrick and Graham, *Population and Economic Development*, p. 53.

74. AMCS, Livros de escrituras da compra e venda de escravos, freguesia da Sé. Occupations of male slaves: domestics, 326 (66.3%); fieldwork, 126 (25.6%); wage earning, 16 (3.2%); artisans, 15 (3.0%); maritime, 7 (1.4%); others, 3 (0.5%). Occupations of female slaves: domestics, 510 (81.5%); fieldwork, 109 (17.4%); wage earning, 5 (0.8%); maritime, 2 (0.3%). Occupations of slaves were not listed in these legal registers until 1861.

75. For figures on slaves in nineteenth-century newspaper advertisements, see Gilberto Freyre, *O escravo nos anúncios de jornais brasileiros do século XIX*, 2nd ed. (São Paulo: Companhia Editora Nacional, 1979). The first monograph on urban domestic slaves in Brazil is Gilberto Freyre's *Sobrados e mucambos* (1936), whose English translation is *The Mansions and the Shanties: The Making of Modern Brazil.*

76. Schwartz, *Sugar Plantations*, pp. 52–53.

77. A. J. R. Russell-Wood, *The Black Man in Slavery and Freedom in Colonial Brazil* (New York: St. Martin's Press, 1982), and personal communication.

78. My research does not support Barbara Trosko's assertion on the time of change in terminology: "With the arrival of the Paraguayan War in 1867, *forro* ceded to the more genetic term *liberto*." See Barbara Rose Trosko, "The Liberto in Bahia before Abolition" (M.A. thesis, Columbia University, 1967), p. 4.

2. The Creation of New Identity, 1808–1831

1. Paul E. Lovejoy, *Transformations in Slavery: A History of Slavery in Africa* (Cambridge: Cambridge University Press, 1983), p. 143. See also Patterson, *Slavery and Social Death*, chapter 4.

2. A. C. de C. M. Saunders, *A Social History of Black Slaves and Freedmen in Portugal, 1441–1555* (Cambridge: Cambridge University Press, 1982), chapter 2.

3. Henry Koster, *Travels in Brazil 1809–1815*, vol. 2 (London: Longman, Hurst, Rees, Ormes, and Brown, 1817), pp. 238–239.

4. Frederick P. Bowser, *The African Slave in Colonial Peru 1524–1650* (Stanford, Calif.: Stanford University Press, 1974), p. 47.

5. Jack Goody, "Writing, Religion, and Revolt in Bahia," *Visible Language* 20, no. 3 (1986): 319–320.

6. Ibid., p. 320.

7. Koster, *Travels in Brazil*, vol. 2, p. 252. My italics.

8. Curtin, *Atlantic Slave Trade*, pp. 184–190.

9. On slave stereotypes and prices in accordance with their "nationalities" in the case of South Carolina, see Daniel C. Littlefield, *Rice and Slaves: Ethnicity and the Slave Trade in Colonial South Carolina* (Baton Rouge: Louisiana State University Press, 1981), chapter 1.

10. Thomas Lindley, *Narrative of a Voyage to Brazil* (London: Printed for J. Johnson, 1805), p. 269.

11. Koster, *Travels in Brazil*, vol. 2, pp. 252–258. See also Lindley, *Narrative of a Voyage to Brazil*, p. 269.

12. Spix and Martius, *Viagem pelo Brasil*, vol. 2, p. 300.

13. See Karasch's largely static treatment of "nations" in early nineteenth-century Rio de Janeiro in her *Slave Life*, chapter 1.

14. Koster, *Travels in Brazil*, vol. 2, pp. 251, 293.

15. "Devassa do levante de escravos occorido em Salvador em 1835," *Anais do Arquivo Público do Estado da Bahia* (hereafter *AAEB*) 38 (1968): 1–142, 32–38. On *malungos*, see Karasch, *Slave Life*, p. 298.

16. Lovejoy, "Background to Rebellion," p. 155.

17. Mintz and Price, *Birth of African-American Culture*, pp. 43, 44: Mintz and Price, *Anthropological Approach*, pp. 22, 23. The "shipmate" relationship has been cited as *malungue* in Trinidad, *mati* in Suriname, and *batiment* in Haiti. See Mintz and Price, *Birth of African American Culture*, p. 44; *Anthropological Approach*, p. 23.

18. Walsh, *Notices of Brazil*, pp. 323–328; Maria Graham, *Journal of a Voyage to Brazil*, pp. 227–228. On the slave market of Rio de Janeiro, see also Karasch, *Slave Life*, chapter 2. Once the slave trade was banned in Brazil, the Valongo itself was declared illegal on November 7, 1831, but much of the business in slaves continued as before, even after 1850. See Karasch, *Slave Life*, p. 36.

19. Lindley, *Narrative of a Voyage to Brazil*, p. 176.

20. A building that formerly housed the slave market on Baixa dos Sapateiros is now owned by the municipal council of Salvador, and has been transformed

into a museum of West African cultures and named Casa de Benin. Founders included the late French anthropologist Pierre Verger.

21. See, for instance, Proposta (December 2, 1828), articles 2 and 8, Presidência da Provincia Conselho Geral da Provincia (Correspondencia recebida), 1829–1834, APB, Seção Histórica, maço 1070–4.

22. The Pelourinho provided slave owners with an ideal place for whipping since whipping was, as the historian Ira Berlin clarifies, "an instrument of social discipline intended to impress not only the immediate victim but also all who witnessed it." See Berlin, "Herbert G. Gutman," p. 45.

23. AMCS, Livro de posturas, no. 119.6, fs. 71, 107 (April 25, 1843).

24. APB, Seção Histórica, maço 2681.

25. Ibid., maço 2951.

26. Marcus J. M. de Carvalho, *Liberdade: rotinas e ruptures do escravismo no Recife, 1822–1850* (Recife: Editora Universitaria de UFPE, 1998), chapter 13. I thank Professor Joseph C. Love for the citation.

27. APB, Seção Histórica, maço 2951.

28. Ibid., maço 2680, caixa 1047.

29. Ibid., maço 2681.

30. APB, Inventários da capital.

31. On the streets of Salvador, see, for instance, Wetherell, *Brazil: Stray Notes from Bahia*, p. 7; and Andrew Grant, *History of Brazil* (London: Printed for Henry Colburn, 1809), p. 208.

32. On *bicho da pé*, see Lindley, *Narratives of a Voyage*, p. 153; and Wetherell, *Brazil: Stray Notes from Bahia*, p. 19.

33. The archives of Santa Casa da Misericórdia da Bahia house a book of registers of slaves and "free Africans." Many of these registers recorded the ethnic mark of the individual African-born. See Arquivo da Santa Casa da Misercórdia da Bahia, Livro de assentamento dos escravos de Santa Casa (B.3.220); Livro do assentamento dos africanos livres à serviço da Santa Casa, 1852–1862 (B.2.200); and Livro de matricula dos africanos livres à serviço da Santa Casa, 1862–1864 (B.2.201).

34. Wetherell, *Brazil: Stray Notes from Bahia*, p. 134. His italics.

35. Ibid., p. 5.

36. Ibid., p. 5.

37. Ibid., p. 54.

38. Henderson, *History of Brazil*, p. 340.

39. Ibid.

40. Wetherell, *Brazil: Stray Notes from Bahia*, p. 5.

41. Biblioteca Nacional do Rio de Janeiro, Rio de Janeiro, Brazil (hereafter BNRJ), II-34.6.57.

42. Spix and Martius, *Viagem pelo Brasil,* vol. 2, p. 300.

43. Nina Rodrigues, *Os africanos no Brasil,* 3rd ed. (São Paulo: Companhia Editôra Nacional, 1945), chapter 6.

44. Donald Pierson, *Negroes in Brazil: A Study of Race Contact at Bahia* (Chicago: University of Chicago Press, 1941), pp. 72–73.

45. For example, many African-born participants, both slave and ex-slave, in the Malê Revolt of 1835 were identified by other people of African birth with their African names only. See the trial and judicial records of the Revolt, many of which were published by the State Archives of Bahia as "Devassa do levante de escravos occorido em Salvador em 1835," *AAEB* 38 (1968): 1–142; and "1835 Insurreição de escravos," *AAEB* 40 (1970): 9–170. See also Prince, "Slave Rebellions," p. 186; and Reis, *Rebelião escrava,* p. 197 (Table 7).

46. Franklin W. Knight and Margaret E. Crahan, "The African Migration and the Origin of an Afro-American Society and Culture," in Crahan and Knight, eds., *Africa and the Caribbean: The Legacies of the Link* (Baltimore: Johns Hopkins University Press, 1979), p. 12.

47. Epstein, *Ethos and Identity,* p. 40.

48. "Devassa do levante," p. 7.

49. Reis, *Rebelião escrava,* p. 190.

50. J. C. Mitchell, "Perceptions of Ethnicity and Ethnic Behaviour: An Empirical Exploration," in Abner Cohen, ed., *Urban Ethnicity* (London: Tavistock Publications, 1974), p. 1.

51. Jacqueline Jones, *Labor of Love, Labor of Sorrow: Black Women, Work, and the Family from Slavery to the Present* (New York, Basic Books, 1985), p. 38. Recent works on slave women in the Caribbean include Hilary McD. Beckles, *Natural Rebels: A Social History of Enslaved Black Women in Barbados* (New Brunswick, N.J.: Rutgers University Press, 1989); Barbara Bush, *Slave Women in Caribbean Society 1650–1835* (Bloomington: Indiana University Press, 1990); and Marietta Morrissey, *Slave Women in the New World: Gender Stratification in the Caribbean* (Lawrence: University Press of Kansas, 1989).

52. Maria Graham, *Journal of a Voyage to Brazil,* p. 133. See also Grant, *History of Brazil,* pp. 235–236; Marjoribanks, *Travels in South and North America,* pp. 94–95.

53. Wetherell, *Brazil: Stray Notes from Bahia,* p. 53; Marjoribanks, *Travels in South and North America,* p. 46.

54. James C. Fletcher and Daniel P. Kidder, *Brazil and the Brazilians: Portrayed in Historical and Descriptive Sketches,* 9th ed. (Boston: Little, Brown, 1879), pp. 475–476.

55. Wetherell, *Brazil: Stray Notes from Bahia,* p. 53. The British traveler Alexander Marjoribanks made a similar observation: "The pole rests upon their bare shoulders, and in order to mark time they have a singular sort of cry as they

proceed along the streets, sung in a kind of melancholy cadence, that proceeding from those in front being on a higher key than from those behind." See Marjoribanks, *Travels in South and North America*, p. 46.

56. AMCS, Livro de posturas, no. 119.1, f. 132.

57. Wetherell, *Brazil: Stray Notes from Bahia*, p. 106. It is only in the late nineteenth century that communication facilities were substantially improved. In 1853, a major steamboat line named the Companhia de Navegação a Vapor Bahiana started service around the Bay of All Saints. Steamboat service along the inland São Francisco River began in 1865. In 1863 the E. F. Bahia–São Francisco rail line reached Alagoinhas, 123 kilometers north of the capital, but it was not until 1896 that the railroad finally connected the capital to the São Francisco River. See Dain Borges, *The Family in Bahia, Brazil 1870–1945* (Stanford, Calif.: Stanford University Press, 1992), pp. 21–22.

58. Wetherell, *Brazil: Stray Notes from Bahia*, p. 26.

59. Borges, *Family in Bahia*, p. 21.

60. Maria Graham, *Journal of a Voyage to Brazil*, p. 145.

61. Spix and Martius, *Viagem pelo Brasil*, p. 290.

62. Wetherell, *Brazil: Stray Notes from Bahia*, pp. 26–27.

63. Ibid., pp. 31, 107–108; Spix and Martius, *Viagem pelo Brasil*, vol. 2, p. 290.

64. Wetherell, *Brazil: Stray Notes from Bahia*, p. 87. Wetherell continued to state: "[I]t is their custom to mix in small quantities of a crystallized substance called 'cong.' in a powdered state, and which is imported from the coast of Africa" (ibid., p. 87). James Prior mentioned the prevailing practice of smoking among the population of the city, particularly the lower class. See Prior, *Voyage along the East Coast of Africa to Mosambique* (London: Printed for St. Richard Phillips, 1819), p. 104.

65. Wetherell, *Brazil: Stray Notes from Bahia*, p. 26.

66. Karasch, "From Porterage to Proprietorship," p. 379. George Gardner stated in 1836 that the small boats and canoes in the bay of Rio de Janeiro were "all manned with African blacks." See Gardner, *Travels in the Interior of Brazil*, p. 4.

67. Grant, *History of Brazil*, p. 29; Wetherell, *Brazil: Stray Notes from Bahia*, p. 139.

68. Lindley, *Narrative of a Voyage to Brazil*, pp. 152–153.

69. Gardner, *Travels in the Interior of Brazil*, p. 78; Tollenare, *Notas dominiais*, pp. 218–222; and Elwes, *Sketcher's Tour*, pp. 97–98.

70. On African American seamen in British America and the theme of African Atlantic communication, see Julius Sherrard Scott III, "The Common Wind: Currents of Afro-American Communication in the Era of the Haitian Revolution" (Ph.D. diss, Duke University, 1986); and W. Jeffrey Bolster, "'To Feel Like a Man': Black Seamen in the Northern States, 1800–1860," *Journal of*

American History 76, no. 4 (1990): 1173–1199; idem, *Black Jacks: African American Seamen in the Age of Sail* (Cambridge, Mass.: Harvard University Press, 1997).

71. Andrade, *A mão de obra*, p. 129.

72. Lyman L. Johnson, "Artisans," in Hoberman and Socolow, eds., *Cities and Society*, p. 240. According to Johnson, analysis of the average prices paid for young unskilled African-born slaves and for skilled slave artisans reveals that profits of 200 or 300 percent were not uncommon, even after the costs of the slave's maintenance were subtracted. See ibid., p. 240.

73. Ibid., p. 240.

74. APB, Inventários da capital.

75. Ewbank, *Life in Brazil*, p. 195. See also Wetherell, *Brazil: Stray Notes from Bahia*, pp. 77–78, 151.

76. I have not found any laws in Salvador forbidding slaves and/or free people of African descent from selling specific commodities. However, in the British Caribbean there were laws stipulating what slaves could sell. These laws were designed to protect poor whites who were trying to make a living in the same way slaves did. See Michael Mullin, *Africa in America: Slave Acculturation and Resistance in the American South and the British Caribbean, 1736–1831* (Urbana: University of Illinois Press, 1992), p. 155. On the slaves' economic activities in the informal market of the Caribbean and mainland North America, see Ira Berlin and Philip D. Morgan, eds., *The Slaves' Economy: Independent Production by Slaves in the Americas* (London: Frank Cass, 1991).

77. Spix and Martius, *Viagem pelo Brasil*, p. 299.

78. Wetherell, *Brazil: Stray Notes from Bahia*, pp. 89–90. According to Wetherell, by 1855 a company had been established to supply the principal portion of the city from pipes through the streets. In 1857, Wetherell mentioned some beautiful public fountains, which had been erected by the new company for supplying the city with water. See ibid., pp. 152–153.

79. AMCS, Livro de posturas, 119.1, fs. 3, 31.

80. Karasch, "Suppliers, Sellers, Servants, and Slaves," p. 271.

81. John Clarke, *Memorials of Baptist Missionaries in Jamaica* (London, 1869), pp. 9–11, cited by Mullin, *Africa in America*, p. 155; Mullin, *Africa in America*, p. 131.

82. Sandra Lauderdale Graham discusses the social landscape of "house" and "street" for female domestic servants, both slave and free, in the city of Rio de Janeiro for the period 1860–1910. In her model, "house" and "street" are dichotomous and function as reciprocal social spheres. See Sandra Lauderdale Graham, *House and Street: The Domestic World of Servants and Masters in Nineteenth-Century Rio de Janeiro* (Cambridge: Cambridge University Press, 1988). For the house/street dichotomy in Brazilian culture, see Roberto

DaMatta, *A casa & a rua: espaço, cidadania, mulher e morte no Brasil* (São Paulo: Brasiliense, 1985).

83. Fox-Genovese discusses the slave woman's dual membership in the plantation household and the slave community in the antebellum South: "Slave women lived between the two worlds of the plantation household and the slave community. . . . Their experiences unfolded two different realities: the domination of their white masters and their relations within the black slave community. Their lives and their identities as women combined their strands into a complex and distinctive pattern. From birth, the slave girl's dual membership in the plantation household and the slave community shaped her identity." See Elizabeth Fox-Genovese, *Within the Plantation Household: Black and White Women of the South* (Chapel Hill: University of North Carolina Press, 1988), p. 146.

84. Women's monopoly of small trade is still widely observed in many Third World cities. See Sidney W. Mintz, "Men, Women, and Trade," *Comparative Studies in Society and History* 13, no. 3 (1971): 247–269; Ximena Bunster and Elsa M. Chaney, *Sellers and Servants: Working Women in Lima, Peru* (New York: Praeger, 1985); and Nancy Rose Hunt, "Placing African Women's History and Locating Gender," *Social History* 14, no. 3 (1989): 363.

85. Marisol de la Cadena, " 'Women Are More Indians': Ethnicity and Gender in a Community near Cuzco," in Brooke Larson and Olivia Harris, eds., with Enrique Tandeter, *Ethnicity, Markets, and Migration in the Andes: At the Crossroads of History and Anthropology* (Durham, N.C.: Duke University Press, 1995), pp. 341–342.

86. Grant, *History of Brazil*, pp. 239–240.

87. Vilhena, *Bahia*, vol. 1, p. 93.

88. Wetherell, *Brazil: Stray Notes from Bahia*, pp. 29–30.

89. For a discussion of food, the concept of pollution, and ethnic identity in the Indian diaspora in Trinidad, see Aisha Khan, "*Juthaa* in Trinidad: Food, Pollution, and Hierarchy in a Caribbean Diaspora Community," *American Ethnologist* 21, no. 2 (1994): 245–269.

90. APB, Seção Histórica, maço 1400, *Postura* of August 18, 1847.

91. Wetherell, *Brazil: Stray Notes from Bahia*, p. 27.

92. Daniel D. Kidder, *Sketches of Residence and Travels in Brazil*, vol. 2 (Philadelphia: Sorin and Ball, 1845), pp. 24–25.

93. Wetherell, *Brazil: Stray Notes from Bahia*, p. 21.

94. AMCS, Livro de Posturas, no. 119.1, f. 122B (November 15, 1785); and Vilhena, *Bahia*, vol. 1, pp. 126–127.

95. Wetherell, *Brazil: Stray Notes from Bahia*, pp. 83–84. The British Reverend Hamlet Clark, visiting Salvador in December 1856, came across a lonely spot in the suburbs, where eighty or more women and girls of color were washing

clothes in a pool of water, and were drying them in the hot sun. He described the scene as "the cruel way in which they murdered the linen, beating it with rough sticks, pointing with stones and amidst a chorus of screams of laughter and noise that was very far removed from English ways!" See Hamlet Clark, *Letters from Spain, Algeria, and Brazil during Past Entomological Rambles* (London: John van Woorst, Paternoster Row, 1867), pp. 105–106. On laundresses in the city of Rio, see Ewbank, *Life in Brazil*, pp. 113–114.

96. In his small, but still interesting, article entitled "Gossip and Scandal," social anthropologist Max Gluckman stresses the important function of gossip in maintaining social groups. See Max Gluckman, "Gossip and Scandal: Papers in Honour of Melville J. Herskovits," *Current Anthropology* 4, no. 3 (1963): 307–316. Gluckman maintains that gossips and scandals "are enjoyed by people about others with whom they are in a close social relationship." He continues: "The right to gossip about certain people is a privilege which is only extended to a person when he or she is accepted as a member of a group or set. It is a hallmark of membership" (ibid., p. 313). On gossip networks, see also A. L. Epstein, "Gossip, Norms and Social Network," in Mitchell, ed., *Social Networks*. Ruth Behar and Sonya Lipsett-Rivera respectively discuss the important function of gossip in controlling women's behaviors for the sake of patriarchalism in the case of colonial Mexico. See Ruth Behar, "Sexual Witchcraft, Colonialism, and Women's Powers: Views from the Mexican Inquisition," in Asunción Lavrin, ed., *Sexuality and Marriage in Colonial Latin America* (Lincoln: University of Nebraska Press, 1989); Sonya Lipsett-Rivera, "A Slap in the Face of Honor: Social Transgression and Women in Late Colonial Mexico," in Lyman L. Johnson and Sonya Lipsett-Rivera, eds., *The Faces of Honor: Sex, Shame, and Violence in Colonial Latin America* (Albuquerque: University of New Mexico Press, 1998).

97. Epstein, *Ethos and Identity*, p. 14.

3. The Representation of Identity, 1808–1831

1. J. da Silva Campos, "Ligeiras notas sobre a vida íntima; costumes e religião dos africanos na Bahia," *AAEB* 29 (1943): 291–309.

2. Rodrigues, *Os africanos*, pp. 174–175. In the mid-1870s such *cantos* were principally located on Rua do Alvo, or Rua dos Nagôs as it was popularly known, and, to a lesser degree, on other streets of Santana parish. A large number of the African-born population congregated in public streets of Santana, Sé, and Pilar parishes. See Campos, "Ligeiras notas," pp. 292–293.

3. Rodrigues, *Os africanos*, p. 175.

4. Campos, "Ligeiras notas," p. 291. In the 1870s, they cut hair for half of a *pataca* (160 *réis*) for every four persons. See ibid., p. 293.

5. Wetherell, *Brazil: Stray Notes from Bahia*, p. 33. Wetherell also stated in 1843: "The blacks have doctors amongst themselves; no matter what ails them, they bind a handkerchief round their heads and consider *that* a cure for all

disorders." See ibid., p. 43. His italics. On the same functions of African-born barber-surgeons in nineteenth-century Rio de Janeiro, see Ewbank, *Life in Brazil*, pp. 282, 293. On barber shops in Rio, see Jean Baptiste Debret, *Viagem pitoresca e histórica ao Brasil*, trans. Sérgio Millet, vol. 1 (São Paulo: Martins and Editora da Universidade de São Paulo, 1972), pp. 151–154.

6. Lindley, *Narratives of a Voyage*, pp. 123–124.

7. Ibid., pp. 71–72.

8. C. R. Boxer, "Some Remarks on the Social and Professional Status of Physicians and Surgeons in the Iberian World, 16th–18th Centuries," *Revista de história de São Paulo* 50, no. 1 (1974): 209. In the years 1741–1749, all thirty-eight licensed barber-surgeons in Salvador were people of African descent: seventeen slaves and twenty-one free blacks or mulattoes. In the years 1810–1822, the thirty-three licensed barber-surgeons in Salvador were composed of twenty slaves and thirteen free men of African descent. See AMCS, vols. 191 and 193, cited by Russell-Wood, *Black Man in Slavery and Freedom*, p. 57. In every city of the U.S. South, barbering was the most important and lucrative work for black men, so that this trade had been closely identified with free blacks by the eve of the Civil War. See Ira Berlin, *Slaves without Masters: The Free Negro in the Antebellum South* (New York: Oxford University Press, 1974), pp. 235–236.

9. Russell-Wood, *Black Man in Slavery and Freedom*, p. 57.

10. See, for instance, Wetherell, *Brazil: Stray Notes from Bahia*, p. 54.

11. Presidência da Provincia Conselho da Provincia (correspondencia recebida), December 2, 1828, article 7, APB, maço 1070-4.

12. Albert J. Raboteau, *Slave Religion: The "Invisible Institution" in the Antebellum South* (New York: Oxford University Press, 1978), p. 15.

13. Vilhena, *Bahia*, vol. 1, p. 134.

14. Arquivo Nacional do Rio de Janeiro, Rio de Janeiro, Brazil (hereafter ANRJ), IJJ9–323, f. 20.

15. On Salvador and Rio de Janeiro as the two major port cities of colonial Brazil, see A. J. R. Russell-Wood, "Ports of Colonial Brazil," in Franklin W. Knight and Peggy K. Liss, eds., *Atlantic Port Cities: Economy, Culture, and Society in the Atlantic World, 1650–1850* (Knoxville: University of Tennessee Press, 1991), pp. 219–229.

16. See, for instance, *O Oculo Mágico*, October 11, 1866, which reported *batuques* in São Miguel, Brotas, and Cabula, where the population of African descent was concentrated. The same article also referred to the funeral feast or celebration which took place among "negros da Costa" in January 1857.

17. Religion of African origins, syncretized with Christianity in the New World through the history of slavery, is called *santería* in Cuba, *shango* in Trinidad, *vaudou* in Haiti. See Raboteau, *Slave Religion*, p. 16. See, for an excellent anthropological study of *santería* in the present-day United States, David Hilary

Brown, "Garden in the Machine: Afro-Cuban Sacred Act and Performance in Urban New Jersey and New York" (Ph.D. diss., Yale University, 1989).

18. Studies on *candomblé* in Bahia include Pierson, *Negroes in Brazil*, chapter 10; Julio Santana Braga, *O jogo de búzios: um estudo da advinação no candomblé* (São Paulo: Editora Brasiliense, 1988); João José Reis, "Magia jeje na Bahia: a invasão do calundo do Pasto de Cachoeira, 1785" *Revista Brasileira de História* 8, no. 16 (1988): 57–81; Fayette Darcell Wimbery, "The African *Liberto* and the Bahian Lower Class: Social Integration in Nineteenth-Century Bahia, Brazil 1870–1900" (Ph.D. diss., University of California at Berkeley, 1989), chapters 4–6; and Rachel E. Harding, *A Refuge in Thunder: Camdomblé and Alternative Spaces of Blackness* (Bloomington: Indiana University Press, 2000).

19. For views on slave cultural independence expressed by colonial authorities and slave owners in eighteenth-century Brazil, see Schwartz, *Sugar Plantations*, p. 484. See also George M. Fredrickson, *The Black Image in the White Mind: The Debate on Afro-American Character and Destiny, 1817–1914* (New York: Harper and Row, 1971); and Celia Maria Marinho de Azevedo, *Onda negra, medo branco: o negro no imaginário das elites no século XIX* (Rio de Janeiro: Paz e Terra, 1987).

20. APB, Livro de registro de testamentos, no. 42, fs. 34–36 (October 13, 1855).

21. Ibid., no. 27, fs. 128–130B (December 18, 1839).

22. Ibid., no. 29, fs. 82B–85. The daughter was her heiress, and also served as executrix of her will. On reunions of African-born kinsfolk in Salvador, see also ibid., no. 13, fs. 61B–68; no. 39, fs. 27–28; no. 40, fs. 76–78; and no. 40, fs. 169B–171B.

23. For the studies of slave families in nineteenth-century Salvador, see, for instance, Kátia M. de Queirós Mattoso, *Família e sociedade na Bahia do século XIX*, trans. James Amado (São Paulo: Corrupio, 1988); idem, "Slave, Free, and Freed Family Structures in Nineteenth-Century Salvador, Bahia," *Luso-Brazilian Review* 25, no. 1 (1988): 69–83.

24. A. J. R. Russell-Wood, personal communication.

25. APB, Seção Judiciária, Livro de registro de testamentos, no. 19, fs. 276B–280B.

26. The 3,516 manumission letters consulted for the years 1808 to 1884 include only four letters in which slaves were recorded as being married. Both in the complete census records of São Pedro Velho parish taken in 1835 and in the surviving census records of Salvador in 1855, no slave was officially recorded as married. The 470 listings in the marriage register of Penha parish for the half century (1808–1857) include only fourteen male slaves and seventeen female slaves who had contracted marriages. Among them there are twelve instances in which both partners were slaves. The marriage register of Conceição da Praia parish for the period 1843–1888 has 763 listings, which do not reveal any marriage in which a slave was one of the partners. See APB, Livros de notas and maço 2880; APB, Seção Histórica, maço 5685, Registro dos fogos e habitantes da freguesia de São Pedro; APB, maços 1549, 1602 and

1605; ACMS, Livros de casamentos, freguesia da Penha; and ACMS, Livros de casamentos, freguesia da Conceição da Praia. It has long been discussed and emphasized in historical literature on Brazilian slavery that in colonial and imperial Brazil, slave marriage was sanctioned by the Church and legally recognized by the State; some travelers from Europe and the U.S. observed and recorded marriage ceremonies for slave couples, which their wealthy owners sponsored. Examples are: Professor and Mrs. Louis Agassiz, *A Journey in Brazil* (Boston: Ticker and Fields, 1868), pp. 129–130; Debret, *Viagem pitoresca*, pp. 174–175. I am grateful to Professor William B. Taylor and Mrs. Barbara Taylor for their generous gift of a rare copy of *A Journey in Brazil*.

27.   Schwartz, *Sugar Plantations*, pp. 387–388; Karasch, *Slave Life*, pp. 287–288.

28.   In view of inheritance, non-property owners, particularly the enslaved who themselves were defined as property and had no legal right to possess any form of property, had no reason to contract matrimony for the succession of property. For instance, few Indian slaves were married in New Mexico for the years 1694–1846 despite the fact that civil and ecclesiastical laws in New Mexico guaranteed them the right to marry freely. See Ramón A. Gutiérrez, *When Jesus Came, the Corn Mothers Went Away: Marriage, Sexuality, and Power in New Mexico, 1500–1846* (Stanford, Calif.: Stanford University Press, 1991), p. 293.

29.   APB, Livros de registro de testamentos. Karasch finds the same preference for the same nation among the enslaved African-born population in early nineteenth-century Rio de Janeiro. See Karasch, *Slave Life*, p. 293.

30.   In Brazil, throughout the colonial and imperial periods, marriage, at least in the official record, referred to church marriage only; no civil marriage was recognized as legal by the State until 1890, when Brazil adopted civil marriage.

31.   ACMS, Livros de batizados, freguesia de Santo Antônio.

32.   Ibid., September 24, 1909; December 10, 1809; December 26, 1809; March 4, 1810; and October 21, 1810. Nineteenth-century Salvador contrasts with the data derived from the four Recôncavo parishes in the eighteenth and early nineteenth centuries. Stephan Gudeman and Stuart B. Schwartz state: "No pattern of godparents from the same African nation can be seen in the documents, and we believe that masters appointed or 'invited' more acculturated slaves to serve as sponsors because of their ability to assist in the baptized's integration into the work force, their defining role." See Stephen Gudeman and Stuart B. Schwartz, "Cleaning Original Sin: Godparenthood and the Baptism of the Slaves in Eighteenth-Century Bahia," in Raymond T. Smith, ed., *Kinship Ideology and Practice in Latin America* (Chapel Hill: University of North Carolina Press, 1984), pp. 51–52.

33.   The only exception in the baptismal records of Santo Antônio parish is ACMS, Livros de batizados, freguesia de Santo Antônio, October 7, 1810.

34.   Manoel Querino, *Costumes africanos no Brasil* (Rio de Janeiro: Civilização Brasileira, 1938), p. 155.

35. Ibid., pp. 154–156.

36. APB, maço 3566/8, cited by Trosko, "The Liberto in Bahia," p. 47.

37. Georges Raeders, *O inimigo cordial do Brasil: o conde de Gobineau no Brasil*, trans. Rosa Freire d'Aguiar (São Paulo: Paz e Terra, 1988), p. 122.

38. In Brazil, throughout the colonial period and the early nineteenth century, black lay sodalities proliferated in areas where a myriad of Africans were intensively imported as slave labor, especially in Bahia, Pernambuco, and Minas Gerais. For African American beneficiary associations during the slavery regime, see Betty M. Kurk, "The African Deviation of Black Fraternal Orders in the United States," *Comparative Studies in Society and History* 25, no. 4 (1983): 559–591.

39. To my knowledge, in the state of Bahia, there is only one existent black sodality whose membership was limited to women: the sodality of Our Lady of the Good Death (irmandade da Nossa Senhora da Boa Morte), which was established by slave women in 1832 in the Recôncavo town of Cachoeira. This black sodality—sisterhood—has never accepted any male members. According to anthropologist Sheila S. Walker, the black sodality of Our Lady of Good Death was established in the Barroquinha Church in Salvador in 1821 and existed in major Bahian towns, but all disappeared except the one in Cachoeira. See Sheila S. Walker, "The Feast of Good Death: An Afro-Catholic Emancipation Celebration in Brazil," *Sage* 3, no. 2 (1986): 27–31, 29. See also Wimbery, "The African *Liberto*," pp. 176–188.

40. Primary criterion for membership of the Santa Casa da Misercórdia of Bahia (founded in Salvador in 1549), was "purity of blood, without any trait of Moorish or Jewish origin, both in the applicant and his wife." Likewise, the Third Order of St. Dominic (founded in 1723), which was established by very successful immigrants from Porto, Viana do Minho, and Lisbon, did not accept Indians, people of African descent, Jews, or even poor whites as its members, and maintained the requirement of "purity of blood" (*limpeza de sangue*). Neither did the Third Order of St. Francis (founded in 1635). See A. J. R. Russell-Wood, *Fidalgos and Philanthropists: The Santa Casa da Misericórdia of Bahia, 1550–1755* (Berkeley and Los Angeles: University of California Press, 1968), p. 124; and João José Reis, *A morte é uma festa: ritos fúnebres e revolta popular no Brasil do século XIX* (São Paulo: Companhia das Letras, 1991), p. 53.

41. A. J. R. Russell-Wood, "Black and Mulatto Brotherhoods in Colonial Brazil: A Study in Collective Behavior," *HAHR* 54, no. 4 (1974): 576.

42. Ibid., p. 595; idem, "Examination of Selected Statutes of Three African Brotherhoods," in Albert Meyers and Diane Elizabeth Hopkins, eds., *Manipulating the Saints: Religious Brotherhoods and Social Integration in Postconquest Latin America* (Hamburg: WAYASBAH, 1988), pp. 224–245; and Manoel Cardozo, "The Lay Brotherhoods of Colonial Bahia," *Catholic Historical Review* 33, no. 1 (1947): 24–30.

43. Stuart B. Schwartz's study of manumission in colonial Bahia does not report a single case in which a slave purchased his or her freedom with a loan from a sodality. See Stuart B. Schwartz, "The Manumission of Slaves in Colonial Brazil: Bahia, 1684–1745," *HAHR* 54, no. 4 (1974): 603–635. Manumission letters registered in Salvador during the nineteenth century do not include such a case either. Wills of ex-slaves included only one case, in which an African-born slave man from Costa da Mina purchased his freedom with a manumission fund borrowed from a black sodality of the Rosary in Lisbon. See Mieko Nishida, "Manumission and Ethnicity in Urban Slavery: Salvador, Brazil, 1808–1888," *HAHR* 73, no. 3 (1993): 385; APB, Seção Judiciária, Livros de registro de testamentos, no. 23, fls. 186–189.

44. Arquivo Histórico Ultramarino (Lisbon), Bahia, papéis avulsos, caixa 48 (July 8, 1733), cited by Stuart B. Schwartz, "Plantations and Peripheries, c. 1580–c. 1750," in Bethell, ed., *Colonial Brazil,* pp. 138–139.

45. This black church was often called the Church of Our Lady of the Rosary of Black People on Shoemakers Street (Igreja de Nossa Senhora do Rosário dos Homens Prêtos da baixa dos Sapateiros) or . . . at the gates of the Carmelite monastery (. . . nas Portas do Carmo) because of its geographical location.

46. "Compromisso da Nossa Senhora do Rosario dos pretos da praya, ano de 1686," chapters 6 and 19, published in A. J. R. Russell-Wood, *Society and Government in Colonial Brazil, 1500–1822* (Brookfield, Vt.: Variorum, 1992), pp. 250–253; Cardoso, "Lay Brotherhoods," pp. 24–30. Chapter 2 of the 1699 statutes of the black sodality of Saint Anthony of Catagerona in São Pedro parish stipulates that a judge, a scribe, a treasurer, a procurator, and an unspecified number of majordomos should be elected by *crioulo* members, while a judge, a scribe, a treasurer, a procurator, and an unspecified number of majordomos also were to be elected by Angolan members. Brazilian-born black women (*crioulas*) and Angolan women should elect their respective officers in the same manner. Manuscript sources on this sodality, including its statutes dated 1699 and 1764, are located in the historical manuscript collection of the Oliveira Lima Library at the Catholic University of America. See Cardozo, "Lay Brotherhoods."

47. Arquivo da Igreja da Nossa Senhora do Rosário dos Homens Prêtos, Salvador, Brazil (hereafter AINS), Livro de entradas dos irmãos (1722–1786). Among those who were admitted to the sodality between 1722 and 1786, only 1,959 members (720 men and 1,239 women) were listed with some indication of legal status and/or origin. They comprised 1,319 slaves (67.3%), 259 ex-slaves (13.2%), and 36 whites (1.8%). African-born members with specific ethnic identifications amounted to 238, while 264 Brazilian-born members were counted. New members of African birth (total 198) were composed of 115 West Africans (103 Gêges, 40 Minas, 10 Nagôs, and 2 Calabars), 69 Angolans, 14 others (13 Benguelas and 1 Mozambique), while Brazilian-born members (total 264) were divided into 142 *crioulos* and 122 mulattoes.

48. For the years from 1798 to 1865 the black sodality of Our Lady of the Rosary in the Pelourinho accepted 1,505 new members. See Jeferson Afonso Bacelar and Maria Conceição Barbosa de Sousa, *O Rosário dos Prêtos do Pelourinho* (Salvador: Fundação do Patrimônio Artistico e Cultura da Bahia, 1974), pp. 15–19. The African-born members were composed of 126 West Africans (97 Gegês, 20 Minas, and 9 Nagô), 35 Angolans, and 11 others (9 Benguelas and 1 Mozambique). The Church has lost the Livro de entradas de irmãos (1798–1865), which Bacelar and Sousa used for their research. This black sodality still keeps a register of admission of new members, listed in alphabetical order, for part of the nineteenth century. This booklet listed 282 members (31 males and 251 females): 176 slaves, 55 ex-slaves, and 51 whites and freeborn people of color. They included 33 African-born (18 Gêges, 4 Angolans, 3 Nagôs, 1 Mina, 1 Congo, 6 unspecified), 36 *crioulos*, 23 mulattoes, and 9 whites. See AINS, Livro de lançamento de irmãos, século XIX. The exact years which this register of admission covered are not mentioned.

49. Arquivo Histórico Ultramarino (Lisbon), Documentos da Bahia, no. 12235, cited by Verger, *Trade Relations*, pp. 464–65; also cited by Russell-Wood, "Black and Mulatto Brotherhoods," p. 573, note 12.

50. Verger, *Trade Relations*, p. 465. According to Pierre Verger, these sodalities were exclusive to specific African nations in their membership (ibid.), but there is no evidence available to support his assertion.

51. Nishida, "Manumission and Ethnicity," pp. 283–284.

52. "Compromisso da Nossa Senhora do Rosario dos pretos da praya, ano de 1686," chapters 6 and 19, published in Russell-Wood, *Society and Government*, pp. 250–253; and AINS, Compromisso da Irmandade da Nossa Senhora dos homens prêtos no ano de 1820. In order to solve the problems derived from internal power struggle and discord, the statutes of the black sodality were modified in 1769, and further chapters were added in 1820. See Russell-Wood, "Examination of Selected Statutes," p. 224.

53. Patricia A. Mulvey, "Black Brothers and Sisters: Membership in the Black Lay Brotherhoods of Colonial Brazil," *Luso-Brazilian Review* 17, no. 2 (1980): 258. In the new statutes of the black sodalities of the Our Lady of the Rosary in the Pelourinho (1820), the scribe and treasurer had to be able to read, write, and count, and this qualification meant that no longer were such elective posts to be exclusively held by whites. This regulation also applied to caretakers. There were some changes in the new statutes. Provision of funds for the purchase of freedom by slave members had been eliminated, but charitable activities themselves had been expanded to reach out to the sick, poor, and imprisoned. Interestingly, they had extended its religious celebrations, with the new annual service held in honor of the patron saint, in addition to the mass and sermon on the third of October, which had been stipulated in the old statutes of 1686. See AINS, Compromisso da Irmandade da Nossa Senhora do homens prêtos no ano de 1820. On the dependent nature of African Brazilian Catholicism in the slavery regime in general, see Roger Bastide, *The Afri-*

can Religions of Brazil: Toward a Sociology of the Interpenetration of Civilizations, trans. Helen Sebba (Baltimore: Johns Hopkins University Press, 1978), pp. 109–125.

54. Russell-Wood, "Black and Mulatto Brotherhoods," p. 587.

55. Wetherell, *Brazil: Stray Notes from Bahia,* pp. 113–114.

56. See Reis, *A morte é uma festa,* p. 54.

57. Bastide, *African Religions,* p. 113. See also Mulvey, "Black Brothers and Sisters," p. 256; Raboteau, *Slave Religion,* p. 24. Out of the 165 black sodalities of colonial Brazil Mulvey studied, 86 were dedicated to Our Lady of the Rosary. See Mulvey, "Black Brothers and Sisters," p. 256.

58. Koster, *Travels in Brazil,* vol. 2, p. 240.

59. Ibid., vol. 2, p. 241. See also ibid., vol. 1, pp. 273–275.

60. Bastide, *African Religions,* p. 113.

61. Ibid., pp. 113, 116.

62. Pierre Verger, *Notícias da Bahia—1850* (São Paulo: Corrupio, 1981), p. 66.

63. Raboteau, *Slave Religion,* pp. 19, 24.

64. The edifice of the church still stands, empty and in a state of disrepair, but the statues of the saints and documents have been stolen. According to Sheila Walker, the first *candomblé* temple in Salvador was established by women from the Barroquinha Church. See Walker, "Feast of Good Death," p. 29.

65. AMCS, Livro de posturas, fs. 119.1, fs. 63, 152 (February 12, 1710). In her sample of 100 wills of ex-slaves (69 men and 31 women) for the period 1863–1890, Kátia Mattoso found two wills of freedmen who stipulated that they be buried in accordance with African customs. See Kátia M. de Queirós Mattoso, *Testamentos de escravos libertos na Bahia no século XIX: uma fonte para o estudo de mentalidades* (Salvador: Centro de Estudos Bahianos, 1979), p. 25 (Table 4).

66. Raboteau, *Slave Religion,* pp. 12–13.

67. In the city of Rio de Janeiro, the American Reverend D. P. Kidder identified the funeral he had witnessed of an African-born person in Engenho Velho in 1839 with the custom held on the Gabon River of Africa. See Fletcher and Kidder, *Brazil and the Brazilians,* p. 136. Also see Conrad, *Children of God's Fire,* pp. 147–149.

68. Prince, "Slave Rebellion in Bahia," pp. 86–151; Verger, *Trade Relations,* pp. 250–294; Schwartz, *Sugar Plantations,* pp. 472–488; Reis, *Rebelião,* pp. 64–83; idem, *Slave Rebellion,* chapter 3; idem, "Slave Resistance in Brazil: Bahia, 1807–1835," *Luso-Brazilian Review,* 25, no. 1 (1988): 111–144, especially 118–124.

69. Gardner, *Travels in the Interior of Brazil,* p. 20. Another example is Koster, *Travels in Brazil,* vol. 2, p. 258.

70. Schwartz, *Sugar Plantations,* p. 475; Lovejoy, *Transformations in Slavery,* pp. 140, 142.

71. Goody, "Writing, Religion, and Revolt," especially p. 333.

72. Schwartz, *Sugar Plantations,* p. 470. *Mu-Kambo* (*mocambo*) is an Ambundu word meaning "hideout." See Stuart B. Schwartz, "The *Mocambo:* Slave Resistance in Colonial Brazil," *Journal of Social History* 3, no. 4 (1970): 316, note 12. *Quilombo* derives from the Angolan term *kilombo.* See Joseph C. Miller, *Kings and Kinsmen: Early Mbundu States in Angola* (Oxford: Oxford University Press, 1976), p. 162 and chapter 8. According to Zoë Strother, who has conducted her field research on art history in Zaire, *kilombo* means the place for boys' initiation ceremonies for the Pende, who originally migrated from Angola and live in rural Zaire near the border with Angola. Strother, personal communication. Studies on fugitive slave communities in colonial Brazil include: R. K. Kent, "Palmares: An African State in Brazil," *Journal of African History* 6, no. 2 (1965): 161–175; Schwartz, "*Mocambo*"; idem, *Slaves, Peasants, and Rebels: Reconsidering Brazilian Slavery* (Urbana: University of Illinois Press, 1992), chapter 4.

73. Schwartz, *Sugar Plantations,* pp. 470–472; idem, *Slaves, Peasants, and Rebels,* pp. 104–109; idem, "*Mocambo.*" For instance, in 1789, fifty of the three hundred slaves of Engenho Santana in Ilhéus (Bahia) fled to the forest to establish a *mocambo* near the *engenho.* Schwartz documents a peace treaty proposal, written by the slaves themselves, stating the conditions under which they would return to slavery. See Stuart B. Schwartz, "Resistance and Accommodation in Eighteenth-Century Brazil: The Slaves' View of Slavery," *HAHR* 57, no. 1 (1979): 69–81.

74. The habit of running away was, of course, not uncommon, as the American medical doctor James McFadden Gaston observed in Salvador at mid-nineteenth century. Iron shackles were sometimes put on slaves' ankles to prevent them from running away. Despite their owners' efforts, slaves took flight, at times on a daily basis. See James MacFadden Gaston, *Hunting a Home in Brazil: The Agricultural Resources and Other Characteristics of the Country—Also, the Manners and Customs of the Inhabitants* (Philadelphia: King, Baird, Partners, 1867), p. 123. Local newspapers advertised such occurrences and the rewards offered by their owners. Slaves "disappeared" while going on errands, or did not bring to owners their daily or weekly wages as wage-earners at the agreed-upon time. It would have been intriguing to study maroon communities in the suburbs of Salvador in relation to the creation of ethnic and gender identities among the fugitive slaves, since the majority of them were African-born men. However, given the lack of documentation, I found it very difficult to research the subject. I thank Professor Joseph C. Love for drawing my attention to identity formation among the maroon slaves.

75. AMCS, Livro de posturas, no. 119.4, fs. 32–32B (November 28, 1733). The municipal council determined a bush captain's daily wage according to the distance from the city to where a fugitive slave was located. For instance, in 1733 he was supposed to be paid 280 *réis* in Itapoam; 320 *réis* at the limits of the city and as far as Soledade, Forte de São Pedro, and Agua dos Meninos;

480 *réis* in Barra, Rio Vermelho, and Brotas; 640 *réis* one league distant from Salvador; 1$280 *réis* three leagues from the owner's house; 2$000 *réis* in Rio Joanes. See ibid.

76. Schwartz, "*Mocambo*," p. 322. For instance, in the case of the *quilombo* known as the Buraco de Tatú ("Armadillo's Hole") located just east-northeast of Salvador and destroyed by a Portuguese-led military expedition in 1763 after twenty years of existence, urban residents of African descent in Salvador helped the *quilombo* inhabitants enter the city at night to steal powder and shot. Ibid., p. 329.

77. Schwartz, *Sugar Plantations*, p. 479.

78. "Officio do Governador Conde da Ponte para o Visconde de Anadia, no qual o informa das provincias que tomara para destruir os *Quilombos*, formados pelos escravos fugidos dos seus senhores. Bahia, 7 de abril de 1807," *Anais de Biblioteca Nacional do Rio de Janeiro* (hereafter *ABNRJ*) 37 (1915): 450–451.

79. Ibid., p. 450.

80. Ibid., p. 450.

81. Schwartz states that the slave who denounced the uprising to the police was "presumably not a Hausa," but does not present any data to support his assumption. See Schwartz, *Sugar Plantations*, p. 480.

82. ANRJ, IJJ9.319, fs. 1, 11–13; "Officio do Governador Conde da Ponte para o Visconde de Anadia, em que lhe da parte das provincias que adoptara para evitar um lavantamento dos escravos contra os brancos, de que tivera denuncia. Bahia, 16 de junho de 1807," *ABNRJ* 37 (1915): 460–461. See also Prince, "Slave Rebellion," pp. 86–96; Verger, *Trade Relations*, p. 288; and Schwartz, *Sugar Plantations*, p. 480.

83. "Dom da Terra chegou, /Cento e cinquenta acabou." See Henderson, *History of Brazil*, p. 339.

84. "Dom da Terra abalou, /Cinco e cinquenta ficou." See ibid., p. 339.

85. Prince, "Slave Rebellion," p. 17; Reis, *Rebelião escrava*, pp. 26–33; idem, *Slave Rebellion*, pp. 13–20; Schwartz, *Sugar Plantations*, pp. 434–436. Bert Barickman discusses the export-oriented agriculture and the slave economy in nineteenth-century Bahia by examining the prices of manioc flour (*farinha*). See B. J. Barickman, *A Bahian Counterpart: Sugar, Tobacco, Cassava, and Slavery in the Recôncavo, 1780–1860* (Stanford, Calif.: Stanford University Press, 1998).

86. ANRJ, IJJ9.318, fs. 9, 12–14. Nina Rodrigues emphasized the important role of the *Obgoni* or *Ohogbo*, a powerful secret society governed by Yorubas in this 1809 uprising, but there is no written evidence extant to support his synthesis. See Rodrigues, *Os africanos*, p. 87.

87. See, for example, APB, Série Ordens Régias, vol. 109, doc. 73A (September 4, 1810).

88. Gardner, *Travels in the Interior of Brazil*, p. 78.

89. ANRJ, IJJ9.322, f. 111.

90. Dent, *Year in Brazil*, p. 246.

91. ANRJ, IJJ9.323, fs. 196–198.

92. Ibid., fs. 280–281.

93. BNRJ, II-34.6.57. The sound of Ave Maria meant eight P.M. See Marjoribanks, *Travels in South and North America*, p. 42. The British merchant Thomas Lindley stated in Salvador (1803): "After sun-set each evening the bells of the churches in Catholic countries slowly toll several times, for all Christians to repeat their Ave-Maria (or prayer to the Virgin), and to return thanks for the benefit of the day. This is so universal, that at the sound of the bell, all passengers stop, uncover their heads, and comply with the ceremony." See Lindley, *Narrative of a Voyage to Brazil*, p. 192.

94. ANRJ, IJJ9. 323, fs. 17–25. See also ANRJ, IJJ9.233, fs. 55–59.

95. BNRJ, II-34.6.57.

96. Ibid. It was a custom in Scotland, Wales, Ireland, and some parts of the North of England, as well as in Salvador, that St. John's Eve was celebrated by bonfires. James Wetherell described it in 1848 as follows: "An immense amount is annually spent in fireworks, which, for some time before the day, are heard exploding in various directions; on the eve the noise becomes universal. Sometimes accidents occur, one description of fireworks used being very dangerous: a charge tightly rammed into a case, which, after gyrating through the air with great force, explodes with a loud report, shattering the tube into pieces. It is called 'buscapé,' from 'buscar'—to seek, to search 'pe,' the foot—and has been known for centuries under this name." See Wetherell, *Brazil: Stray Notes from Bahia*, pp. 23–24. St. John's Day, strategically placed six months before Christmas, celebrates the birth of St. John Baptist and the summer solstice. St. John was transplanted to the New World, and in each country throughout Latin America, it was adapted to the particular character developed there. In Venezuela, for instance, St. John was adopted by the large black population in coastal plantations and has become commonly known as "the saint of the blacks" in the area called Barvovento. See David M. Guss, "The Selling of San Juan: The Performance of History in an Afro-Venezuelan Community," *American Ethnologist* 20, no. 3 (1993): 452–453. In a village named Curiepe, the original St. John, called San Juan Congo, which had been replaced by the pale-skinned San Juan Bautista at least by 1870, was said to be black but was in fact light-skinned with Caucasian features, including blond hair. The anthropologist David M. Guss discusses that it was the absence of color that made San Juan such a powerful symbol of it; the blackness he represented was that of poverty and oppression since the arrival of the first slaves in the early 1500s. San Juan might not have appeared black but he was indeed poor, with his broken fingers, lack of toes, and irregular skin (ibid., p. 465).

97. Schwartz, *Slaves, Peasants, and Rebels*, p. 139 and p. 157, note 4.

98. Henderson, *A History of Brazil*, p. 344; and Patricia Ann Aufderheide, "Order

and Violence: Social Deviance and Social Control in Brazil 1780–1840" (Ph.D. diss., University of Minnesota, 1976), p. 76.

99. On the theme of communication among peoples of African descent in colonial British America and the Caribbean at the revolution, see Julius Scott, "Common Wind." In Julius Scott's thesis, sailors of African descent played a significant role as the agent of news on the Haitian Revolution in the formation of "Afro-America" in the revolutionary era. One may wonder, however, how the geographical boundary of "Afro-America" could be defined in the revolutionary era. For instance, Genovese discusses New World slave rebellions in the Age of Revolution, including those in non-Anglo America. See Genovese, *From Rebellion to Revolution.*

100. Prince, "Slave Rebellion," pp. 117–125.

101. Ibid., p. 130.

102. Verger, *Trade Relations,* p. 293.

103. Ibid., p. 310, note 24.

104. On slave uprisings from 1822 to 1831, see APB, Seção Histórica, maço 2845 (Insurreição de escravos); Verger, *Trade Relations,* pp. 292–293; Prince, "Slave Rebellion," pp. 126–145.

105. ANRJ, IJ1.705; APB, maço 2845, fs. 11–12B. See Prince, "Slave Rebellion," pp. 146–151; Verger, *Slave Relations,* p. 294.

106. Schwartz, *Sugar Plantations,* p. 475. See chapter 1 for a lengthier discussion.

4. The Re-creation of Identity, 1808–1831

1. Sidney W. Mintz, "Tasting Food, Tasting Freedom," in Wolfgang Binder, ed., *Slavery in the Americas* (Würzburg: Könighausen and Neumann, 1993), p. 257.

2. Studies on manumission in colonial and imperial Brazil have covered regions (Bahia and Paraíba), and specific towns and cities (the city of Rio de Janeiro, Paraty, Sabará, Campinas, and Cachoeira and São Felix of the Bahian Recôncavo). See Schwartz, "Manumission," pp. 603–635; Kátia M. de Queirós Mattoso, "A propósito de cartas de alforria na Bahia, 1779–1850," *Anais de História* 4 (1972): 23–52; Trosko, "The Liberto in Bahia"; Nishida, "Manumission and Ethnicity"; Diana Soares de Galliza, *O declínio da escravidão na Paraíba 1850–1888* (João Pessoa: Editora Universitária, 1979), chapter 4; Karasch, *Slave Life,* chapter 11; Sidney Chalhoub, "Slaves, Freedmen and the Politics of Freedom in Brazil: The Experiences of Blacks in the City of Rio," *Slavery and Abolition* 10, no. 3 (1989): 64–84; idem, *Visoes da liberdade: uma história das últimas décadas da escravidão na corte* (São Paulo: Companhia das Letras, 1990); James Patrick Kiernan, "The Manumission of Slaves in Colonial Brazil: Paraty, 1789–1822" (Ph.D. diss., New York University, 1976); Kathleen Joan Higgins, "The Slave Society in Eighteenth-Century Sabará: A Community Study in Colonial Brazil" (Ph.D. diss., Yale University, 1987), chapter 4; Robert Wayne Slenes, "The Demography and Economics of Brazilian Slavery: 1850–

1888" (Ph.D. diss., Stanford University, 1975), chapter 10; Peter L. Eisenberg, "Ficando livre: as alforrias em Campinas no século XIX," *Estudos Ecônomicos* 17, no. 2 (1987): 175–216; and Wimbery, "The African *Liberto*," chapter 2. For studies on manumission in other parts of Latin America, see Bowser, *African Slave in Colonial Peru*, chapter 10; idem, "The Free Person of Color in Mexico City and Lima: Manumission and Opportunity, 1650–1850," in Stanley L. Engerman and Eugene D. Genovese, eds., *Race and Slavery in the Western Hemisphere: Quantitative Studies* (Princeton, N.J.: Princeton University Press, 1975); Lyman L. Johnson, "Manumission in Colonial Buenos Aires, 1776–1810," *HAHR* 59, no. 2 (1979): 258–279.

3. Koster, *Travels in Brazil*, vol. 2, p. 230. See also ibid., vol. 1, p. 404.

4. Lei N. 2040 of September 28, 1871, Art. IV, *Colleção das leis do Imperio do Brazil de 1871* (Rio de Janeiro: Tipografico Nacional, 1871), part I, p. 149; Robert Edgar Conrad, *The Destruction of Brazilian Slavery 1850–1888* (Berkeley and Los Angeles: University of California Press, 1972), p. 191; idem, "Nineteenth-Century Brazilian Slavery," in Robert Brent Toplin, ed., *Slavery and Race Relations in Latin America* (Westport, Conn.: Greenwood Press, 1974), pp. 154–155; Manuela Carneiro da Cunha, "Silences of the Law: Customary Law and Positive Law on the Manumission of Slaves in 19th Century Brazil," *History and Anthropology* 1, pt. 2 (1985): 427–443, especially pp. 428–429.

5. Koster, *Travels in Brazil*, vol. 2, p. 231.

6. Ibid., pp. 231–232, note.

7. Manuela Carneiro da Cunha, "Silences of the Law," p. 434. My italics.

8. Ibid., pp. 434–438.

9. APB, Livros de notas and maço 2880. Concerning the advantage of Brazilian-born slaves in manumission, see Schwartz, "Manumission," p. 612; Karasch, *Slave Life*, p. 352; Kiernan, "Manumission of Slaves," p. 92; Higgins, "Slave Society," p. 213; and Eisenberg, "Ficando livre," pp. 189–191.

10. APB, Livros de notas and maço 2880. On the constant 1:2 male-female ratio among the manumitted in Bahia for 1684–1745, 1779–1850, and 1813–1850, see Schwartz, "Manumission," p. 611; Mattoso, "A propósito," p. 41; Arnold Kessler, "Bahian Manumission Practices in the Early Nineteenth Century" (paper presented to the American Historical Association, San Francisco, 1973), cited in Schwartz, "Manumission," p. 611. The same sex ratio is found in Rio de Janeiro (1807–1831), Paraty (1789–1822), and Lima (1580–1650). See Karasch, *Slave Life*, p. 345; Kiernan, "Manumission of Slaves," p. 86; and Bowser, "Free Person," p. 350. Higher proportions of women among the manumitted are found in other cities and towns, such as Sabará, Minas Gerais (1710–1809), Campinas, São Paulo (1799–1887), Mexico City (1580–1650), and Buenos Aires (1776–1810). See Higgins, "Slave Society," pp. 205–207; Eisenberg, "Ficando livre," pp. 184–185; Bowser, "Free Person," p. 350; and Johnson, "Manumission in Colonial Buenos Aires," p. 262.

11. APB, Livros de notas and maço 2880; AMCS, Livros de escrituras da compra e venda de escravos, freguesia da Sé; APB, Inventários da capital (1808–1888). On the nearly equal distribution of geographic and ethnic origins of the African-born slave population among the manumitted, see Schwartz, "Manumission," pp. 612–614; Karasch, *Slave Life*, p. 345; and Kiernan, "Manumission of Slaves," p. 93.

12. In the mining town of Sabará, Minas Gerais, for the period 1710–1809, more than twice as many Costa da Mina slaves were freed as from the Congo-Angola region, despite the fact that the former outnumbered the latter only by approximately 9 percent in the inventories dating from 1725 to 1808. See Higgins, "Slave Society," p. 216. See, also Russell-Wood, *Black Man in Slavery and Freedom*, pp. 122–123.

13. APB, Livros de notas and maço 2880. Payment for freedom was made in the Brazilian currency of *real* (*réis*). The manumission letters I consulted for this study do not include a case in which the price for freedom was paid in silver *dobras*, or any other type of currency.

14. On the prices of manumitted slaves in nineteenth-century Salvador, see Kátia M. de Queirós Mattoso, Herbert S. Klein, and Stanley L. Engerman, "Trends and Patterns in the Prices of Manumitted Slaves: Bahia, 1819–1888," *Slavery and Abolition* 7, no. 1 (1986): 59–67. On the difference between estimated value and sales price in Paraty, see Kiernan, "Manumission of Slaves," p. 137.

15. AMCS, Livros de escrituras de compara e venda de escravos, freguesia da Sé.

16. APB, Livros de notas and maço 2880.

17. APB, maço 2898, Relação dos africanos . . . Santana, 1849. Unfortunately there is no way of making connections between the price of freedom and daily wages by occupations based on the data mentioned in the manumission letters, which rarely state the occupation or skills of the slave to be freed. Among 3,516 manumission letters for the entire period 1808–1884, only 69 state the occupations of slaves. The letters represent 46 men and 23 women: 29 African-born, 29 Brazilian-born, and 11 whose birthplaces were not stated. The men's occupations include 13 artisans, 9 domestics, 8 transporters, 8 field hands, 4 barber-surgeons, and 4 wage-earners; the women's are 11 domestics, 10 field hands, and 2 wage-earners. Letters of liberty (manumission letters) rarely mention the occupation or skills of the slave to be freed. See APB, Livros de notas and maço 2880. Few ex-slaves mentioned their occupations in their wills, either. See APB, Livros de registro de testamentos.

18. APB, Livro de registro de testamentos, no. 13, fs. 8B–15 (January 28, 1825).

19. Galliza, *Declínio da escravidão*, p. 150.

20. The term "trade-in" is borrowed from Karasch, *Slave Life*, pp. 343 and 358.

21. APB, Seção Judiciária, Livro de notas da capital, no. 306, May 14, 1852.

22. Among the wills of ex-slaves, seven ex-slaves, all African-born, declare that they had provided their owners with substitute slaves, but only one was identi-

fied in terms of "nation." APB, Livros de registro de testamentos, no. 4, fs. 5B–9B; no. 9, fs. 101B–106; no. 16, fs. 156–161; no. 17, fs. 145B–149B; no. 28, fs. 98B–101; no. 28, fs. 122–125B; and no. 47, fs. 28–30B.

23. Maria and Thereza, both Nagô, in place of Maria, Nagô (APB, Livro de notas, no. 206, May 31, 1822); and two newly arrived African-born slave women, with no specific names nor places of origin, in place of Anna, Nagô (ibid., no. 206, June 8, 1822).

24. Bricklayer in APB, Livro de notas, no. 160, July 15, 1809; chair carrier in ibid., no. 242, April 10, 1832; field worker in ibid., no. 295, February 3, 1851; and stevedore in ibid., no. 306, May 14, 1852.

25. APB, Livro de notas, no. 160, July 15, 1809. The same settlement: ibid., no. 242, April 10, 1832; ibid., no. 304, May 7, 1852.

26. Joaquim was replaced by his namesake Joaquim (APB, Livro de notas, no. 272, March 9, 1841); and Caetana, *crioula*, replaced by another Caetana, Nagô, in the same occupation of fieldwork (ibid., no. 295, February 3, 1851).

27. APB, Livro de notas, no. 293, May 22, 1821; ibid., no. 238, February 16, 1832.

28. Instituto Geográfico e Histórica da Bahia, Salvador, pasta 28, doc. 11, cited by Schwartz, "Manumission," pp. 626–627 (note 36).

29. African-born ex-slaves who were engaged in the transatlantic slave trade: APB, Livro de registro de testamentos, no. 19, fs. 276B–280B; ibid., no. 28, fs. 98B–101B. See also chapter 3.

30. Miller, "Slave Prices," pp. 45, 47; and Mattoso, Klein, and Engerman, "Trends and Patterns," p. 66 (note 9).

31. Schwartz, "Manumission," p. 626; Karasch, *Slave Life,* p. 358; Higgins, "Slave Society," p. 247.

32. Karasch, *Slave Life,* p. 358.

33. The practice of substitution took place in Bahia (1684–1745), the city of Rio de Janeiro (1808–1850), and Sabará of Minas Gerais (1789–1822). See Schwartz, "Manumission," p. 626; Karasch, *Slave Life,* p. 358; and Higgins, "Slave Society," pp. 247–248. Kátia Mattoso refers to substitution but does not provide any interpretation: "Slaves had to pay for their freedom in hard cash, metal coin or paper money, either in a lump sum or by installments. Some slaves redeemed themselves by giving another slave to masters." See Mattoso, *To Be a Slave in Brazil,* p. 158.

34. Kiernan, "Manumission of Slaves," especially p. 148; Galliza, *O declínio da escravidão,* chapter 4. Judith Lee Allen, who conducted her archival research in 1987–1989 in Salvador and Cachoeira, found only four cases of substitution among approximately 1,700 manumission letters registered in the towns of the Bahian Recôncavo in the nineteenth century. Allen, personal communication.

35. Koster, *Travels in Brazil,* vol. 2, pp. 266–267.

36. William D. Phillips, *Slavery from Roman Times,* p. 28. On the *peculium,* see also Patterson, *Slavery and Social Death,* pp. 182–186.

37. Carl Campbell, "John Mohammed Bath and the Free Mandingos in Trinidad: The Question of Their Repatriation to Africa 1831–38," *Journal of African Studies* 12, no. 4 (1975): 472.

38. Maria Graham, *Journal of a Voyage to Brazil,* p. 108.

39. APB, maço 647, Arollomento dos africanos libertos . . . Conceição da Praia, 1846; APB, maço 2898, Relação dos africanos libertos . . . Santana, 1849.

40. APB, maço 6472, Arollomento dos africanos libertos que rezedem nesta freguesia da Conceição da Praia, January 31, 1846.

41. APB, maço 2898, Relação dos africanos libertos existentes nesta freguesia, Santana, February 11, 1849. The total number of African-born freedmen is 133.

42. Andrade, *A mão de obra escrava,* p. 129; and APB, Inventários da capital.

43. APB, maço 6472, Arollomento dos africanos libertos . . . Conceição da Praia; ibid., maço 2898, Relação dos africanos libertos . . . Santana.

44. APB, Livro de registro de testamentos, no. 40, fs. 19–21 (April 14, 1849); ibid., no. 48, fs. 116–118B (August 21, 1873).

45. APB, Livro de registro de testamentos, no. 28, fs. 98B–101B (August 20, 1827).

46. Ibid., no. 11 (September 24, 1824), fs. 32B–35B.

47. Ibid., no. 19, fs. 276B–280B.

48. Walsh, *Notices of Brazil,* vol. 2, p. 362.

49. See, for instance, J. Michael Turner, "Les Brésiliens—The Impact of Former Brazilian Slaves upon Dahomey" (Ph.D. diss., Boston University, 1975), pp. 102–125; Pierre Verger, *Formation d'une société brésilienne au Golfe du Bénin au XIXème siècle* (Dakar: Centre de Hautes Etudes Afro-Ibéro-Américaines de L'Université de Dakar, 1969). On the commercial role of Luso-Africans in Angola, see Miller, *Way of Death,* chapter 8.

50. See, for example, the recollection of one elderly Bahian-born man of African descent, in Pierson, *Negroes in Brazil,* pp. 240–242.

51. APB, Livro de registro de testamentos, no. 23, fs. 146B–149 (October 13, 1833).

52. Ibid., no. 25, fs. 83–85B (March 30, 1837).

53. Some slaves, especially those of Brazilian birth, had been given family names before manumission. See Schwartz, *Sugar Plantations,* p. 402.

54. APB, Livros de registro de testamentos.

55. Schwartz, *Sugar Plantations,* p. 402.

56. APB, maço 2898, Relação dos africanos libertos existentes nesta freguesia, Santana, February 11, 1849; APB, Seção Histórica, maço 6472, Alloroment dos africanos libertos que rezedem nesta freguezia da Conceião da Praia, January 31, 1846.

57. Oliveira, *O liberto,* p. 41 (Table 2). Due to the rapid transformation of the larger society from slave society to slave-owning society, which started to take place in Salvador during the 1840s (see my discussions in chapter 1) and was

spurred by the termination of the transatlantic slave trade (1851), the percentages of slave owners among the ex-slave property owners declined considerably after the mid-nineteenth century. For the period of 1850–1890, only 35.2 percent of men (45 out of 128) and 57.9 percent of women (45 out of 95) were slave owners among the ex-slave population who registered their wills. See ibid.

58. My interpretation deviates from Karasch on slaveholding as practiced by African-born ex-slaves. She states: "One other factor that appears to have encouraged ex-slaves to own slaves is that while the African trade continued, they had the opportunity to rescue their own people from being enslaved to Brazilians. This pattern is suggested in the *negros de ganho* records in which Yorubas owned other Yorubas as slaves." See Karasch, *Slave Life*, p. 211.

59. APB, Livros de registro de testamentos. On *crias* as heirs, see, for example, ibid., no. 43, fs. 50–52. On the legal arrangement of coartação, see Schwartz, "Manumission," pp. 627–628. Cf. On the custom of *coartación* in Spanish America, see Hubert H. S. Aimes, "Coartación: A Spanish Institution for the Advancement of Slaves into Freedom," *Yale Review* 17 (1909): 412–431; Herbert S. Klein, *Slavery in the Americas: A Comparative Study of Virginia and Cuba* (Chicago: University of Chicago Press, 1967), pp. 196–200.

60. APB, Livros de registro de testamentos, nos. 3–34.

61. APB, Livro de registro de testamentos, no. 5, fs. 202B–206. Ana Maria died on October 15, 1815.

62. Ibid., no. 31, fs. 154–157B (February 6, 1844).

5. The Convergence of Identity, 1831–1880

1. Decreto de 14 de dezembro de 1830, *Collecção de leis do Imperio do Brazil de 1830* (Rio de Janeiro: Tipografico Nacional, 1876), part I, pp. 96–98.

2. APB, livros de escrituras de compra e venda de escravos, freguesia da Sé; APB, Inventários da capital.

3. Reis, *Rebelião escrava*, p. 16.

4. Studies on the Malê revolt of 1835 include Etinne Ignace, "A revolta dos Malés (24 para 25 de Janeiro de 1835)," *Revista de Instituto Geografico e Histórico da Bahia* 14, no. 33 (1907): 129–149; Rodrigues, *Os africanos*, chapter 2 (Os negros maometanos no Brasil; originally published in the *Jornal do Comércio do Rio de Janeiro*, dated November 2, 1900); R. K. Kent, "African Revolt in Bahia: 24–25 January 1835," *Journal of Social History* 3, no. 4 (1970): 334–356; Prince, *Slave Rebellion*, pp. 152–224; Reis, *Rebelião escrava;* idem, *Slave Rebellion;* idem, "Slave Resistance," pp. 124–132; and Lovejoy, "Background to Rebellion."

5. On the miraculous Church of Bonfim, James Wetherell observed in 1856: "Numbers of devotees, particularly blacks and mulattoes, dressed in their best and with bare feet, are seen wending their way each to present a candle as

an offering. . . . Wax models of arms, legs, breasts, & c., with different diseases simulated thereon, are suspended round the room. . . . It was formerly the custom of the sailors belonging to the slave vessels to bring one of their sails to be blessed previous to departure; or having vowed a sail when in distress, they would escort with bare feet the sail, tied up with garlands of flowers, to the Church, and then, after offering the same, redeem it. Upon the ceiling is a large allegorical painting representing, amongst other things, sailors in the act of presenting a sail to Christ." See Wetherell, *Brazil: Stray Notes from Bahia*, pp. 121–122. See also Lindley, *Narrative of a Voyage to Brazil*, pp. 190–192. According to the British medical doctor Robert Dundas, the "higher classes" of the inhabitants of Bahia resorted to the suburb of Bonfim for sea-bathing, during the hottest months of the year, namely December, January, February, and March. See Dundas, *Sketches of Brazil*, p. 240.

6. Verger, *Trade Relations*, p. 294.

7. "Devassa do levante," pp. 61–62.

8. Ibid., p. 63. According to Nina Rodrigues, the name of "Aruna" was a retention of the Arabic term "Alufa," which means teacher or priest. Rodrigues, *Os africanos*, p. 94.

9. The expression "white man's land" seems to have been commonly used among the population of African descent in nineteenth-century Salvador. One old returnee from Bahia in Lagos, named Francisco, mentioned to Father Baudin during his stay for 1874–1875 that he had been born in Bahia, "in the *terra dos brancos*," and continued to say, "I was happy then, in that bounteous land of Brazil! What beautiful churches, what lovely houses!" See Manuela Carneiro da Cunha, "Introduction," in Marianno Carneiro da Cunha, *Da senzala ao sobrado: arquitetura brasileira na Nigéria e na República Popular do Benin* (São Paulo: Nobel, 1985), p. 42.

10. "1835 Insurreição de escravos," pp. 9–170.

11. Prince, "Slave Rebellion," p. 169.

12. Ibid., p. 177, based on APB, maço 2847 (Insurreição de escravos, 1835), fs. 1–18.

13. Verger, *Trade Relations*, p. 303.

14. Goody, "Writing, Religion, and Revolt," p. 324.

15. Parkinson to the Duke of Wellington, FO 13/21 (Bahia, January 29, 1835), cited by Goody, "Writing, Religion, and Revolt," p. 324. On anti-British feelings prevailing among Brazilians because of Britain's interference with the slave trade, see Marjoribanks, *Travels in South and North America*, p. 47.

16. On the severe shortage of women in New World maroon societies, see Richard Price, "Introduction: Maroons and their Communities," in idem, ed., *Maroon Societies: Rebel Slave Communities in the Americas*, 2nd ed. (Baltimore: Johns Hopkins University Press, 1979), pp. 18–19.

17. Reis, *Rebelião escrava*, p. 172.

18. "Devassa da levante," p. 135. Slaves were obliged to return home after the sound of Ave Maria, namely eight o'clock at night, and were prohibited from going out after nine o'clock.

19. Reis, *Rebelião escrava,* p. 172.

20. Ibid.

21. See the testimony by Pacífico in the court, in "Devassa da levante," pp. 84–85.

22. "1835 Insurreição," p. 40.

23. "Devassa da levante," pp. 72–73. See Verger, *Trade Relations,* pp. 300–301.

24. "1835 Insurreição," p. 13.

25. Bastide, *African Religions,* p. 106; Lovejoy, "Background to Rebellion." Lovejoy's synthesis is largely based on a sample of 108 slaves from the Central Sudan who were sold into the transatlantic slave trade. See ibid., pp. 176–180.

26. Rodrigues, *Os africanos,* pp. 108–119; Prince, "Slave Rebellion," p. 234.

27. Reis, *Rebelião escrava,* parte 2; idem, *Slave Rebellion,* part 2.

28. Vincent Monteil, "Analyse de 25 documents arabes des Malés de Bahia (1835)," *Bulletin de l'Institut Fondanetake d'Afrique Noir,* tomo 29, série B, no. 1–2 (1967): 88–98; and Rolf Reichert, *Os documentos Arabes do Arquivo do Estado da Bahia* (Salvador: Universidade Federal da Bahia, 1970).

29. Mariane Ferme, personal communication.

30. Goody, "Writing, Religion, and Revolt," pp. 328–329.

31. Eugene D. Genovese, *From Rebellion to Revolution: Afro-American Slave Revolts in the Making of the Modern World* (Baton Rouge: Louisiana State University Press, 1979), p. 44.

32. Goody, "Writing, Religion, and Revolt," p. 332.

33. Ibid., p. 333.

34. Genovese, *From Rebellion to Revolution,* p. 32. Genovese continues: "In the hands of a skillful anti-Christian leader the religious cry could be made to separate the slaves from the white community and thus transform every rising into a holy war against the infidel. When master and slave appealed to the same God, the same book, the same teachings, the task of Nat Turner's became much more difficult. . . . The difference came not with the abstract character of the Christian tradition but with the reduction of revolutionary potential inherent in the deeper separation of religion from class and especially ethnicity" (ibid.).

35. ANRJ, IJ1.707, no. 9.

36. Verger, *Trade Relations,* pp. 314–316.

37. APB, Seção Legislativa, Assembleia legislativa provincial, Registros de leis approvadas pela assembleia, no. 1, Lei 8, fs. 9–16.

38. Ibid., fs. 11–11B (Article 8).

39. Ibid., fs. 14B–15 (Article 17).

40. APB, Livro de registro de testamentos, no. 40, fs. 29B–32 (August 31, 1859). See also ibid., no. 40, fs. 186–188B (June 5, 1860); ibid., no. 43, fs. 50–52 (August 11, 1863); ibid., no. 46, fs. 172B–175 (March 25, 1868); ibid., no. 47, fs. 28–30 (August 13, 1872).

41. APB, Seção Legistlativa, Assembleia legislativa provincial, Registros de leis approvadas pela assembleia, no. 1. f. 15.

42. Ibid., Lei 14, fs. 28B–30.

43. APB, Inventários da capital.

44. Titulos de residencia à africanos libertos, APB, Seção Histórica, maço 5664, f. 1.

45. *British and Foreign State Papers*, vol. 40 (London: James Ridway & Sons, Picadilly, 1850–1851), pp. 428–429.

46. ANRJ, IJ1.707, no. 32; Verger, *Trade Relations*, p. 316.

47. Verger, *Trade Relations*, pp. 317–322.

48. Ibid., p. 563, note 3.

49. Manuela Carneiro da Cunha, *Negros, estrangeiros: os escravos libertos e sua volta à Africa* (São Paulo: Editora Brasiliense, 1985), p. 80.

50. APB, Projecto de Lei no. 19 à Assembléia Legistrativa da Província, 1851, Art. 15, cited by Trosko, "The Liberto in Bahia," p. 37.

51. On back-to-Africa movements from Salvador, see Lorenzo D. Turner, "Some Contacts of Brazilian Ex-Slaves with Nigeria, West Africa," *Journal of Negro History* 27, no. 1 (1942): 55–67; Pierson, *Negroes in Brazil*, pp. 238–239; Richard D. Ralston, "The Return of Brazilian Freedmen to West Africa in the 18th and 19th Centuries," *Canadian Journal of African Studies* 3, no. 3 (1969): 577–592; Verger, *Formation d'une société Brésilienne;* idem, *Trade Relations*, chapter 16; J. Michael Turner, "Les Brésiliens"; Manuela Carneiro da Cunha, *Negros, estrangeiros;* idem, "Introduction"; and Lisa A. Lindsay, "'To Return to the Bosom of their Fatherland': Brazilian Immigrants in Nineteenth-Century Lagos," *Slavery and Abolition* 15, no. 1 (1994): 22–50.

52. Fletcher and Kidder, *Brazil and the Brazilians*, p. 136.

53. Raeders, *O inimigo cordial do Brasil*, p. 122.

54. Mariano Carneiro da Cunha studies the Luso-Brazilian architecture of these West African coastal towns in the nineteenth century. See Mariano Carneiro da Cunha, *Da senzala ao sobrado*.

55. John Duncan, *Travels in Western Africa, in 1845 & 1846, Comprising a Journey from Whydah, through the Kingdom of Dahomey, to Adofoodia, in the Interior*, vol. 1 (New York: Johnson Reprint Corporation, 1967 [1847]), p. 138.

56. Ibid., vol. 1, p. 185.

57. On the "return" movement from Cuba, see, for instance, Rodolf Saracino, *Los que volvieron a Africa* (Havana: Editorial de Ciencias, 1988).

58. Duncan, *Travels in Western Africa*, vol. 1, p. 186; and Jean Herskovits Kopytoff, *A Preface to Modern Nigeria: The "Sierra Leoneans" in Yoruba, 1830–1890* (Madison: University of Wisconsin Press, 1965).

59. APB, Livros de notas and maço 2880.

60. APB, Livros de registro de testamentos; ACMS, Livros de batizados, freguesia de Santo Antônio; and ACMS, Livros de casamentos, freguesia de Conceição da Praia, freguesia de Penha.

61. APB, Livro de registro de testamentos, no. 31, fs. 132B–135B.

62. Ibid., no. 10, fs. 91–96B (June 12, 1823); ibid., no. 29, fs. 103–107 (March 3, 1838); ibid., no. 31, fs. 87–89B (April 6, 1846); ibid., no. 40, fs. 29B–32 (February 13, 1857); ibid., no. 52, fs. 145B–149B (February 21, 1873); ibid., no. 61, fs. 168B–170 (August 15, 1887).

63. APB, Livros de notas and maço 2880.

64. APB, Livro de registro de testamentos, no. 3, fs. 142B–145B (November 1, 1841).

65. Ibid., no. 6, fs. 231–235 (May 2, 1816).

66. Ibid., no. 51, fs. 141B–144B.

67. She named all of her legitimate and natural children and her six grand-children (children of her legitimate children) as her heirs. Ibid., no. 22, fs. 271–273B.

68. Ibid., no. 41, fs. 64–65B (November 26, 1861). For grandfathers, see also ibid., no. 30, fs. 63 (October 19, 1840); ibid., no. 41, fs. 64–65B (November 26, 1861); ibid., no. 52, fs. 39–41 (March 9, 1877).

69. Ibid., no. 5, 206B–210. On grandmother figures, see also ibid., no. 5, fs. 25B–28B (March 17, 1815); ibid., no. 22, fs. 4B–8 (July 29, 1832); ibid., no. 22, fs. 52–55B (October 9, 1832); ibid., no. 31, fs. 102B–105 (February 27, 1839); ibid., no. 34, fs. 8–11B (January 7, 1837); and ibid., no. 51, fs. 101–104 (July 27, 1867).

70. Ibid., no. 30, fs. 57–59B.

71. Sandra Lauderdale Graham reports, albeit based on two civil court records, on a similar case of church marriage and separation of an African-born ex-slave couple in nineteenth-century Rio de Janeiro, and discusses the meanings of honor for women among the urban poor. See Sandra Lauderdale Graham, "Honor among Slaves," in Johnson and Lipsett-Rivera, eds., *Faces of Honor*.

72. APB, Livro de registro de testamentos, no. 46, fs. 43–45B.

73. Legitimate children born to African-born ex-slaves: ibid., no. 42, fs.160B–163B; ibid., no. 44, fs. 161–163B; ibid., no. 47, fs. 107–109; ibid., no. 40, fs. 188B–190B. Among the 325 wills of ex-slaves, 214 (94 men and 120 women) never had any children.

74. APB, Livro de registro de testamentos, no. 49, fs. 165B–168.

75. ACMS, Livros de casamentos, freguesia da Conceição da Praia.

76. APB, Livros de registro de testamentos, no. 43, fs. 16–18; ibid., no. 44. fs. 106B–109. Other examples of matrimony of longtime common-law spouses before

death include: ibid., no. 14, fs. 192–96 (June 8, 1847); ibid., no. 60, fs. 55–58 (December 20, 1884); ibid., no. 61, fs. 71B–77 (July 21, 1886). The expression "illicit" union was commonly used in wills to refer to common-law marriage unsanctified by holy matrimony.

77. Linda Lewin, "Natural and Spurious Children in Brazilian Inheritance Law from Colony to Empire: A Methodological Essay," *Americas* 48, no. 3 (1992): 363–368.

78. ACMS, Livros de batizados, freguesia de Santo Antônio.

79. APB, Livros de notas and maço 2880.

80. The *crioula* Antônia, seventeen years of age, was manumitted on payment of 900$000 *réis* by her godfather José de São João, Nagô (APB, maço 2880, February 6, 1879).

81. APB, Livros de registro de testamentos.

82. Ibid., no. 19, fs. 214–217B (January 7, 1830).

83. Ibid., no. 23, fs. 270B–274 (September 23, 1832).

84. APB, Livros de registro de testamentos.

85. Ibid.

86. Ibid., no. 44, fs. 195–198.

87. Ibid., no. 40, fs. 19–21.

88. Criminal records discussing kinship and other networks exclusively among African-born ex-slaves include: APB, Autos Crimes, 3552.4 (1865); and 3559.10 (1872).

89. Manuela Carneiro da Cunha, "Introduction," p. 18. On the importance of kola nuts as a trade commodity in Africa, see Paul E. Lovejoy, *Caravans of Kola: The Hausa Kola Trade 1700–1900* (Zaria, Nigeria: Ahmadu Bello University Press, 1980).

90. Some African-born ex-slaves still went back to their hometowns in the interior, such as Abeokuta, Ilesha, and Oyo, despite ongoing wars and high risk of re-enslavement. Manuela Carneiro da Cunha reports an oral tradition that Pa Callisto and his parents were manumitted in Bahia and went back to Ilesha, their hometown, where they were re-enslaved. Callisto's father is said to have committed suicide to escape from captivity. See Manuela Carneiro da Cunha, "Introduction," p. 64, note 4.

91. *Diário da Bahia*, May 7, 1868; *Jornal da Bahia*, February 23, 1857; and *Diário da Bahia*, April 29, 1863. See also J. Michael Turner, "Les Brésiliens," pp. 55–63.

92. One example is Antônio de Silva, whose owner was Antônio Vieira da Silva (*Jornal da Bahia*, March 5, 1857).

93. APB, Livro de registro de testamentos, no. 46, fs. 188–191B.

94. Ibid., no. 52, fs. 39–41.

95. Manuela Carneiro da Cunha, *Negros, estrangeiros*, pp. 152–204.

96. Verger, *Trade Relations*, p. 544.

97. Manuela Carneiro da Cunha, *Negros, estrangeiros*, p. 214.

98. APB, Livros de notas and maço 2880.

99. Manuela Carneiro da Cunha, *Negros, estrangeiros*, pp. 210–216.

100. Lorenzo D. Turner, "Some Contacts," which was based on his interviews conducted in Salvador, 1941–1942.

101. J. Michael Turner, "Les Brésiliens," p. 83.

102. APB, Livros de notas and maço 2880.

6. The Creation of Disparate Identity, 1808–1851

1. Mintz, "Tasting Food, Tasting Freedom," p. 257. I concur with Mintz: "The vast differences between the enslaved and those who were born into slavery are too often ignored." See ibid., p. 270, note 1.

2. APB, Quadro dos nascimentos da freguesia da Penha (1844), maço 1549.

3. ACMS, Livros de batizados, freguesia de Santo Antônio, from which I consulted data for two out of every ten years (1809–1810, 1828–1829, 1838–1839, 1848–1849, 1858–1859, and 1868–1869).

4. AMCS, Livros de escrituras de compra e venda de escravos, freguesia da Sé. All four cases of father-child transaction took place in the 1860s.

5. Ibid., no. 82.6, December 7, 1867.

6. APB, Livros de notas and maço 2880.

7. APB, Livro de notas, no. 116, January 25, 1811.

8. Ibid., no. 272, Nov. 17, 1841; and ibid., no. 275, October 30, 1841.

9. APB, Livros de notas and maço 2880.

10. APB, Livro de registro de testamentos, no. 38, fs. 177B–179B (September 21, 1848). See also ibid., no. 35, fs. 16–18 (May 18, 1850).

11. APB, Livros de notas and maço 2880.

12. APB, Livro de registro de testamentos, no. 28, fs. 98B–101B (August 20, 1827). See also ibid., no. 30, fs. 142B–145B (November 1, 1841); ibid., no. 44, fs. 135–137 (November 10, 1863); and ibid., no. 58, fs. 65B–68 (April 18, 1882).

13. Ibid., no. 51, fs. 185B–189B.

14. Lewin, "Natural and Spurious Children," p. 389.

15. APB, Livro de registro de testamentos, no. 52, fs. 39–41.

16. Ibid., no. 41, fs. 64–65B (November 26, 1861). For grandfathers, see also ibid., no. 30, fs. 63 (October 19, 1840); and ibid., no. 41, fs. 64–65B (November 26, 1861).

17. Ibid., no. 5, 206B–210. On grandmother figures, see also ibid., no. 5, fs. 25B–28B (March 17, 1815); ibid., no. 22, fs. 4B–8 (July 29, 1832); ibid., no. 22, fs. 52–

55B (October 9, 1832); ibid., no. 31, fs. 102B–105 (February 27, 1839); ibid., no. 34, fs. 8–11B (January 7, 1837); and ibid., no. 51, fs. 101–104 (July 27, 1867).

18. ACMS, Livros de batizados, freguesia de Santo Antônio. After mid-century, a higher percentage of Brazilian-born slaves were baptized with both godfathers and godmothers; women seem to have begun to take a more active role in fictive kinship.

19. ACMS, Livros de batizados, freguesia de Santo Antônio, February 2, 1810; May 14, 1810; October 7, 1810; December 13, 1813.

20. APB, Livros de notas and maço 2880. Grandmothers: Anacleta, *crioula*, daughter of Thomara (already dead), *crioula* slave of the same owner, with 150$000 *réis* from her grandmother, Joaquina, Nagô; and Thedolina, 11-year-old *parda* with money from her grandmother, Mana, of African birth. APB, Livro de notas, no. 297, July 1, 1851; ibid., no. 416, March 27, 1872. Godparents: only one of the godparents was identified as African-born; José de São João, Nagô, paid the price of Antônia, 17-year-old *crioula* (900$000 *réis*). See APB, maço 2880, February 6, 1879. In some cases, relations of purchasers of freedom to the slaves were not mentioned in the manumission letters. For instance, two Brazilian-born sisters, Euporoma (6 years old) and Justina (9 years old), daughters of their owner's former slave, Verdina, a *crioula*, were liberated with 1:200$000 *réis* donated by Manuel Joaquim Gomes Vilças, because he "appreciated the services" not only of their mother but also of their grandmother. In 1880, Guirina, a 23-year-old *crioula*, received her letter of liberty on payment of 800$000 *réis*: 400$000 *réis* from herself and another 400$000 *réis* from Margarida dos Sassos, who had rented out Guirina for fieldwork. In the case of Luís, *crioulo*, George Harris Duder paid 950$000 *réis* for his freedom, but on condition that Luís had to serve him for seven years. See APB, Livro de notas, no. 416, April 17, 1872; APB, maço 2880, February 16, 1880; ibid., November 13, 1879. On the purchasers of freedom for Brazilian-born child slaves in Rio de Janeiro, see Karasch, *Slave Life*, pp. 347–350.

21. APB, Livros de notas and maço 2880.

22. Nishida, "Manumission and Ethnicity," p. 374. In Bahia for the earlier period 1684–1745, Brazilian-born ex-slaves made up 69 percent of the total freed, while African-born ex-slaves were only 31 percent. See Schwartz, "Manumission," p. 612. On the advantage of Brazilian-born slaves in manumission in other parts of Brazil, see Karasch, *Slave Life*, p. 352; Kiernan, "Manumission of Slaves," p. 92; Higgins, "Slave Society," p. 213; and Eisenberg, "Ficando livre," pp. 189–191.

23. APB, Livros de notas and maço 2880. Concerning the advantage of Brazilian-born slaves in manumission, see Schwartz, "Manumission," p. 612; Karasch, *Slave Life*, p. 352; Kiernan, "Manumission of Slaves," p. 92; Higgins, "Slave Society," p. 213; and Eisenberg, "Ficando livre," pp. 189–191.

24. Schwartz, "Manumission," p. 619.

25. APB, Livros de notas and maço 2880.

26. In this study, I classify those of more than 15 years of age as falling into the category of "adult," based on the age for working and military service for males and reproduction and domestic responsibility for females. I regard as "children" those who are identified by diminutives such as *crioulinho/crioulinha, pardinho/pardinha,* and *mulatinho/mulatinha,* but whose ages are not specified.

27. APB, Livros de notas and maço 2880. Brazilian-born child slaves rarely purchased their freedom. Among those of Brazilian birth who purchased freedom, only 8.1 percent of males and 7 percent of females were children. See APB, Livros de notas and maço 2880.

28. AMCS, Livros de escritura de compra e venda de escravos, freguesia da Sé. On the advantage of children, see Schwartz, "Manumission," pp. 615–616; Kiernan, "Manumission of Slaves," p. 102; Eisenberg, "Ficando livre," p. 192; Bowser, "Free Persons," pp. 350–351.

29. APB, Livros de notas and maço 2880. Eleven boys and 16 girls belong to this category for 1808–1884.

30. Manoel, *crioulo,* son of the female slave. See APB, Livro de notas, no. 164, January 25, 1811.

31. On high child slave mortality in Brazil, see, for instance, Merrick and Graham, *Population and Economic Development,* p. 61; Conrad, *World of Sorrow,* pp. 14–15.

32. APB, Livros de notas and maço 2880. I regard all of those who were classified as *pardos, cabras, mulatos,* and *mestiços* together as "mulattoes" in contrast to *crioulos.*

33. AMCS, Livros de escritura de compra e venda de escravos, freguesia da Sé.

34. APB, Inventários da capital.

35. APB, Livros de notas and maço 2880. Concerning the advantage of mulatto slaves in manumission, see Schwartz, "Manumission," p. 618; Kiernan, "Manumission of Slaves," p. 92; Higgins, "Slave Society," p. 215; Eisenberg, "Ficando livre," p. 187; and Johnson, "Manumission in Colonial Buenos Aires," pp. 264–265.

36. See, for instance, ACMS, Livros de casamentos, freguesia da Penha 1808–1857; and freguesia da Conceição da Praia (1843–1888). The marriage records in early nineteenth-century Rio de Janeiro show the same tendency: Marriages that crossed color and civil status barriers were uncommon. See Karasch, *Slave Life,* p. 291.

37. In the first national census of 1872, 30 percent of the white population in Brazil was registered as married, whereas only 8 percent of the slave population was married. The percentage of the married among the legally free (freed and free-born) population of color was significantly higher than among slaves, whereas within the broad category of free people of color, free "mulattoes" enjoyed a slight advantage over free "blacks." See Merrick and Graham, *Population and Economic Development,* pp. 58–60.

38. Dain Borges discusses Bahian endogamy among elite families for the period 1800–1870, as a means of not dividing inheritance and also as a patriarchal strategy to preserve family continuity. See Borges, *Family in Bahia*, pp. 240–241.

39. APB, maço 5685, Registro dos fogos . . . São Pedro (1835).

40. APB, Livro de registro de testamentos, no. 28, pp. 148–150B.

41. Verena Martinez-Alier, *Marriage, Class and Color in Nineteenth-Century Cuba: A Study of Racial Attitudes and Sexual Values in a Slave Society* (London and New York: Cambridge University Press, 1974), chapter 6.

42. In the colonial Mexican city of Antequerra (Oaxaca), which was a slave-owning society but never a slave society, such group boundaries were situational and flexible, and individual cross-group mobility always existed. Children were classified with regard to "social race" at baptism, and frequently separate registers were kept for Spaniards, Indians, and *castas* (a generic term for all mixed bloods). Yet, the same individuals were categorized or identified themselves in different ways in different situations. Marriage was often contracted across socioracial lines. See John K. Chance and William B. Taylor, "Estate and Class in a Colonial City: Oaxaca in 1792," *Comparative Studies in Society and History* 19, no. 4 (1977): 454–487.

43. Martinez-Alier, *Marriage, Class and Colour,* chapter 7. On marriage and family honor in colonial Mexico, see Patricia Seed, *To Love, Honor, and Obey in Colonial Mexico: Conflicts and Marriage Choice, 1574–1821* (Stanford, Calif.: Stanford University Press, 1988); Ann Twinan, *Public Lives, Private Secrets: Gender, Honor, Sexuality, and Illegitimacy in Colonial Spanish America* (Stanford, Calif.: Stanford University Press, 1999).

44. Verger, *Trade Relations,* p. 465; and idem, *Notícias da Bahia,* p. 65. On the establishment of the mulatto sodality of Our Lord of Good Jesus of the Cross (irmandade de Nosso Senhor Bom Jesus da Cruz) in 1751 and its oral tradition, see Ignácio Accioli de Cerqueira e Silva, *Memórias históricas e políticas da Bahia,* vol. 5 (Salvador: Imprensa Oficial do Estado, 1931), p. 241.

45. The Tailors' Revolt has been identified by some historians as the first slave uprising in Brazil, but does not seem to have represented the interests of the general enslaved population. Studies on the Tailors' Revolt include: Afonso Ruy, *A primeira revolução social brasileira (1798),* 2nd ed. (Salvador: Tipografico Beneditina Ltda, 1951); Kátia M. de Queirós Mattoso, *Presença francesa no movimento democrático bahiano de 1798* (Salvador: Editora Itapuã, 1969); Donald Ramos, "Social Revolution Frustrated: The Conspiracy of the Tailors in Bahia, 1798," *Luso-Brazilian Review* 13, no. 1 (1976): 74–90; Schwartz, *Sugar Plantations,* pp. 476–478; Judith Lee Allen, "Tailors, Soldiers, and Slaves: The Social Anatomy of a Conspiracy" (M.A. thesis, University of Wisconsin–Madison, 1987).

46. Allen, "Tailors, Soldiers, and Slaves," p. 8. Allen did not distinguish between free-born and ex-slaves among the free *pardos.*

47. Ramos, "Social Revolution Frustrated," p. 78.

48. Anne Pérotin-Dumon, in her study of the Lesser Antilles for the years 1789–1794, successfully discusses the emergence of politics among the free and enslaved male population of African descent. In revolutionary Guadeloupe, different groups of people adopted the key concepts, such as "liberty" and "freedom," but interpreted and used them for different purposes. See Anne Pérotin-Dumon, "The Emergence of Politics among Free-Coloreds and Slaves in Revolutionary Guadeloupe," *Journal of Caribbean History* 25, nos. 1–2 (1991): 100–135.

49. Schwartz points out that the Tailors' Revolt seems to fit into the model that historians Michael Craton and Eugene D. Genovese respectively draw on to document an important change in the type or nature of slave rebellions during the Age of Revolution. Craton maintains that in the British Caribbean, maroon-style rebellions led by "unassimilated" African-born slaves in the earlier period were replaced by movements led by elite creole slaves. Genovese, in his comparative study of slave rebellions in the New World, maintains: "Until the Age of Revolution the slaves did not challenge the world capitalist system within which slavery itself embedded. Rather, they sought escape and autonomy—a local, precapitalist social restoration. When they did become revolutionary and raise the banner of abolition, they did so within the context of the bourgeois-democratic revolutionary wave." See Schwartz, *Sugar Plantations,* pp. 472–473; Michael Craton, *Testing the Chains: Resistance to Slavery in the British West Indies* (Ithaca, N.Y.: Cornell University Press, 1982); Genovese, *From Rebellion to Revolution,* p. xxi. Most recently, Michael Mullin attempts to establish a typology to explain changes in major slave rebellions in Anglo America (namely the American South and the West Indies) between 1736 and 1831 by setting up three historical stages of "acculturation" for the slave population. These are: "the unseasoned" (from the 1730s to the 1760s); "plantation slaves" (from the late 1760s to the early 1800s); and "the assimilated" (from the late 1760s to the second quarter of the nineteenth century). See Mullin, *Africa in America,* especially pp. 268–273. On American slavery in the revolutionary era (1770–1823), see David Brion Davis, *The Problem of Slavery in the Age of Revolution* (Ithaca, N.Y.: Cornell University Press, 1975). On slave resistance in the American South during the same period, see Sylvia R. Frey, *Water from the Rock: Black Resistance in a Revolutionary Age* (Princeton, N.J.: Princeton University Press, 1991).

50. Schwartz discusses the distinction between African-born and Brazilian-born, as well as between *crioulos* and mulattoes, resulting in different political actions. See Schwartz, *Sugar Plantations,* p. 473.

51. Michael C. McBeth, "The Brazilian Recruit during the First Empire: Slave or Soldier?" in Dauril Alden and Warren Dean, eds., *Essays Concerning the Socioeconomic History of Brazil and Portuguese India* (Gainesville: University Press of Florida, 1977), p. 71.

52. Joan E. Menzar, "The Ranks of the Poor: Military Service and Social Differen-

tiation in Northeast Brazil, 1830–1875," *HAHR* 72, no. 3 (1992): 335–351. Menzar argues that the Quebra Quilos revolt, which took place in northeast Brazil in November and December of 1874, was a manifestation of the desire of the poor "honorable" working people to maintain their status separate from slaves and "undesirables." See ibid., pp. 347–351.

53. F. W. O. Morton, "The Military in Bahia, 1800–1821," *Journal of Latin American Studies* 7, no. 2 (1975): 257–258. A royal decree of 1822 stipulated that all Brazilian single males between the ages of 18 and 35 were subject to service in the army, whereas the so-called nonrecruitment law exempted the following categories: married men and only sons; overseers and administrators of cattle ranches, plantations, and brick factories; seamen; merchants; students; and cattle herders, bricklayers, carpenters, and fishermen as long as they "actually exercised their craft and were well behaved." When the national guard was created on August 14, 1831, all Brazilian men between 18 and 60, but only from families whose annual incomes qualified them to vote, became subject to national guard service. This financial qualification distinguished the national guard from the army. See Menzar, "Ranks of the Poor," pp. 337–340.

54. Russell-Wood, *Black Man in Slavery and Freedom*, p. 86.

55. Maria Graham, *Journal of a Voyage to Brazil*, p. 141. Maria Graham praised the black regiment in Salvador as "unquestionably the best trained, and most serviceable, as a light infantry." See ibid., p. 141.

56. APB, Ordens régias 54 (January 30, 1754); Arquivo Histórico Ultramarino (Lisbon), Bahia, papéis avulsos, caixa 66 (December 8, 1756) and maço 18 (May 11, 1756), cited by Stuart B. Schwartz, "The Formation of a Colonial Identity in Brazil," in Nicolas Canny and Anthony Pagden, eds., *Colonial Identity in the Atlantic World, 1500–1800* (Princeton, N.J.: Princeton University Press, 1987), p. 48.

57. Kátia M. de Queirós Mattoso, *Bahia, século XIX: uma província no império* (Rio de Janeiro: Editora Nova Fronteira, 1992), p. 404; Julita Scarano, "Black Brotherhoods: Integration or Contradiction?" *Luso-Brazilian Review* 16, no. 1 (1979): 11; and Maria Inés Côrtes da Oliveria, *O liberto*, pp. 84–85.

58. Mattoso, *Bahia, século XIX*, pp. 401, 400.

59. Oliveira, *O liberto*, p. 84.

60. APB, Livros de registro de testamentos, nos. 35–61. This confirms the findings of Kátia Mattoso in her study of 200 wills of ex-slaves in Salvador. According to her analysis, for the years 1790–1826 those who did not belong to any sodality numbered only 14.9 percent of men and 17 percent of women. These relatively low percentages escalated to 98.5 percent for men and 87 percent for women for the period 1863–1890. See Mattoso, *Testamentos de escravos libertos*, p. 23 (Table 2). Mattoso consulted 100 wills of ex-slaves for each period: 53 men and 47 women for 1790–1826 and 31 men and 69 women for 1863–1890. Oliveira's study of 482 wills of ex-slaves for 1790–1890 strongly supports this point and furthermore indicates a gradual process of change in ex-slaves' atti-

tudes toward lay sodalities. The percentages of those who did not mention membership in any sodality are 21.6 percent (men) and 18.5 percent (women) for 1790–1830; 50.0 percent (men) and 42.4 percent (women) for 1830–1850; and 96.1 percent (men) and 84.2 percent (women) for 1850–1890. See Oliveira, *Liberto*, p. 84.

61.   APB, Livros de registro de testamentos.

62.   AINS, Livro de termo e resolução, f. 104. These data do not have any breakdown by legal distinction, birthplace, or color. Among the ex-slaves who registered their wills, there were 13 men and 20 women who held memberships in this specific black sodality for 1808–1849, but for 1850–1888 only one was a member of this sodality. See APB, Livros de registro de testamentos.

63.   Wetherell, *Brazil: Stray Notes from Bahia*, p. 79.

64.   C. R. Boxer, *Women in Iberian Expansion Overseas 1415–1815: Some Facts, Fancies and Personalities* (New York: Oxford University Press, 1975), chapter 6, relates the popularity of the cult of the Virgin Mary to the notion of the basic inferiority of women in colonial Iberian Society. William B. Taylor discusses the historical process in which the Virgin of Guadalupe, a representation of the Virgin Mary, became the symbol of future Mexico before independence. See William B. Taylor, "The Virgin of Guadalupe in New Spain: An Inquiry into the Social History of Marian Devotion," *American Ethnologist* 14, no. 1 (1987): 9–33. See also William B. Taylor, *Magistrates of the Sacred: Priests and Parishioners in Eighteenth-Century Mexico* (Stanford, Calif.: Stanford University Press, 1996), chapter 11. On the indigenous population's response to Christianity in the case of late colonial Mexico, see Stephanie Wood, "Adopted Saints: Christian Images in Nahua Testaments of Late Colonial Toluca," *Americas* 47, no. 3 (1991): 259–294; and James Lockhart, *The Nahuas after the Conquest: A Social and Cultural History of the Indians of Central Mexico, Sixteenth through Eighteenth Centuries* (Stanford: Stanford University Press, 1992), chapter 6. I am grateful to Professor William B. Taylor for allowing me to read two chapters of his book before publication. On the cult and veneration of the Virgin Mary in general, see Hilda Graef, *Mary: A History of Doctrine and Devotion* (Westminster: Christian Classics and London: Sheed & Ward, 1985 [1963 (Part 1) and 1965 (Part 2)]); and Marina Warner, *Alone of All Her Sex: The Myth and the Cult of the Virgin Mary* (New York: Alfred A. Knopf, 1976).

65.   Borges, *Family in Bahia*, pp. 58 and 63.

66.   Wetherell, *Brazil: Stray Notes from Bahia*, p. 24.

67.   ACMS, Livros de batizados, freguesia de Santo Antônio. In Brazil, church practice was codified in the synod in 1707 and published in the *Constituiçoes primeiras do Arcebispado na Bahia* in 1720. According to this code, baptism was to be given to newborn infants by a parish priest within eight days of birth, and each child was to have only one godmother (over the age of 12) and one godfather (over the age of 14). The baptism of newly arrived and unacculturated slaves called for special religious instruction to ensure that they under-

stood their obligations as members of the church. See Schwartz, *Slaves, Peasants, and Rebels*, p. 139.

68. The staff of the Arquivo da Cúria Metropolitana de São Salvador da Bahia (ACMS), personal communication.

69. From the twelfth century on, increased importance was given to the Virgin Mary in accordance with the ongoing feminization process of religious language. Women continued to be perceived as physiologically and spiritually weaker, defective in body and moral fortitude, but as being equally worthy of salvation. See Caroline Walker Bynum, *Jesus as Mother: Studies in the Spirituality of the High Middle Ages* (Berkeley, Los Angeles, and London: University of California Press, 1982), p. 135.

70. Taylor, *Magistrates of the Sacred*, chapter 11 and personal communication.

71. Taylor, *Magistrates of the Sacred*, chapter 11.

72. Schwartz, *Slaves, Rebels, and Peasants*, p. 139.

73. Ibid., pp. 139 and 150. The practice of baptizing children with the Virgin Mary as godmother took place in other parts of Brazil during the nineteenth century. See Gudeman and Schwartz, "Cleaning Original Sin," p. 52; Renata Pinto Venâncio, "Nos limites da sagrada família: illegitimidade e casamento no Brasil colonial," in Ronaldo Vanifes, ed., *História e sexualidade no Brasil* (Rio de Janeiro: Graal, 1986), pp. 113–121; Elizabeth Anne Kuznesof, "Sexual Politics, Race and Bastard-Bearing in Nineteenth-Century Brazil: A Question of Culture or Power," *Journal of Family History* 16, no. 3 (1991): 256; Schwartz, *Slaves, Peasants, and Rebels*, p. 150; Robert M. Levine, "'Mud-Hut Jerusalem': Canudos Revised," *HAHR* 68, no. 3 (1988): 525–576. According to Marcia Elisa de Campos Graf this custom was common in nineteenth-century southern Brazil. Maria Elisa de Campos Graf, personal communication.

74. The historian Suzanne Desan discusses the re-emergence of lay Christianity in the case of revolutionary France. See Suzanne Desan, *Reclaiming the Sacred: Lay Religion and Popular Politics in Revolutionary France* (Ithaca, N.Y.: Cornell University Press, 1990).

75. Verger, *Trade Relations*, p. 465.

76. Arquivo da Sociedade Protetora dos Desvalidos, Salvador, Brazil (hereafter ASPD), Livro de termos do ano de 1832; Verger, *Trade Relations*, pp. 457–459; and Júlio Santana Braga, *Sociedade protetora dos desvalidos: uma irmandade de côr* (Salvador: Ianamá, 1987). Not only did both Verger and Braga misidentify Manoel Victor Serra and the founding member of the sodality as free (or freed) Africans, but they misinterpreted the primary purpose of the Protective Society as an emancipation pool (*junta de alforria*). Their argument was grounded on the presence of the safe box, which still exists in the Society, but sodalities often had safe boxes, such as the case of the black sodality of Our Lady of the Rosary in the Pelourinho. For example, see chapter 18 of its statutes (1820): AINS, Compromisso da Irmandade da Nossa Senhora do homens prêtos no ano de 1820.

77. ASPD, Livro de termos e acordãos, f. 7B (August 4, 1833).

78. Compromisso da Irmandade do Glorioso São Francisco de Paula Filial à Matriz de Nossa Senhora do Pilar, de crioulos livres nascidos no Imperio do Brazil, ano de 1844, Arquivo da Venerável Ordem Terceira de Nossa Senhora do Monte do Carmo (Salvador, Brazil). I am grateful to Professor A. J. R. Russell-Wood for the copy of this *compromisso*.

79. The popularity of the cult of the Virgin of Guadalupe, patron saint of Mexico, especially among the indigenous population, is attributable to the alleged miraculous appearance of the Virgin in December 1531. Her church was subsequently built at a historically special place, which had been sacred to the Aztec maize goddess. See George M. Foster, *Culture and Conquest: America's Spanish Heritage* (New York: Wenner Gren Foundation for Anthropological Research, 1960), p. 207.

80. Russell-Wood, "Examination," pp. 247–248; idem, "Black and Mulatto Brotherhoods," pp. 577–578.

81. Compromisso da Irmandade do Glorioso São Francisco de Paula (1844), chapters 21–32, Arquivo da Venerável Ordem Terceira de Nossa Senhora do Monte de Carmo; and Russell-Wood, *Black Man in Slavery and Freedom*, p. 152.

82. In the remaining census records of 1855, among the free population, 52.2 percent of the couples who shared the same households were not married. See Mattoso, *Família e sociedade*, p. 82.

7. The Labyrinth of Identity, 1851–1888

1. Brasil, *Recenseamento da população*, pp. 508 and 510.

2. AMCS, Livros de escrituras da compra e venda de escravos, freguesia da Sé, nos. 82.1–82.20; APB, Seção Judiciária, Inventários da capital (1808–1888).

3. Brasil, *Recenseamento da população*, pp. 308, 310.

4. Conrad, *Destruction of Brazilian Slavery*, chapters 9–12.

5. Emília Viotti da Costa, *The Brazilian Empire: Myths and Histories* (Chicago: Dorsey Press, 1988), p. 147.

6. APB, Livros de notas and maço 2880.

7. APB, Seção Judiciária, Autos Crimes, 3531.8. On Bahian abolitionism and abolitionist societies, see Pierson, *Negroes in Brazil*, pp. 54–59. On abolitionism in Brazil, see Conrad, *Destruction of Brazilian Slavery*, pp. 121–277; Robert Brent Toplin, *The Abolition of Slavery in Brazil* (New York: Atheneum, 1972).

8. Compra e venda de escravo para a Guerra do Paraguay 1867, APB, Seção Histórica, maço 2970; Trosko, "Liberto in Bahia," p. 30 and footnote 48.

9. Conrad, *Destruction of Brazilian Slavery*, pp. 90–117; Toplin, *Abolition of Slavery*, pp. 20–21.

10. APB, Livro de notas, no. 411, August 8, 1871; ibid., no. 411, August 12, 1871; ibid., no. 416, August 21, 1817.

11. APB, Livro de notas, no. 711, March 20, 1883.

12. APB, Seção Judiciária, Autos Crimes, no. 2360.5.

13. Chalhoub, "Slaves, Freedmen and the Politics of Freedom," p. 78. See also idem, *Visões da liberdade,* chapter 2.

14. Sandra Lauderdale Graham, "Slavery's Impasse: Slave Prostitutes, Small-Time Mistresses, and the Brazilian Law of 1871," *Comparative Studies in History and Society* 33, no. 4 (1991): 669–694. On slave prostitution in nineteenth-century Rio de Janeiro, see, for instance, Luiz Carlos Soares, *Rameiras, ilhoas, polacas . . . : A prostituição no Rio de Janeiro do século XIX* (São Paulo: Editora Atica, 1992), chapter 5.

15. Lauderdale Graham, "Slavery's Impasse," p. 676.

16. Brasil, *Recenseamento da população,* pp. 510, 512.

17. Merrick and Graham, *Population and Economic Development,* p. 59.

18. Slenes, "Demography and Economics," p. 420, Table 9.2.

19. Merrick and Graham, *Population and Economic Development,* p. 59, particularly Table IV-3 and note 5. Robert Conrad cites the same data as proof that ex-slaves rushed to register their marital status once they obtained their freedom, but does not pay any attention to the problem in the Brazilian census data. See Conrad, *World of Sorrow,* p. 13.

20. Brasil, *Recenseamento da população,* pp. 508, 510.

21. The percentage of self-identified mulattoes continued to grow in post-emancipation Salvador: from 35.1% (1890) to 38.4% (1944), while that of the *prêto* population did not change (26.3% for both 1890 and 1940). See Kim D. Butler, *Freedoms Given, Freedoms Won: Afro-Brazilians in Post-Abolition São Paulo and Salvador* (New Brunswick, N.J.: Rutgers University Press, 1998), p. 134, Table 7. Needless to say, these census data do not suggest a scale of further racial mixture but demonstrate Afro-Brazilians' continuing denial of blackness and eagerness to pass as mulattoes.

22. Dain Borges states that the usage of *crioulo* became impolite in Bahia after the turn of the twentieth century. See Borges, *Family in Bahia,* p. 292.

23. In present-day Salvador, the term *prêto,* which is regarded as extremely pejorative, is rarely used to refer to a dark-skinned person, unless it is intended to offend the person.

24. APB, Autos Crimes, 2594.2. Conducting his research in the late 1930s, the U.S. sociologist Donald Pierson stated that the term *negro* was "seldom heard in Bahia," since it was regarded as "*a palavra pesada,* a harsh, even offensive term." See Pierson, *Negroes in Brazil,* p. 138. Pierson recorded terms and popular expressions for various phenotypes among the mulatto population. Ibid., pp. 135–138.

25. Manoel Francisco dos Santos, *Discurso Proferido na Sociedade Protetora dos Desvalidos* (1876), APB, maço 5306.

26.   I was very fortunate to learn interesting oral history in person from longtime
      members of the Society for the Protection of the Needy on many occasions,
      although I had not planned to conduct interviews. Our conversations usually
      took place in the main meeting room of the Society for the Protection of the
      Needy in the afternoons over cool *maté* tea with much sugar, which I was
      generously offered whenever I visited there for consultation of their historical
      documents. Those old members, all Afro-Brazilian men, gathered around one
      by one and started to speak to me about their histories, which must have been
      constructed and reconstructed since the days of slavery, together with their
      activities as members of this association and their individual experiences as
      "black" Bahians. My gratitude goes to Sr. Aloisío Conceição Rocha and his
      fellow members of the Society for the Protection of the Needy as well as his
      cousin Padre Rocha. Sr. Rocha, who is a devoted Catholic, has been also ac-
      tively engaged in *candomblé* throughout his life, although he does not hold
      the title of *pai de santo.* Every one of those members of the Society for the
      Protection of the Needy conveyed to me "in an individual way the collective
      experience of a conquered people," and revealed "his experiences as they are
      embodied in, and embody, the history of his society," as Mintz describes his
      Puerto Rican informant named Tazo in his monograph entitled *Worker in
      the Cane.* See Sidney W. Mintz, "The Sensation of Moving, while Standing
      Still," *American Ethnologist* 16, no. 4 (1989): 792. Also, as Mintz perceives his
      relationship with Tazo (ibid., pp. 794–795), I feel the people of the Society for
      the Protection of the Needy had "chosen" me; I happened to "come along"
      when those individuals were ready to tell their stories. See Sidney W. Mintz,
      Worker in the Cane: A Puerto Rican Life History (New York: W. W. Norton,
      1974 [1960]).

27.   *Estatutos da Sociedade Protetora dos Desvalidos* (1873), titulo 1 and art. 9, pub-
      lished by Braga, in *Sociedade protetora,* pp. 79–89. I was not able to consult the
      original copy of the *Estatutos* (1873), since Sr. Rocha, who is in charge of their
      Archives, was unable to locate it during my research period.

28.   Wetherell, *Brazil: Stray Notes from Bahia,* p. 85.

29.   ASPD, Livro de matriculas (1870–1950); Documentos dos anos (1870–1874).

30.   *Estatutos da Sociedade Protetora dos Desvalidos* (1873), art. 11.

31.   The first female member of the Society for the Protection of the Needy, who
      was an elderly lady but in excellent health in June 1989, came to the headquar-
      ters relatively often, but just briefly each time, during my research, but she
      never joined the table where the male members and I gathered for talks.

32.   Anani Dzidzienyo, "Africa-Brazil: Ex Africa Semper Aliquid Novi," in Larry
      Crook and Randall Johnson, eds., *Black Brazil: Culture, Identity, and Social
      Mobilization* (Los Angeles: UCLA Latin American Studies Center, University
      of California, 1999) and personal communication.

33.   *Estatutos da Sociedade Protetora dos Desvalidos* (Salvador: *Sociedade Protetora
      dos Desvalidos,* 1974).

34. The term *mestiço* was employed in the Brazilian national censuses of 1890 but was again replaced by *pardo* in 1940. See Butler, *Freedoms Given, Freedoms Won,* p. 134. Today *mestiço* is not used commonly.

35. Daphne Patai, *Brazilian Women Speak: Contemporary Life Stories* (New Brunswick, N.J.: Rutgers University Press, 1988), pp. 12–15. Patai capitalizes the terms as White and Black, while I put them in quotation marks.

36. Patai, *Brazilian Women Speak,* p. 11. For an excellent discussion of color and gender identity among Afro-Brazilian women, see John Burdick, *Blessed Anastácia: Women, Race, and Popular Christianity in Brazil* (New York: Routledge, 1998), chapter 1.

37. Carl N. Degler, *Neither Black nor White: Slavery and Race Relations in Brazil and the United States* (Madison: University of Wisconsin Press, 1986 [1971]), chapter V.

38. Virginia R. Domínguez, *White by Definition: Social Classification in Creole Louisiana* (New Brunswick, N.J.: Rutgers University Press, 1986).

39. The Brazilian Institute of Geography and Statistics (IBGE) decided in 1980 to begin analyzing and publishing racial data in dichotomous form by dividing the population into whites (*brancos*) and blacks (*prêtos*). According to George Reid Andrews, in São Paulo, Rio de Janeiro, and the states of southern Brazil, such a North American dichotomous vision of race hierarchy as blacks versus whites "corresponds not just to 'objective' statistical indicators but to subjective Brazilian perceptions of race as well." Andrews, *Blacks and Whites in São Paulo,* pp. 250–251. Since the turn of the 1970s, many demographers, both Brazilians and non-Brazilians, have discussed "racial inequalities" in Brazil based on quantitative analysis of census data. The Brazilian sociologist Nelson do Valle Silva, in particular, maintains that the complex web of color terminology can be reduced into three categories: blacks, *pardos,* and whites, and concludes that the race-related differences between blacks and *pardos* are far less significant than the difference between "whites" and "non-whites." See Nelson do Valle Silva, "Updating the Cost of Not Being White in Brazil," in Pierre-Michel Fontaine, ed., *Race, Class, and Power in Brazil* (Los Angeles: Center for Afro-American Studies, University of California, Los Angeles, 1980). See also Carlos Hasenbalg, Nelson do Valle Silva, and Márcia Lima, *Cor e estratifição social* (Rio de Janeiro: Contra Capa Libraria, 1999).

40. David L. Marcus and Lennox Samuels, "Melting Pot Coming to a Boil," *Dallas Morning News,* January 16, 1994, p. 31A. My italics. I am grateful to Professor William B. Taylor for a copy of the article. This newspaper article does not specify the original Portuguese word that has been translated as "black."

41. Recent studies on blackness and racial identity in Latin America include Guss, "Selling of San Juan"; Winthrop R. Wright, *Café con leche: Race, Class, and National Image in Venezuela* (Austin: University of Texas Press, 1990); Peter Wade, *Blackness and Race Mixture: The Dynamics of Racial Identity in Colombia* (Baltimore: Johns Hopkins University Press, 1993); idem, "The

Cultural Politics of Blackness in Colombia," *American Ethnologist* 22, no. 2 (1995): 341–357; Aline Helg, *Our Rightful Share: The Afro-Cuban Struggle for Equality, 1886–1912* (Chapel Hill: University of North Carolina Press, 1995); and Alejandro de la Fuente, *A Nation for All: Race, Inequality, and Politics in Twentieth-Century Cuba* (Chapel Hill: University of North Carolina Press, 2001).

42. Guss, "Selling of San Juan," p. 466.

43. For recent studies on the *movimento negro*, see Andrews, *Blacks and Whites in São Paulo*, pp. 146–207; Michael James Mitchell, "Racial Consciousness and the Political Attitudes and Behavior of Blacks in São Paulo" (Ph.D. diss., Indiana University, 1977); Michael George Hanchard, *Orpheus and Power: The Movimento Negro of Rio de Janeiro and São Paulo, Brazil, 1945–1988* (Princeton, N.J.: Princeton University Press, 1994); and Butler, *Freedoms Given, Freedoms Won*. See also Larry Crook and Randall Johnson, eds., *Black Brazil: Culture, Identity, and Social Mobilization* (Berkeley and Los Angeles: University of California Press, 1999); Michael Hanchard, ed., *Racial Politics in Contemporary Brazil* (Durham, N.C.: Duke University Press, 1999); Antonio Sérgio Alfredo Guimarães and Lynn Huntley, eds., *Tirando a máscara: ensaios sobre o racismo no Brasil* (São Paulo: Paz e Tera, 2000).

44. Melissa Nobles maintains: "The umbrella term *movimento negro* subsumes a variety of activities and organizations that are held together only by the term *negro*, which glosses over the regional, class, political, and ideological divisions between and among them. More important, the use of 'black movement' conceals the absence of a broadly shared understanding of 'black' and to whom 'black' should be applied." See Melissa Nobles, *Shades of Citizenship: Race and Censuses in Modern Politics* (Stanford, Calif.: Stanford University Press, 2000), p. 146. See also Rebecca Reichmann, "Introduction," in Rebecca Reichmann, ed., *Race in Contemporary Brazil: From Indifference to Inequality* (University Park: Pennsylvania State University Press, 1999), pp. 14–20; Abdias do Nascimento, *Brazil Mixture or Massacre? Essays in the Genocide of a Black People*, trans. Elisa Larkin Nascimento, 2nd ed. (Dover, Mass.: Majority Press, 1989); Abdias do Nascimento and Elisa Larkin Nascimento, *Africans in Brazil: A Pan-African Perspective* (Trenton, N.J.: Africa World Press, 1992); idem, "Reflexões sobre o movimento negro no Brasil, 1938–1997," in Guimarães and Huntley, eds., *Tirando a máscara*.

45. Reichmann, "Introduction," p. 11. Reichmann states: "In accord with the official version, the *negro* acknowledges and welcomes African identity, embracing Africa's cultural contributions to Brazilian life. In a departure from the received ideology, however, the *negro's* consciousness is heightened about the significance of ethnicity (rather than color) and, regardless of his or her own statues, identifies with the subjugation of black people in Brazil." See ibid, p. 11.

46. Ibid., p. 2, note 3.

47. Andrews, *Blacks and Whites in São Paulo*, chapters 6 and 7. Andrews discusses

a tendency among light-skinned Afro-Brazilians, who identify themselves as mulattoes, to emphasize their social superiority over darker-skinned Afro-Brazilians. See ibid., pp. 178–179.

48. Anani Dzidzienyo, personal communication.

49. For psychological studies on mulatto identity in present-day Brazil, see, for instance, Eneida de Almeida Reis, "Mulato: negro-não-negro e/ou branco-não-branco: un estudo psicossocial sobre identidate" (M.A. thesis, Pontícia Universidade Católica, 1997).

50. Based on substantial in-depth interviews with Afro-Brazilian women I have conducted in the city of São Paulo (1997–2001), I have discussed the remarkable lack of racial consciousness among the urban poor, especially among the migrant population from the Northeast, most of whom identify themselves as *morenos* (dark-complexioned), not *negros*. See Mieko Nishida, "Voices of Otherness: 'Black' and 'Japanese' Women in São Paulo, Brazil" (paper presented at the Latin American Studies Association Congress, Washington, D.C., September 6–8, 2001); "Gender, Race, and Ethnicity in Urban Brazil: 'Black' and 'Japanese' Women in São Paulo" (paper presented at the American Historical Association Annual Meeting, San Francisco, Calif., January 3–6, 2002).

Conclusion

1. See, for instance, Viotti da Costa, *Brazilian Empire*, pp. 239–243.

2. Ira Berlin, "Time, Space, and the Evolution of Afro-American Society on British Mainland North America," *AHR* 85, no. 1 (1980): 44–78; and Curtin, *Atlantic Slave Trade*, p. 268 (Table 77).

3. Nobles, *Shades of Citizenship*, p. 68. Although socially, as African Americans, they have not been regarded as a separate racial group from blacks, mulattoes have always occupied an ambiguous yet very important position in American culture. See, for instance, Judith R. Berzon, *Neither Black nor White: The Mulatto in American Fiction* (New York: New York University Press, 1978). Berzon maintains that "the key elements in distinguishing the mulatto from the full-blooded blacks are sociological and psychological rather than biological" and defines the mulatto as "an individual who reaps certain advantages and disadvantages in his interaction with both blacks and whites, advantages and disadvantages which are a direct result of his mixed racial heritage." See ibid., p. 8.

4. On the multiracial movement in the United States, see Nobles, *Shades of Citizenship*, pp. 130–145. The movement no longer exits today.

5. For discussions on diasporas, see, for instance, Khaching Tölölyan, "Rethinking Diaspora(s): Stateless Power in the Transnational Movement," *Diaspora* 5, no. 1 (1996): 3–36; James Clifford, *Routes: Travel and Translation in the Late Twentieth Century* (Cambridge, Mass.: Harvard University Press, 1997), pp. 244–277; Smadar Lavie and Ted Swedenburg, eds., *Displacement, Diaspora, and Geographies of Identity* (Durham, N.C.: Duke University Press,

1996); and Robin Cohen, *Global Diaspora: An Introduction* (Seattle: University of Washington Press, 1997).

6. Monica Schuler, *"Alas, Alas, Kongo": A Social History of Indentured African Immigration into Jamaica, 1841–1865* (Baltimore: Johns Hopkins University Press, 1980).

7. George Gmelch, *Double Passage: The Lives of Caribbean Migrants Abroad and Back Home* (Ann Arbor: University of Michigan Press, 1992).

8. The original Japanese term *dekasegi* refers to a seasonal labor migration or migrant to big cities within Japan. By 1991, the population of Japanese Brazilians numbered around 1.2 million, out of whom some 100,000 had migrated to Japan. For major legal issues concerning *dekassegui* (the Brazilian term) see Masato Ninomiya, org., *"Dekassegui": Gensho ni kansuru Simpojium Hokokusho* (São Paulo: Sociedade Brasileira de Cultura Japonesa, 1993). As of the year 2001, 250,000 Japanese Brazilians are said to be working in Japan.

9. See, for instance, "In Japan, Bias is an Obstacle Even for the Ethnic Japanese," *New York Times,* November 13, 1991; and "Sons and Daughters of Japan, Back from Brazil," *New York Times,* November 27, 2001. Japanese journalists have published numerous small accounts on Japanese Brazilian migrant workers in Japan, such as "Kyuzo-suru Nikkei Brajiru-jin: 'Sokoku' Nippon de Hataraku" ("The increasing number of Japanese Brazilians, working in their 'homeland'"), *Asahi Shimbun Weekly AERA,* March 19, 1991, pp. 46–48. Japanese American novelist Karen Tei Yamashita, author of the highly acclaimed *Brazil-Maru* (1993) on Japanese immigration to Brazil, has just published a book on Japanese Brazilian *dekassegui* workers based on her observations during her six-month stay in Nagoya, Japan in 1997. See Karen Tei Yamashita, *Circle K Cycles* (Minneapolis: Coffee House Press, 2001). Recent scholarly monographs on *dekassegui* workers in Japan include Takayuki Tsuda, "Strangers in the Ethnic Homeland: The Migration, Ethnic Identity, and Psychological Adaptation of Japan's New Immigrant Minorities" (Ph.D. diss., University of California at Berkeley, 1996); Joshua H. Roth, "Defining Communities: The Nation, the Firm, the Neighborhood, and Japanese Brazilian Migrants in Japan" (Ph.D. diss., Cornell University, 1999). Other studies on *dekassegui* include Keiko Yamanaka, "Return Migration of Japanese-Brazilians to Japan: The Nikkeijin as Ethnic Minority and Political Construct," *Diaspora* 5, no. 1 (1996), pp. 65–98; idem, "'I will go home, but when?' Labor Migration and Circular Diaspora Formation by Japanese Brazilians in Japan," in Mike Douglas and Glenda S. Roberts, eds., *Japan and Global Migration: Foreign Workers and the Advent of a Multicultural Society* (New York: Routledge, 2000); Yoko Sellek, "Nikkeijin: The Phenomenon of Return Migration," in Michael Weiner, ed., *Japan's Minorities: The Illusion of Homogeneity* (New York: Routledge, 1997); Reimei Yoshioka, *Por que migramos do e para o Japão: os exemplos dos barrios das Alianças dos atuais dekasseguis* (São Paulo: Massao Ohno Editor, 1995); Renato Mikio Moriya, *Fenômeno dekassegui: um olhar sobre os adolescentes que ficaram,* with a preface by Paul Negri (Rôndorina: Edições CEFEL, 2000); and

Daniel Touro Linger, *No One Home: Brazilian Selves Remade in Japan* (Stanford, Calif.: Stanford University Press, 2001).

10. I am currently working on a book-length manuscript on Afro-Brazilian and Japanese Brazilian women in twentieth-century São Paulo, which is tentatively entitled: "The (Re) Making of Gender, Race, and Ethnicity: 'Black' and 'Japanese' Women in São Paulo, Brazil, 1888–2000." Part of my research has been published as a Working Paper in Latin American Studies Series by the University of Maryland at College Park as *Japanese Brazilian Women and Their Ambiguous Identities: Gender, Ethnicity, and Class in São Paulo* (2000). I am grateful to the Latin American Studies Center of the University of Maryland at College Park and the Center's director, Saúl Sosnowski, for a postdoctoral fellowship I was awarded for the 1997–1998 academic year.

11. See, for my detailed discussions on the subject, Mieko Nishida, "Diasporic Identities in Transformation: Repatriation Movements from Brazil and to West Africa and Japan" (paper presented at the Latin American Studies Association Congress, Miami, Florida, March 16–18, 2000).

12. One such example was published in a national newspaper. Rudy E. Carlino, author of this very short essay, wrote of her experience with a taxi driver in Turkey where she once lived: "I could see his look of perplexity: His passenger was a Chinese-looking woman, with an Italian name, born in the Philippines, and she was an American?" See her essay in the section "Life Is Shot: Autobiography as Haiku," *Washington Post,* February 3, 2002, p. F1.

13. Jan Arat Scholte, "The World of Collective Identities in a Globalizing World," *Review of International Political Economy* 3 (Winter 1996): 565–607, 575. I am grateful to David J. Bachner for the citations, a copy of his draft pages from his book manuscript on global education, and his continuing interest in my study.

Bibliography

Manuscript Sources

Salvador, Brazil

Arquivo da Cúria Metropolitana de São Salvador da Bahia
Arquivo da Igreja de Nossa Senhora do Rosário dos Homens Prêtos
Arquivo Municipal da Cidade do Salvador
Arquivo Público do Estado da Bahia
Arquivo da Santa Casa da Misercórdia da Bahia
Arquivo da Sociedade Protetora dos Desvalidos

Rio de Janeiro, Brazil

Arquivo Nacional do Rio de Janeiro
Biblioteca Nacional do Rio de Janeiro

Newspapers

Diário da Bahia (Salvador, Brazil)
Jornal da Bahia (Salvador, Brazil)
O Oculo Mágico (Salvador, Brazil)

Published Primary Sources

Abé-Lallemant, Robert. *Reise durch Nord =Brasilien im Jahre 1859.* 2 vols. Leipzig: F. D. Bradhaus, 1860.
———. *Viagem pelo norte do Brasil no anno de 1859.* Trans. Eduard de Lima Castro. 2 vols. Rio de Janeiro: Instituto Nacional do Livro, 1961.
Agassiz, Louis, Professor and Mrs. *A Journey in Brazil.* Boston: Ticker and Fields, 1868.
Almeida, Candino Mendes de. *Codigo philippino ou ordenações e leis do Reino de Portugal.* 14th ed. Rio de Janeiro: Typographia do Instituto Philamathico, 1870.
Bandinel, James. *Some Accounts of the Trade in Slaves from Africa as Connected with Europe and Africa.* London: Longman, Brown, 1862.
Brasil, Diretoria Geral de Estatística. *Recenseamento da população de Imperio do Brazil a que se procedeu no dia 1 de agosto de 1872.* Rio de Janeiro: Leuzinger, 1873–1876.
British and Foreign State Papers, vol. 40 (London: James Ridway & Sons, Picadilly, 1850–1851), pp. 428–429.
Burgess, Wilson. *Narrative of a Recent Visit to Brazil, to Present an Address on the Slave-*

Trade and Slavery, Issued by the Religious Society of Friends. London: Edmund Marsh, 1853.

Candler, John, and Wilson Burgess. *Narrative of a Recent Visit to Brazil to Present an Address on the Slave-Trade and Slavery, Issued by the Religious Society of Friends.* London: Edmund Marsh, 1853.

Christie, W. D. *Notes on Brazilian Questions.* London: Macmillan, 1865.

Clark, Edwin. *A Visit to South America: With Notes and Observations on the Moral and Physical Features of the Country, and the Incidents of the Voyage.* London: Dean and Son, 1978.

Clark, Hamlet. *Letters from Spain, Algeria, and Brazil during Past Entomological Rambles.* London: John van Woorst, Paternoster Row, 1867.

Collecção de leis do Imperio do Brazil. Rio de Janeiro: Tipografico Nacional, 1831–1888.

Debret, Jean Baptiste. *Viagem pitoresca e história ao Brasil.* Trans. Sérgio Millet. 3 vols. in 2 tomes. São Paulo: Martins and Editora da Universidade de São Paulo, 1972.

Dent, Hastings Charles. *A Year in Brazil with the Notes on the Abolition of Slavery, the Finances of the Empire, Religion, Meteorology, Natural History.* London: Kegan Paul, Trench, 1886.

"Devassa do levante de escravos occorido em Salvador em 1835." *Anais do Arquivo Público do Estado da Bahia* 38 (1968): 1–142.

Duncan, John. *Travels in Western Africa, in 1845 and 1846: Comprising a Journey from Whydah, through the Kingdom of Dahomey, to Adofoodia, in the Interior.* 2 vols. New York: Johnson Reprint Corporation, 1967 [1847].

Dundas, Robert. *Sketches of Brazil: Including New Views on Tropical and European Fever, with Remarks on a Premature Decay of the System Incident to Europeans on Their Return from Hot Climates.* London: John Churchill, 1852.

"1835 Insurreição de escravos." *Anais do Arquivo Público do Estado da Bahia* 40 (1970): 9–170.

Elwes, Robert. *A Sketcher's Tour round the World: Illustrations from Original Drawings by the Author.* London: Hurst and Blackett, 1854.

Ewbank, Thomas. *Life in Brazil; A Journal of a Visit to the Land of the Cocoa and the Palm.* New York: Harper and Brother, 1856.

Fala receitada da Assembléia Legislativa (falas e relatorios dos presidentes em exercio da Provincia). Bahia, 1839–1889.

Fletcher, James C., and Daniel P. Kidder. *Brazil and the Brazilians: Portrayed in Historical and Descriptive Sketches.* 9th ed. Boston: Little, Brown, 1879.

Gardner, George. *Travels in the Interior of Brazil Principally through the Northern Provinces and the Gold and Diamond Districts during the Years 1836–1841.* London: Milford House, 1987 [1846].

Gaston, James McFadden. *Hunting a Home in Brazil: The Agricultural Resources and Other Characteristics of the Country—Also, the Manners and Customs of the Inhabitants.* Philadelphia: King, Baird, Partners, 1867.

Graham, Maria Dundas (Lady Maria Calcott). *Journal of a Voyage to Brazil and Residence There, during Part of the Years 1821, 1822, 1823.* New York: Frederick A. Praeger, 1969 [1824].

Grant, Andrew. *History of Brazil: Comprising a Geographical Account of That Country,*

Together with a Narrative of the Most Remarkable Events Which Have Occurred There since the Discovery; A Description of the Manners, Customs, Religion, & C. of the Natives and Colonists; Interspersed with Remarks on the Nature of Its Soul, Climate, Production, and Foreign and Internal Commerce. London: Printed for Henry Colburn, 1809.

Hartt, Charles Frederick. *Geology and Physical Geography of Brazil.* Boston: Fields, Osgood, 1870.

Henderson, James. *A History of the Brazil: Comprising Its Geography, Commerce, Colonization, Aboriginal Inhabitants, & C. & C. & C.* London: Longman, Hurt, Rees, Orme, and Brown, 1821.

Kidder, Daniel P. *Sketches of Residence and Travels in Brazil.* 2 vols. Philadelphia: Sorin and Ball, 1845.

Koster, Henry. *Travels in Brazil 1809–1815.* 2 vols. London: Longman, Hurst, Rees, Orme, and Brown, 1817.

Lindley, Thomas. *Narrative of a Voyage to Brazil.* London: Printed for J. Johnson, 1805.

Marjoribanks, Alexander. *Travels in South and North America.* 5th ed. London: Simpkin, Marshall, 1854.

"Officio do Governador Conde da Ponte para o Visconde de Anadia, no qual o informa das provincias que tomara para destruir os *Quilombos,* formados pelos escravos fugidos dos seus senhores. Bahia, 7 de abril, 1807." *Anais da Biblioteca Nacional do Rio de Janeiro* 37 (1915): 450–451.

"Officio do Governador Conde da Ponte para o Visconde de Anadia, em que lhe da parte das provincias que adoptara para evitar um lavantamento dos escravos contra os brancos, de que tivera denuncia. Bahia, 16 de junho de 1807." *Anais da Biblioteca Nacional do Rio de Janeiro* 37 (1915): 460–461.

Prior, James. *Voyage along the Eastern Coast of Africa to Mosambique, Johanna, and Quiloa to St. Helena; to Rio de Janeiro, Bahia and Pernambuco in Brazil in the Nisus Frigate.* London: Printed for St. Richard Phillips, 1819.

Rugendas, João Maurício. *Viagem pitoresca através do Brasil.* Trans. Sérgio Millet. São Paulo: Livraria Martins Editora, 1972.

Spix, Johann B. von, and Carl Friedrich P. von Martius. *Viagem pelo Brasil.* Trans. Lúcia Furquim Lahmeyer. 2nd ed. 4 vols. Rio de Janeiro: Impresa Nacional, 1938.

Tollenare, L. F. de. *Notas dominiais.* Recife: Governo do Estado de Pernambuco, 1979.

Walsh, Robert. *Notices of Brazil in 1818 and 1829.* 2 vols. London: Fredrick Westley and A. H. Davis, 1830.

Wetherell, James. *Brazil. Stray Notes from Bahia: Being Extracts from Letters, &.c, during a Residence of Fifteen Years.* Ed. William Hadfield. Liverpool: Webb and Hunt, 1860.

Secondary Sources

Accioli de Cerqueira e Silva, Ignácio. *Memórias históricas e políticas da Bahia.* 6 vols. Salvador: Imprensa Oficial do Estado, 1931.

Aimes, Hubert H. S. "Coartación: A Spanish Institution for the Advancement of Slaves into Freedom." *Yale Review* 17 (1909): 412–431.

Alden, Dauril. "Late Colonial Brazil, 1750–1808." In Leslie Bethell, ed., *Colonial Brazil*. Cambridge: Cambridge University Press, 1987.

Algranti, Leila Mezan. *O feitor ausente; estudo sobre a escravidão urbana no Rio de Janeiro de 1808 a 1821*. Petrópolis: Vozes, 1988.

Allen, Judith Lee. "Tailors, Soldiers, and Slaves: The Social Anatomy of a Conspiracy." M.A. thesis, University of Wisconsin–Madison, 1987.

Amaral, José Alvares do. "Cronicas dos Acontecimentos da Bahia (1809–1828)." *Anais do Arquivo Público do Estado da Bahia* 16 (1938): 50–95.

Andrade, Maria José de Souza. *A mão de obra escrava em Salvador 1811–1860*. São Paulo: Corrupio, 1988.

Andrews, George Reid. *The Afro-Argentines of Buenos Aires, 1800–1900*. Madison: University of Wisconsin Press, 1980.

———. *Blacks and Whites in São Paulo, Brazil 1888–1988*. Madison: University of Wisconsin Press, 1991.

Andrews, George Reid, Emília Viotti da Costa, and Franklin W. Knight. "George Reid Andrews, *Blacks and Whites in São Paulo, Brazil, 1888–1988*. Madison, WI: University of Wisconsin Press, 1991. Introduction, Two Comments, and a Rejoinder by the Author." *Luso-Brazilian Review* 29, no. 2 (1992): 141–158.

Aufderheide, Patricia Ann. "Order and Violence: Social Deviance and Social Control in Brazil 1780–1840." Ph.D. diss., University of Minnesota, 1976.

Azevedo, Celia Maria Marinho de. *Onda negra, medo branco: o negro no imaginário das elites no século XIX*. Rio de Janeiro: Paz e Terra, 1987.

Azevedo, Thales de. *Povoamento da cidade do Salvador*. 2nd ed. São Paulo: Companhia Editora Nacional, 1955.

Bacelar, Jeferson Afonso, and Maria Conceição Barbosa de Sousa. *O Rosário dos Prêtos do Pelourinho*. Salvador: Fundação do Patromônio Artístico e Cultura da Bahia, 1974.

Barickman, B. J. *A Bahian Counterpart: Sugar, Tobacco, Cassava, and Slavery in the Recôncavo, 1780–1860*. Stanford, Calif.: Stanford University Press, 1998.

Barman, Roderick J. *Brazil: The Forging of a Nation, 1798–1852*. Stanford, Calif.: Stanford University Press, 1988.

Barth, Fredrik. "Introduction." In Fredrik Barth, ed., *Ethnic Groups and Boundaries: The Social Organization of Cultural Difference*. Bergen–Oslo: Universitets Forlaget, and London: George Allen and Unwin, 1969.

Bastide, Roger. *The African Religions of Brazil: Toward a Sociology of the Interpenetration of Civilizations*. Trans. Helen Sebba. Baltimore: Johns Hopkins University Press, 1978.

Beckles, Hilary McD. *Natural Rebels: A Social History of Enslaved Black Women in Barbados*. New Brunswick, N.J.: Rutgers University Press, 1989.

Behar, Ruth. "Sexual Witchcraft, Colonialism, and Women's Powers: Views from the Mexican Inquisition." In Asunción Lavrin, ed. *Sexuality and Marriage in Colonial Latin America*. Lincoln: University of Nebraska Press, 1989.

Berkhofer, Robert F., Jr. *A Behavioral Approach to Historical Analysis*. New York: Free Press, and London: Collier-Macmillan, 1969.

Berlin, Ira. "Herbert G. Gutman and the American Working Class." In Herbert G.

Gutman, *Power and Culture: Essays on the American Working Class,* ed. Ira Berlin. New York: Pantheon Books, 1987.

———. *Slaves without Masters: The Free Negro in the Antebellum South.* New York: Oxford University Press, 1974.

———. "Time, Space, and the Evolution of Afro-American Society on British Mainland North America." *American Historical Review* 85, no. 1 (1980): 44–78.

Berlin, Ira, and Philip D. Morgan, eds. *The Slaves' Economy: Independent Production by Slaves in the Americas.* London: Frank Cass, 1991.

Berzon, Judith R. *Neither Black nor White: The Mulatto Character in American Fiction.* New York: New York University Press, 1978.

Bethell, Leslie. *The Abolition of the Brazilian Slave Trade: Britain, Brazil and the Slave Trade Question 1807–1869.* Cambridge: Cambridge University Press, 1970.

———. "The Independence of Brazil." In Leslie Bethell, ed., *Brazil: Empire and the Republic, 1822–1930.* Cambridge: Cambridge University Press, 1989.

Bethell, Leslie, and José Murilo de Carvalho. "1822–1850." In Leslie Bethell, ed., *Brazil: Empire and the Republic, 1822–1930.* Cambridge: Cambridge University Press, 1989.

Blassingame, John W. *The Slave Community: Plantation Life in the Antebellum South.* Revised and enlarged ed. New York and Oxford: Oxford University Press, 1979.

Boles, John B. *Black Southerners 1619–1869.* Lexington: University Press of Kentucky, 1983.

Bolster, W. Jeffrey. *Black Jacks: African American Seamen in the Age of Sail.* Cambridge, Mass.: Harvard University Press, 1997.

———. "'To Feel Like a Man': Black Seamen in the Northern States, 1800–1860." *Journal of American History* 76, no. 4 (1990): 1173–1199.

Borges, Dain. *The Family in Bahia, Brazil 1870–1945.* Stanford, Calif.: Stanford University Press, 1992.

Boon, James A. *Other Tribes, Other Scribes: Symbolic Anthropology in the Comparative Study of Cultures, Histories, Religions, and Texts.* Cambridge: Cambridge University Press, 1982.

Boschi, Caio César. *Os leigos e o poder (Irmandades leigas e política colonizadora em Minas Gerais).* São Paulo: Editora Ática, 1986.

Bott, Elizabeth. *Family and Social Network: Roles, Norms, and External Relationships in Ordinary Urban Families.* London: Tavistock Publications, 1959.

Bowser, Frederick P. *The African Slave in Colonial Peru 1524–1650.* Stanford, Calif.: Stanford University Press, 1974.

———. "The Free Person of Color in Mexico City and Lima: Manumission and Opportunity, 1650–1850." In Stanley L. Engerman and Eugene D. Genovese, eds., *Race and Slavery in the Western Hemisphere: Quantitative Studies.* Princeton, N.J.: Princeton University Press, 1975.

Boxer, C. R. *The Golden Age of Brazil 1695–1750: Growing Pains of a Colonial Society.* Berkeley and Los Angeles: University of California Press, 1962.

———. *Race Relations in the Portuguese Colonial Empire 1415–1825.* Oxford: Clarendon Press, 1963.

———. "Some Remarks on the Social and Professional Status of Physicians and Surgeons in the Iberian World, 16th–18th Centuries." *Revista de história de São Paulo* 50, no. 1 (1974): 197–219.

———. *Women in Iberian Expansion Overseas 1415–1815: Some Facts, Fancies and Personalities.* New York: Oxford University Press, 1975.

Braga, Júlio Santana. *O jogo de búzios: un estudo da adivinação no candomblé.* São Paulo: Editora Brasiliense, 1988.

———. *Sociedade protetora dos desvalidos: uma irmandade de cor.* Salvador, Bahia: Ianamá, 1987.

Breen, T. H. "Creative Adaptations: Peoples and Cultures." In Jack P. Greene and J. R. Pole, eds., *Colonial British America: Essays in the New History of the Early Modern Era.* Baltimore: Johns Hopkins University Press, 1984.

Breen, T. H., and Stephen Innes. *"Myne Owne Ground": Race and Freedom on Virginia's Eastern Shore, 1640–1676.* New York: Oxford University Press, 1980.

Britto, Eduard A. de Calda. "Levantes de prêtos na Bahia." *Revista do Instituto Geográfico e Histórico da Bahia* 10, no. 20 (1903): 69–94.

Brown, David Hilary. "Garden in the Machine: Afro-Cuban Sacred Act and Performance in Urban New Jersey and New York." Ph.D. diss., Yale University, 1989.

Bunster, Ximena, and Elsa M. Chaney. *Sellers and Servants: Working Women in Lima, Peru.* New York: Praeger, 1985.

Burdick, John. *Blessed Anastácia: Women, Race, and Popular Christianity in Brazil.* New York: Routledge, 1998.

Burke, Peter. *History and Social Theory.* Ithaca, N.Y.: Cornell University Press, 1993.

Bush, Barbara. *Slave Women in Caribbean Society 1650–1835.* Bloomington: Indiana University Press, 1990.

Butler, Kim D. *Freedoms Given, Freedoms Won: Afro-Brazilians in Post-Abolition, São Paulo and Salvador.* New Brunswick, N.J.: Rutgers University Press, 1998.

Bynum, Caroline Walker. *Jesus as Mother: Studies in the Spirituality of the High Middle Ages.* Berkeley, Los Angeles, and London: University of California Press, 1982.

Cadena, Marisol de la. "'Women Are More Indians': Ethnicity and Gender in a Community near Cuzco." In Brooke Larson and Olivia Harris, eds., with Enrique Tandeter, *Ethnicity, Markets, and Migration in the Andes: At the Crossroads of History and Anthropology.* Durham, N.C.: Duke University Press, 1995.

Campbell, Carl. "John Mohammed Bath and the Free Mandingos in Trinidad: The Question of Their Repatriation to Africa 1831–38." *Journal of African Studies* 12, no. 4 (1975): 467–495.

Campos, J. da Silva. "Ligeiras notas sobre a vida intima; costumes e religião dos africanos na Bahia." *Anais do Arquivo Público do Estado da Bahia* 29 (1943): 291–309.

Canny, Nicholas, and Anthony Pagden, eds. *Colonial Identity in the Atlantic World, 1500–1800.* Princeton, N.J.: Princeton University Press, 1987.

Cardoso, Fernando Henrique. *Capitalismo e escravidão no Brasil meridional: o negro na sociedade escravocrata do Rio Grande do Sul.* São Paulo: Difusão Européia do Livro, 1962.

Cardozo, Manoel S. "The Lay Brotherhoods of Colonial Bahia." *The Catholic Historical Review* 33, no. 1 (1947): 12–30.

Carneiro, Edison. *Ladinos e crioulos.* Rio de Janeiro: Editôra Civilização Brasileira, 1964.

Carroll, Patrick J. *Blacks in Colonial Veracruz: Race, Ethnicity, and Regional Development.* Austin: University of Texas Press, 1991.

Carvalho, Marcus J. M. de. *Liberdade: rotinas e ruptures do escravismo no Recife, 1822–1850.* Recife: Editora Universitaria de UFPE, 1998.

Chalhoub, Sidney. "Slaves, Freedmen and the Politics of Freedom in Brazil: The Experiences of Blacks in the City of Rio." *Slavery and Abolition* 10, no. 3 (1989): 64–84.

——. *Visões da liberdade: uma história das últimas décadas da escravidão na corte.* São Paulo: Companhia das Letras, 1990.

Chance, John K., and William B. Taylor. "Cofradias and Cargos: An Historical Perspective on the Mesoamerican Civil-Religious Hierarchy." *American Ethnologist* 12, no. 1 (1985): 1–26.

——. "Estate and Class in a Colonial City: Oaxaca in 1792." *Comparative Studies in Society and History* 19, no. 4 (1977): 454–487.

Clifford, James. *Routes: Travel and Translation in the Late Twentieth Century.* Cambridge, Mass.: Harvard University Press, 1997.

Cohen, Abner. *Custom and Politics in Urban Africa: A Study of Hausa Migrants in Yoruba Towns.* Berkeley and Los Angeles: University of California Press, 1969.

——. *Two Dimensional Man: An Essay on the Anthropology of Power and Symbolism in Complex Society.* London: Routledge and Kegan Paul, 1974.

Cohen, Abner, ed. *Urban Ethnicity.* London: Tavistock Publications, 1974.

Cohen, Anthony P. "Of Symbols and Boundaries; or, Does Erti's Greatcoat Hold the Key?" in Anthony P. Cohen, ed., *Symbolising Boundaries: Identity and Diversity in British Cultures.* Manchester: Manchester University Press, 1986.

——. *Self Consciousness: An Alternative Anthropology of Identity.* New York: Routledge, 1994.

——. *The Symbolic Construction of Community.* London: Tavistock Publications, 1985.

Cohen, David W., and Jack P. Greene, eds. *Neither Slave nor Free: The Freedmen of African Descent in the Slave Societies of the New World.* Baltimore: Johns Hopkins University Press, 1972.

Cohen, Robin. *Global Diaspora: An Introduction.* Seattle: University of Washington Press, 1997.

Collier, Jane Fishburne, and Sylvia Junko Yanagisako, eds. *Gender and Kinship: Essays toward a Unified Analysis.* Stanford, Calif.: Stanford University Press, 1987.

Conrad, Robert Edgar. *Children of God's Fire: A Documentary History of Black Slavery in Brazil.* Princeton, N.J.: Princeton University Press, 1983.

——. *The Destruction of Brazilian Slavery 1850–1888.* Berkeley and Los Angeles: University of California Press, 1972.

——. "Neither Slave nor Free: The *Emancipados* of Brazil, 1818–1868." *Hispanic American Historical Review* 53, no. 1 (1973): 50–70.

——. "Nineteenth-Century Brazilian Slavery." In Robert Brent Toplin, ed., *Slavery and Race Relations in Latin America.* Westport, Conn.: Greenwood Press, 1974.

——. *World of Sorrow: The African Slave Trade to Brazil.* Baton Rouge: Louisiana State University Press, 1986.

Cope, R. Douglas. *The Limits of Racial Domination: Plebeian Society in Colonial Mexico City, 1660–1720.* Madison: University of Wisconsin Press, 1994.

Costa, Iraci del Nero da. *Arraia-miúda: um estudo sobre os não-proprietários de ecravos no Brasil*. São Paulo: MGSP Editores Ltda., 1992.

Cox, Edward L. *Free Coloreds in the Slave Societies of St. Kitts and Grenada, 1763–1833*. Knoxville: University of Tennessee Press, 1984.

Crahan, Margaret E., and Franklin W. Knight, eds. *Africa and the Caribbean: The Legacies of a Link*. Baltimore: Johns Hopkins University Press, 1979.

Craton, Michael. *Testing the Chains: Resistance to Slavery in the British West Indies*. Ithaca, N.Y.: Cornell University Press, 1982.

Crook, Larry, and Randall Johnson, eds. *Black Brazil: Culture, Identity, and Social Mobilization*. Los Angeles: UCLA Latin American Studies Center, University of California, 1999.

Cunha, Manuela Carneiro da. *Antropologia do Brasil: mito, história, etnicidade*. São Paulo: Brasiliense, 1986.

———. "Introduction." In Marianno Carneiro da Cunha, *Da senzala ao sobrado: arquitetura brasileira na Nigéria e na República Popular do Benin*. São Paulo: Nobel, 1985.

———. *Negros, estrangeiros: os escravos libertos e sua volta à Africa*. São Paulo: Editora Brasiliense, 1985.

———. "Silences of the Law: Customary Law and Positive Law on the Manumission of Slaves in the 19th Century Brazil." *History and Anthropology* 1, pt. 2 (1985): 427–443.

Cunha, Mariano Carneiro da Cunha. *Da senzala ao sobrado: arquitetura brasileira na Nigéria e na República Popular do Benin*. São Paulo: Nobel, 1985.

Curtin, Philip D. *The Atlantic Slave Trade: A Census*. Madison: University of Wisconsin Press, 1969.

Curtin, Philip D., ed. *Africa Remembered: Narratives by West Africans from the Era of the Slave Trade*. Madison: University of Wisconsin Press, 1967.

DaMatta, Roberto. *A casa & a rua: espaço, cidadania, mulher e morte no Brasil*. São Paulo: Brasiliense, 1985.

Davis, David Brion. *The Problem of Slavery in the Age of Revolution 1770–1823*. Ithaca, N.Y.: Cornell University Press, 1975.

Degler, Carl N. *Neither Black nor White: Slavery and Race Relations in Brazil and the United States*. Madison: University of Wisconsin Press, 1986 [1971].

Desan, Suzanne. *Reclaiming the Sacred: Lay Religion and Popular Politics in Revolutionary France*. Ithaca, N.Y.: Cornell University Press, 1990.

Dzidzienyo, Anani. "Africa-Brazil: Ex Africa Semper Aliquid Novi." In Larry Crook and Randall Johnson, eds., *Black Brazil: Culture, Identity, and Social Mobilization*. Los Angeles: UCLA Latin American Studies Center, University of California, 1999.

———. "Brazil." In Jay A. Sigler, ed., *International Handbook on Race and Race Relations*. New York: Greenwood Press, 1987.

———. "Brazilian Race Relations Studies: Old Problems, New Ideas?" *Humboldt Journal of Social Relations* 19, no. 2 (1993): 109–129.

Domínguez, Virginia R. *White by Definition: Social Classification in Creole Louisiana*. New Brunswick, N.J.: Rutgers University Press, 1986.

Eisenberg, Peter L. "Ficando livre: as alforrias em Campinas no século XIX." *Estudos Ecônomicos* 17, no. 2 (1987): 175–216.

Elkins, Stanley M. *Slavery.* 3rd ed. Chicago: University of Chicago Press, 1978 [1959].

Ellison, Ralph. *Invisible Man.* New York: Vintage, 1982 [1952].

Eltis, David. *Economic Growth and the Ending of the Transatlantic Slave Trade.* New York: Oxford University Press, 1987.

———. *The Rise of African Slavery in the Americas.* Cambridge: Cambridge University Press, 2000.

Eltis, David, and James Walvin, eds. *The Abolition of the Atlantic Slave Trade: Origins and Effects in Europe, Africa, and the Americas.* Madison: University of Wisconsin Press, 1981.

Epstein, A. L. *Ethos and Identity: Three Studies in Ethnicity.* London: Tavistock Publications, 1978.

———. "Gossip, Norms and Social Network." In J. Clyde Mitchell, ed., *Social Networks in Urban Situations: Analyses of Personal Relationships in Central African Towns.* Manchester: Manchester University Press, 1969.

———. "The Network and Urban Social Organization." *Rhodes-Livingstone Journal* 29 (1961): 29–62.

Fernandes, Florestan. *A integração do negro na sociedade de classes.* 2 vols. São Paulo: Dominus Editôra, 1965.

Fields, Barbara. *Slavery and Freedom on the Middle Ground: Maryland during the Nineteenth Century.* New Haven, Conn.: Yale University Press, 1985.

Filho, Luís Viana. *O negro na Bahia.* 3rd ed. Rio de Janeiro: Nova Fronteira, 1988.

Finley, M. I. "Slavery." In *International Encyclopedia of the Social Sciences,* vol. 14, 307–314. New York: Macmillan and Free Press, 1968.

Flexor, Maria Helena. *Oficiais mecânicos na cidade do Salvador.* Salvador: Prefeitura Municipal do Salvador, 1974.

Flory, Rae Jean Dell. "Bahian Society in the Mid-Colonial Period: The Sugar Planters, Tobacco Growers, Merchants, and Artisans of Salvador and the Recôncavo." Ph.D. diss., University of Texas at Austin, 1978.

Flory, Rae Jean Dell, and David Grant Smith. "Bahian Merchants and Planters in the Seventeenth and Early Eighteenth Centuries." *Hispanic American Historical Review* 58, no. 4 (1978): 571–594.

Flory, Thomas. *Judge and Jury in Imperial Brazil, 1808–1871: Social Control and Political Stability in the New State.* Austin: University of Texas Press, 1981.

Foster, George M. *Culture and Conquest: America's Spanish Heritage.* New York: Wenner-Gren Foundation for Anthropological Research, 1960.

Fox-Genovese, Elizabeth. "Placing Women's History in History." *New Left Review* 133 (1982): 5–29.

———. *Within the Plantation Household: Black and White Women of the South.* Chapel Hill: University of North Carolina Press, 1988.

Fragoso, João Luís R. and Manolo G. Florentino, "Melcelino, filho de Inocência crioula, neto de Joana Cabina: um estudo sobre famílias escravas em Paraíba do Sul." *Estudos Econômicos* 17, no. 2 (1987): 151–173.

Fredrickson, George M. *The Black Image in the White Mind: The Debate on Afro-American Character and Destiny, 1817–1914.* New York: Harper and Row, 1971.

Frey, Sylvia R. *Water from the Rock: Black Resistance in a Revolutionary Age.* Princeton, N.J.: Princeton University Press, 1991.

Freyre, Gilberto. *The Mansions and the Shanties: The Making of Modern Brazil*. Trans. and ed. Harriet de Onís. New York: Alfred A. Knopf, 1963.

——. *The Masters and the Slaves: A Study in the Development of Brazilian Civilization*. Trans. Samuel Putman. New York: Alfred A. Knopf, 1946.

——. *O escravo nos anúncios de jornais brasileiros do século XIX*. 2nd ed. São Paulo: Companhia Editora Nacional, 1979.

Fuente, Alejandro de la. *A Nation for All: Race, Inequality, and Politics in Twentieth-Century Cuba*. Chapel Hill: University of North Carolina Press, 2001.

Galliza, Diana Soares de. *O declínio da escravidão na Paraíba 1850–1888*. João Pessoa: Editora Universitária, 1979.

Genovese, Eugene D. *From Rebellion to Revolution: Afro-American Slave Revolts in the Making of the Modern World*. Baton Rouge: Louisiana State University Press, 1979.

——. *Roll, Jordan, Roll: The World the Slaves Made*. New York: Vintage Books, 1976.

Gluckman, Max. "Analysis of a Social Situation in Modern Zululand." *Bantu Studies* 14 (1940): 1–30, 147–174.

——. "Gossip and Scandal: Papers in Honour of Melville J. Herskovits." *Current Anthropology* 4, no. 3 (1963): 307–316.

Gmelch, George. *Double Passage: The Lives of Caribbean Migrants Abroad and Back Home*. Ann Arbor: University of Michigan Press, 1992.

Golden, Claudia Dale. *Urban Slavery in the American South, 1820–1860*. Chicago: University of Chicago Press, 1976.

Goody, Jack. "Writing, Religion, and Revolt in Bahia." *Visible Language* 20, no. 3 (1986): 318–343.

Gorender, Jacob. *O escravismo colonial*. 4th ed. São Paulo: Atica, 1978.

Goulart, Maurício. *A escravidão Africana no Brasil (Das origins à extinção do trafico)*. São Paulo: Alfa-Omega, 1975.

Graef, Hilda. *Mary: A History of Doctrine and Devotion*. Westminster: Christian Classics, and London: Sheed and Ward, 1985 [1963 (Part 1) and 1965 (Part 2)].

Graham, Richard. "Brazilian Slavery Re-examined: A Review Article." *Journal of Social History* 3, no. 4 (1970): 431–453.

——. *Patronage and Politics in Nineteenth-Century Brazil*. Stanford, Calif.: Stanford University Press, 1990.

——. "Slave Families on a Rural Estate in Colonial Brazil." *Journal of Social History* 9, no. 3 (1976): 382–402.

Graham, Richard, ed. *The Idea of Race in Latin America, 1870–1940*. Austin: University of Texas Press, 1990.

Greene, Jack P. *Imperatives, Behaviors, and Identities: Essays in Early American Cultural History*. Charlottesville: University Press of Virginia, 1992.

——. *The Intellectual Construction of America: Exceptionalism and Identity from 1492 to 1800*. Chapel Hill: University of North Carolina Press, 1993.

——. *Pursuits of Happiness: The Social Development of Early Modern British Colonies and the Formation of American Culture*. Chapel Hill: University of North Carolina Press, 1988.

Gudeman, Stephen, and Stuart B. Schwartz. "Cleaning Original Sin: Godparenthood and the Baptism of the Slaves in Eighteenth-Century Bahia." In Raymond T.

Smith, ed., *Kinship Ideology and Practice in Latin America.* Chapel Hill: University of North Carolina Press, 1984.

Guimarães, Antonio Sérgio Alfredo, and Lynn Huntley, eds. *Tirando a máscara: ensaios sobre o racismo no Brasil.* São Paulo: Paz e Terra, 2000.

Guss, David M. "The Selling of San Juan: The Performance of History in an Afro-Venezuelan Community." *American Ethnologist* 20, no. 3 (1993): 451–473.

Gutiérrez, Rámon A. *The Political Legacies of Columbus: Ethnic Identities in the United States.* Working Papers no. 16. College Park, Md.: Department of Spanish and Portuguese, University of Maryland at College Park, 1995.

——. *When Jesus Came, the Corn Mothers Went Away: Marriage, Sexuality, and Power in New Mexico, 1500–1846.* Stanford, Calif.: Stanford University Press, 1991.

Gutman, Herbert G. *The Black Family in Slavery and Freedom, 1750–1925.* New York: Vintage Books, 1977 [1976].

——. "Interview with Herbert Gutman." In MARHO, Henry Abelove, et al., eds., *Visions of History.* New York: Pantheon Books, 1983.

——. *Power and Culture: Essays on the American Working Class.* Ed. Ira Berlin. New York: Pantheon Books, 1987.

Hahner, June E. *Poverty and Politics: The Urban Poor in Brazil, 1870–1920.* Albuquerque: University of New Mew Mexico Press, 1986.

Hall, Gwendolyn Mildo. *Africans in Colonial Louisiana: The Development of Afro-Creole Culture in the Eighteenth Century.* Baton Rouge: Louisiana State University Press, 1992.

Hanchard, Michael George. *Orpheus and Power: The Movimento Negro of Rio de Janeiro and São Paulo, Brazil, 1945–1988.* Princeton, N.J.: Princeton University Press, 1994.

Hanchard, Michael George, ed. *Racial Politics in Contemporary Brazil.* Durham, N.C.: Duke University Press, 1999.

Handler, Jerome S. *The Unappropriated People: Freedmen in the Slave Society of Barbados.* Baltimore: Johns Hopkins University Press, 1974.

Handler, Richard. "Is 'Identity' a Useful Cross-Cultural Concept?" In John R. Gills, ed., *Commemorations: The Politics of National Identity.* Princeton, N.J.: Princeton University Press, 1994.

Handlin, Oscar. *Boston's Immigrants: A Study in Acculturation.* Revised and enlarged ed. Cambridge, Mass.: Harvard University Press, 1981.

Harding, Rachel E. *A Refuge in Thunder: Camdomblé and Alternative Spaces of Blackness.* Bloomington: Indiana University Press, 2000.

Hasenbalg, Carlos, Nelson do Valle Silva, and Márcia Lima. *Cor e estratifição social.* Rio de Janeiro: Contra Capa Libraria, 1999.

Helg, Aline. *Our Rightful Share: The Afro-Cuban Struggle for Equality, 1886–1912.* Chapel Hill: University of North Carolina Press, 1995.

Hemming, John. *Red Gold: The Conquest of the Brazilian Indians.* Cambridge, Mass: Harvard University Press, 1978.

Henretta, James A. "Social History as Lived and Written." *American Historical Review* 84, no. 5 (1979): 1293–1322.

Higgins, Kathleen Joan. *"Licentious Liberty" in a Brazilian Gold-Mining Region: Slav-*

ery, Gender, and Social Control in Eighteenth-Century Sabará, Minas Gerais. University Park: Pennsylvania State University Press, 1999.

———. "The Slave Society in Eighteenth-Century Sabará: A Community Study in Colonial Brazil." Ph.D. diss., Yale University, 1987.

Higman, B. H. *Slave Populations of the British Caribbean 1807–1834.* Baltimore: Johns Hopkins University Press, 1984.

Hobsbawm, Eric J. *Nations and Nationalism since 1780: Programme, Myth, Reality.* 2nd ed. Cambridge: Cambridge University Press, 1992.

Hobsbawn, Eric J., and Terence Ranger, eds. *The Invention of Tradition.* Cambridge: Cambridge University Press, 1983.

Horton, James Oliver. *Free People of Color: Inside the African American Community.* Washington, D.C.: Smithsonian Institute Press, 1993.

Hünefeldt, Christine. *Paying the Price of Freedom: Family and Labor among Lima's Slaves, 1800–1854.* Berkeley and Los Angeles: University of California Press, 1994.

Hunt, Nancy Rose. "Placing African Women's History and Locating Gender." *Social History* 14, no. 13 (1989): 359–379.

Ianni, Octavio. *As metamorfoses do escravo.* 2nd ed. São Paulo: Editora Hucitec, 1988.

———. *Escravidão e racismo.* 2nd ed. São Paulo: Editora Hucitec, 1988.

Ignace, Etinne. "A revolta dos Malés (24 para 25 de Janeiro de 1835)." *Revista de Instituto Geografico e Histórico da Bahia* 14, no. 33 (1907): 129–149.

Inikori, Joseph E., and Stanley L. Engerman, eds. *The Atlantic Slave Trade: Effects on Economics, Societies, and Peoples in Africa, the Americas, and Europe.* Durham, N.C.: Duke University Press, 1992.

Isaac, Rhys. "Ethnographic Methods in History: An Action Approach." *Historical Methods* 13, no. 1 (1980): 43–61.

———. *The Transformation of Virginia 1740–1790.* Chapel Hill: University of North Carolina Press, 1982.

Jacobson-Widding, Anita. "Introduction." In Anita Jacobson-Widding, ed., *Identity: Personal and Socio-cultural.* Uppsala, Sweden: Acta Universitatis Upsaliensis, 1983.

Johnson, Lyman L. "Artisans." In Louisa Shell Hoberman and Susan Migden Socolow, eds., *Cities and Society in Colonial Latin America.* Albuquerque: University of New Mexico, 1986.

———. "Manumission in Colonial Buenos Aires, 1776–1810." *Hispanic American Historical Review* 59, no. 2 (1979): 258–279.

Jones, Jacqueline. *Labor of Love, Labor of Sorrow: Black Women, Work, and the Family from Slavery to the Present.* New York: Basic Books, 1985.

Joyner, Charles. *Down by the Riverside: A South Carolina Slave Community.* Urbana and Chicago: University of Illinois Press, 1984.

Karasch, Mary C. "From Porterage to Proprietorship: African Occupations in Rio de Janeiro, 1808–1850." In Stanley L. Engerman and Eugene D. Genovese, eds., *Race and Slavery in the Western Hemisphere: Quantitative Studies.* Princeton, N.J.: Princeton University Press, 1975.

———. *Slave Life in Rio de Janeiro 1808–1850.* Princeton, N.J.: Princeton University Press, 1987.

———. "Suppliers, Sellers, Servants, and Slaves." In Louisa Schell Hoberman and Susan Migden Socolow, eds., *Cities and Society in Colonial Latin America*. Albuquerque: University of New Mexico Press, 1986.

Kennedy, John. "Bahian Elites, 1750–1822." *Hispanic American Historical Review* 53, no. 39 (1973): 415–439.

Kent, R. K. "African Revolt in Bahia: 24–25 January 1835." *Journal of Social History* 3, no. 4 (1970): 334–356.

———. "Palmares: An African State in Brazil." *Journal of African History* 6, no. 2 (1965): 161–175.

Kessler, Arnold. "Bahian Manumission Practices in the Early Nineteenth Century." Paper presented to the American Historical Association, San Francisco, 1973.

Khan, Aisha. "*Juthaa* in Trinidad: Food, Pollution, and Hierarchy in a Caribbean Diaspora Community." *American Ethnologist* 21, no. 2 (1994): 245–269.

Kiernan, James Patrick. "The Manumission of Slaves in Colonial Brazil: Paraty, 1789–1822." Ph.D. diss., New York University, 1976.

Kilson, Martin L., and Robert I. Rotberg, eds. *The African Diaspora: Interpretative Essays*. Cambridge, Mass.: Harvard University Press, 1976.

Klein, Herbert S. *African Slavery in Latin America and the Caribbean*. New York: Oxford University Press, 1986.

———. "African Women in the Atlantic Slave Trade." In Claire C. Robertson and Martin A. Klein, eds., *Women and Slavery in Africa*. Madison: University of Wisconsin Press, 1983.

———. *The Middle Passage: Comparative Studies in the Atlantic Slave Trade*. Princeton, N.J.: Princeton University Press, 1978.

———. *Slavery in the Americas: A Comparative Study of Virginia and Cuba*. Chicago: University of Chicago Press, 1967.

Knight, Franklin W. *Slave Society in Cuba during the Nineteenth Century*. Madison: University of Wisconsin Press, 1970.

Knight, Franklin W., and Margaret E. Crahan. "The African Migration and the Origin of an Afro-American Society and Culture." In Margaret E. Crahan and Franklin W. Knight, eds., *Africa and the Caribbean: The Legacies of a Link*. Baltimore: Johns Hopkins University Press, 1979.

Knight, Franklin W., and Peggy K. Liss, eds. *Atlantic Port Cities: Economy, Culture, and Society in the Atlantic World, 1650–1850*. Knoxville: University of Tennessee Press, 1991.

Kondo, Dorinne K. *Crafting Selves: Power, Gender, and Discourses of Identity in a Japanese Workplace*. Chicago: University of Chicago Press, 1990.

Kopytoff, Jean Herskovits. *A Preface to Modern Nigeria: The "Sierra Leonians" in Yoruba, 1830–1890*. Madison: University of Wisconsin Press, 1965.

Kraay, Hendrik. "'As Terrifying as Unexpected': The Bahian Sabinada, 1837–1838." *Hispanic American Historical Review* 42, no. 4 (1992): 501–527.

Kurk, Betty M. "The African Derivation of Black Fraternal Orders in the United States." *Comparative Studies in Society and History* 25, no. 4 (1983): 559–591.

Kuznesof, Elizabeth Anne. "Sexual Politics, Race and Bastard-Bearing in Nineteenth-Century Brazil: A Question of Culture or Power." *Journal of Family History* 16, no. 3 (1991): 241–260.

———. "Sexuality, Gender and the Family in Colonial Brazil." *Luso-Brazilian Review* 30, no. 1 (1993): 119–132.

Lauderdale Graham, Sandra. "Honor among Slaves." In Lyman L. Johnson and Sonya Lipsett-Rivera, eds., *The Faces of Honor: Sex, Shame, and Violence in Colonial Latin America.* Albuquerque: University of New Mexico Press, 1998.

———. *House and Street: The Domestic World of Servants and Masters in Nineteenth-Century Rio de Janeiro.* Cambridge: Cambridge University Press, 1988.

———. "Slavery's Impasse: Slave Prostitutes, Small-Time Mistresses, and the Brazilian Law of 1871." *Comparative Studies in History and Slavery* 33, no. 4 (1991): 669–694.

Lavie, Smadar, and Ted Swedenburg, eds. *Displacement, Diaspora, and Geographies of Identity.* Durham, N.C.: Duke University Press, 1996.

Leach, Edmund. *A Runaway World?* London: British Broadcasting Corporation, 1968 [1967].

Lebsock, Susanne. *The Free Women of Petersburg: Petersburg, Virginia 1784–1820.* New York: Norton, 1984.

Levine, Lawrence W. *Black Culture and Consciousness: Afro-American Folk Thought from Slavery to Freedom.* Oxford: Oxford University Press, 1978.

Levine, Robert M. "'Mud-Hut Jerusalem': Canudos Revised." *Hispanic American Historical Review* 68, no. 3 (1988): 525–576.

Lewin, Linda. "Natural and Spurious Children in Brazilian Inheritance Law from Colony to Empire: A Methodological Essay." *Americas* 48, no. 3 (1992): 351–396.

———. *Politics and Parentela in Paranaíba: A Case Study of Family-Based Oligarchy in Brazil.* Princeton, N.J.: Princeton University Press, 1987.

Lindsay, Lisa A. "'To Return to the Bosom of Their Fatherland': Brazilian Immigrants in Nineteenth-Century Lagos." *Slavery and Abolition* 15, no. 1 (1994): 22–50.

Linger, Daniel Touro. *No One Home: Brazilian Selves Remade in Japan.* Stanford, Calif.: Stanford University Press, 2001.

Lipsett-Rivera, Sonya. "A Slap in the Face of Honor: Social Transgression and Women in Late Colonial Mexico." In Lyman L. Johnson and Sonya Lipsett-Rivera, eds. *The Faces of Honor: Sex, Shame, and Violence in Colonial Latin America.* Albuquerque: University of New Mexico Press, 1998.

Littlefield, Daniel C. *Rice and Slaves: Ethnicity and the Slave Trade in Colonial South Carolina.* Baton Rouge: Louisiana State University Press, 1981.

Lockhart, James. *The Nahuas after the Conquest: A Social and Cultural History of the Indians of Central Mexico, Sixteenth through Eighteenth Centuries.* Stanford: Stanford University Press, 1992.

Lockhart, James, and Stuart B. Schwartz. *Early Latin America: A History of Colonial Spanish America and Brazil.* Cambridge: Cambridge University Press, 1983.

Lovejoy, Paul E. "Background to Rebellion: The Origins of Muslim Slaves in Bahia." *Slavery and Abolition* 15, no. 2 (1994): 151–180.

———. *Caravans of Kola: The Hausa Kola Trade 1700–1900.* Zaria, Nigeria: Ahmadu Bello University Press, 1980.

———. *Transformations in Slavery: A History of Slavery in Africa.* Cambridge: Cambridge University Press, 1983.

Lugar, Catherine. "The Merchant Community of Salvador, Bahia 1780–1830." Ph.D. diss., State University of New York at Stony Brook, 1980.

Machado, Maria Helena Pereira Toledo. *Crime e escravidão: trabalho, luta e resistência nas paulistas 1830–1888*. São Paulo: Editora Brasiliense, 1987.

Maestri, Mário. "Consideração sobre o cativeiro do 'negro da terra' no Brasil quinhentista." *Estudos Ibero-Americanos* 16, no. 1–2 (1990): 197–210.

Marchant, Alexander. *From Barter to Slavery: The Economic Relations of Portuguese and Indians in the Settlement of Brazil, 1500–1580*. Baltimore: Johns Hopkins University Press, 1942.

Marcílio, Maria Luiza. "The Price of Slaves in XIXth Century Brazil: A Quantitative Analysis of the Registration of Slave Sales in Bahia." In *Studi in memoria di Federigo Melis*, 5 vols., vol. 5, 83–97. Paris: Giannini Editore, 1978.

Martinez-Alier, Verena. *Marriage, Class and Color in Nineteenth-Century Cuba: A Study of Racial Attitudes and Sexual Values in a Slave Society*. London: Cambridge University Press, 1974.

Mattoso, Kátia M. de Queirós. *Bahia: a cidade do Salvador e seu mercado no século XIX*. São Paulo: Hucitec, 1978.

———. *Bahia, século XIX: uma província no império*. Rio de Janeiro: Editora Nova Fronteira, 1992.

———. *Entre esclave au Brésil: XVIe–XIXe*. Paris: Hachette, 1979.

———. *Família e sociedade na Bahia do século XIX*. Trans. James Amado. São Paulo: Corrupio, 1988.

———. *Presença francesa no movimento democrático bahiano de 1798*. Salvador: Editora Itapuã, 1969.

———. "A propósito de cartas de alforria na Bahia, 1779–1850." *Anais de História* 4 (1972): 23–52.

———. "Slave, Free, and Freed Family Structures in Nineteenth-Century Salvador, Bahia." *Luso-Brazilian Review* 25, no. 1 (1988): 69–83.

———. *Testamentos de escravos libertos na Bahia no século XIX: uma fonte para o estudo de mentalidade*. Salvador: Centro de Estudos Bahianos, 1979.

———. *To Be a Slave in Brazil, 1550–1888*. Trans. Arthur Goldhammer. New Brunswick, N.J.: Rutgers University Press, 1986.

Mattoso, Kátia M. de Queirós, Herbert S. Klein, and Stanley L. Engerman. "Trends and Patterns in the Prices of Manumitted Slaves: Bahia, 1819–1888." *Slavery and Abolition* 7, no. 1 (1986): 59–67.

McBeth, Michael C. "The Brazilian Recruit during the First Empire: Slave or Soldier?" In Dauril Alden and Warren Dean, eds., *Essays Concerning the Socioeconomic History of Brazil and Portuguese India*. Gainesville: University Press of Florida, 1977.

Mello, Pedro C. de. "Expectation of Abolition and Sanguinity of Coffee Planters in Brazil, 1871–1881." In Robert William Fogel and Stanley L. Engerman, eds., *Without Consent or Contract: The Rise and Fall of American Slavery*. Conditions of Slave Life and the Transition to Freedom: Technical Papers. 2 vols. New York: W. W. Norton, 1992.

Menard, Russell, and Stuart B. Schwartz. "Why African Slavery? Labor Force Transitions in Brazil, Mexico, and the Carolina Lowcounty." In Wolfgang Binder, ed., *Slavery in the Americas*. Würzburg: Königshausen and Newman, 1993.

Menzar, Joan E. "The Ranks of the Poor: Military Service and Social Differentiation in Northeast Brazil, 1830–1875." *Hispanic American Historical Review* 72, no. 3 (1992): 335–351.

Merrick, Thomas W., and Douglas H. Graham. *Population and Economic Development in Brazil: 1800 to the Present*. Baltimore: Johns Hopkins University Press, 1979.

Metcalf, Alida C. *Family and Frontier in Colonial Brazil: Santana de Parnaíba, 1580– 1822*. Berkeley, Los Angeles, and Oxford: University of California Press, 1992.

Meyers, Albert, and Diane Elizabeth Hopkins, eds. *Manipulating the Saints: Religious Brotherhoods and Social Integration in Postconquest Latin America*. Hamburg: WAYASBAH, 1988.

Miers, Suzanne, and Igor Kopytoff, eds. *Slavery in Africa: Historical and Anthropological Perspectives*. Madison: University of Wisconsin Press, 1977.

Miller, Joseph C. *Kings and Kinsmen: Early Mbundu States in Angola*. Oxford: Oxford University Press, 1976.

———. "Slave Prices in the Portuguese Southern Atlantic, 1600–1830." In Paul E. Lovejoy, ed., *Africans in Bondage: Studies in Slavery and Slave Trade*. Madison: University of Wisconsin Press, 1986.

———. *Way of Death: Merchant Capitalism and the Angolan Slave Trade 1730–1830*. Madison: University of Wisconsin Press, 1988.

Mintz, Sidney W. "Defining Black and White." *Johns Hopkins Magazine* 46, no. 5 (1994): 8, 10.

———. "A Melting Pot—Sort of." *Johns Hopkins Magazine* 46, no. 4 (1994): 24–25.

———. "Men, Women, and Trade." *Comparative Studies in Society and History* 13, no. 3 (1971): 247–269.

———. "The Sensation of Moving, while Standing Still." *American Ethnologist* 16, no. 4 (1989): 786–796.

———. "Tasting Food, Tasting Freedom." In Wolfgang Binder, ed., *Slavery in the Americas*. Würzburg: Königshausen and Neumann, 1993.

———. *Worker in the Cane: A Puerto Rican Life History*. New York: W. W. Norton, 1974 [1960].

Mintz, Sidney W., and Richard Price. *An Anthropological Approach to the Afro-American Past: A Caribbean Perspective*. Philadelphia: Institute for the Study of Human Issues, 1976.

———. *The Birth of African-American Culture: An Anthropological Perspective*. Boston: Beacon Press, 1992.

Mintz, Sidney W., and Eric R. Wolf. "An Analysis of Ritual Co-Parenthood (Compadrazgo)." *Southwestern Journal of Anthropology* 6, no. 4 (1950): 341–368.

Mitchell, J. Clyde. *The Kalela Dance: Aspects of Social Relationships among Urban Africans in Northern Rhodesia*. Manchester: Manchester University Press, 1956.

———. "Perceptions of Ethnicity and Ethnic Behaviour: An Empirical Exploration." In Abner Cohen, ed., *Urban Ethnicity*. London: Tavistock Publications, 1974.

———. *Tribalism and the Plural Society*. London: Oxford University Press, 1960.

———. "Tribe and Social Change in South Central Africa: A Situational Approach." *Journal of Asian and African Studies* 5 (1970): 83–101.

Mitchell, J. Clyde, ed. *Social Networks in Urban Situations*. Manchester: Manchester University Press, 1969.

Mitchell, Michael James. "Racial Consciousness and the Political Attitudes and Behavior of Blacks in São Paulo." Ph.D. diss., Indiana University, 1977.

Monteil, Vincent. "Analyse de 25 documents arabes des Malés de Bahia (1835)." *Bulletin de l'Institut Fondanetake d'Afrique Noir*, tomo 29, série B, no. 1–2 (1967): 88–98.

Moreno Fraginals, Manuel, Herbert S. Klein, and Stanley L. Engerman. "The Level and Structure of Slave Prices on Cuban Plantations in the Mid-Nineteenth Century: Some Comparative Perspectives." *American Historical Review* 88, no. 5 (1983): 1201–1218.

Morgan, Philip D. "British Encounter with Africans and African-Americans, circa 1600–1780." In Bernard Bailyn and Philip D. Morgan, eds., *Strangers within the Realm: Cultural Margins of the First British Empire*. Chapel Hill: University of North Carolina Press, 1991.

Moriya, Renato Mikio. *Fenômeno dekassegui: um olhar sobre os adlescentes que ficaram*, with a preface by Paul Negri. Rôndorina: Ediçoes CEFEL, 2000.

Morrissey, Marietta. *Slave Women in the New World: Gender Stratification in the Caribbean*. Lawrence: University Press of Kansas, 1989.

Morrison, Toni. *The Bluest Eye*. New York: Plum, 1994 [1970].

Morton, F. W. O. "The Military in Bahia, 1800–1821." *Journal of Latin American Studies* 7, no. 2 (1975): 249–269.

Mullin, Michael. *Africa in America: Slave Acculturation and Resistance in the American South and the British Caribbean, 1736–1831*. Urbana: University of Illinois Press, 1992.

Mulvey, Patricia A. "Black Brothers and Sisters: Membership in the Black Lay Brotherhoods of Colonial Brazil." *Luso-Brazilian Review* 17, no. 2 (1980): 253–279.

———. "The Black Lay Brotherhoods of Colonial Brazil." Ph.D. diss., City College of New York, 1976.

———. "Slave Confraternities in Brazil: Their Role in Colonial Society." *Americas* 39, no. 1 (1982): 39–68.

Mura, David. *Turning Japanese: Memories of a Sansei*. New York: Doubleday, 1991.

Nascimento, Abdias do. *Brazil Mixture or Massacre? Essays in the Genocide of a Black People*. Trans. Elisa Larkin Nascimento. 2nd ed. Dover, Mass.: Majority Press, 1989.

Nascimento, Abdias do, and Elisa Larkin Nascimento. *Africans in Brazil: A Pan-African Perspective*. Trenton, N.J.: Africa World Press, 1992.

———. "Reflexões sobre o movimento negro no Brasil, 1938–1997." In Antonio Sérgio Alfredo Guimarães and Lynn Huntley, eds., *Tirando a máscara: ensaios sobre o racismo no Brasil*. São Paulo: Paz e Terra, 2000.

Nascimento, Anna Amélia Vieira. *Dez freguesias da cidade do Salvador: aspectos sociais e urbanos do século XIX*. Salvador: Fundação Cultural do Estado da Bahia, 1986.

Nash, Gary B. *Forging Freedom: The Formation of Philadelphia's Black Community, 1720–1840*. Cambridge, Mass.: Harvard University Press, 1988.

Nazzari, Muriel. *Disappearance of the Dowry: Women, Families, and Social Change in São Paulo, Brazil (1600–1900)*. Stanford, Calif.: Stanford University Press, 1991.

Ninomiya, Masato, org. *"Dekassegui": Gensho ni kansuru Simpojium Hokoku-sho.* São Paulo: Sociedade Brasileira de Cultura Japonesa, 1993.

Nishida, Mieko. "Diasporic Identities in Transformation: Repatriation Movements from Brazil and to West Africa and Japan." Paper presented at the Latin American Studies Association Congress, Miami, Florida, March 16-18, 2000.

———. "From Ethnicity to Race and Gender: Transformations of Black Lay Sodalities in Salvador, Brazil." *Journal of Social History* 32, no. 2 (Winter 1998): 329-348.

———. "Gender, Race, and Ethnicity in Urban Brazil: 'Black' and 'Japanese' Women in São Paulo." Paper presented at the American Historical Association Annual Meeting, San Francisco, CA, January 3-6, 2002.

———. *Japanese Brazilian Women and Their Ambiguous Identities: Gender, Ethnicity, and Class in São Paulo.* Latin American Studies Working Paper no. 5. Latin American Studies Center, University of Maryland at College Park, 2000.

———. "Manumission and Ethnicity in Urban Slavery: Salvador, Brazil, 1808-1888." *Hispanic American Historical Review* 73, no. 3 (1993): 361-391.

———. "Voices of Otherness: 'Black' and 'Japanese' Women in São Paulo, Brazil." Paper presented at the Latin American Studies Association Congress, Washington, D.C., September 6-8, 2001.

Nobles, Melissa. *Shades of Citizenship: Race and Censuses in Modern Politics.* Stanford, Calif.: Stanford University Press, 2000.

Oboler, Suzanne. *Ethnic Labels, Latino Lives: Identity and the Politics of (Re)Presentation in the United States.* Minneapolis: University of Minnesota Press, 1995.

Oliveira, Maria Inês Côrtes de. *O liberto: o seu mundo e os outros.* São Paulo: Corrupio, 1988.

Palmié, Stephan. "Ethnogenetic Processes and Cultural Transfer in Afro-American Slave Populations." In Wolfgang Binder, ed., *Slavery in the Americas.* Würzburg: Königshausen & Newman, 1993.

———. "Slave Culture and the Culture of Slavery in North America: Some Remarks on Historiography and the Present State of Research." In Wolfgang Binder, ed., *Slavery in the Americas.* Würzburg: Königshausen & Newman, 1993.

———. "Spics or Spades? Racial Classification and Ethnic Conflict in Miami." *Amerikastudien/American Studies* 34 (1989): 211-221.

Patai, Daphne. *Brazilian Women Speak: Contemporary Life Stories.* New Brunswick, N.J.: Rutgers University Press, 1988.

Patterson, Orlando. *Slavery and Social Death: A Comparative Study.* Cambridge, Mass.: Harvard University Press, 1982.

Pérotin-Dumon, Anne. "The Emergence of Politics among Free-Coloreds and Slaves in Revolutionary Guadeloupe." *Journal of Caribbean History* 25, nos. 1-2 (1991): 100-135.

Phillips, Caryl. *Crossing the River.* New York: Vintage, 1993.

Phillips, William D., Jr. *Slavery from Roman Times to the Early Transatlantic Trade.* Minneapolis: University of Minnesota Press, 1985.

Pierson, Donald. *Negroes in Brazil: A Study of Race Contact at Bahia.* Chicago: University of Chicago Press, 1941.

Preston, James J., ed. *Mother Worship: Theme and Variations.* Chapel Hill: University of North Carolina Press, 1982.

Price, Richard, ed. *Maroon Societies: Rebel Slave Communities in the Americas*. 2nd ed. Baltimore: Johns Hopkins University Press, 1979.

Prince, Howard M. "Slave Rebellion in Bahia 1807–1835." Ph.D. diss., Columbia University, 1972.

Querino, Manoel. *Costumes africanos no Brasil*. Rio de Janeiro: Civilização Brasileira, 1938.

Raboteau, Albert J. *Slave Religion: The "Invisible Institution" in the Antebellum South*. New York: Oxford University Press, 1978.

Raeders, Georges. *O inimigo cordial do Brasil: o conde de Gobineau no Brasil*. Trans. Rosa Freire d'Aguiar. São Paulo: Paz e Terra, 1988.

Ralston, Richard D. "The Return of Brazilian Freedmen to West Africa in the 18th and 19th Centuries." *Canadian Journal of African Studies* 3, no. 3 (1969): 577–592.

Ramos, Donald. "Social Revolution Frustrated: The Conspiracy of the Tailors in Bahia, 1798." *Luso-Brazilian Review* 13, no. 1 (1976): 74–90.

Ranger, Terence. *The Invention of Tribalism in Zimbabwe*. Gweru, Zimbabwe: Mambo Press, 1985.

Reichert, Rolf. *Os documentos arábes do Arquivo do Estado da Bahia*. Salvador: Universidade Federal da Bahia, 1970.

Reichmann, Rebecca. "Introduction." In Rebecca Reichmann, ed., *Race in Contemporary Brazil: From Indifference to Inequality*. University Park: Pennsylvania State University Press, 1999.

Reis, Eneida de Almeida. "Mulato: negro-não-negro e/ou branco-não-branco: un estudo psicossocial sobre identidate." M.A. thesis, Pontícia Universidade Católica, 1997.

Reis, João José. "A elite baiana face os movimentos sociais, Bahia: 1824–1840." *Revista de História* 54, no. 108 (1976): 342–384.

———. "Magia jeje na Bahia: a invasão do calundo do Pasto de Cachoeira, 1785." *Revista Brasileira de História* 8, no. 16 (1988): 57–81.

———. *A morte é uma festa: ritos fúnebres e revolta popular no Brasil do século XIX*. São Paulo: Companhia das Letras, 1991.

———. *Rebelião escrava no Brasil: a história do levante dos malês (1835)*. 2nd ed. São Paulo: Editora Brasiliense, 1987.

———. *Slave Rebellion in Brazil: The Muslim Uprising of 1835 in Bahia*. Trans. Arthur Brakel. Baltimore: Johns Hopkins University Press, 1993.

———. "Slave Resistance in Brazil: Bahia, 1807–1835." *Luso-Brazilian Review* 25, no. 1 (1988): 111–144.

Reis, João José, and Eduard Silva. *Negociação e conflito: a resistência negra no Brasil escravavista*. São Paulo: Companhia das Letras, 1989.

Reiter, Rayna Rapp, ed. *Toward an Anthropology of Women*. New York: Monthly Review, 1974.

Robertson, Claire C., and Martin A. Klein. "Women's Importance in African Slave Systems." In Claire C. Robertson and Martin A. Klein, eds., *Women and Slavery in Africa*. Madison: University of Wisconsin Press, 1983.

Robertson, Claire C., and Martin A. Klein, eds. *Women and Slavery in Africa*. Madison: University of Wisconsin Press, 1983.

Rodrigues, Nina. *Os africanos no Brasil*. 3rd ed. São Paulo: Companhia Editôra Nacional, 1945.

Rosaldo, M. Z., and L. Lamphere, eds. *Women, Culture, and Society.* Stanford, Calif.: Stanford University Press, 1974.

Roth, Joshua H. "Defining Communities: The Nation, the Firm, the Neighborhood, and Japanese Brazilian Migrants in Japan." Ph.D. diss., Cornell University, 1999.

Ruiz, Vicki. *Cannery Women, Cannery Lives: Mexican Women, Urbanization, and the California Food Processing Industry, 1930–1950.* Albuquerque: University of New Mexico Press, 1987.

Russell-Wood, A. J. R. "Aspectos da vida social das irmandades leigas da Bahia no século XVIII." *Universitas*, no. 6/7 (1970): 189–204.

———. "Black and Mulatto Brotherhoods in Colonial Brazil: A Study in Collective Behavior." *Hispanic American Historical Review* 54, no. 4 (1974): 567–602.

———. *The Black Man in Slavery and Freedom in Colonial Brazil.* New York: St. Martin's Press, 1982.

———. "Colonial Brazil." In David W. Cohen and Jack P. Greene, eds., *Neither Slave nor Free: The Freedmen of African Descent in the Slave Societies of the New World.* Baltimore: Johns Hopkins University Press, 1972.

———. "Examination of Selected Statues of Three African Brotherhoods." In Albert Meyers and Diane Elizabeth Hopkins, eds., *Manipulating the Saints: Religious Brotherhoods and Social Integration in Postconquest Latin America.* Hamburg: WAYASBAH, 1988.

———. *Fidalgos and Philanthropists: The Santa Casa da Misericórdia of Bahia, 1550–1755.* Berkeley and Los Angeles: University of California Press, 1968.

———. "Ports of Colonial Brazil." In Franklin W. Knight and Peggy K. Liss, eds., *The Atlantic Port Cities: Economy, Culture, and Society in the Atlantic World, 1650–1850.* Knoxville: University of Tennessee Press, 1991.

———. "Prestige, Power, and Piety in Colonial Brazil: The Third Orders of Salvador." *Hispanic American Historical Review* 69, no. 1 (1989): 61–89.

———. *Society and Government in Colonial Brazil, 1500–1822.* Brookfield, Vt.: Variorum, 1992.

———. "Women and Society in Colonial Brazil." *Journal of Latin American Studies* 9, no. 1 (1977): 1–34.

Russell-Wood, A. J. R., ed. *From Colony to Nation: Essays on the Independence of Brazil.* Baltimore: Johns Hopkins University Press, 1977.

Ruy, Afonso. *A primeira revolução social brasileira (1798).* 2nd ed. Salvador: Tipografio Beneditina Ltda. 1951.

Saffioti, Heleieth I. B. *Women in Class Society.* Trans. Michael Vale. New York: Monthly Review Press, 1978.

Santos, Juanita Elbein dos. *Os nàgô e a morte: pàde, àsèsè e o culto egun na Bahia.* 4th ed. Petrópolis: Vozs, 1986.

Saracino, Rodolfo. *Los que volvieron a Africa.* Havana: Editorial de Ciencias, 1988.

Saunders, A. C. de C. M. *A Social History of Black Slaves and Freedmen in Portugal, 1441–1555.* Cambridge: Cambridge University Press, 1982.

Scarano, Julita. "Black Brotherhoods: Integration or Contradiction?" *Luso-Brazilian Review* 16, no. 1 (1979): 1–17.

——. *Devoção e escravidão: a irmandade de nossa senhora do Rosário dos Prêtos do distrito diamantino no século XVIII.* 2nd ed. São Paulo: Ed. Nacional, 1978.

Scholte, Jan Arat. "The World of Collective Identities in a Globalizing World." *Review of International Political Economy* 3 (Winter 1996): 565–607.

Schuler, Monica. *"Alas, Alas, Kongo": A Social History of Indentured African Immigration into Jamaica, 1841–1865.* Baltimore: Johns Hopkins University Press, 1980.

——. "Ethnic Slave Rebellion in the Caribbean and the Guianas." *Journal of Social History* 3 (1970): 374–385.

Schwartz, Stuart B. "The Formation of a Colonial Identity in Brazil." In Nicolas Canny and Anthony Pagden, eds., *Colonial Identity in the Atlantic World, 1500–1800.* Princeton, N.J.: Princeton University Press, 1987.

——. "Indian Labor and New World Plantations: European Demands and Indian Responses in Northern Brazil." *American Historical Review* 83, no. 3 (1978): 43–78.

——. "The Manumission of Slaves in Colonial Brazil: Bahia, 1684–1745." *Hispanic American Historical Review* 54, no. 4 (1974): 603–635.

——. "The *Mocambo:* Slave Resistance in Colonial Brazil." *Journal of Social History* 3, no. 4 (1970): 313–333.

——. "Plantations and Peripheries, c. 1580–c. 1750." In Leslie Bethell, ed., *Colonial Brazil.* Cambridge: Cambridge University Press, 1987.

——. "Recent Trends in the Study of Slavery in Brazil." *Luso-Brazilian Review* 25, no. 1 (1988): 1–25.

——. "Resistance and Accommodation in Eighteenth-Century Brazil: The Slave's View on Slavery." *Hispanic American Historical Review* 57, no. 1 (1979): 69–81.

——. *Slaves, Peasants, and Rebels: Reconsidering Brazilian Slavery.* Urbana: University of Illinois Press, 1992.

——. *Sovereignty and Society in Colonial Brazil: The High Court of Bahia and Its Judges, 1609–1751.* Berkeley and Los Angeles: University of California Press, 1973.

——. *Sugar Plantations in the Formation of Brazilian Society, Bahia, 1550–1835.* Cambridge: Cambridge University Press, 1985.

Scott, Joan. "Gender: A Useful Category of Historical Analysis." *American Historical Review* 91, no. 5 (1986): 1053–1075.

Scott, Julius Sherrard, III. "The Common Wind: Currents of Afro-American Communication in the Era of the Haitian Revolution." Ph.D. diss., Duke University, 1986.

Scott, Rebecca J. "Exploring the Meaning of Freedom: Postemancipation Societies in Comparative Perspective." *Hispanic American Historical Review* 68, no. 3 (1988): 407–428.

——. *Slave Emancipation in Cuba: The Transition to Free Labor 1860–1899.* Princeton, N.J.: Princeton University Press, 1985.

Seed, Patricia. *To Love, Honor, and Obey in Colonial Mexico: Conflicts and Marriage Choice, 1574–1821.* Stanford, Calif.: Stanford University Press, 1988.

Sellek, Yoko. "Nikkeijin: The Phenomenon of Return Migration." In Michael Weiner, ed., *Japan's Minorities: The Illusion of Homogeneity.* New York: Routledge, 1997.

Silva, Maliene Rosa Nogeira da. *Negro na rua: a nova face de escravidão.* São Paulo: Hucitec, 1988.

Silva, Maria Beatriz Nizza da. *Sistema de casamento no Brasil colonial.* São Paulo: EDUSP, 1984.

Silva, Nelson do Valle. "Updating the Cost of Not Being White in Brazil." In Pierre-Michel Fontaine, ed., *Race, Class, and Power in Brazil.* Los Angeles: Center for Afro-American Studies, University of California, Los Angeles, 1980.

Sio, Arnold A. "Marginality and Free Coloured Identity in Caribbean Slave Society." *Slavery and Abolition* 8, no. 2 (1987): 166–182.

Skidmore, Thomas. "Bi-racial U.S.A. vs. Multi-racial Brazil: Is the Contrast Still Valid?" *Journal of Latin American Studies* 25, no. 2 (1993): 373–386.

———. *Black into White: Race and Nationality in Brazilian Thought.* New York: Oxford University Press, 1974.

———. "Racial Ideas and Social Policy in Brazil, 1870–1940." In Richard Graham, ed., *The Idea of Race in Latin America.* Austin: University of Texas Press, 1990.

Slenes, Robert Wayne. "The Demography and Economics of Brazilian Slavery: 1850–1888." Ph.D. diss., Stanford University, 1975.

———. "Escravidão e família: padroes de casamento e estabilidade familiar numa comunidade escrava." *Estudos Econômicos* 17, no. 2 (1987): 217–227.

———. "Lares negros, olhos brancos: história da família escrava no século XIX." *Revista Brasileira de História* 8, no. 16 (1988): 189–203.

Smith, Raymond T., ed. *Kinship Ideology and Practice in Latin America.* Chapel Hill and London: University of North Carolina Press, 1984.

Soares, Luiz Carlos. "Os escravos de ganho no Rio de Janeiro do século XIX." *Revista Brasileira de História* 8, no. 16 (1988): 107–142.

———. *Rameiras, ilhoas, polacas . . . : a prostituição no Rio de Janeiro do século XIX.* São Paulo: Editora Atica, 1992.

Sousa, Paulo Cesar. *A Sabinada: a revolta separatista da Bahia (1837).* São Paulo: Editora Brasiliense, 1987.

Souza, Laura de Mello e. *O diabo e a terra de Santa Cruz: feitiçaria e religiosidade popular no Brasil colonial.* São Paulo: Companhia das Letras, 1986.

Stein, Stanley J. *Vassouras, a Brazilian Coffee County, 1850–1900: The Roles of Planter and Slave in a Plantation Society.* Princeton, N.J.: Princeton University Press, 1985 [1957].

Stuckey, Sterling. *Slave Culture: Nationalist Theory and the Foundations of Black America.* New York: Oxford University Press, 1985.

Tannenbaum, Frank. *Slave and Citizen: The Negro in the Americas.* New York: Alfred A. Knopf, 1947.

Tavares, Luís Henrique Dias. *Comércio proibido de escravos.* São Paulo: Editora Atica, 1988.

Taylor, William B. "Between Global Process and Local Knowledge: An Inquiry into Early Latin American Social History." In Olivier Zunz, ed., *Reliving the Past: The Worlds of Social History.* Chapel Hill: University of North Carolina Press, 1985.

———. *Drinking, Homicide, and Rebellion in Colonial Mexican Villages.* Stanford, Calif.: Stanford University Press, 1979.

———. *Magistrates of the Sacred: Priests and Parishioners in Eighteenth-Century Mexico*. Stanford, Calif.: Stanford University Press, 1996.

———. "The Virgin of Guadalupe in New Spain: An Inquiry into the Social History of Marian Devotion." *American Ethnologist* 14, no. 1 (1987): 9–33.

Thompson, E. P. *The Making of the English Working Class*. New York: Vintage Books, 1966 [1963].

Thornton, John. *Africa and Africans in the Making of the Atlantic World, 1400–1680*. Cambridge: Cambridge University Press, 1992.

Tölölyan, Khaching. "Rethinking Diaspora(s): Stateless Power in the Transnational Movement." *Diaspora* 5, no. 1 (1996): 3–36.

Toplin, Robert Brent. *The Abolition of Slavery in Brazil*. New York: Atheneum, 1972.

Trosko, Barbara Rose. "The Liberto in Bahia before Abolition." M.A. thesis, Columbia University, 1967.

Tsuda, Takayuki. "Strangers in the Ethnic Homeland: The Migration, Ethnic Identity, and Psychological Adaptation of Japan's New Immigrant Minorities." Ph.D. diss., University of California at Berkeley, 1996.

Turner, J. Michael. "Les Brésiliens—The Impact of Former Brazilian Slaves upon Dahomey." Ph.D. diss., Boston University, 1975.

Turner, Lorenzo D. "Some Contacts of Brazilian Ex-Slaves with Nigeria, West Africa." *Journal of Negro History* 27, no. 1 (1942): 55–67.

Twinan, Ann. *Public Lives, Private Secrets: Gender, Honor, Sexuality, and Illegitimacy in Colonial Spanish America*. Stanford, Calif.: Stanford University Press, 1999.

Vail, Leroy, ed. *The Creation of Tribalism in Southern Africa*. London: James Currey, 1989.

Venâncio, Renata Pinto. "Nos limites da sagrada família: illegitimidade e casamento no Brasil colonial." In Ronaldo Vanifes, ed., *História e sexualidade no Brasil*. Rio de Janeiro: Graal, 1986.

Verger, Pierre. *Flux e Reflux de la Traite des Negres entre le Golfe De Bénin et Bahia de Todos os Santos du Xvii au Xix Siècle*. 3 vols. Paris: Mouton, 1968.

———. *Fluxo e refluxo do tráfico de escravos entre o Golfo do Benin e a Bahia de Todos os Santos, dos séculos XVII a XIX*. Trans. Tasso Gadzanis. 2nd ed. São Paulo: Editora Corrupio, 1987.

———. *Formation d'une société Brésilienne au Golfe du Bénin au XIXème Siècle*. Dakar: Centre de Hautes Etudes Afro-Ibéro-Américanes de L'Université de Dakar, 1969.

———. *Notícias da Bahia—1850*. São Paulo: Corrupio, 1981.

———. *Os libertos: sete caminhos na liberdade de escravos da Bahia no século XIX*. São Paulo: Corrupio, 1992.

———. *Trade Relations between the Bight of Benin and Bahia from the 17th to 19th Century*. Trans. Evelyn Crawford. Ibadan, Nigeria: Ibadan University Press, 1976.

Vilhena, Luís dos Santos. *A Bahia no século XVIII*. 3 vols. Bahia: Editôra Itapuã, 1969.

Viotti da Costa, Emília. *The Brazilian Empire: Myths and Histories*. Chicago: Dorsey Press, 1988.

———. *Crowns of Glory, Tears of Blood: The Demerara Slave Rebellion of 1823*. New York and Oxford: Oxford University Press, 1994.

———. *Da senzala à colônia*. 2nd ed. São Paulo: Livraria Editora Ciências Humanas Ltda., 1967.

Wade, Peter. *Blackness and Race Mixture: The Dynamics of Racial Identity in Colombia*. Baltimore: Johns Hopkins University Press, 1993.

———. "The Cultural Politics of Blackness in Colombia." *American Ethnologist* 22, no. 2 (1995): 341–357.

Wade, Richard C. *Slavery in the Cities: The South 1820–1860*. New York: Oxford University Press, 1964.

Walker, Sheila S. "The Feast of Good Death: An Afro-Catholic Emancipation Celebration in Brazil." *Sage* 3, no. 2 (1986): 27–31.

Warner, Marina. *Alone of All Her Sex: The Myth and the Cult of the Virgin Mary*. New York: Alfred A. Knopf, 1976.

Wimbery, Fayette Darcell. "The African *Liberto* and the Bahian Lower Class: Social Integration in Nineteenth-Century Bahia, Brazil 1870–1900." Ph.D. diss., University of California at Berkeley, 1989.

Wood, Peter H. *Black Majority: Negroes in Colonial South Carolina from 1670 through the Stono Rebellion*. New York: Alfred A. Knopf, 1974.

Wood, Stephanie. "Adopted Saints: Christian Images in Nahua Testaments of Late Colonial Toluca." *Americas* 47, no. 3 (1991): 259–294.

Wright, Winthrop R. *Café con leche: Race, Class, and National Image in Venezuela*. Austin: University of Texas Press, 1990.

Yamanaka, Keiko. " 'I will go home, but when?' Labor Migration and Circular Diaspora Formation by Japanese Brazilians in Japan." In Mike Douglas and Glenda S. Roberts, eds., *Japan and Global Migration: Foreign Workers and the Advent of a Multicultural Society*. New York: Routledge, 2000.

———. "Return Migration of Japanese-Brazilians to Japan: The Nikkeijin as Ethnic Minority and Political Construct." *Diaspora* 5, no 1 (1996): 65–98.

Yamashita, Karen Tei. *Brazil-Maru*. Minneapolis: Coffee House Press, 1993.

———. *Circle K Cycles*. Minneapolis: Coffee House Press, 2001.

Yanagisako, Sylvia Junko. "Family and Household: The Analysis of Domestic Groups." *Annual Review of Anthropology* 8 (1979): 161–205.

———. *Transforming the Past: Tradition and Kinship among Japanese Americans*. Stanford, Calif.: Stanford University Press, 1985.

Yoshioka, Reimei. *Por que migramos do e para o Japão: os exemplos dos barrios das Alianças dos atuais dekasseguis*. São Paulo: Massao Ohno Editor, 1995.

Index

Conceição da Praia, 57; in the Pelourinho, 58–59, 89, 148; in Santo Antônio, 89; and on Rua de João Perreira, 90); of Saint Anthony of Catagerona in the chapel of São Pedro, 57; of Saint Benedict (in Conceição da Praia, 60; in the Saint Francis monastery, 61; and in the Carmelite monastery, 90); of Saint Ephigenia in the Carmelite monastery, 90

Black Soul, 155

Blackness, 13

Boxer, Charles C., 6, 136

Brazil: "discovery" of (1500), 13; independence of (1822), 2; republic of (1889), 2; transition from mercantilism to free trade (1808), 2, 65

Brazilian identity, 113

Brazilian succession law, 110

Brazilian-born slaves, 123–130; kinship and fictive kinship, 124–127; manumission of, 127–130; skin color, 129

Brazilians: in Lagos, 115–116, 118, 158; in Japan, 163–164

Brazilwood, 13

British-Brazilian Mixed Commission, 16

British privilege, 97

Bush captain, 63

Cabra, 26, 131

Caboclo, 26

Cadena, Marisol de la, 44

Cafre (Kaffir), 6

Caixa de empréstimo, 55

Candomblé, 96; *casa de candomblé,* 51

Canto, 48–50

Carneiro da Cunha, Manuela, 75

Carta de alforria, 73

Carurú, 45

Carvalho, Marcus J. M. de, 34

Categorization, 3, 46

Chalhoub, Sidney, 145

Civil marriage, 146

Class exclusivity, 155

Cohen, Anthony P., 5

Cohen, David W., 6

Color, 9, 26, 129, 131, 146–147, 153–154, 162; coding system, 6; labels of, 7

Comadre, 94, 95, 96

Common-law marriage: among ex-slaves, 109; among slaves, 108

Companheiro/companheira, 109

Congo, 31, 32

Conto, 2

Consensual unions among slaves, 53–54

Coparent, 110, 111

Côr. See Color

Count of Arcos, D. Marcos de Noronha, 37, 66, 67

Count of Gobineau, Joseph Arthur de Gobineau, 55, 104

Count of Ponte, João de Saldanha de Gama, 63, 65

Coparents of the fig tree, 67

Crahan, Margaret E., 38

Creolization, of diverse African cultures, 4

Cria, 88, 102; *cria forro,* 113

Crioulo, 26, 123, 133, 134, 135, 138, 141, 147, 148, 160

Crioulo livre, identity formation of, 134–141

Crioulo sodalities, 138–141, 161

Curtin, Philip D., 31

Day of the Kings, 49

Dekassegui, 163

Diaspora communities, formation of, 163

Domínguez, Virginia R., 154

Donatary system, 14

Duncan, John, 105

Egba, 38

El Mina, 31

Elkins, Stanley, 74

Elwes, Robert, 42

Emancipado, 15, 25

Engenho, 18, 66

Engerman, Stanley L., 23

Engomadeira, 46

Enslavement, 30

Epstein, A. L., 3, 47

Escravo, 6

Ethnic: affiliation of the individual, 36; category, 47; communication networks, 52; gathering and grouping, 48–51; identity, 32–38, 49, 62, 70, 157–159; labels, 5; origins, 26; solidarity, 8; symbol, 36

Ethnicity: definition of, 38; in New World slavery, 38

Etlis, David, 18

Ewbank, Thomas, 43

Falúa, 42

Ferme, Mariane, 99

MIEKO NISHIDA is Assistant Professor of History at Hartwick College in Oneonta, New York. She held a Predoctoral Research Fellowship at the Carter G. Woodson Institute of the University of Virginia and a Rockefeller Foundation Postdoctoral Fellowship at the Institute of Latin American Studies of the University of Texas at Austin.